Poison

GALT
NIEDERHOFFER

Poison

ST. MARTIN'S PRESS ≈ NEW YORK

POISON. Copyright © 2017 by Galt Niederhoffer. All rights reserved. Printed in the United States of America. For information, address St. Martin's Press, 175 Fifth Avenue, New York, N.Y. 10010.

www.stmartins.com

Designed by Anna Gorovoy

The Library of Congress Cataloging-in-Publication Data is available upon request.

ISBN 978-1-250-08529-0 (hardcover)
ISBN 978-1-250-08530-6 (ebook)

Our books may be purchased in bulk for promotional, educational, or business use. Please contact your local bookseller or the Macmillan Corporate and Premium Sales Department at 1-800-221-7945, extension 5442, or by email at MacmillanSpecialMarkets@macmillan.com.

First Edition: November 2017

10 9 8 7 6 5 4 3 2 1

FOR ELIZABETH, JOY, NADINE, AND MICHELLE

ACKNOWLEDGMENTS

Elizabeth, Joy, Nadine, Michelle

Rob and Alexia

Sylvie, Ben S., Alexandra, Gretchen, Becky, Jen, Tina, Nan, Corinne, Paul, Galaxy, Dustin, Cara, Jon E., Randy S., Koreen, Sarah, Zosia, Evan, Felicia, Christa, Francoise, Liv, Paula, Allison, Ben W., Dana, Richard, Mike, Elliot F., Randy W., Tommee, Samara, Billy, Sean L., Bingo, Arturo, Benji, Sheena, Sean C., Lucinda, Ivy, Sheila, Todd, Tara, Nicola, Amy, Jeremy, Nicole, and Dori

Mom and Jim

G.E.M.

PROLOGUE

This story takes place in a home, if such a concept can be trusted, a home in which a family lives and loves one another. In this home, the family wakes every morning and goes to sleep every night together. They cook, they eat, they sleep, they play. Everyone gives and everyone takes. Family is the ultimate symbiosis. They are part of that most perfect of machines in which everyone shares the common goal of survival and, when they achieve it, the luxuries that surpass it.

It's a busy and productive life if the family tableau is, in fact, an accurate portrait. Houseplants, bookshelves, abstract art, kids doing homework in various corners. The artifacts of their very own culture. Children fight over toys, food, equitable distribution. Parents fight over bills, sex, equitable distribution. The parents pour their work into a home they hope will outlast them, a home built to weather storms, time, love, and other fluctuations. They try to make it durable. They try to make it matter.

This is the social contract writ large: love, marriage, family—a dowry of domestic virtues with all its gleaming assets. If a family is lucky, that luck compounds with annual interest. If a family is unlucky, it begins to crack at the surface. The luck of a family depends on the consent of every member of the unit. When one member fails to fill his role, the structure caves around him.

But when a family functions well, there are few things that are stronger. The family itself is a force, an unbreakable alliance. The drive to survive compels the most intricate defense and the most ferocious offense. A family is glued together by a central pact for self-preservation, and it runs on something stronger than loyalty, something more powerful than common interest, a goal whose realization is as important as its failure is dire. Life and death. These are the two possible outcomes that stand on either side of the family endeavor, the ultimate punishment and the best of all possible rewards. This is the unique property of blood and not water.

It is a perfect system, like the always-rising moon, the petals of a flower, a system whose beauty derives from its shape and the fact that it always happens. But not every family achieves this most coveted state. Nature shares its blessings on an uneven basis.

The Connor family has achieved this enviable state of nirvana. Something delicious simmers on the stove. The dishwasher murmurs. Laundry circles. The daily rotation of domestic life rolls on, as with any perfect machine, until a circuit breaks and the machine ceases to function.

Part I

ONE

It's Thursday night, just after six, and Cass does the things of a mother. She decapitates a head of broccoli and drops it into a pot of boiling water. She opens the lid on a vat of rice and nearly burns her face off. She kneels to check the chicken, sweating in the oven. She hacks an onion with a knife, achieving, in three swift blows, a painless execution. She balances a call for work with the needs of her toddler, who is feet away on the floor, demolishing a wooden tower. She mutes the phone and calls upstairs to the older kids to please come down for dinner. She unmutes the phone just in time to utter something useful. The kids tumble down the stairs, enmeshed in their own struggle. The sitter, at six on the dot, abandons her post at the tower and makes her evening exit, the speed and precision of which sometimes feels to Cass like a jailbreak.

Despite the initial shudder of knowing that she is outnumbered, Cass softens when the sitter leaves, relieved by the privacy and power of being alone with her children. She could do anything with these kids, teach them any new concept, any new religion. She could tell them blue is green, that gender is a construct, that God does not exist, that God is perfect. It's a dizzying amount of power. There is no one to check or balance this power—only the mother and the father. In any other situation—work, government, or religion—this would be a recipe for disaster. For Cass, it is a sacred gift, a vocation and an honor, the chance to start and end her day with her three most important people, three human beings who share her big trusting eyes and the rest of her genetic makeup.

The hours between six and nine include several obligations: dinner, homework, piano practice, bathing, brushing teeth, bedtime book, just ten more minutes of LEGOs, please, pile in for a snuggle. This time is often chaotic. But it is routine, and routine offers its own meditation. It is regimen and ritual. Cass lives for this time, and it lives by her supervision. She texts her husband before sitting down to dinner.

"Home soon? Kids are hungry." She leaves the phone on the counter, deposits the baby in the high chair, and begins her nightly sermon. "All right, people."

The kids take their seats. Cass dismembers the chicken.

"I want to wait for Ryan," says Pete.

"Not tonight. It's getting late."

"I'm not eating until he gets here."

"Then I guess you're not eating."

The standoff between mother and son ends in the usual fashion, with a heartfelt attempt at mutiny followed by a decisive maternal triumph, along with a tacit relief in the imperviousness of the ruling power dynamic. As the kids begin to eat, Cass breathes more slowly. She is like a mother cat, purring when her children are close—double that when they are eating a healthy dinner. She cuts and mashes chicken for the baby while Pete covertly transfers his portion to his sister. Cass takes a bite of her own and pretends not to notice.

A noxious buzz interrupts the quiet. Cass starts—as though it is not just the sound of her phone but rather she and her husband are wired for instant communication. She makes a show of disinterest and then, as the kids consider the meal, she stands and crosses the room to read her husband's message.

"Stuck at work."

She puts the phone down. The news is not uncommon. Ryan's workload as an architect is cyclical, and his schedule can sometimes resemble a bear going in and out of hibernation. But the frequency of late nights over the last few months has been a source of minor frustration. She makes a conscious effort to unfurrow her brow and sits down with the children.

Cass looks different from how she expected to look at forty, her body further along in its natural expiration. She is a woman who has already seen most of life's great highlights: a childhood with plenty of laughter and toys, summer nights in cars with sunburned boys, all-nighters in a college dorm lined with books and posters, a flurry of years rushing around in tall heels and short dresses, childbirth, three times, every one a revelation, a pink and wailing infant, eyes, chest expanding, the first precious moments of motherhood, when life reveals its purpose, and all the stages of undress in between from all dressed up to naked.

She has spent nights hunched over library tables, always the hungry student, hours scribbling to meet deadlines in a newspaper office, chipping away at the keyboard and ceiling, weeks sprinting down city sidewalks, chasing news and stories and then, years later, on these same streets, chasing after her children. She has slowed her pace to a waddle as her belly and ankles widened, and years, standing at playground swings, pushing her babies into midair and launching them in their childhoods. At forty, she has lain naked in the arms of at least ten men she thought she loved for a moment, fallen in love with three of these men, married two, and buried her first husband. She has lain on the floor of her kitchen, weeping, begging for respite from each passing minute, slept in rocking chairs next to a crib, nursing each child to sleep, to grow, so content as not to notice as these nights became a decade. She has kneeled at the grave of the husband she mourned and at the altar of the one who came after.

At forty, she is more beautiful than she imagined and more exhausted than she cares to acknowledge. Her eyes have tiny tributaries at the outside corners, laugh lines that she knows result, in fact, from both tears and laughter. She is tall and lean from years of running, miles docked burning baby weight and tamping back the sparks of worry. Her hair is blondish by design, with an ashy, silver timbre, and this, combined with her light eyes, makes Cass look certain even when she is worried. She is stately, if slightly spent, wise, if slightly wizened, exceptionally sexy or elegant depending on the makeup. She has the light eyes of an optimist, eyes that see human nature at its best, if not at its truest. Her smile bears the permanent twist of a woman who has heard more stories than most and lived even more. She has the curves that kindness gives a face, and the angles wrought by hardship. She is lithe but has the heft of a woman who has had and held unfathomable sadness.

Time has passed. The kids are settled. Alice stares down her homework upstairs, writing and rewriting the topic sentence of a paragraph. Her teacher's question: What is the relationship of Huck Finn and Jim? Fraught, Cass explains. As close as lovers, and as doomed as any other rivals. Pete faces off with "Für Elise," teetering through the first phrases. From the baby's room emerge the sounds of a child in the last stage before slumber: the rustle of blankets, a request for water, followed by the hush of slower breaths. The Connor kids wind their way through their evening vesper.

A floor below, the rush of air, barely louder than a whisper. The kids, attuned to this sound, leap from their spots and race to the front door to greet their stepfather, Ryan.

Cass attempts the near-impossible feat of demanding quiet without raising her volume. She follows the kids down the stairs, reaching them just as Ryan greets his waiting fan club. When he enters, he stands still and braces himself for their momentum. The kids stop at his feet, pausing just long enough to let him take off his jacket, and then they follow him, a celebrity and his entourage, as he makes his way to the kitchen.

"Baby sleeping?" Ryan asks. He deposits a kiss on Cass's cheek.

The baby calls out. Cass sighs. Sleep has been disrupted. It will take double the time to begin the cycle from its onset.

The balance Cass works to achieve is often toppled in this fashion, calm traded for a new energy, the Ryan vibration, but she doesn't really mind. In fact, she has come to believe it is best for her children. A measure of chaos, she tells herself, has its place next to order. Ryan is her antidote, and she is his better judgment. Their roles are at times so distinct, their functions so opposite in the household that she has come to feel that all families would benefit from this division of labor. She knows she lacks an ingredient in herself, like bread without enough yeast, and that her kids might end up flat were she to raise them without it.

Still, it is not without some effort that Cass makes the transition between the night's hard-earned quiet and Ryan's easy disruption.

"Ryan," she says.

"Hi, sweetheart." His eyes are tired.

"Long day?" she says. She replaces his jacket as it slips from the hook behind them.

"You say that as though it's over."

"Late meeting?"

"New proposal. I thought we were gonna check work at the door." He smiles, diluting the comment.

"We did say that." She studies him, tests his facial expressions, replays his last statement. Something's off—a smell, a glance, eyes too quickly averted.

"Chicken's still warm," she says. "Rice is on the counter."

"Perfect," he says and kisses her again. "You are."

They do this a lot, this sweet routine as a kind of penance, a way of acknowledging the goodness of life, the battles they have weathered—alone and together. They have reached the goals they set for themselves, and so they observe this simple rite, the return of the father to the home, the reunion of husband and wife with the same earnest gratitude of reformed sinners.

Cass turns and walks up the stairs to collect the now-crying baby. The rumble of feet as Alice and Pete follow Ryan to the table.

"Homework finished?" Ryan asks.

"Yup," says Pete.

"Teeth brushed?"

"Completed," says Alice.

He picks up the lifeless broccoli. "Vegetable consumption?"

"Excessive," says Alice.

An expectant grin and a perfect pause from Ryan. "Then I guess you deserve ice cream!"

Before Cass clears the top step, before she has scooped up the baby, a cry of delight is followed by a rumble of muffled laughter, then the patter of feet crossing the floor, the rustle of coats being tugged off hooks, jackets pulled over pajamas, then the door and the rush of night as Alice and Pete follow Ryan out the door like rats after the Pied Piper.

"Ryan, it's a school night," she calls out.

But now the house is silent, except for the sound of the closing door and the victorious giggles of Ryan and the kids as they gallop toward the empty playground on the corner.

Cass gathers the baby now, listens to the silence. So what if Ryan sometimes stands in the way of a good night's sleep? Grief had made her dull. Grief had made her boring. Her husband of a decade died seven years prior after fighting an aggressive case of Hodgkin's lymphoma. What her kids need more than anything now is to feel lighthearted. And that is exactly how they seem when Cass finds them in the playground, hands sticky with ice cream, eyes bright with excitement. The school is a quarter mile from the house at the top of the hill they live on, and its playground is a second backyard for the Connors. Its convenience is sweetened by the freezer full of sweets at the adjacent market. Ryan and Pete stand in the dark, racing remote-control helicopters. Alice watches from a bench, calling the winner. The pavement is shiny as the bay, an endless black horizon. Neon lights dart overhead, Portland's version of comets.

Cass sits down next to her daughter. Alice abandons her duties to feed the baby ice cream. She unwinds his scarf and unzips a garment that looks like something between a sleeping bag and jacket. At two years old, Sam is small and round, the size of a large puppy. He has his mother's eyes and his father's temperament, and so, despite his sweet plump face, he has a formidable presence. As the baby of the family, he is everybody's darling, benefiting from the apprenticeship of his older sibs and the constant flow of attention. He enjoys his ice cream almost as much as the undivided focus of his sister.

Ryan is deep in planning mode, describing a new adventure.

"I have to go away next week."

"What for?" says Pete.

"Business trip."

"Bummer."

"Maybe you can skip school and come."

"Ryan, don't taunt him," says Cass.

"I'm not. I'm totally serious." Ryan swerves his hand to the right.

Pete takes his eye off his helicopter, and it crashes. And he's down. That's all it takes with Pete to ignite an obsession—one endorsement from Ryan, the promise of adventure. He becomes Ryan's unwitting lobbyist, missionary, and disciple, badgering his mother until that belief takes on the force of revolution.

"One day I'll take you diving," says Ryan. "I'll show you the Great Barrier Reef. The biggest structure in the world made by living creatures. Coral. The best architects on earth. It's so big you can see it from outer space. We gotta go soon before it's all gone. Swallowed by global warming. Alice, you in?" he continues.

"No, thanks," she says. "I prefer to stay where I'm less likely to be devoured."

Alice takes another lick of ice cream. She is at that special age where magic and logic hold equal weight—and neither wields as much power as vanilla with rainbow sprinkles. She is young enough to be vulnerable to charm but smart enough to recognize manipulation. Reward, punishment, ultimatum, deprivation—these are, of course, the same tacks she uses on her brother. But at ten, she is still at the mercy of the best incentive, the call of the unknown, the pull of adventure.

"Suit yourself," says Ryan.

Alice feigns indifference.

Cass instinctively tenses. The last time she heard him say, "Suit yourself," she came home to find Alice and Pete covered in paint, assisting Ryan as he "painted the house," the living room walls splattered like a Jackson Pollock canvas.

"Guess we'll just go on our own." Sometimes the plans Ryan makes are met with some resistance. But he knows how to double defense into a new offense. There is an electric quality to Ryan's attention and a penalty for dissenters, the ability to shine light into a room and cause the world to feel as though it has suffered a blackout in his absence.

Alice frowns. Even if the prize had no pull before, its withdrawal has given it value.

Cass begins to collect their trash, pack up scarves and mittens.

"We'll pick this up tomorrow," says Ryan.

"When?" asks Pete, his face falling.

"Don't worry, man. We got plenty of time."

"But you're leaving Monday."

"I'll only be gone for a week," he says. "And then you're stuck with me. Forever."

Cass watches closely now as Ryan leads Pete further. She allows it because she feels it is necessary for Pete to learn how to razz and be razzed, to spar and be sparred with, that relaxation, recreation, and play is as essential for a child as a well-balanced diet. And mostly because she knows Ryan will make good on his promise. Given the choice between a promise-breaker and a promise-keeper, she will take the latter. A few hours of sleep is a small price to pay for her son's second chance at a father.

"Can we, Mom?"

Ryan shrugs. He knows he's won now.

"You can't go on this trip," she says, "but we can start planning our holiday vacation. We're due to go back to the Dunmore. I've been craving those milk shakes."

"Hooray!" cries Pete. He jumps up and down. Even Alice is smiling.

Cass concedes defeat once again, but now with open delight. After years of grief, the trade of her will for her children's joy is one she is willing to make.

Cass walks to her husband's side, awards him with an adoring smile, the smile of a co-conspirator, a trusted ally. She grasps his hand and imparts, in a grasp, all her love, her thanks, her adoration. He doubles the force of her grasp, as if raising her love in a bet, then tugs her gently toward their home, leading the family they have made, the family they have formed together. It is a perfect moment, its contentment sweetened by the tears that came before it.

Travel plans gain fervor now in the empty school yard as descriptions of pink coral give way to a discussion of diving gear and the current color—blue or purple—of ink on stamps on passports. But now Ryan is ready to release the reins to his partner. Cass commands the group and begins the trip back home, anxious to resume the bedtime ritual, this time aided by hard-earned fatigue and fulfillable dreams of pirates and mermaids.

It is nearly eleven, and Cass and Ryan lie in bed, unwinding. In a faded blue T-shirt and cotton briefs, Ryan looks somehow too carnal for a marital bedroom. Cass wears a short silk nightgown and a gray cardigan sweater, the glasses she wore in college. She reads while he scans his device. Domestic bliss, the modern version. A breath of air rushes in the window. Cass burrows deeper under the covers.

"More travel again so soon." She is going for disinterest. "Which project is this?"

"The new one I told you about. Second home. Usual bullshit. 'Hidden Harbor,' Jamaica."

She flips the page in her novel. "Sounds exotic."

He turns to her suddenly. "Why don't you come? Just us? A quick vacation?"

"You know I can't miss class," she says. "I teach every day but Monday."

"I guess I'll just have to bring back some of that Jamaican magic. Make us some more of those cookies. We'll do another staycation. Go back to the Lakehouse. Would you like that, babe?" He kisses her neck, slides his hand from her shoulder to her stomach. "Remember those?"

"Do I ever."

"Those will take the edge off."

"Who says I'm edgy?" She pushes his hand away playfully and turns the light off.

TWO

It is just after dawn, and Cass is choking on her husband. She tries to make her mouth small. She tries to excel at gagging. He comes violently. She ingests. Wipes her face off.

From the anonymity of this act, it would seem these two are strangers. A snake delivering venom. Not husband and wife sneaking one in before the kids wake up on a Friday morning.

"Thanks," he says. He walks out of the bedroom.

Cass catches her breath. On hands and knees at the foot of the bed, she is an uncomfortable mixture of feminine and ferocious.

In the bathroom, Cass splashes her face with cold water, the timeless cure-all. She looks in the mirror and touches a heart-shaped locket, given to her by her husband. It is both a reminder and a talisman. To remind her to act from love. And to ward off evil spirits.

Cass hurries down the hall, stops, closes an open window. The chill of winter is early this year. Climate change has turned hot to cold. Either that or the Connors live in their own special orbit.

Ryan chops an apple with a large knife. An egg explodes in a pan. Scalding water descends over ground coffee. The basic tasks of domestic life are a slip away from hazard. We are in a civil space again. But this is a modern home. Mommy is on a work call, and Daddy is doing the cooking.

"Pete! Alice! Breakfast!" says Ryan.

Cass juggles a call for work with her true calling. She picks up a trail of toys from the floor, fastens a toothpick to a gumdrop model of the atom, stops a child to tie his shoe, and kisses her husband before ushering the whole troop to breakfast. The Connor family sits down to eat. Ryan and Cass exchange a sheepish grin. Squeaky clean after a filthy morning.

Now, for family obligations.

"Surreptitious," says Ryan.

"In secret," says Pete.

"Dormant."

"Wait! I know this one."

Cass takes her seat at the table. "Like a volcano."

"Hidden under the surface," says Pete, beaming.

"Hirsute," says Ryan.

"Hairy!" says Pete. At seven, Pete is a sucker for any discussion of creatures. In this, Pete and Ryan find a soaring common interest.

"You sure this is the vocab for *Robin Hood*? Sounds more like *Zombie Apocalypse*."

"Kind of the same story," says Alice. "If you think about it." Alice, at ten, is a hybrid herself, somewhere in between the knowing of adults and the innocence of children.

Cass smiles and hands Alice the model of the atom, post-triage.

"You fixed it!"

Cass's next stop is Sam. At two, he is equally fascinated by his sibs and the mashed banana on his high chair. Cass sits down to feed him.

"That's my cue," says Ryan.

"Already?" says Cass.

"It's nearly eight."

She checks the clock. "It's only ten after."

"I want to get in before Kevin. Make some headway on the proposal. Pete, good luck on the quiz. Alice, give 'em hell today." He stops and plants a kiss on Sam's head.

Alice watches her stepdad.

Cass clocks a note of envy. "Parents' night tonight," she says. "Meet you there at six thirty."

"You want to go solo?" Ryan asks. "I'll stay home and watch them."

"Already asked one of my students."

He smiles. He's been chided.

"Is there anything you don't do well?" he says.

"Only the things you do better." Cass follows her husband out into the foyer, intercepting him at the door as he puts on his jacket.

They speak in a different tone now, with no witnesses, the private space of grown-ups.

"Big day?" she asks.

"Massive. What time do you teach?"

"Eleven."

"Teach our children well," he says.

"I shall try."

"You sure schooled me this morning."

An X-rated squeeze, a laugh, and a kiss. These two have their own language. And a constantly shifting role: who wears the pants in the family.

"I may be a little late tonight," he says.

She raises her brow, playful but stern. "Please don't be."

And he's gone. Cass watches the door for a moment. Then she's back on duty.

"All right, guys. Ten minutes."

Cass ushers the kids to the car, a general and her army. Alice carries the science project. Pete recites his vocab list. Cass manages the chaos, strapping the baby into his car seat. The house that stands behind them, a blue Victorian with black shutters, is as picturesque as the Connor family, an example of what can be attained with hard work, a little luck—and a low-interest mortgage.

Cass pulls out of the driveway and peers in the rearview. The sight of her kids is like medicine, the ultimate comfort. A happy, hearty brood ranging from tween to toddler. Alice is as willowy as she is moody, her hormones stretching her legs every night as well as her emotions. Pete is as sweet as he is sensitive, his round face and big eyes, circles in the same ripple of water. And Sam, like all youngest sibs, gets the best of both nature and nurture. In addition to their similar features, the common threads woven through each sibling by their mother, all three kids have the distinct look of children who are well-loved and nourished—translucent skin, rosy cheeks, and legs with an appealing ratio of fat to muscle. They share so many features, in fact— high foreheads, saucer eyes, and easy smiles—that few can tell that one of the three has a different father.

"Anyone know who left the upstairs window open?"

Pete shrugs.

"No idea," says Alice.

Cass stops at a light, surveys her surroundings. Two years after moving from New York, she still occasionally feels like she's in a foreign country.

Cumberland, Maine, is a lush and quiet satellite of Portland, with just enough access to the city to feel connected and just enough distance to feel protected. The town spans several miles of prime Casco Bay frontage, with the glass bay in the east and, in the north, evergreen forests. The bayside is dotted with colorful Capes and Victorians and a perpetual drizzle that amplifies the glow of light from their porches. The houses are built with wide clapboards, well-kept lawns, and modest proportions. The windows light up like fireflies every night as hardworking professionals file in, returning to the comfort of their wonderful, boring project. It is the closest Cass has ever seen to a Norman Rockwell painting. A town filled with people enmeshed in living their lives, as opposed to the people she knew in New York, for whom living their lives was a business.

Cass finds Mainers to be refreshingly honest. Like the people of America's old Midwest—realists, literalists, and skeptics. Maine, like Missouri, the original "show-me" state, is a population of unfailingly practical people, for whom a claim is not true unless it can be proven. And so, Cass joins the locals in their loving disdain for the weather—the short summers, the early chill, the reliably brutal winter, and, in the spring and fall, the near-constant drizzle. When the weather grows cold enough to see one's breath in the house (by mid-November), she rejoices in what locals call "the coastal effect," whereby the towns closest to the bay are spared the most extreme fluctuations due to the clash of warmer bay air with the frigid wind from the mountains.

Occasionally, when she misses home, she drives her car to Fort Williams Park, a jewel of the Maine coastline. She parks by the water, and then she runs away from the beach and back, as though she is on a pilgrimage and the lighthouse is her beacon. Like so many rituals, this habit has become a compulsion. Cass makes a point to drive there once a week, to run from the beach into the trails, through the gardens and the arboretum. And when the kids are restless at night, she turns on their nightlights and tells them that they too have a beacon. A beacon, she explains, is an unflinching guide that will never leave them.

"Like the North Star for sailors," Pete chimes in.

"Yes," says Cass.

"A bright light. An unflinching guide," says Alice. "A signal or a warning."

"Like a parent," says Pete.

"Yes." Cass smiles. "Like a parent." And the weight gives out in her stomach as she is struck anew by the enormity of her obligation. And the simple fact that, if she dies, her children will be left in darkness.

Fifteen minutes later, Cass pulls into the parking lot at the Bayside School. Earnest, windswept students balance backpacks, balls, and musical instruments. The smell of fresh-cut grass sails in on a breeze from the bay. As Cass watches her kids walk in the school doors, she exhales the daily mix of relief and nostalgia. Seeing them, content and engaged, folding into friends and classmates, helps silence the occasional question of whether it was the right decision to move so far from home, so far from friends and family. Doubts quelled, she continues downtown to tend to her own students.

Cass stands in the front of a classroom at the local university, University of Southern Maine or USM to its students. Her students, aspiring journalists, sport garden-variety piercings, concert T-shirts, and millennial arrogance. Cass writes on the board in capital letters: REPORTING ON THE FEMALE WITNESS. She takes a step back from the board, looks at the phrase, then walks back, erases, and rewrites: DESTROYING THE FEMALE WITNESS. She ignores the nervous laughter and gasps of her female students.

"Today we're going to look at trends in the reporting of female testimony. Let's look at this example. The DA has charged a man with sexual assault. The victim is the only witness. How does the defense destroy the testimony against him?"

A student cautiously raises her hand. "Is the victim telling the truth?"

"Does it matter?" asks Cass.

She has their attention now. Someone coughs. One student looks visibly uncomfortable, a thin, comely girl named Jean with short dark hair, rosy cheeks, black jeans, and a black denim jacket. Jean does not look amused. Jean looks outraged.

"Dredge something up," says Daniel. "Find some dirt. Catch her in a lie."

"Okay," says Cass. "Can you be more specific, Daniel?"

"History of drug use. A mental disorder. Better yet, a sex tape." Daniel does little to disguise the smile that this concept conjures. Retro glasses and overly groomed sideburns make him look a little more sinister than hipster.

"That's vile," says Jean.

"Well, hold on, Jean. Every person is entitled to a vigorous defense. Come on, guys. There's a playbook for this. How do you discredit a female witness?" Cass turns back to the chalkboard. "One: mental illness. You poke holes in the reliability of her observations and statements."

"The oldest defense in the book," says Daniel. " 'She crazy!' "

The students laugh. Except for Jean and another girl named Anna. Anna, even with cherubic blond curls, has the intensity of a prosecutor. She usually sits in the front row and takes copious notes. Sometimes she records the entire class on a recorder.

Cass occasionally marvels at the awesome potential of her female students. Would that they understood the power they hold, the power conferred by youth, intelligence, and beauty. This generation, she often notes, shares a confidence hers didn't. She only hopes she can direct them to an accurate awareness.

"Without a wound or a bruise," says Cass, "most assault cases come down to hearsay. He said. She said. Mental illness is a charge that's easy to make and hard to shed. What else?" She writes numbers on the chalkboard. "Two: fabrication. Describe the testimony as a lie. For a lie, you need a motive. The witness made it up due to jealousy, revenge, or, better yet, for money. Where have we seen this work?"

"The Cosby case," says Anna. "Thirty women. Thirty years."

"Yes," says Cass. "Good."

"It's like a bad light bulb joke," says Jean. "How many women have to report a crime before one person believes them?"

"It's true that this claim can make an assault charge dead on arrival. Why? A lot of people think women make up crimes for attention."

A collective cringe from all the students.

Cass writes the number three on the board, followed by the word *Inculpation*.

"What else?"

"Blame the victim," says Anna.

"Yes," says Cass. "Inculpation. Incriminate the victim. Her skirt was too short. She got too drunk. She wandered into the wrong locker room. Basically, she asked for it. Where have we seen this?"

"Pretty much every single rape case," says Jean.

"It's true," says Cass. "Shared inculpation works like a charm, not only discrediting the victim but often reducing the perpetrator's sentence. Okay, what else?"

The students are growing more uncomfortable.

"Charge her with something," says Daniel. "Criminalize the victim. Resisting arrest. Faking a police report. A theft that she committed."

"Yes," says Cass. "Shift the blame. Turn the tables. Change the focus. Who has employed this strategy?"

"The president of the United States?"

Laughter all around.

"Shocking but true. He confessed to numerous assaults on an audio recording. Then he denied it and passed it off as a joke. When his victims corroborated the account, he said his victims were lying. Fabrication. Then he said they were too ugly to merit his interest. Inculpation."

Anna and Jean are shaking their heads in unanimous revulsion. Cass sees their indignation. And raises the ante.

"Congratulations, you guys. You now know the playbook. How to destroy female testimony in four moves or less. What makes this possible?"

"Systemic baked-in misogyny in our legal system from the communities to the courts, from the policy to the precincts?" says Anna.

"Bingo!" says Cass.

The students shift uncomfortably in their seats, unsettled by the statements. Cass has made her point. Jean and Anna are proud to have assisted.

Cass sits in the USM office later. Her office is adorned by framed clippings. *Atlantic Monthly. Mother Jones.* A degree from the Columbia Journalism

School. A call comes in on her phone. Caller ID: DAD. She declines the call. Enough drama for one morning without talking to her father. Jean pokes her head in.

"Okay if I bring ingredients for s'mores when I babysit tonight?"

Cass softens, tamping back the reflexive anger that comes from seeing her father's number. "They would love it."

"See you at five thirty."

Cass waits in the car outside the Bayside School doors. A breeze scatters October leaves and the hair of outpouring students. Pete and Alice straggle out, looking a bit like runners after a track meet. Alice's ponytail is loose to her chin, and Pete's backpack needs a quick zip to deter a cascade of pencils.

"Nine out of ten?" Cass says.

"How'd you know?" says Pete.

"They got you on *dormant*?"

Pete's eyes widen.

"Mom, you're scary," says Alice.

"Nice work, Pete. How was your day, Al?"

Alice shrugs. She palms a piece of paper, crumples it up, and throws it in the trash, hopes no one noticed.

"You want to talk about it?" says Cass.

"Maybe later," says Alice.

Cass stalls and grabs the crumpled paper from the trash, stuffs it in her pocket.

"Got some good news," she says, lightening the mood.

"What?" says Alice.

"Jean's coming tonight. She said something about marshmallows and graham crackers. Wonder what she's planning . . ."

Pete beams. Even Alice cracks a smile.

Cass stands alone at a busy school function. She is trying to hide at the cheese table, feeling a little lost among the power couples.

"My favorite . . . a cave-aged cheddar paired with a two-year-old box wine."

She turns around, smiling. "I was dreading this without you," she says. "You know I wouldn't miss it," says Ryan.

A parent waves at Cass.

"Oh, God, here comes that Allen guy."

"Where is he now?"

"Four o'clock. Keep talking. Keep talking—"

"Allen, great to see you," says Ryan. "We loved the pictures you posted from your family trip building schools for indigenous children in the Amazon."

Another mother approaches, recusing Cass from this conversation. Nora is the same age as Cass but looks a bit younger with brown hair in a bob, long bangs, light eyes, and twiggy legs the size of her daughters'.

"Thank you," says Cass.

"How are you?" says Nora.

"Pretty good. I've been—"

"I literally woke up screaming. I have three deals closing, and two kids were up before six this morning. You make it look so easy." Nora is a real estate broker, the petite grande dame of Cumberland. The two women met this way, when Nora sold Cass and Ryan their house.

Cass smiles. "I just try to do my screaming in private. Where's Dave?"

"Probably in the broom closet, banging the art teacher. Ryan?"

Cass turns to find him. He is not where he was a moment ago. She scans the room. Nora spots him first.

"Busted."

He is talking to a pretty young redhead who wears overalls splattered with paint over a thin white tank top. Ryan looks up, waves at Cass. He holds up a painting of Pete's. A perfect family portrait. Yellow sun, cobalt sky, a mom, a dad, and three children. Except in Pete's rendering, everyone has curious sizes. Ryan is the largest, followed by Pete. Everyone else is tiny. Cass, however, is distracted by the current vignette's vivid colors. The art teacher's adorably tousled red hair and Ryan's white teeth as he laughs at her joke. It must have been really funny.

THREE

Cass and Ryan's first date nearly didn't happen. Cass had been home that night in her Brooklyn apartment, working on a story that would become both her treatise and her swan song: SEASON OF THE WITCH: THE RISE OF INSTITUTIONAL MISOGYNY FROM POLITICS TO PRECINCT. Cover story of *The New York Times Magazine.* Single byline. Cass Phillips, legal reporter. It was the most exhaustive piece she wrote as a journalist before taking a hiatus from work for something more important—specifically, two things. And it earned its place in a frame above her desk, even if her subsequent pieces never filled the space that surrounded it. She was working, in pajamas, when a friend sent her an SOS text asking if she would meet her at the bar on the corner. She was headed to a friend's birthday party and did not want to arrive "looking so single."

"Please," said the friend. "You never know. You might meet someone."

Moved by a combination of duty and procrastination, Cass knocked on the door of her neighbor, a grad student and occasional babysitter, asked for an hour of supervision, then swapped her bra for a lacier model, pulled on the nearest pair of jeans, and joined the other single moms of the world in search of the elusive dream of starting over, or what her friend incessantly referred to as "getting back out there."

Skeptical as she was of the idea, Cass tried on the bettor's logic of every woman who walks into a bar, that past odds do not predict the future, that one has an equal chance, every night, of finding one's soul mate. Sometimes, the idea of a soul mate seemed less fanciful than the specimen she was after: a man who loved her enough to join *her* family project, a family she started with another person; a man who loved her enough to abandon his biological imperative. On this night, she would meet a man game for both options.

Her friend, all dolled up and blown out, did want for some sort of decoy. Heavy eyeliner made her look more like a wounded raccoon than a wanton doe waiting for the buck with the biggest antlers. And so, when a man approached the two, Cass instinctively retreated. This only drew him closer. She did her best to deflect his attention, but he was relentless. Within twenty minutes, even the friend was rooting for Cass and Ryan.

Cass was immediately struck by Ryan's wit and his charm, his dogged drive and intelligence, both of which were on display in his pursuit of her affection. His looks gave him—put simply—an unfair advantage: dark brown hair, clear green eyes, and a smile that made a girl feel the sun had simply closed up shop and gone fishing for the summer. His voice, a boyish tenor, was somewhat hypnotic. That night, Ryan displayed the tenacity that she would soon learn was his nature.

They chatted passionately. Pheromones swirled. Sexual chemistry combusted. A fireworks show of common interests lit up their compatibility detectors. An "accidental" brush of his hand sent heat from her throat to her stomach. They both loved spaghetti and scrambled eggs and popcorn with extra butter! They both loved the Beatles and Raymond Carver! It did not take long for this promising array of shared likes to create that special aura. And so, when Cass's friend stood up to go to the bathroom, Ryan seized the moment. He asked if he could see Cass again and kissed her before she answered. The kiss caused such an electric jolt as to make her speechless. Ryan left soon after, claiming a work emergency, and Cass remained silent, if only because she was still unable to utter a complete sentence. He left as suddenly as he appeared, like some sort of caped crusader, leaving the prickle of bourbon on her lips, the smell of his laundry detergent on her clothes, and a taste of the future.

He called her the next day and invited her to meet for an encore. She hit up the neighbor to watch the kids again despite the short notice. An early autumn chill had already scattered leaves across the sidewalks, but as Cass walked to their date, the path before her may as well have been littered with roses. Ryan and Cass sat down at the bar on her corner, and things grew blurry long before they'd ordered their first cocktail.

"Do you like music?" he asked.

"Excuse me?"

"You know. Songs. Singing. You into that?"

"Isn't everyone?" said Cass.

"No, not everyone. There are people, for example, who actually hate it."

"Why would anyone hate music?"

"Because they're too sensitive. They can't bear it. Their nerves are too raw to withstand other people's emotions. Or something."

"Weird," she said. She stared at him, unnerved by the concept. But the truth was she had spent the better part of the last three years doing precisely that: shutting out all emotion.

"Except for the Beatles," he said. "They have a knack for making heartbreak seem pretty awesome."

She had to agree. "It's like they live in a world where human suffering never gets too awful."

The next ten years of their lives had been set on a course, and they both knew it.

"Oh shit."

"What?" she said.

"It's just . . ." He shook his head, wincing. "I can already tell how this is going to end."

"Oh no. You can? How?"

"Badly. Tragically. Violently. In a cloud of indignity and a blaze of glory."

"Bad like gore and violence? Or bad like pain and heartbreak?"

"Both."

"Oh no," said Cass, smiling. "How sad. How scary. How tragic."

He stared at her as though he were trying to solve an equation. "I know what we should do."

"What?"

"We need to take precautions."

"Precautions?"

"We need to make a list. Ten things."

"Ten things?"

"Ten things to do before we break up."

"To avoid breaking up?"

"Hopefully. Yes. Maybe if we do all these things, we might just stay to-gether." He grabbed the pen lying on the bill and started writing on a nap-kin. "Ten things to do before we break up."

"That might keep us together?"

"They may or may not."

"Why bother if it's doomed?"

"Try to look on the bright side."

Cass scanned the bar for the first time in several hours. The customers were thinning out, the candle on their own table nearing its last flicker. The bourbon she was drinking no longer tasted sour. And still, she took another drink and agreed to take the wager.

"Pessimists see the world like this."

He picked her drink off the table and poured half of it into his empty glass. Now both of them were half full. And half empty. "How do you see the world?"

Cass took a sip. "Blurry."

They toasted and both took a gulp.

"Number one: make out in a taxi while crossing the Manhattan Bridge, silhouetted by the New York skyline and a pink-and-gray sunset."

Cass smirked. "That's a little elaborate. Number two: read *The Sunday Times* in bed, cover to cover. We can read the Travel Section and plan all the trips we'll never get to take together."

"Number three: go diving in the Great Barrier Reef."

"Number four: take a walk on a deserted beach."

"Number five: scream at one another."

"Number six: hold each other and cry."

"Number seven: kiss and make up."

"Number eight: get married and have a child."

"Wait, that's two."

"Oh, you're right."

"A child?"

"Yes."

"No way. Never."

"Oh. Wow. Really? That's too bad."

"Number nine: say, 'I'm sorry.'"

"Wait. We need to talk about this. I have two children."

"Yes, I know. Are you saying you want to have a child with me?"

"No, I'm not saying that. I'm saying—"

"That's really sexy. I'll have to think about that."

She inhaled deeply. "Number ten: say goodbye."

"No, I don't want to say goodbye."

She looked into those eyes.

"Come on. Let's get out of here."

"Where are we going?"

He smiled. "I know this really beautiful bridge."

And before she knew it, they were speeding across the Manhattan Bridge, toward the New York skyline, silhouetted by a pink-and-gray sunset, kissing and kissing and kissing.

She woke up the next morning, heartily hungover. They exchanged some awkward niceties. He made her a cup of coffee. An hour later, she was sprinting down Atlantic, thanking her neighbor for the twelve-hour shift and racing to make it home before the kids woke up in the morning.

At work, she struggled to think of anything else for the next eight hours. A text arrived at six thirty while she and the kids were eating dinner.

"One down. Nine to go."

She stared at the phone. He was nothing if not charming.

"You free Saturday? Heard there's a good concert."

She put down the phone, smiling.

With coupledom came a new world view. Two cynics abandoned their grim outlooks. It was an end to the sadness of recent years, the beginning of a happy ending. Ryan and Cass were perfect together, not because either one was perfect but because they fit so well together, one craving the other's demands, the other craving being needed. Her grief understood his loneliness.

His damage understood her sadness. Together they felt as calm as a lakeside cabin. Sex, of course, played its part in this feeling of contentment. Sex in every position, location, and coordinate. Sex in cars, closets, taxis, stairwells, front seats, back seats, chairs, hallways, alleys, beds, and bathtubs. No spot, no time, no potential passerby could curb their appetite. It was sex that made Cass wonder how she had lived without it. Sex that made her rush home from work, wake at any hour. Sex that made her forget years of heartbreak. Oxytocin worked its special magic, proving itself the world's most potent panacea, upper, aphrodisiac, sedative, and amnesiac.

It renewed her faith in pleasure itself, a sensation she had written off as the delusion of a younger woman. She had long since replaced the pursuit of love with the decision that life must be understood in a relativistic fashion, with gradations of pain to be borne, withstood, waited out and ultimately, with the grace of detachment, without that thing called *judgment*. This grim outlook replaced the trusting nature of the pre-tragedy Cass until it offered a kind of respite, leveling all experience to just that, experience, and sapping it of expectation. Ironically, it was this penchant to trust that made her capable, once again, of suspending disbelief and expectations.

For Ryan, the relationship renewed his faith in the intimacy he had avoided, not only because it was his first experience with both but because he was somewhat shocked to find scintillating conversation and every pornographic position in the same woman. For a while, this mutual wonder worked, gluing them with the strongest adhesive. Cass was able to forget all the women who came before her. And Ryan was carried by his awe for Cass, all these new sensations and, even more shocking, his ongoing exclusive interest. Their love felt to them as it does to so many, as though they were love's sole inventor, as if they had discovered a new element in the periodic table.

But all this togetherness—the chemistry, the connection—all of it paled in comparison to another love affair altogether. When Ryan was with Cass's kids, when Ryan presided at the dinner table, telling stories about his travels, when Ryan caroused with Alice and Pete, commandeered elaborate snowball fights, led them down to the lake like a mallard with his ducklings, when Ryan made pancakes on Saturday mornings and the whole family crowded round the table like a team of hungry athletes, it triggered a deep primal urge in Cass, the most basic maternal instinct. It spread a feeling from her heart to her toes of all-consuming rightness.

Surely, there was a name for this: peace of mind, domestic bliss, contentment? The knowledge that her kids were healthy and happy, that she had fulfilled her duties, provided exactly what they needed: a mother and a father. The whole gang might be riding bikes, playing in the park, or just sitting at home, watching a movie, and she would find herself wearing the same stupid grin of people exiting a yoga class, high on meditation. Ryan was good for her kids. Her kids were good for Ryan. She was like a cavewoman who had brought a medicinal root back to her cubs, the ultimate gatherer to her marksman, except in this case, she had gathered something much better than a root: she had brought back—and trapped—a hunter.

One year later, and a small courthouse wedding behind them, Cass and Ryan's baby was born, and all the conditions surrounding his birth were quickly forgotten.

Ryan liked to say a new sun rose in the sky the day Sam was born. That's how drastically his world shifted. Far from those fathers who struggle with attachment during the newborn phase, Ryan was fixed on Sam from the first night like a laser on a target. Call it paternal instinct, or narcissism—for him, there was no distinction. Time spent away from Sam was wasted. Time spent with Sam was precious. Sam gave Ryan's life meaning, story, purpose. For Cass, it was all good news, happiness to the third power. Sam was the perfect final ingredient to their burgeoning family, the last pinch of salt in a simmering dish, the connecting thread, the strongest adhesive. Watching a relationship bloom between her baby and her husband was just as potent as watching love blossom between Ryan, Pete, and Alice but with the added pleasure of a newborn. Here was the product of her love with a man she adored, a cooing bundle in her arms and a sibling for her son and daughter.

Their first year as a family of five arrived with all its wonders—followed by the usual stresses. Muffled versions of "I told you so" turned into louder squabbles over the inequities of the nighttime feed, time to go to the gym, relax, read, take a shower, financial stress over the cost of groceries, child care, doctors, square footage, the nightly yelps of older kids awoken by younger siblings—all the inevitable tumbling pins of two working parents attempting the work-life juggle. Parents of newborns find themselves in a tricky position, in need of extra energy just when the right to a full night's sleep has been temporarily suspended. And so a month of couples' counseling turned into six and then twelve months. And new problems replaced old ones—the cost of square footage in Brooklyn, the dragon-like daily growth and need for space of three children, the cost of health insurance, education, not to mention the simple quest to get two kids to school on time every morning, shoelaces tied and stomachs sated.

There were other more menial matters as well, more carnal kinds of competition, such as the difficulty of shedding baby weight and the seemingly endless crop of taut younger women strolling through flea and farmers' markets in Brooklyn like gazelles on the Serengeti, and the threat of their intrusion into the periphery of the gaze of her husband. So did these concerns begin to collude with her late-night internet surveys and the ever-present allure of real estate listings in Seattle, San Francisco, Portland! Who could not picture their own family, crowded round the dining room table of a well-priced four-bedroom, lounging in these "sun-lit" living rooms, thriving in these "charm-filled" Victorians, Colonials, and Craftsmans, kids enrolled in the "best public school district" in the nation? And so Ryan and Cass went the way of so many before them, so many self-respecting families when faced with these options: they took a plea bargain, exonerated each other, and sentenced themselves to a more "livable city," if not the actual suburbs.

FOUR

By all accounts, that first year was a good year for the Connors. The move came with new jobs for both parents, Cass's as a professor in the journalism department at USM, Ryan in a snazzy architecture firm, an industry with as much business in Portland as the prior decade's lobstermen. Whereas Cass's previous work required an enormous amount of travel, she quickly found that the new job required an enormous amount of staying in the same position, standing at the front of a classroom of big-eyed aspiring journalists, defending the viability of print to the post-digital revolution, debating the best way to get their blogs in front of the "right person," and then, after class, sitting at a desk in a basement office, fielding students' questions of what was it like and how did you get your start working at a real-life city paper?

The job, if a slight demotion from legal reporter at *The Times* and frequent contributor to *Mother Jones*, was, in truth, the perfect graduation, allowing Cass to balance the hustle of work with the hush of home for the first time since giving birth to Alice. It offered a long-overdue respite from the working mother's juggle—the one that leaves mothers breathless from the first waking gasp to the first moment of sleeping relaxation. It was, for Cass, nothing less than a long-overdue vacation. As rewarding as her career had been, as impressive as her advances within it, so was the fact that her hard work now enabled her to coast for a few years in Portland while focusing on her kids and husband.

For Ryan, the move was the culmination of the work of a decade, a long-coveted career change after working in a city design firm, suffering the Pharaoh-style exploitation of its younger generation. The way he talked about leaving his firm, he may as well have been released from prison. The slaves of New York, he liked to say, were used up until they were no longer useful, whipped and scourged by their superiors, their best ideas snatched without credit, held captive in marble offices, forced to eat greasy takeout until their meticulous blueprints etched red lines into their faces. It was, for Ryan, a welcome relief to leave behind this culture. And so the move was characterized by all sorts of reverent chatter, phrases like "quality of life," and "making up for lost time," dreamy plans to cook more, hike more, read more, buy a kayak.

Cass's family was less enthusiastic about the move to Portland. They opposed the idea of Cass moving the kids hundreds of miles away. At first Cass was taken aback by their reaction, but she had come to learn that grief brings out the best or the worst in people, not much in between bottomless generosity or callous judgment. Her own family was not immune to the polarities of human nature. Her father, Marty, suffered from some of the more unappealing isms—egotism, narcissism, solipsism, and good old-fashioned chauvinism. He was born of a generation that tolerated, as opposed to respected, women, charging women with the crime of original sin and, after the malice of temptation, for adding insult to injury with their irascible, emotional natures. Three wives and several affairs provided ample proof of his theory, and a trail of increasingly bitter wives, each with more naked financial goals and more recent college graduations.

Cass's mother, Dale, though well meaning, was similarly challenged, as reverential of social norms as her ex-husband was oblivious to them. And the disparity between her hopes and dreams created an angst quelled only by the right daily dosage. She was consumed with a set of expectations that

Cass had always maddeningly flouted, starting with her choice to use the name *Cass* instead of *Cassandra*, followed by her favoring combat boots and red lipstick in high school, followed by her decision to embed herself in Croatia and write about the refugee crisis. The mother-daughter relationship had always teetered between tortured and tattered. The death of Cass's first husband was no less an insult to Dale than Cass's decision to marry Ryan years later.

When Cass fell in love with Ryan, her mother did not hide her aversion. This grew to equal opportunity animosity directed at both Cass and Ryan.

"What specifically don't you like," Cass had asked, "other than the fact that he's not Jason?"

"I don't know," her mother had quipped. "There's just something about him. And frankly, I think it reflects poorly on you that you're so quick to get back on the saddle."

At first Cass took the criticism with a measure of understanding, but she never forgot the comment. Her relationship with her mother worsened as her relationship with Ryan developed. Over time, she stopped confiding in her mother altogether, whether commiserating over a minor quibble or consulting on a major life decision. Negative reinforcement is a powerful force. She stopped calling to avoid hearing four words ("I told you so") more than any explicit conversation. Little by little, the rift between mother and daughter widened into a chasm. When Sam was born, Cass's mother sent a note and a present, but to this day, she had yet to visit their new home in Portland or to meet her youngest grandson. Perhaps because of these tenuous bonds and a toxic family upbringing, Cass was particularly open to the idea of starting fresh in a different part of the country.

The choice had proven a good one.

Two years after moving to Portland, the kids were settled in their school, laying sturdy roots with friends, digging into their schoolwork, and buttressing these foundations with their own interests—soccer, dance, music. The house finally looked like a home, the floors collaged with faded rugs, walls adorned with mosaics of children's paintings, rooms sprouting with houseplants, musical instruments, and a sofa that transformed the living room into a den fit for hibernation. The house still needed work—the inspection revealed some kinks in the basement foundation, a leak in the roof, and a burgeoning termite problem—which was not ideal given all the other flux.

But the defects of the house made it more affordable, and so they took their lumps—taking on a mortgage that was cramped, if not crippling, with the hope that real estate values would appreciate faster than their cost of living. They bet the farm on the farm, draining their savings into an asset that would either set them up for life, or sink them.

Occasionally, they checked in with each other, assessing the choice to move as they lay in bed, the house finally quiet.

"Do you still think we're doomed?" Ryan asked.

Cass smiled and ignored him, continued reading.

He ignored her attempt to ignore him. "Do you still think we're doomed?" he repeated.

She shook her head. "Don't be ridiculous."

He stared at her, smiling, flirting, then frowned at her disinterest. He leaned in suddenly, grabbed her book, dislodging her reading glasses in the process.

"Hey, what are you doing?" she said. She stared at him, defiant.

"Do you or don't you?" he repeated.

"Do I or don't I what?"

"Do you or don't you think we're doomed?"

She stared at him, eyes narrowed. It was this ability to turn from interested to intense, from asking to demanding in a moment that made Ryan so endearing—and occasionally unsettling. "Doomed to live in paradise," she said, ending the face-off, thereby inviting his lips onto hers and quashing any doubts that they had made the right decision.

Their house was built in the classic Victorian construction, two stories, four bedrooms, a dormer attic made for hiding, ornate, if tired, trim on the roof that looked like a storybook cottage or, when decked with Halloween garb, decidedly haunted. There was plenty of room for a sizable family to burrow in without rubbing elbows, and a trim backyard for everyone to spill into in the summer. The house was built into a hill, two stories in the front and three in the back, with a grade so steep as to make room for a third floor below. The "hidden" half-underground floor made it feel a bit like a home for a family of elves, as did the abundance of children spilling into the back-yard in the summer. It was painted a pleasing dusty blue with black trim that matched its slate roof. It was, in every way, the embodiment of the Connor family—apparently perfect on the outside with hidden depth and complexity. Both sides of the house boasted a different point of view; a window that opened inches above the ground, putting the viewer at eye level with grass. Or, if you stood on your toes on the top floor, a view of the vast bay in the distance.

A house without a view of the bay would have sufficed, but Ryan was persuasive. His argument was simple: if they were going to live their dream, they might as well do it in their dream house. It was time, he told Cass, to "start living their best life." She knew him well enough to understand his true meaning. Not so much financial ambition as growing up, as he described it, the poor kid in a world of privilege. Nonetheless, she wanted this for him, wanted to help him achieve success on his terms, and so she agreed when he asked her to dip into her savings for the down payment. In fact, it was more of a dive than a dip into the money left to her by her husband, but better to put it in a solid asset than leave it vulnerable to spending. The deed named Ryan and Cass as joint tenants with rights of survivorship. God forbid something happen to one, his or her half of the house would automatically transfer to the one still standing.

The house grew increasingly incomplete as you walked up the stairs, creating the sense that you were traveling back in time as you ascended. The first floor housed the kitchen, the living room, and a dining room table. The kitchen was an amalgam of appliances bought on Craigslist: cabinets salvaged from the prior owners and a large refrigerator that intermittently buzzed and vibrated. The floor itself looked something like a quilt of wooden patchwork because of all the places walls had been removed and flooring replaced with plywood. Cass yearned to sand the floors or at least paint them white, but Ryan opposed the idea, insisting that he liked it as is. She suspected he opposed the idea simply because he hadn't thought of it himself.

The second floor was more of a mess, as it contained one empty room, not only empty of furniture but empty of flooring. Ryan's first demolition project had been to remove a spiral staircase that rose from the first to second floor, the removal of which he began on a Friday night at ten with a pickax. For a week, the family lived with a ten-by-ten-foot hole in the ceiling, joking about how lucky they were that the hole wasn't in the roof and how the placement of a pole would turn their home into a firehouse. Eventually, Ryan enlisted a team of local workers to close up the hole and haul out the staircase.

But Ryan had only begun his endeavors in home improvement. The wall between the living room and kitchen was his next target.

"One day, I'm just gonna take it down. I'm gonna do it with a hammer." And, as Ryan tended to do, he made good on his promise.

On a Sunday morning, Cass, Alice, and Sam returned from the grocery store to find the house in a state of chaos. Walls that were there when she left two hours before were no longer. Electrical wires swung from the ceiling like exotic jungle branches. Flurries of white drywall dust coated the kitchen appliances. Metal framing spiked from tufts of insulation. Ryan stood in the middle of this mess, wild with exhilaration, grunting as he hacked at a wall with an ax, a one-man demolition. It was as though a hurricane had blown through the house, except the hurricane was her husband.

"What are you doing?" Cass said. She instinctively stepped in front of the kids, backing them into the hall behind her.

Ryan beamed, like a hunter with his fallen target, his face white from the drywall dust, his UC–Berkeley sweatshirt soaked with perspiration. "This wall was driving me nuts," he said.

"So you took the whole room down?"

"I got a little carried away."

Cass surveyed the room, imagined their children playing in this hazardous death zone. "Ryan, the kids can't be in here. Everything in here is dangerous. The kitchen isn't functional anymore. The air in here is toxic."

"Yeah," he said, still holding the ax. "I thought of that."

"Are you sure this wasn't a structural wall?" She eyed a tenuous pillar that no longer reached the ceiling, the wires swaying beside it.

"Yeah," he said. "Certain." And then, approaching the pillar, he said, "If it was, better we know that now. This thing looks like it needs a replacement."

Cass surveyed the scene, moved by the cold comfort. "Where are we going to sleep?" she said. "I'm picking Pete up from soccer in twenty minutes."

He stood in silence, fixed on her like a drunk man trying to regain balance. "Don't worry," he said. "I'll clean it up, I promise. Take 'em to the park for a little while. I'll have it fixed by dinner." He scurried away to find a broom and began sweeping like a possessed beaver.

Cass watched him begin in total indignation. She might as well have stumbled into the house and found her husband in her dress and heels, dancing in front of the mirror. But something shifted in her as she watched his frantic cleaning: sympathy and begrudging respect for his ambition. He wanted, needed a happy home so badly he would stop at nothing. Here he was, using the tools that men use, the few at a man's disposal for construction, instead of destruction. And so he should be forgiven, she decided, for passionate effort. God bless him for taking this on. Most men expected others to do their work for them.

"If you want a piece of pie, you gotta pick the apples."

She shook her head, resigned, but the sight of him made her laugh.

"Keep them out of the house a few hours. I'll have it back to normal. By dinnertime, I'll have the kitchen totally up and running."

Months passed before the walls were sealed up, framed, dry-walled, and plastered, this time by a professional team under an engineer's guidance. In the meantime, Ryan fashioned a temporary kitchen, turning the house into his own architecture school for the children and teaching the family the pleasures of in-home camping. He taped garbage bags to the walls, forming a crude insulation, and reconfigured the kitchen appliances in the newly open space so that the entire living room was oriented around a central kitchen island. While the neighbors covered their kitchen counters in slabs of slate and granite, Ryan borrowed from the subfloor and laid a plank of plywood.

The kitchen was command central for Ryan's experiments, the ultimate realm for his transformation from Peter Pan to Pater. Long gone were the "medicinal" pot cookies Ryan made Cass during their courtship. Now, Ryan's culinary feats were fit for a family of five, all manner of meats grilled in the backyard in the summer, hearty pastas and soups in the winter, and all year round, come Saturday morning, his famous pancake breakfast. Ryan was never happier than when he was barking orders at his family, transforming his stepkids into sous-chefs, enlisting the kids to crack an egg, to prep or peel vegetables, bossing them around like the chef of a three-star Michelin restaurant. Pete was usually tasked with cleaning while Alice took on more advanced work, chopping, or, much to Cass's horror, transferring heated items. The kids rejoiced in the responsibility, the drama, and the magic. Cass reveled in their delight, usually from the sidelines, enjoying the reprieve to nurse the baby. The division of labor worked. Together they made elaborate meals for family dinners and Sunday breakfasts. The quality of these meals, which ranged from spotty to very good, was secondary to the process. In cooking, as with home improvement, Ryan walked a fine line between safety and hazard, between the outcome and the adventure.

Pasta-making was perhaps their most successful project. Alice cleaned the work surface, wiping down the wooden counter. Pete prepped the ingredients, the perfect trifecta: flour, olive oil, water. Together they built a pyramid of flour, poured olive oil and water to form a lake in the center, and carefully mixed these disparate substances in a quiet meditation. When satisfied, they rolled the dough into sheets as thin as cotton fabric and fed them into a contraption with the patience of weavers. The least successful experiment was apple cider caramel. A molten drop of caramel erupted from the pot and landed on Pete's cheek. The trip to the emergency room and the scar from the burn only slightly soured the sweetness of the candy-making chapter.

As is true with any chef, Ryan's attention to his tools verged on the obsessive. He had an enormous array of gadgets more sophisticated than a typical domestic kitchen—a terrifying collection of knives, a menacing sharpener, zesters, graters, basters, mandolines, a squadron of pots and pans, and a large vat called an immersion circulator that looked and sounded like an indoor aquarium. Those who carelessly handled or improperly cleaned these tools would suffer Ryan's wrath, with Ryan reprimanding the offending borrower without mercy, or searching the house for the person who had placed a knife in the dishwasher instead of washing and drying it by hand.

Sometimes Ryan's passion for cooking unnerved Cass. Kitchen experiments could spin out of control, turning the kitchen into a postapocalyptic landscape. Though the kids loved the chaos, Cass sometimes found it disconcerting. It was this wild, manic, slightly unhinged side to her husband that sometimes made her feel she lived with a man in whom lurked a vaguely maniacal demon. When planning a pig roast, boiling molten sugar for caramel, or soaking cashews for homemade nut milk, he sometimes veered from charming chef to fanatical mad scientist. The pig he brought home from the local butcher looked alarmingly more like a fetus than a piglet. The nuts he soaked for almond milk reaped quarts of toxic liquid.

The evolutionary attributes of such a man were not lost on Cass—a man who could build a fire and cook a good meal, make a decent living and even better pancakes, frame a wall and lay the foundation for a fort with the kids. What better partner could she dream up? What better role model for her sons and her daughter? Ryan was the ultimate modern man, a well-rounded composite of the often bifurcated male and female virtues, a man as comfortable in the kitchen as he was in the shed, as graceful on a bicycle as he was in the bedroom. And so Cass tried to be graceful too with the inevitable clunks of this role reversal. So what if he asserted control of domains she might have wanted to claim for herself—namely, the kitchen? So what if he seemed to be better at most anything he took on, from scrambled eggs to roast chicken? Competition was a healthy force in the kitchen, at least, and perhaps it could be similarly applied to parenting.

It did occur to Cass that this competition might one day veer from rivalry to something more rancorous—and that Ryan's contributions, while often helpful, did slightly encroach on certain spheres traditionally reserved for the mother. Worse, it sometimes occurred to her that his ambition might ultimately end their marriage; that when her beauty and reproductive role were exhausted, she might be reduced to obsolescence. For example, what if, once she finished nursing Sam, Ryan decided he was the better parent, the only parent necessary, that Cass had served her use and was now disposable? He was not without awareness of other younger specimens in their environment. But such dire Darwinian prophecies seemed more fitting for a mongoose than a man, more likely for a wolf than this wanderer who had stationed himself in her kitchen, and so she squelched her misgivings as the same kind of rivalry that rankled her own children. Instead, she counted her blessings. This new man and all that he came with—a home undivided by maternal and paternal roles, by the gender norms prescribed by pink and blue lines, by any expectations whatsoever—was a man, a home, a life that a generation of women had fought for, a life that allowed her to focus on what she loved the most—her kids and her work and her husband.

FIVE

Cass wakes with a start just before sunrise. A noise outside? One of the kids? She bolts out of bed, riled. She hurries down the hall, pulling on her bathrobe. The window is open again. She closes it, bothered. She checks the kids' rooms. They are asleep. All is well. All is quiet.

"Ginger," she calls. Still moving quickly, she continues down the stairs in her nightgown and sweater. In the kitchen, she checks cabinets, opens closet doors. She bursts out the back door into the backyard. "Ginny," she calls. "Ginger."

Scanning the yard, she spots a neighbor's fence and a swinging dog door. She looks around, then up. The family cat is perched at the top of a telephone post.

Minutes later, Cass walks back down the hall, holding the cat, only slightly breathless.

She gets back into her bed, more confused than before, addresses her sleeping husband.

"Did you leave the upstairs window open?"

"Nope."

"Cat got out," she says.

"Something must've spooked her."

"What does she know that we don't?" says Cass.

"That sleep is not allowed in this house anymore."

"Nora said there was a burglary in Bayview."

"Maybe you should dust for prints, Miss Marple." He turns to his wife, kisses her neck, but she does not engage. He rolls over and goes back to sleep, now as annoyed as she is.

The Connors are not morning people. Waking occurs in phases, beginning with a ten-minute incubatory stage that looks a lot like sleeping. Alice's entrance is the most dramatic. Her hair is in a tornado, as though she has averted being sucked into the sky by a vacuum and escaped with only this evidence of her nearness to natural disaster. Pete's arrival is less dramatic, more of a saunter than an entrance, in which he migrates from the bedroom to the kitchen like a coastal bird, stopping at a pile of LEGOs, poking around a bit before advancing to the breakfast table. The baby wakes up in a spectacular blaze of tears and laughter, followed by an onset of delight that is brighter than summer sunshine. It will be another twenty minutes before the whole group is assembled.

Finally, they achieve that precarious moment just before hunger overwhelms and lateness becomes inevitable. But the fragile stasis is interrupted by an urgent message: Ryan calling from upstairs, upset about something.

"Cass!" Footsteps increase in volume as he marches down the stairs and enters the kitchen.

"What is the matter?" Cass asks.

"She ruined another shirt. That's like a thousand dollars in damage." Ryan holds up a crisp blue dress shirt, the color of a baby's bonnet. "We need to find someone new."

"Ryan, what happened?" Cass says. She looks at the empty stairs.

"Marta destroyed a brand-new shirt. These shirts can't go in the dryer."

Marta works part-time for the Connors, watching Sam when Cass teaches and helping to ferry the older children from school to sports and playdates. A mother herself, she has large brown eyes, graying black hair, and a soothing demeanor. She focuses on Sam, pitches in around the house, and otherwise helps Cass solve the daily mathematical challenge of getting three kids to and from three different places. She has not been working long, only started at the beginning of Cass's semester but, from Ryan's critique, seems destined not to stay much longer.

"You're always saying you need more clean shirts," Cass says, trying humor.

"Now I have one fewer."

"She was just trying to help." Cass smiles again, a last attempt at resolution.

"She broke my LEGOs too," Pete adds. He is always happy to second Ryan. His mother's temper accelerates as soon as she's outnumbered.

Ryan knows this. "Do you know how much time it takes to put those together?"

"Time and effort," says Pete.

"Exactly. Time and effort. I want her out by the end of the week." He is like a politician this way, seizing opportunities, capitalizing on weakness. It is almost athletic. "Promise you'll find someone better."

"It's not easy to find someone good."

"Apparently," says Ryan. He is walking toward the door, signaling, without the usual niceties, the end of the conversation.

"Maybe you shouldn't buy such expensive shirts," Cass says. Sometimes self-defense and counterattack have no distinction.

"Maybe you should find someone experienced to be in our home and watch our children."

Ryan is at the door now. He laces his shoes and puts on his jacket, leaving for work without a goodbye—knowing this will hurt her more than any comment.

"*My* children," Cass mutters. She says this for her own satisfaction.

The kids look up as the front door slams, from their breakfast to their mother. They are waiting for him to come back, for the door to open again, and for him to burst in, smiling, saying, "I was just kidding!" But he doesn't. They check their mother's eyes, which do a poor job of hiding disappointment, but she deflects their looks with a valiant performance.

"Someone woke up on the wrong side of bed," she says, smiling. "No dessert for Ryan tonight."

The kids take this as license to laugh. They cautiously relinquish their concern and go back to eating. Cass, too, returns to the business of breakfast, combating her own emotion with a rigorous focus on the wooden beam in the kitchen. The beam has a large splinter that descends from the top down the pillar.

Focusing on the day ahead distracts her from this revelation. She teaches tonight and needs Ryan to pitch in with child care. As the kids finish their breakfast, Cass drifts upstairs for a round of reconnaissance. She walks to the bathroom, stands at the sink, and opens the medicine cabinet. She removes Ryan's prescription bottle and palms it, a biweekly habit, then conducts the measurement by which she can tell if he has taken his daily dose from the change in the weight of the bottle. The bottle feels as heavy as the last time she checked, a few days prior. She reads the label more carefully now, noting the name of the med and the prescribing doctor, Dr. Lugner.

Ryan is seeing a new therapist due to the onslaught of work and life stress he has lamented, and what he has acknowledged as an increasingly short temper. The anxiety med, while generally leveling, has the unfortunate effect of either curbing his temper or, when days are missed, making him prone to erratic moods and anger. With new concern, she walks downstairs, utters a five-minute warning to the children. Hoisting the baby to her hip, she hurries out the front door. A morning like this will ruin her day when a simple exchange can correct it.

Ryan is sitting in his car, typing into his cell phone. The look on his face is inscrutable, the look of a man writing an important work email or planning where to meet his mistress.

"Don't forget. I teach tonight," Cass says, approaching.

"You're kidding. Can't Marta stay?" he asks.

"She has to leave at six."

"You realize she is affecting my work. Who would you rather get fired?"

"You or me?" Cass asks.

"Me or her," says Ryan.

"Hmm," she says, pretending to think. "Marta helps out a lot with the kids. Tell you what," Cass says. "If you get fired, I'll fire her."

Anger in Ryan looks like a smile before it looks like a snarl. His breathing sharpens.

"I'm sorry," she says. Retreat is her only move now. The words work a strange magic on Ryan, defusing his anger.

"Meet me at six at the office," he says. It is a concession. "But promise you'll find someone better. Promise you'll have someone new by Monday."

"I'll do my best," Cass says. "I have work today also."

He makes the half-mean, half-irresistible look that turns Cass into a puddle. Is it possible his cruelty turns her on, or just that she is addicted to the challenge of losing and earning back his affection?

Cass watches Ryan drive away and asks herself this question: How did she get to this place—was it slow or sudden? How did she fall so far afield from a happy marriage? Did everyone deviate gradually from a life they knew and loved to one that defied recognition? The only thing she knew for sure was that this switch escaped detection. She and Ryan have been married for three years. They have three children. They have lived in Portland for one of these years. Somewhere, though she could not say when, her confidence—and their marriage—faltered.

Standing at her front door, she takes a mental inventory of what she knows at this moment. One: she is not a child anymore. She is a grown-up. Therefore, she is not helpless. Two: she has all the clothes she needs, an assortment of skirts and dresses, tights and socks, shirts and sweaters. She has enough bras and underwear to get through a week without doing laundry, enough lace to pull together a respectable outfit for a date with ten minutes' warning—and enough makeup (rose blush, pink-hued lipstick, gray eyeliner, black mascara, matte foundation). She has enough friends to go out once a week, get dressed up once a month, enough passion in her marriage to have sex once a week, and occasionally, if the baby's nap conspires, in the afternoon on a Sunday. She has a job, she has a home, she has children, friends, and relations. She knows her children's shoe sizes, their favorite flavors of cake and ice cream. She knows her best friends' birthdays. She has, in a drawer in the laundry room, Band-Aids, scissors, Scotch tape, pens, and paper. She has saved all her kids' artwork. She keeps a cabinet stocked with crayons, paints, and Magic Markers. She has a bulletin board with a calendar marked with all her children's schedules. She has high black heels for an evening out, appropriate shoes for the classroom, hats and scarves and mittens, a bucket of umbrellas, and, somewhere in a box upstairs, Christmas ornaments, snowsuits, sleds, a Boogie Board, and, farther in the attic, shoe boxes stuffed with yellowing photographs of ancestors and exes.

She has things that she can count. Things that she can count on and by which she can be counted. She is depended on by a precious few and has those she can depend on. She has everything she needs to survive. She has the capacity for her and her kids to subsist in their home in a natural disaster. Water, batteries, canned food. She has achieved a self-sufficient state; she is not dependent on another person for sustenance and protection. She is depended upon by three people for food, water, sleep, hugs, kisses, and guidance, transportation to soccer practice, dance class, playdates, and sleepovers. She depends on someone only for the luxuries of advanced civilizations, companionship, love, sex, and conversation. She has achieved adulthood.

This realization gives her great comfort. More than comfort. Relief. The feeling after comfort. The hope that after comfort is lost, comfort can be recovered. The same feeling she gets when she loses her keys, that she is now locked out of her life, with as much hope to re-enter as a trespasser. But then, as she fumbles in her pocket, desperate to find her phone, to call a neighbor, a friend, a locksmith, she finds her keys in her pocket. Her belongings still belong to her. All may not be well in the world, but she still has access.

Stilled, she turns and walks back into her house to collect her children.

The phone rings. She sees the Westchester area code and declines the caller. It is her father, and he is calling to talk about work, to pepper her with his worries. To make sure she is doing all she can to get into the tenure track, taking on a bigger class load, meeting often with her superiors, trying to publish. He is calling to project his aspirations onto his daughter, while simultaneously demeaning her for falling short, for failing his lifelong goal of having a son simply by being a daughter. No, she will not be answering. Enough gender politics for one morning.

Cass and Nora are out for a run after school drop-off. Nora has asked if she can join in Cass's weekly routine, and Cass has agreed in an effort to expand her friend base beyond one acquaintance. It is one of those rare breathtakingly clear days in Portland. The sky is a crystal ball. The future is sunny.

"I can't believe you do this every day," says Nora.

"Need it to stay sane," says Cass.

Nora struggles to keep up. "You're in really good shape," she says. "What else have you been doing?"

"Just running."

"After your husband?"

"Nora!"

"Most I've run in the last year is to catch my kids in the playground."

"There is no better workout."

"They should give us awards," says Nora, "throw us a party. And this year's award goes to . . . Every Working Mother."

"Dream on," says Cass.

"That reminds me," says Nora. "I'm throwing something for Halloween. For grown-ups. Costumes. You're coming."

They run past majestic bay-view homes, uniform in their grandeur. The Victorian era was a good one for architecture.

"Would you guys ever sell?" Nora asks.

"The house? No. We're just getting settled."

"It needs so much work."

"It's good for Ryan. He needs a project."

"Other than the move, the job, the beach house, and the stepkids?"

"He's happiest when he's busy."

They hit a patch of uneven terrain. Cass slows down, cuing Nora about the roots and rocks underfoot.

"I just got the most amazing listing," she says. "Water views. Totally mint."

"Ryan would never sell."

"It's only his decision?"

"No, but we're enjoying the process. Besides, I've already gone through it. When Jason died, the sale of the house was . . . a lot to deal with."

"You're tenants in common. On the deed. I remember from the contracts." Nora has either missed or chosen against delving into the subject of Cass's deceased husband.

"You trying to get me to leave Ryan?"

"No, just don't drop dead."

"What?"

"The house would automatically transfer to him. Not the children."

Cass comes to a full stop. "You really don't like my husband."

"Don't be ridiculous," she says. "I love Ryan. I just believe a woman should be able to pick up and leave at any moment. Feminism, bitches."

Cass stares at Nora. This has gotten awkward. "I'd better go," she says. "I teach at noon."

"You should be sainted," says Nora.

Cass peels off, heading back toward their neighborhood. Nora starts walking.

It is just after five o'clock, and Cass is on her way to Ryan's office. She texts him as she gets in the car.

"Heading to you now," she says. "See you at six." He will need to be punctual. She is on a tight schedule.

The usual chaos of dinner is doubled on nights when Cass teaches. Tonight, it is augmented by confusing logistics. Cass has made last-minute arrangements in light of the scheduling conflict. The older kids will go home from school with a friend. And Cass will bring the baby when she drives to the city, dropping him off with Ryan at his office before racing to USM for her seminar at six thirty. Ryan will pick up Pete and Alice at their friend's house, drive the baby back home, and, if he keeps his end of the bargain, Cass will return home after class to a calm and quiet house, purring with sleeping children. But first she must drive a fussy baby into the city in rush-hour traffic. By the time they've reached the city, he is wailing at maximum volume, which makes the late hour and the lack of response from Ryan all the more unnerving.

It's quarter of six, and there has been no answer to any texts or emails. Cass picks up her phone and dials. No answer. She dials again. Time is passing quickly.

"Ryan. Where are you? I teach at six thirty."

And then again, five minutes later: "I'm going to have to take the baby to class if you don't surface."

With some effort, she parks and carries the baby into the building. It is one of the glass-and-steel buildings in the newly fashionable Arts District, buildings that seem to evidence radical changes in engineering, apparently standing on pillars of glass or rubber, with steel draped in the same way as canvas. Other than these architectural feats, the building has no distinct personality and produces no further indications of Ryan's whereabouts, other than the blank look of the main desk receptionist and the photos on the desk of Stephanie, Ryan's over-tanned, underage, also absent assistant. Stephanie is younger than Cass realized and prettier than Ryan described, with the bleached-blond hair of a sorority girl and the manly muscles of—who knew it was a sport?—a championship "bikini competitor." An array of contest photos, ass splayed, tan sprayed, reveals his assistant's hobby, along with a recent win at the "twenty-five and under conference" in Miami! No such luck for Cass, however, who is still failing at the simple task of finding her husband.

Another ten minutes pass with no sign of Ryan. No answer on any screen. Texts, calls, silence. Ryan has disappeared, either into a closed-door meeting or an alien abduction. Facing the special panic reserved for working mothers, Cass flips the switch designed to help in emergencies. Usually, this adrenal gland kicks in for manageable disasters, like having to change a diaper while pressing mute in the middle of a conference call while in a public restroom. And usually, the call goes off with only minor reputational damage with an awkward, self-deprecating apology about a babysitter's untimely departure and halfhearted patronizing murmurs from others that "we've all been there." But today's work-life emergency offers no such respite. She has one of two options: cancel class and be docked for irresponsible behavior, or take the baby to class and pray that the smug millennials have mercy on her and deem her child care malfunction more endearing than tragic. And that they don't complain to the dean that their teacher is wasting their parents' tuition.

One last lifeline. Cass is nearly too proud to call her.

"Nora Hall Real Estate," says her assistant. "Home is where the heart is."

Cass hangs up and starts the car. "Looks like you're coming to class, kiddo."

Her students are unfortunately less compassionate than she hopes. They smirk with the dispassion reserved for the young and wealthy. But Cass will not be shamed. She is not so easily broken. She fixes her hair, wipes baby drool off her shirt, and, with Sam on her hip, walks gamely to the chalkboard. Sam makes an adorable sound, much to her students' amusement. But Cass is stone-faced. No special treatment for mothers. She delivers a solid attempt at a lecture, intermittently holding Sam on her hip and placing him on the floor with a stack of pens and paper. Finally a young female student takes pity on her situation, taking Sam by the hand and leading him out of the classroom. He goes quietly with one last heartbreaking glance at his mother. It is an act of mercy but comes too late for salvation. For the last half hour of class, Cass abandons her lecture to classroom discussion, but she is too distracted to offer much, her attention divided between Sam's babbling just outside the door and flickers of rage and concern over the whereabouts of her husband.

By the time class is over, Cass is exhausted. She leaves the university building, upset and depleted. She carries Sam in her arms, balancing her bag, books, and his belongings. Now, as opposed to during the class, Sam is calmly sleeping.

Ryan is standing outside when they emerge from the building. He is leaning against his car like a high school suitor and lunges toward Cass when he sees her, opening his arms to take the baby. She instinctively holds Sam tighter and keeps walking.

"Where were you?" she asks.

"I'm so sorry, Cass. I got trapped on a call. It was a total disaster."

She continues walking. "You're right. It was a disaster."

"I nearly lost my job today."

"That makes two of us," she says. "I showed up to class with a toddler."

Ryan takes Cass's anger and matches it with defiance.

"Look, I need to keep my job unless you're planning to pay the mortgage. Last time I checked, your teaching salary did not cover our expenses."

"Why don't you start by telling me where you were instead of trying to make me feel bad."

Ryan looks down, takes a long breath. "Kevin called me in for a conference call at the last minute. He's up my ass already. I had to show up. I know that's no excuse, babe. I should have called. I've been so stressed. Scared. I'm under a lot of pressure. I really don't need more."

And just like that, in a matter of seconds, he has deployed his classic tactics: shifting the blame, turning the tables, and transforming his apology into further evidence of Cass's failure.

"I accept your apology," says Cass.

They drive home in separate cars, Cass stopping to pick up the kids at the neighbors'. Cass heads straight upstairs with the sleeping baby and falls asleep on the chair in his room, determined not to speak to Ryan until the next morning.

It is two o'clock, and Cass is at her nightly vigil. Tonight she is riled by unanswered questions. Cass doesn't need much sleep. She has always prided herself on this. She has never been able to sleep on command, either for a nap or for the night. She is a sleep anorexic. She needs less sleep than most to get through the day, to complete basic bodily functions. She has spent so many afternoons watching children nap in their cribs. She has spent so many nights watching men sleep in her bed. First boyfriends, and then husbands. She has traded envy for their apparent respite into pride in her deprivation, pride in how little she needs to survive, pride in the fact that she can make do with less than most people—or, seen differently, make more of fewer resources.

So heavy and hearty is Ryan's sleep as she crosses the room, removes his cell phone from its cord, and crosses the threshold of trust to lock herself in the bathroom, which is, for all intents and purposes, the interrogation room. She moves confidently in this haven of hers, this hell of her own making. There it sits in its factual glory like the mercury in a thermometer: an email from Ryan to a male colleague earlier in the day, in which Ryan excuses himself from the very call he claims detained him.

"Cover for me on the call?" he writes. "I've got a doctor's appointment."

But before she has considered the implications of this statement, the proof and countervailing evidence, she has darted out of the bathroom, away from her torture and its chamber and marched down the hall to the bedroom, where she crouches on the edge of the bed, shaking Ryan's shoulder.

"Where were you this afternoon?" Cass is saying.

"I told you. I was on a call."

She is still shaking him. Or now, she is just shaking. "Where were you really?"

"Cass, don't do this. We've been through this already."

"I saw the email, Ryan. You told Kevin to cover for you. You told him you had a doctor's appointment. Why don't you try again, and this time tell the truth from the beginning."

Ryan sighs and turns away. It is the sigh of a confessor. It is the sigh of someone who has done something he knows will not be forgiven.

"Why did you say you were on a call?"

"Because," he says. He sounds like a child, and he knows it.

"Because what?"

"Because," he says, "I knew you wouldn't believe the truth. That would be too easy."

"You what?" she said. This would not do. This turning of the tables, this process by which, in seconds flat, his crime became her crime, and worse, a crime for which she would be sentenced, punished. No one but the two of them will witness this double insult, the manner in which insult turns to injury. Only two witnesses, one liar and one listener to debate the veracity of each other's statements. A jury of two defendants does not make for due process. And so she says it again, as though for a jury, as though restating his lie will force him to admit the absurdity of his statements. "You lied because I wouldn't believe the truth? That doesn't make sense, Ryan."

"You're right. It doesn't make sense, Cass. But that's where we're at now. That's what you've driven me to. You overreact to everything."

Cass is lost, torn between his explanation and her intuition. "Stop. Stop turning the tables."

And then, at just the moment when she expects a confession, he says, "I'm trying to confide in you, Cass. You're too obsessed to listen. I'm having a really hard time at work. There's so much pressure on me. Three kids, the insurance, the mortgage," he continues. "I could lose my job, Cass. I wish you could be more supportive."

Cass feels herself doing it, trying on his version. She is doing this against her will, helping Ryan lie to her, colluding in her own deception. Now the charges have changed again: she is no longer just the suspicious wife, driven crazy with paranoia, but has failed him with a dearth of tenderness, the most basic female virtue.

"I wish you had some compassion for my situation."

"What is your *situation*?" says Cass.

"That I could lose my job right now." A single tear slides down his cheek, gets caught in his stubble.

"Why?" she says, regaining strength. "Because you're fucking your assistant?" This is the first time she has said this out loud, truly considered it in earnest, made the mental passage from the purgatory of presumption to the hell of provable wrongdoing. But after seeing the photos of Stephanie's aerosol tan and manly muscular body, countless photos in painted-on pencil skirts, and then, ass splayed, legs oiled, arms flexed in her winning poses as reigning bikini champ of South Florida—and of course, her conspicuous absence, Cass can no longer dismiss the most obvious possibility, the biggest cliché in the marriage textbook. Common sense has begun its dull rap on her intuition.

"There's no affair, Cass. The only crime here is your mistrust. That's what's destroying our marriage."

Once again, she finds herself in a cage of her own making, questioning her conclusions, regretting the confrontation. He turns away, and she sits on the bed, replaying the conversation, reviewing every word he has said, as though for a legal record. Which was the comment that made him snap, which word, which moment? Has her mistrust become so corrosive as to conjure a fictitious affair, dream up an imaginary mistress? Or is she trapped in some middle ground with shared inculpation? If he has indeed been unfaithful, does she bear some of the burden? Did she drive him to it by fearing it, by scrutinizing him so cruelly, by expecting the worst from him, and chasing him like a vengeful ghost in a haunted cemetery? In seconds, she has flipped from conviction to confusion, from self-respect to self-loathing. One of three things is possible: her husband is having an affair; she has imagined the whole proceeding; or her incessant nagging has driven him into the arms of another woman, in retaliation. None of these possibilities is good. All roads lead to heartbreak. Regardless, trust has been breached. The only question is who bears *more* of the blame, Ryan or Cass, his or her betrayal.

The fight continues into the night without resolution. By three o'clock, both are in tears, exhausted from physical fatigue and emotional depletion. Just before dawn, Ryan turns the tide with a dramatic mea culpa, insisting he wants to make things work and begging for forgiveness. He does this without confessing per se, but rather with a promise—a pledge to be a better man, better husband, better person—in a wholesale prostration that is, for all intents and purposes, a willing act of submission, the last act of a fight like this, a total surrender. But despite the apparent win for Cass, the fight is a loss for both opponents, and they fall asleep, weakened both as people and a couple.

SIX

It's morning, and Cass drops the kids at school with the usual set of emotions—pride, relief, a flash of sadness, and bone-deep exhaustion. Alice is unnerved this morning because she has not finished her homework. Pete is happy to join a throng of kids chasing one another around the school courtyard. The baby is home with Marta, the unlucky sitter who, according to Ryan's decree, has been put on notice and has exactly two more days of employment. Cass is depleted from the late-night fight. She is just about to drive away when Alice appears at the car, rapping on the window.

"What?" says Cass.

"Mom!" she says. Her mouth is moving, but sound is silenced.

Cass lowers the window.

"Mom," says Alice.

"What, sweetie?"

"You have our backpacks."

Cass turns to the passenger seat, sees the bags in question, two lumps of blue and green with the customary fluorescent patches. Would that every item of evidence, every guilty party, was so easily spotted in a lineup.

Alice opens the car door, heaves both bags onto her shoulders. "Get some sleep, Mom," she says and slams the car door behind her. And then, as she sprints into school, "Love you!" for good measure.

Cass feels as unsettled at work as she did at drop-off. She needs ten minutes for basic hygiene and mental restoration. Instead, she arms herself with caffeine—three tea bags in the morning's dosage—and a splash of icy water on her eyes in the bathroom, and sets aside her grading deadlines for another urgent project. She logs into a website she has used with some success on various occasions to find sitters since moving to Portland. She pulls up an old job description: "Seeking Nanny for Three Great Kids to Help Working Parents."

She scrolls through a list of applicants, scans their eyes and smiles, profiling for intelligence and kindness, if these two qualities can be profiled, or better yet, if either one can predict behavior. She stars a gray-haired granny, a smiling Peruvian woman, and stops on the post of a young brunette with unusually wide-set eyes and a toothy smile that is equal parts welcoming and feral, with even more inviting young breasts that seem likely to entice her husband to push her into a closet. Cass moves on quickly. She scrolls back to the elderly lady in a pastel caftan, her friendly face all but obscured by bushy black eyebrows. Unfortunately, further review reveals she speaks mostly German and describes herself as "deeply religious"—a good candidate either for proselytizing or kidnapping her children.

Five more minutes are spent sifting through a dispiriting roster, evaluating with no particular criteria other than gut instinct a parade of women who look, in turns, cute and creepy. It is not beyond her self-awareness to acknowledge the potential flaws in her logic, but she still has the conviction of most women to know this saying usually applies: always trust your gut. A knock on the door—the first student lined up for office hours—interrupts her planning.

"Who is it?" she says.

"It's Daniel," he says.

"Come on in," says Cass. "Just getting settled."

She grabs the ungraded pile, frantically flips through in search of Daniel's latest. She takes a last glance at the sitter site, appraises the paltry submissions, then chides herself for her pettiness and moves back to the pretty young one. If Ryan is going to cheat, better he do it under her roof than in some tawdry hotel room. At least that way she will have proof of his indiscretion. Amused and chilled by the idea of conducting this real-time experiment, she turns her attention to Daniel.

"I was just rereading your piece," says Daniel, "'Season of the Witch.' It's really amazing."

"Thank you, Daniel," says Cass. "How long do you need for the extension?"

Daniel smiles, mortified by his transparence.

"Friday work for you?" he asks.

"That'll be fine," says Cass. Even when distracted, she's got excellent intuition.

Daniel leaves, and Cass resumes her previous project. She opens the sitter site, scrolls through the pics, and emails the feral brunette to set up an appointment.

A few minutes later, she receives an email:

> My name is Marley, I think I would be the perfect fit for your family! Please take a look at my résumé and let me know if you agree. I look forward to hearing from you! Marley

Cass sits in a coffee shop in downtown Cumberland. She is starting to have a feeling that she has had a handful of times when visiting foreign countries, on the first day of high school, or when she watched the towers go down on a television affixed to a wall in a train station. A bit like an astronaut trapped in orbit, condemned to watch but not to inhabit, estranged enough to notice things for the first time, close enough to see them—but now, with no entitlement, rather the fear, the knowledge that she has lost access to something dear and familiar.

It is not a coincidence, she considers now, that she is feeling this way on this day of all days. Today is Cass's birthday. She has made a decision to ignore it, not only because her husband seems to have forgotten but because this decree exonerates him—and her—from further introspection. This year, she will not engage in the ritual rumination, the taking of stock, the making of lists, the plaintive hand-wringing and navel-gazing, that she gave up her career too quickly, made that trade that mothers make, fractured her ambition, leaning on the crutch of her children. No, she will not be indulging in this. Today she will go only so far as to listen to the music in the café and stare melancholically out the window.

The coffee shop is painted a lovely shade of gray, a color as soothing as the activities that take place within it. Pleasant music shares the air with a breeze from the bay. Lively people in warm clothes drink things that soothe or invigorate. They talk, they drink, they laugh and chat. They communicate. Cass feels somehow unlike the people in this room. She feels loneliest in public places. The isolation she has come to know is bearable when she is alone. When she is surrounded by others enmeshed in their lives, it is harder to shake the sense that she is a satellite condemned to her own private orbit.

A chipper smile interrupts Cass's dreary notion. A young woman—at twenty-four, she is more a girl than a woman. She is wearing a checked collared shirt over a camisole and leggings, and a pair of lace-up round-toe boots that look like something from a Victorian novel. She looks less horsey in person than in her photos but still distinctly rural. She has the face and hair of a girl, but the confidence of an older woman, and the wrinkles in her forehead that suggest time in the sun or intense life experience. She calls the waiter to their table and orders coffee with impressive command. From the intensity of her need for caffeine, Cass assumes, she is currently working a late shift or a grad student. But before Cass has time for any further assumptions, she launches into a compelling audition, revealing, in addition to her good looks, a charming Southern accent.

"In my previous position, I was expected to oversee the pickup of two children in the household and to manage the supervision of after-school logistics. I supervised and assisted with homework, kept the house clean and tidy, made healthy meals and snacks for the kids, and otherwise kept things running smoothly so that the mom and dad could be the best kind of parents and the best kind of wife and husband."

"Wow. Can I quote that?" Cass cannot help but acknowledge the appeal of the accent. She has come to consider the South in the same manner of most New Yorkers, as the battleground of a disquieting time in American history, the birthplace of a few estimable writers, and now, a food destination. And yet, she cannot help but see this woman through the eyes of her husband. She has come to see much of her life through his eyes, as though imagining his thoughts will lead her to anticipate his actions. Either way, it has made a drastic change in her thinking, making her into a man of sorts, trapped in a woman's body, conscious of every curve of the women in her midst, every rise and narrow in their hips, thighs, and lips. It has made her an Olympic judge of sorts in the sport of being a woman, fixing constant unscrupulous attention to the flaws and virtues of her own gender. Her mind has become a cubist collage of the cut-up bodies, shapes, mouths, breasts, thighs, eyes, cheekbones, waists, and asses of women. And so, much to her own dismay, she now sees this woman as her husband would see her, charmed by her girlish figure, lulled by her Southern belle accent, endeared by her frequent "yes, ma'ams" and "oh, my goodnesses" while she stifles the disquieting image of Ryan, pushing her tits-first against a wall and pressing himself into her girlish round ass while she squeals like a Southern piglet.

"I'm so glad to hear my skills are in keeping with your values."

Cass regards her with hope and suspicion. Is this girl for real? Could she save her home, her kids, her marriage? Or would she be the nail in the coffin?

"How are you today?" Marley asks. She asks this with earnest interest.

"I'm fine. Thanks for asking."

"You don't sound so sure," she says.

Cass exhales. "Kind of a rough morning."

"Sorry to hear that. Hopefully, the day's improving."

"Actually, it's my birthday today."

"Oh, my goodness! Happy birthday. I bet your husband has something special planned."

"Probably," Cass lies. "Something low-key with the family." And now, Cass's expert move: deflection. "It says here you're a nurse practitioner." Another thought occurs to Cass. Is it possible to be too good to be true? Are there diminishing returns for goodness? Can you be so good as to be awful?

"Yes, I completed my license two summers ago. But"—she hesitates, struggling with something—"I guess I'll just go ahead and say it. I have leu-kemia."

"Oh, dear," says Cass.

"No," says the girl. "I didn't mean it that way. I'm actually very healthy. I only wanted to share my reason for wanting to do this. The medication I take means it won't be possible for me to have children. So I've decided to put my degree aside to devote my time on this earth to the thing that gives me the most fulfillment." A pause.

Cass waits, as though it's a game and she is expected to provide the answer.

"Children."

"Oh." It is a word that may be the most honest reflection of human won-der. Cass stomachs a sensation that is becoming familiar. She feels and foils the distinct impression that they have deviated in some way from knowable human behavior. Her senses know the discrepancy before her conscious mind does, just as a computer detects fraud in a bank account balance long before the owner realizes she has lost her wallet.

"Did I mention I play the guitar?"

"You do? Alice has been wanting to learn for forever."

"I grew up playing violin, cello, and guitar. All things strings."

"Wonderful," says Cass.

"I've taught every kid I've worked for."

This girl is too good to be true, a modern Mary Poppins. Now, Cass struggles to find the words for her next question. Are you strong? Are you weak? Are you able to work normal nine-to-five hours? Are you prone to re-lapse? Are you healthy right now? And of course, as a mom, at the front of her mind: Is it okay for you to be around children? But because none of these questions seem appropriate or organic, she arrives instead at this awkward declaration. "I can't begin to imagine the obstacles you've faced because of the illness. And I want you to know, if you work with us, you can always let me know your needs . . ." She trails off. "What I mean is if you work with our family, you'll be part of our family also."

Marley smiles, apparently moved. A thread of compassion connects the two women.

Cass struggles to word one final practical question. "You okay with light housework?"

"I'm a total laundry Nazi." Marley smiles. "Never shrunk a shirt to date."

Cass smiles. "When can you start?"

Game and round to Little Miss Sunshine, but a victory all around.

Cass returns to find the house in a state of chaos. The move a year ago has not aided the family's sense of stasis. Boxes still line most walls, creating an internal warren. Books and frames are piled nearby like roots sprouting from the center. And still, despite the implicit flux of the environment, there is charm to the endeavor, a palpable creative energy that makes the house feel like a place with endless, if potentially hazardous, possibility for adventure. At the moment, the kids have fashioned an airplane from a cardboard box and unused copper pipes, and they're pushing themselves across the room looking like a very large and lethal insect. It's hard to tell today's energy from the usual buzz at the Connors', but something is decidedly afoot. Long gone is the doom and gloom of the morning. Everyone's grinning, keeping a secret.

"Oh, good, you're home," Ryan says as Cass enters. She hangs her coat on the hook and heads inside for the usual survey, the rapid-fire assessment of her kids' level of hunger, energy, and excitement. But Ryan stops her where she stands, placing both hands on her shoulders. He kisses her firmly on the lips and smiles in a decisive way, apparently a changed person.

Cass stares at Ryan, mystified by the transformation.

Ryan meets her skepticism with renewed conviction. "Take a shower. Put on a dress. We're leaving in ten minutes."

"But who will watch the kids?" Cass asks.

Alice and Pete grin in their usually failed attempt to keep a secret. The act of keeping a secret is as much fun as the knowledge in their possession.

A delighted squeal from the baby serves as one last tipoff.

Cass's student, Jean, appears from her hiding place in the hall. "Surprise!" she says.

"Oh, hi!" says Cass. "Where'd you come from?" She is too surprised to compliment Jean's out-of-school attire, black combat boots offset by an abundance of black eyeliner.

"Ryan arranged it."

Cass looks to her smiling husband, his beaming co-conspirators.

"Happy birthday, Mom," says Pete.

Cass grins back at them. "How exciting," she says. Then to Ryan, "Could've sworn you'd forgotten."

Another kiss is exchanged, this one more passionate, lust mixed with suppressed rage and buried affection.

"Happy birthday, Cass."

All is forgiven.

Cass and Ryan sit in a restaurant in downtown Portland. An old church has been converted into the latest food cathedral with soaring exposed beams and reclaimed crosses, competing with hulking Jonah crab and dewy local produce. He's made a massive effort in tonight's festivities, eclipsing a heartfelt apology with an elaborate celebration. Wine, delicious food, a small black box with a blue ribbon. And if things go as planned: amnesia followed by absolution.

They're in the Old Port section of the city on the north side of Portland Harbor, the Atlantic Northeast's answer to Brooklyn. But it's somehow better here because of the local bounty of fish, farm, and fowl, more eccentric fashion, and of course, the city's burgeoning music scene and opioid epidemic. It all feels more heartfelt, less contrived for effect than back in Brooklyn. Cass has cleaned up well, dressing quickly for the occasion. She is wearing a slim black dress that cinches at the waist, sleeveless with leather piping on the collar, and buttons that unfold mischievously just below her collarbone. Ryan looks handsome, as he always does to her, in a crisp oxford shirt with a lavender check that offsets his mossy eyes, her favorite tweedy gray jacket, and his dark brown hair slicked back like a matinee idol.

"Happy birthday, babe. It's been a long road," Ryan says. He lifts his glass and gazes at Cass in a way that makes her feel at once loved, understood, and desired.

"Yes, it has." She smiles back at Ryan, returns his desire with her own. Whoever says marriage gets boring doesn't know her husband. Four years into the relationship, she is more attracted to him than when she first met him, when he devoured her in an alley—and then a stairwell, a bathroom, and standing at the door of her bedroom. He sucked the pain right out of her, put something new inside her, an addiction that needed feeding, a new wound that needed healing.

"Often rocky," he goes on. He is giving one of his speeches, one of the rhetorical tours that makes Ryan so addictive, in which he tiptoes above propriety, teetering masterfully between dignified and disreputable comments. It creates the same effect on Cass as a brilliant comic, and so she stays braced for shock, pain, or something devilishly inappropriate, so unsure of where his next words will turn that she is primed for tears or laughter.

"Always an adventure," she says. She is making an effort at coyness. She is trying to make him work for this, but it isn't easy. It feels too good to slide back into these feelings. Despite the way he torments her, she is addicted to Ryan, hooked on how he makes her feel—known, tested, challenged—and therefore somehow worth it.

"We're getting to the scenic part," he says.

"With you, it's always a pleasure."

"Cass, I don't deserve you, but I'm determined to be better." His tone is serious now, drained of coyness.

She smiles. Contrition is too good a gift, a bonus on top of the pleasure of his attention. This is the honeymoon period, sweeter because of the recent fight, pleasure made more potent by the pain prior.

Ryan reaches for her hand across the table like a drowning swimmer. "I'm such a fuckup, Cass. People like me aren't good at relationships. My parents didn't teach me."

"We have some time to figure it out. Copy the normal people."

"Everyone thinks the way out of a fight is a compromise. Everyone's right and everyone's sorry. But you've been right, and I've been wrong. You've been perfect, and I've been a moron."

The waiter stops and offers wine.

"More for him," says Cass.

"Cass, I'm serious. It's not the wine. It's me. I finally get it."

"We should come to this restaurant more often."

Now he's holding both of her hands. His grasp is tight, desperate. "This family is my life, Cass. I love your kids so much, and I would"—his eyes widen—"I would kill for that baby. If I lose him . . ." He trails off. "If I lose him, I'd have nothing. I promise I'll get it right. It won't take long. All I need is . . ." He pauses. "All I need is forever."

She's smiling now in spite of herself. Her face is warm. Ryan's love feels like sunshine. And remorse feels even hotter. She returns his grasp with the same force, ignoring the age-old adage about drowning swimmers. The rescuer should save herself or else run the risk of being pulled to the bottom.

"Please give me a chance to deserve you. Give me a chance to be better."

He's grinning now mischievously. She can't resist his seduction. Before the second course is served, he's got his hand up her dress under the table.

She loves the way he makes her feel, like she's sixteen and she just snuck out of her parents' house in the suburbs and she's in a car, going eighty down dark, slick streets with the boy in her high school class who is rumored to be, depending on the witness, a pyromaniac or a poet. They leave the restaurant, laughing, drunk, high on food and laughter, basking in the full-body warmth of someone you know and love, the high of reconciliation. And things continue in this way—sexy, sweet, and playful—as they walk from the restaurant to the car, tripping in the shadows. He takes advantage of a peal of laughter to push her up against a building, hiking her skirt up to her thighs, hoisting her up against the wall and descending on her with all the force of a demonic angel.

Back at home, they make love, this time without the drama. Now it is the quiet and adoring sex of two best friends, two members of the same family, two people committed to the same goal, who have weathered yet another storm, friends who have remembered and renewed a promise.

"Just love. Just love," Ryan says. "That's all we have to do. It's that simple."

Cass nods as she comes. The full weight of Ryan eclipses her doubts until all she feels is pleasure. What price would she pay to love this man forever? What amount would she give to spend her life with Ryan? If pressed, if forced to decide right now, she would give anything. They fall asleep just like this, his body crushing her body, his body inside her body, touching her heart, her soul, her organs. She has made a devil's deal again. Will this time be forever?

SEVEN

It's Saturday, and the Connors are in the early stages of a beloved family ritual, packing up the car for the weekend and lighting out for freedom. The constellation of islands north of Portland provide all manner of adventure, all accessible by ferry, all within an hour or two of every Portland doorstep. When Cass first discovered this, it felt like her secret, like so many things that became possible after meeting Ryan. The islands were like nothing she had seen before: forests of fir, compact peaks rising out of navy-blue water, a hidden world of exploration for those lucky enough to cross these enclosed harbors—that is, until she realized the secret was known to every resident of Portland. But right now, she is back in the zone where all of life feels precious, every little thing feels like a dose of good fortune. Ryan and Cass are back in the best version of their relationship, when even the simplest action, the most familiar pastime—waking up in her husband's arms, drinking a cup of coffee he makes her, driving as a family to the beach—feels new and special.

"I think I met a good person," Cass says as they near the ferry.

"For what?" says Ryan.

"A new sitter."

"That's a relief."

"She's so perfect it's almost weird. She's either a real-life Mary Poppins or a professional con."

"You and your theories," Ryan says. "Time to call the doctor." But his tone is back to the playful version.

"Mrs. Doubtfire . . ." Cass says.

"Promise me you'll hire her," he says. "Anyone would be better."

The whole family is peaceful as they set out on their journey. The kids read and draw in the back seat, enjoying the breeze through the window, fielding minor squabbles during the twenty-minute wait to drive their car onto the ferry. Finally the ferry whistle blows, and the boat sets out for the island. Wind sets their hair aloft and spirits even higher as they forge across Penobscot Bay, turning toward the northern islands. The children spend the morning gazing into the water, taking turns at the front of the boat, competing to be the first to see the island. They occasionally take breaks from their post to play with the pets of the other passengers and decide which of the dogs on the boat they would most like to take home with them. Two hours later, they file out of the boat and traipse onto the windy dock, transformed in mind and body.

Pete and the baby toddle out, rush to score a wagon. Cheeks flushed, the kids sprint down the dock to the beach and stay like this for hours. They play and run and laugh and shriek from afternoon to evening, until the blue sky turns to gray, the gray clouds turn silver, until the last minutes of winter light, when shadows and darkness blur the same way as the surf and the ocean. Reluctantly they gather their scattered belongings, socks and jackets soaked by seaweed and water, and slowly make their way to the house, lit by the Atlantic. Violet and silver light give way to the chill of evening.

The Connor family unspools into a simple A-frame cabin. It is bleached by salt water and loving use, if not perfect upkeep. The house was inherited by Ryan from his mother, if *inherited* is a word that applies to something given from one living person to another. Ryan and his mother have not spoken in over a decade. The mere mention of her name causes him to stop speaking altogether. Like so many things about Ryan, even the transfer of the house is shrouded in darkness, a story with gaps or at least many parts that have been stricken from the record.

Ryan's mother left his father when Ryan was a baby. She packed up a wood-paneled station wagon and an oblivious toddler and moved to a Portland suburb to raise her child with the help of neighbors and cousins. A struggling, hardworking woman frayed into a frazzled single parent with a penchant for married men and too many drinks before dinner. A quiet, antisocial child grew into a gifted but angry teenager, and the relationship between mother and child—you can see where this is going—grew increasingly fractured. Concern over the wrong kind of friends and the regular kind of trouble rose tension in the house to a boil from a simmer. By the time Ryan was sixteen, his mother was calling his father on a weekly basis, explaining that Ryan had become an untenable situation and demanding that he resurface as a parent or at least pitch in with a monthly payment.

A trial stay at his father's was an even bigger failure. And sixteen-year-old Ryan returned home before the month was over, angrier and more indignant, with new daddy issues to add to the growing maternal disaster. Ryan and his mother would spend only one more month together. A fight whose subject he now forgot or preferred never to mention marked their last conversation. Harsh words were exchanged on the topic—a party and rumors of drug use—and soon it blossomed into the stuff of after-school specials. In the heat of this argument, Ryan's mother threw him out of the house. It was the last night he would spend under the roof of either parent. He stayed in his car for the next month and then at the home of a girlfriend, another child of divorce with a more lenient parent.

Other than a handful of conversations about college tuition, this was the last time Ryan spoke to his mother. Which is not to say that she didn't try. Throughout college, she called once a week, leaving messages on the answering machine in his dorm room or with his roommates, writing letters, and sending packages that were never opened. During architecture school, she drove up once and asked if she could take him out to dinner. She made one last-ditch effort to reconcile after graduation, sending a package to his first design firm with a box of ties and the transfer of the deed of the cabin. But Ryan was long gone now, and forgiveness had exceeded its statute of limitations. He had started a new life, safe from the turbulence of his mother, a life buttressed by a new career, a promising position at a hot design firm, a decent biweekly paycheck, and all the pleasures available to a gainfully employed twenty-eight-year-old man in a big city. He had no need for a ramshackle cabin in a distant cove on a dreary island or the long-overdue apologies of a woman he no longer needed. Truth be told, he was ashamed of his mother. The ties she sent seemed cheap and crass compared to the ones worn by his colleagues—bright shiny silks in pink, orange and gray, blue and silver—unlike the dark and heavy synthetic fabrics she sent him.

Like most of the houses on this rustic, windswept island, Ryan's cabin looks as though it could topple in a strong wind or current. The house is a wooden A-frame built in the sixties from a kit and looks like a house of cards compared to the rugged heft of the substantial Victorians that dot the island, which were built a hundred years prior. The wood is thin, the walls are warped, and the bathroom and kitchen are spare, but this house feels more like a home to the Connors than anywhere they have lived before, scattered with board games and puzzles, decorated with the children's drawings and drying towels. And every time they arrive, the whole group changes, lightens. They grow closer and more entwined, like a family of cats, curled up in a laundry basket.

This evening, the house enjoys the hush of physical exhaustion. The older kids listen, on repeat, to their favorite album, collaborating on a jigsaw puzzle of a gum-ball machine with more detail than the Sistine Chapel, while Sam adds a competitive element to the game by hiding puzzle pieces under the sofa cushions. Ryan tinkers in the back with a new project—he is teaching himself how to update the plumbing in the outdoor shower. Cass putters in the kitchen, making some very basic pasta. Her mind is still for the first time in months, unburdened by any discernible thoughts other than the most mundane: boil water, turn off stove, drain pasta. When things are calm like this, she cannot remember any other version. When life is good with Ryan, there is nothing better.

Perhaps they have finally scaled the last peak in their marriage, set off across a peaceful plateau filled with lakes and meadows. She wonders if they have passed some test, finished a painful growth spurt. She starts to imagine contentment, a world in which the best is to come and the worst is behind them. But an odd and unwelcome image catches her eye as she cleans the counter: a tiny circle of black hair, and then another. She picks it up, holds it to her eyes. It is wiry and tightly coiled. Recognizing what it is, she feels suddenly nauseous. Repulsed, she flicks the hair into the sink and hovers, uncertain for a moment, like a confused hummingbird; then she tries to flick the thought out of her head, carries the steaming bowl to the table, and joins her family for dinner.

An hour or two have passed, and Cass takes a shower. She feels like a woman in a movie, a woman in the reflexive stage of bathing after trauma. Is it an attempt to wash off the pain or to reinstate ownership of one's own body? The kids are reading in their room, or sneaking some time with a laptop movie. The baby is asleep—no sounds emerge from his room other than peaceful rhythmic breathing. Ryan lies in the bed in a T-shirt and his gray cotton briefs, holding his phone like a shield and watching something that seems, from the sporadic moans and shrieks emanating from his phone, to be extremely violent.

Cass knows all too well the details of Ryan's sexual preference. He has always liked to do it on the counter; backward, forward, one leg up, calf slung over his shoulder. Less so since the baby was born, but occasionally late on a Saturday night when the kids are sleeping and the house is quiet, as they sat, decompressing in the kitchen, him fussing with the furniture, her loading the dishwasher. And then, without warning, he would be behind her, lifting her skirt, wetting her with his fingers, and inserting himself without a word as though it was the next phase on the quick rinse of the dishwasher, as though it was his right to grab her ass and grip it calmly, then mash her breasts against the wood counter as he pounded her body.

Now, against her will, she begins to test various theories. If the hair belongs to Stephanie, it is from the root. Over-bleached hair is likely to break due to all that damage. But these strands are long and black, longer than the root of hair in need of touch-up highlights, and no blond in sight. Is it possible it belongs to someone else? she now considers. That she was wrong about Stephanie and Ryan is fucking someone else entirely? That Stephanie is one of many? Or has she truly lost her mind and missed some reasonable explanation?

Cass tries to wrangle her thoughts and dispel the new image, but like so many crimes of the heart, it has already made an indelible mark, like the shape of a bare bulb on the retina after facing it in a basement. And even before she can do the work of denial or self-inflicted amnesia, she is staring at more disgusting proof. It is as though he has set a trail for her, a sinister treasure hunt in which each bread crumb leads closer to a trap, closer to certain ruin.

Clumping up the shower drain is another nasty blockage: swirls of black hair fill the grate like hundreds of tiny spiders. She crouches to see them better. The hair is dark, the shade somewhere between brown and black. It's thick and wiry as pubic hair, but long enough to be from someone's head. It obstructs the shower drain in clumps, as though it has accumulated over time, or come from a person who sheds more hair than most people. Cass fights her gag reflex as she reaches into the drain and removes it. Repulsed, she releases a clump from her hand and flushes it down the toilet, but as it starts to swirl away, she reaches in and grabs it. She rescues and saves several strands with this desperate gesture as though the rescue of this hair will amount to the rescue of her self-respect, the salvation of her marriage. She pulls her hand from the toilet water, dripping and covered by the hair of a stranger, the hair of her husband's lover. She wonders which is more disgusting: the ugly facts she must now confront or the person she has become in the process.

Cass enters the bedroom where Ryan is lounging. Intermittent zombie sounds punctuate the silence. It's fine that he loves zombie shows, like every other male carnivore, but the fact that he finds it relaxing, that he likes to fall asleep to this—tonight this strikes her as disturbing. The world abounds with options—porn, football, boxing—for condoned male violence. She enters the room and stands at the door, watching him for a moment, then holds up the hair like a prosecutor showing evidence to a jury. The force of her pose is undermined slightly by the fact that a minute passes before Ryan acknowledges her presence.

"What's this?" she says.

He doesn't look up. More shrieking. Moaning. Howling. "What's what?" he says. He looks up now.

"This," she says.

He squints and leans toward her. His stomach muscles sharpen. "What do you have there, Sherlock?"

"Don't talk to me like that," she says. It is a toothless but valiant effort.

"I thought we came here to relax. I thought we had moved past this." He goes back to his entertainment.

"Ryan, this isn't your hair. This belongs to a woman."

"Go easy on me, Cass. The stress is making my hair fall out." He grunts something between a laugh and a sneer. Cass ignores the deflection.

Ryan looks up finally and stares at Cass with utter loathing, as though she is vile and filthy, as though she is an untouchable and he is something royal. "I'm done with your paranoia," he says. "I told you I was finished."

But Cass is amped now. She won't be cowed or bullied. Cass is bolstered by the thing in her hands, the weight of physical evidence, the heft of empirical data. She is holding a grenade, and Ryan is an enemy soldier. They are in a four-walled room. He is in a corner. "Ryan, whose hair is this? Ryan, who did you bring here?"

Ryan looks back at his phone, retreating into his next move. The best defense is indifference. "I'm not going to live like this anymore. I am sick of your sickness."

"Stop turning the tables, Ryan. Don't tell me it's paranoia. I'm looking at it. Holding it. In my hand. It's not yours or mine. Now tell me whose the fuck this is, or I'm waking the children and leaving the island."

A minute passes in silence with no grenade thrown, no words between them. Nothing but the sporadic sounds of humans eating human flesh while Cass is eaten alive by the lies of her husband.

"There are no boats off the island right now," he tells her.

"I'll borrow one from the harbor," she says. "I'll row a boat across the bay. I'll steal one if I have to."

"You're so far gone."

"You've said that, Ryan. And I don't believe you."

"You're nuts."

"Am I?" she says. "Or am I onto you?"

"You've lost it, Cass. You can't trust your own judgment."

"No, I haven't. And yes, I can. It's you who can't be trusted."

"Listen to yourself, Cass. You can't tell the difference anymore between appropriate and inappropriate behavior."

"If I'm crazy, you drove me to it," she says. Her arms are on her hips now. Her stance is defiant.

Ryan nods and reclines. His face softens so that he looks almost gentle.

"Don't tell me what's appropriate," she says. "You're a cheater and a liar."

Another moment passes in which Ryan does nothing. He has defused his anger, like a bomb whose code is punched seconds before explosion. He sits up on the bed now in the most inviting manner, as though entreating a child to join him for a bedtime story.

"I rented the house, Cass. I put it up on one of those sites and got a bunch of offers. In fact, I made a really good deal. Paid a month of the mortgage. There were people here over Labor Day. A nice Jewish family. With dark brown hair. Are you happy now, Raymond Chandler?"

"Why didn't you tell me about this?" she says. "You never mentioned a summer rental."

"Why *would* I tell you about this?" he says. "Do you have any idea how many things I do on a daily basis to take care of our family, our finances?"

This, it must be said, is a sophisticated pivot. But still a variation on a theme, a 3.0 version. He has moved from "I didn't do it" to "You imagined that I did it," skipped "You made me do it" this time, and gone on to "You are guilty of doing something ten times worse." Cass is baffled, immobilized for the moment, if only by the flair of Ryan's pyrotechnics.

Ryan pats the spot on the bed next to where he is sitting, as though the fight has not occurred, as though he is sitting on the beach and inviting her to watch the sunset.

But Cass does not sit. She remains standing. She knows what he is doing now. He's trying to distract her, trying to make her feel guilty. This is his favorite strategy, a tactic designed to sedate the advancing party. But tonight she will not fall for it. Tonight she will not feel feelings. Tonight she has something stronger. Facts and conviction. Tonight she has this hair in her hands, slicing the pads on her fingers. Tonight her heart is split in two, and the intensity of the pain will make her stronger.

"I'm done with this," Cass says. "The yelling, the lies, the secrets. This is the last time you'll bully me, intimidate me for asking, threaten me for knowing. Try to make me doubt my own perceptions. Twist the facts. Shift the blame. Blame the victim."

"That's it," he says. "We're finding you a shrink on Monday."

Ryan shakes his head and sighs in an apparent surrender, as though he has finally accepted her characterization. It is an unexpected withdrawal, a triumph for Cass. He lies down on the bed again, stretches his legs, theatrically fluffs a pillow. Then the bomb accelerates and descends to zero. Ryan springs from the bed and lunges at Cass, pinning her against the wall with the force and skill of an assassin. His hands close in around her neck like metal on a buckle. With each second, he presses in, pushing deeper into her skin, as though to touch the muscle.

Her back is against the wall. His chest is crushing her chest. He is pushing the force of his weight into her body, using his body as a weapon, the wall as his accomplice. His eyes are large and shiny. His mouth is wet and open. "You are going to exit my life."

"Stop. Let go. You're hurting me," she whispers. It is hard to breathe now. Her neck is cinched, constricted.

He pushes farther into her, slowly and with power, as though he is a bulldozer and she is a mound of dirt in the path before him.

"Let go. I can't breathe," she says.

He somehow gets taller. "How dare you speak to me like that after everything I do for you, the sacrifices I've made for you and your children."

One small shove against the wall to punctuate the sentence and then he walks back to the bed, leaving Cass crouching, breathless. Ryan reclines again, settling into the pillow, facing Cass but staring at the wall as though he can see through her. It could be called a hundred-yard stare, that amazing feat of vision, but in fact it is Cass who now can see the future.

Cass sits on the floor and struggles to get her bearings. The sound of her children sleeping nearby, the feel of the wall against her back—these are the first, the best ways to orient herself and confirm her presence.

As unsettling as Ryan's rage was, so is Cass's reaction. It makes her feel equal parts aroused and alarmed, repelled and attracted, damaged and valued. It is wilderness itself that she sees in him, more than the type she has glimpsed in most men—and the feeling is narcotic. In Ryan, it is more pronounced, the snarl more sudden, the growl more ferocious. But it is all part of knowing, of loving this man, all part of being with Ryan. She feels pressed to take the good with the bad. Who is she to be exempt from life's imperfections? And so she becomes guilty, first, of looking away, then tolerating her own degradation.

She sits like this on the floor for several minutes. Reality shifts slightly, she learns, when your safety is threatened, when oxygen is diminished and the flow of blood to the brain is slowly constricted. In place of calm is high alert. In place of time are endless minutes. In place of normal low-res life is total saturation, excruciating detail. This is what is meant, Cass decides, when people describe "being present." Everything is heightened. Images are sharpened. Her brain is buzzing like a high, but with no euphoria, just the focus. The flimsy wood of the wall, the way it creaks when she leans on it, the itch on her left eyebrow, the way the big toe of her bottom foot and pinkie from her top one interlock on her crossed feet, the prickle of cold air on her skin as the wind comes in from the ocean.

And yet with this precision comes consuming confusion. A mental replay of a match, a play-by-play in slow motion, a person on a losing streak, but here, there is no referee, just you and your decisions. The thing that's lost is you. What follows is a gradual return to one's senses. Time resumes its normal speed. The wall no longer makes a creak, or you no longer notice. The cold no longer feels like something present, incarnate. Now it is just you and him, two people in a room, one on the bed, one on the floor, a universe between them.

There are things to attend to now. New details to reconcile, new questions: Why does a woman stay a day with a man she knows is capable of violence? Culpable of violence. He is now culpable of violence. Does that mean you are culpable too? For causing it, as he tells you. For imagining it, for deserving it. Or simply for staying? Does that make you complicit? And now the newly minted hashtag. Why, dear woman, did you stay? Because you are afraid of him or afraid of losing him? Or worse, did you get off on it? Did it make you high? Feel alive? Make you feel special, wanted? Did you, in fact, like it? Are you, in fact, by staying, subscribing to a repeat performance? A better question than #WhyIStayed: How did you escape alive?

Adding to the confusion of questions are so many statements. A new list of pros and cons. Reasons to be grateful: a growing family, a lovely home, all the comforts of lucky people. To bitch about his flaws could be construed as a lack of perspective. She has certainly lived through enough to know that no life is perfect. She has been taught to take the bad with the good, to focus on the positive. To work through it. Just as anger plays into her love, so does love excuse his anger. Ryan is a textbook case: the son abandoned by his dad, the teenage boy who rebelled against the mom who let it happen. The foregone father. How could she not see his temperament as the outcome of others' failures?

Ryan is sleeping now. Peaceful as a child. Cass stands from her place on the floor, regaining her indignation. She pads across the room, removes his phone from its cord, and, in the blue light of the quiet house, resumes her investigation. But she is stopped at first attempt by a changed password. Perhaps it would be foolish for him to trust her at this point, but the act reveals more than any clue. Why would a person have reason to hide if not to cover proof?

The Connors take the early ferry home the next morning. The kids are light and free of cares, but Cass and Ryan are changed by the night that passed between them. They have crossed an invisible line, traveled too great a distance. There's no turning back after words like this, no unhearing or unseeing. His mouth so close to her mouth, shining with saliva. Strands of wiry brown-black hair slicing the tips of her fingers.

On the ferry, Cass imagines her family from an outside perspective, a family in a photo, the yellow bruise of time spreading on their outlook. There is a palpable distance now between the wife and husband like the volcanic islands that rise from the Penobscot Bay between here and Portland. Once they were connected, but a substance pooled between them—ash, water, blood, tears—time's inevitable insults.

Cass stands at the front of the boat, both hands on the railing. She imagines the breeze is a windstorm. The only thing to do is wait for relief from nature and the energy for renewed effort. Alice, sharp as a satellite, sees the storm approaching. She watches her mother's eyes but says nothing. The chill follows them all the way home as the boat docks in the terminal and cars file off the ferry. With the baby asleep, the car ride home is quiet. As though all of them have seen a ghost in their dreams. Or the devil.

Cass sits in the back with Sam. He has fallen asleep on her chest. It seems wiser to sit with him in the back, forming a human seat belt, than risk waking him up while transferring him to the car seat. She watches Ryan as he drives, his forearm resting on the wheel, a repose that is defiant. He scans the road like a predator. The strength of his gaze, the breadth of his hand—he has this edge on her. He takes his phone with one hand and Cass grows alert, watching his fingers move across the keypad. She clocks the shape, the movement he makes, and thereby sets his changed passcode to memory.

She repeats these four numbers to herself like a lullaby she sings to her baby. She holds Sam close as the car winds along the bay back to home and its promise of safety.

It's Monday now. A day has passed, and the chill has begun to thaw at the Connors. Ryan is doling out smiles again on a limited basis, enough to make his distance felt but to offer the glimmer of forgiveness. Cass sprints from her afternoon class to school pickup. At three o'clock, a crowd of moms descend on the Bayside School, looking like a swarm of aliens in their post-workout spandex. Ghouls and goblins dangle over the front door in preparation for the upcoming holiday. The kids emerge in a throng of tangled hair and unrepentant exuberance. You can almost feel their energy, see their spirits like auras around them. They are caught between childhood innocence and adult awareness, and they grasp both sides with the fervor of falling climbers.

Cass sees Nora and, on instinct, tries to dodge her. The prospect of conversation—even with friends—feels like an invasion, requiring that she answer honestly to questions like "How are you?" or worse, pretend all is well and walk away with the knowledge that she is a liar. But Nora, all smiles, approaches before she can avoid her.

"Where the hell have you been?" says Nora.

"What? Oh, we went to the beach for the weekend," says Cass. Not enough time or energy to conjure anything more delightful.

"I haven't seen you in ages," says Nora. She bats off a child's cello case with the skill of a major-league player. "What's going on? You're tiny."

"Really? Do I look thin?" Cass says. She knows she's in a wretched state when even this comment fails to cheer her.

"Very." Nora is one to talk. She looks typically flawless. Her bright blue eyes peer out from the fringe of her bangs and a nest of carelessly draped scarves. She looks chic in a corduroy skirt that would be too short on any other woman. The fact that three kids came out of this body seems wholly impossible.

"I guess stress is the best diet." No smile for what would usually be welcome information.

"Cass, what's wrong?" says Nora.

"Nothing," says Cass.

Nora frowns, waits for the truth.

"Just going through some shit at home."

"Some shit? Or some little shit?"

Cass sighs. She hates to admit that Nora was right. This woman, who is barely more than an acquaintance, sees through her bullshit. They have known each other only a year and yet, by virtue of their recent move, this makes Nora Cass's closest friend in Cumberland.

"Sorry to hear that," Nora says.

Another child swipes past her. Now it's one of Cass's on a mission for frozen yogurt. Cass expertly denies this request without missing a word of conversation.

"I could be imagining it," Cass says.

"Is that what he told you? That's like right out of a textbook."

"Seriously. It could be nothing."

"It never is," says Nora.

The kids surround their mothers, this time with more fervor. They're clamoring for something sweet, and they will not be dissuaded.

"Can Jake and I go to the park?" says Pete.

"Can I go get ice cream with Laura?" says Alice.

"We can go to the park for a while," says Cass, "but we need to be home by five."

"We'll talk later," says Nora.

"Yes. Please," says Cass. She is grateful for Nora's warmth, grateful for a friend amid such isolation. Cass starts to gather her children.

"Wait. Take this," says Nora. She reaches into her bag, fumbles for something.

"It's okay. We've already tried it."

"What?"

"Couples counseling," says Cass.

"No, not that," says Nora. She is still riffling through her bag. Keys. Lip gloss. Wallet. "Remember last year when my housekeeper was stealing from me? Bags, shoes, jackets."

"I think so," says Cass. "We had just moved here."

"This guy helped me through it," says Nora.

"A shrink?"

"Oh, no. Much better." She smiles. "An amazing hacker."

"Oh." Cass plants her feet to steel herself against the tugs of her children. She waits for her to elaborate. Nora has her full attention.

"He can clone a phone," Nora whispers.

"What does that mean?" says Cass.

"You will get everything he gets. You will see everything he sees."

"You're kidding," says Cass.

"Swear to God. Modern technology, baby."

"Is that legal?"

"If it's not, it should be. He's doing a public service. He's like Robin Hood for jilted housewives."

"How does he do that?" Cass asks.

"He can basically break into anyone's phone as long as he's on the same network. He can get you anything you need. Texts, emails, calls. Apps, accounts, porn, purchases, chats. All communication."

Cass begins to nod, a smile gracing her lips for the first time in as long as she can remember. She is feeling lighter now, so much so that when her kids tug her again, she takes their hand and matches their excitement. "Thank you, Nora."

"Anything for the cause," she says. "One more off the streets for our children." And then, before they part, she adds, "You know I'm always here to talk. You can call me at any hour. Show up on my doorstep."

"Let's hope it doesn't come to that."

"It's a standing offer."

Cass smiles and hugs her friend. She wants to convey her gratitude—not only for the referral but for taking her to heart, for seeing the anguish in her eyes and treating her like a sister. Feminism, bitches.

It's nighttime now. The house is quiet. Everyone is asleep. Cass lies in bed, waiting for full respite. She can hear the release of tension when her children and husband enter deep sleep. In. Out. In. Out. An intake and an expression. When she hears these sounds, she stands and pads down the hall and texts Nora's referral.

"Nora said I should get in touch."

This seems the best way to begin. He responds in under a minute. "Glad to help a friend of Nora's."

"Looking for the same kind of thing. Someone to help me organize my computer."

"Text me your address," he writes. "I can meet tomorrow."

They arrange to meet the following night. He says he'll text her when he's close and to look for a blue Toyota.

Cass goes to sleep with the prospect of relief. To know Ryan's moves when he does, to have proof of her suspicions—feels like nothing short of a cure. A headlamp in the lightless cave she currently inhabits. Could it be salvation for their marriage? She wonders if she will miss the search, the deduction and the inference, the quest that has been her mission, the fear that has been her companion. She wonders if she will feel remorse, if this crime has its own retribution. But contrition is canceled out by the perks of incentive. And guilt is quickly usurped by the thrill of potential. Making a clone of Ryan's phone feels like salvation, tantamount to being inside his head, and right now, she needs this insight more than she needs water. This is what all women need, she decides. Perfect information. And so tonight she falls asleep, dreaming of perfection. No nightmares this evening. No thoughts of her namesake, Cassandra.

It's afternoon, and Cass is feeling better. It's the last week of October, and the leaves are vibrant—red, orange, purple, and yellow of the highest magnification. The air is cool and grazes her face like cold water. Cass loves nothing more than to find an hour in between her classes to steal kisses from her son, to squeeze his pliant tummy, to traipse with him up ladders and down slides like a busy penguin. His favorite game is a version of cat and mouse, except here with a surrogate monster. Amnesty is won, in this case, simply by repetition. In it, he runs up the slide, arms out, escaping from Cass's monster, and then, once atop the jungle gym, he invites her to join him.

"Be a nice monster now!" he yells. At which point she heeds the call and sprints up the slide, transformed. Would that she and her husband could achieve the same role reversal.

Cass knows, now from experience, how rapidly time passes, and so she holds this time sacred and makes sure to spend time alone with each of her three children. It is not always possible to stanch the flow of her students' queries and deadlines, but thanks to the phone, the invention that brings the office to the playground, she can, if necessary, take a work call while climbing up a jungle gym ladder.

Now she coyly mutes her phone while Sam sprints down a ramp to announce his triumph. Another child approaches—a sturdy boy with a thicket of curls followed by his father. The father has large pronounced eyebrows that immediately conjure a raccoon. He has long, dark hair that is either badly in need of a wash or intentionally dreaded. He looks like a guy she remembers from college with similarly unfortunate hygiene whom Cass and her friends used to refer to as "Dreaded Danny." This man now stands in front of Cass, smiling at her as though she is a dear acquaintance.

"We should have a playdate," he says.

Cass has not heard him. She is still focused on the call she missed, wondering if it was important—and watching her son and another little boy. They are staring each other down like miniature cowboys, trying to assert climbing rights to the same ladder.

"For them." He nods at the kids.

"Sure. That would be great," she says.

"Not that the two of us don't deserve to run around in a padded room together."

Cass looks more closely now. Is this guy funny or creepy? She instinctively discounts anyone who wears sunglasses while they're talking. She sees it as a sign of disrespect for one person to remain obscured during conversation. His eyebrows are unusually large, circling his eyes like a nocturnal animal.

"Funny," she says and tries to laugh.

"I'm Aaron, your next-door neighbor." He removes his sunglasses now, as though he has just remembered. "A.k.a. the creepy dad at the playground. Sorry about that. I'm basically blind."

"Oh. No worries," says Cass.

"We met when you were moving in," he says. "My son is two also."

"Right. Of course. Gray house. White shutters." She smiles as though she really cares, like it's all coming back to her. In fact, she does not care at all and does not want to talk to him any longer than she has to.

"Your light is on a lot," he says.

"Excuse me?"

"The light in your bedroom window. It's on at all hours."

"Oh," she says. "You noticed?"

"Be hard not to." He gestures at his nearby house, the distance between his and her bedroom windows.

"Insomniac," she admits.

He nods. "Card-carrying member."

"I've tried everything," she says. "Working, reading, laundry. I try to make the time productive."

"Our washer-dryer is broken," he says.

"Oh," she says. "That's too bad. You can borrow ours if you need to."

He smiles, tilts his head in a show of appreciation. "You should text me next time. We'll keep each other company. We could even call each other. Like kids with Campbell Soup cans."

"Funny," she says.

"Or we could just exchange numbers."

She smiles as though she did not hear. "Maybe next time."

Aaron forms the tight, admonished smile to which men are accustomed, the same smile men make in bars when an advance is rebuked by indifference. "Till then," he says, saving face. "Don't forget. Delicates for denim." He takes his son by the hand and heads out of the playground.

Cass smiles politely at the eccentric exit. She watches him leave, slightly unnerved. His gait is odd, distinctive. Large rhythmic strides like he's walking to the beat of music. Then she focuses her full attention on her son. Cass and Sam spend the next hour playing on the slide, hurling themselves through space in a simple celebration of being together.

EIGHT

It's ten o'clock, and the house is back in its sleep cycle. Children breathe in and out, their breaths marking the seconds between life and its adjournment. Ryan is deep in sleep, a pillow over his eyes. Cass stands in her bedroom, checking the window. Finally, the sound of tires on gravel. A blue Toyota pulls up to the curb. Cass leans in to the glass and then silently leaves the bedroom. The stairs are cold through her socks as she hurries down to meet him.

A plump man in his midthirties sits at the wheel. He has the thick jaw, stout comportment, and feline eyes of a Russian. Cass slips into this stranger's car, breathless with excitement. She is unsure where to look and so she looks out the window and focuses on a tree whose drying leaves dangle from their branches like a scab on an elbow.

"You have it?" he asks.

She hands him the phone.

"You know the password?"

"Two. Zero. One. Zero." She is touched and furious as she realizes Ryan has used their anniversary as his new passcode. "Fucker."

"What?" says the man.

"Oh, it's just . . . he used our anniversary."

The man removes a wire from his bag, connects one side to his computer, the other side to Ryan's phone.

"This is legal, right?"

He does not answer.

It occurs to Cass that they have not yet exchanged names, and she wonders if Nora has, in fact, given her access to a world that is darker than she'd realized.

"Are you a former spy?" she asks.

He does not answer.

She regrets both the tone and question. She realizes this is the one question you should never ask a spy, particularly if you want that spy to give a clear indication. She decides to remain silent. She has learned this lesson. Frivolity is not becoming for a woman her age, not in this situation. It is time to replace frivolity with focus. She watches his computer power up, its green light flickering in the dark car. "How long does this take?"

He does not answer. The light glows on his face. He unhooks the wire that connects the phone and the computer. Disappointment drops from Cass's head to her stomach.

"Did it work?"

"I have what I need," he says. "I'll reach out in a couple of days and tell you where to meet me." He returns the phone.

Cass sits for a moment, unsure whether to shake his hand or say thank you, and then she opens the door and gets out of the car and hurries back across her porch to her sleeping family.

Cass returns to the house, her thoughts speeding.

Tomorrow, Ryan will leave for his trip. Would that she had the tools in time to follow him on his journey. She imagines a world in which she owns this power of observation, imagines an end to lies, to uncertainty, humiliation. She imagines how Pandora felt, offered the chance to see the future, not with psychic power, but knowledge of all things, from all perspectives. Of course, she knows there is a price. How do you go on with daily life when you know how you're going to die? Wait? Avoid? Resist? Resign? Kill time? What did Pandora do? Look away? Lean in? Open her eyes?

It is afternoon, and a new car is idling in front of the Connors'. The house has not seen this much activity since the day a moving truck transported their life from Brooklyn. Ryan is getting ready to leave, still upstairs, packing. The kids are waiting near the door with the nervy, unsettled energy of animals before a rainstorm. They get this way before goodbyes—when Ryan and Cass go out at night or before he leaves for a trip—as though they can tell the future by reading their parents' expressions.

Ryan rushes down the stairs and drops his bag at the door. The kids surround him and intercept, making heartfelt pleas to be brought along, last requests for presents.

"Why does everyone look so serious?" he says.

"They miss you when you travel," says Cass.

"I'm only gone for a week," he says. "I'll barely have time to put down my bags and buy presents."

"You said we were going to take me," says Pete.

Occasionally, this happens: Ryan finds himself in a corner, a cage of his own construction, when one of the many plans he suggests gains its own momentum.

"And I meant it. Tell your mom to book the tickets for Christmas vacation."

"That's not for ages," Pete says.

"It's less than two months away," says Ryan.

"You see."

But Ryan has already moved on to the baby, holding him and gazing with total adoration. He throws him into the air while the driver approaches to help with his luggage.

Cass looks on as Pete watches Ryan shower attention on Sam. She steps toward Pete and puts her arms around him.

"You're back Friday?" Cass says.

Ryan puts down the baby. "Yes, Cass."

"Can you send me your flight information?"

"It's ridiculous that I have to."

"What?"

"Report to you like a teenager."

Cass bristles at his words, the usual characterization. His outrage fuels her outrage, his anger her indignation. She can't help entertain the usual question: Is it possible this is all her fault, that she has created the problem, that her mistrust is the root of their ills, as opposed to his indiscretions?

Ryan picks up on her self-doubt. He has a portable detector. He jumps at the chance to gain leverage, to compound Cass's gnawing doubt with the renewed possibility that she is unbearably paranoid and he is entirely innocent.

"Why don't you do something nice for yourself? Book a massage at the Lakehouse?" He is moving toward her and smiling now. When Ryan shines his light on you, all the world is summer.

"Maybe I will."

He opens his arms, and she collapses into them. And again, she feels herself giving in, giving away her convictions for the prize of Ryan's attention. She is like a puppy the way she begs for affection, so quickly trading her beliefs for one kind gesture.

"Do it for me, if not yourself," he tells her. He holds her face and strokes her forehead. She looks up and into his eyes. They are light and gray now like a mirror. "If you want this to work, you're going to have to work on your issues."

Cass pulls away quickly. Why must he always do this? Take every chance to create shame, turn the sweetest moment into a chance for degradation. "This is about trust," she says, "not some made-up mental illness."

Ryan smiles and pulls her back. "You said it. I didn't."

"You know what I mean," Cass says.

"Yes, I do." He kisses her on the forehead.

Now he turns back to the children who stand on the porch, waiting. He hugs each kid in rapid succession like a pope receiving disciples, then descends into the waiting car and sets out for the airport. Cass and the kids watch his car pull out of the driveway. It might as well be a funeral hearse based on their look of dejection. Ryan waves, and they raise their arms, swaying at the horizon. The car recedes, rises up the hill, turns left, and again the street is still and silent. As they turn and walk back into the house, Cass cannot shake the image of Ryan, waving with a look of love, smiling with deception.

Later, as she lies in bed, she imagines his destination: a beach town shaded by mirrored condos, dirty sand paced by aging men and plastic bimbos, where crooked businessmen come for the tax shelters and cheating husbands come for asylum. A smoke-stained hotel room, decorated in beige and salmon, a waiting bucket of cheap champagne, melted ice, and the gasps of her husband's lover as she stands above him and he drags his tongue through her.

At the kitchen table, later that night, Cass "works on her issues." She considers Ryan's advice, his diagnosis. Perhaps, he is right on one count. She is stressed, taxed to the limit. She is like some fey Victorian woman, suffering from hysteria and hot flashes, banished to convalesce for the summer, prescribed to follow a program of sunshine, salt water, and the occasional electric convulsant. Long live Frances Farmer. Was she a credible or crooked witness to her own perceptions? Or merely a canvas for wildly distorted opinions?

It is with this doubt, her innate skepticism coupled with her conviction, that Cass considers the validity of Ryan's thesis. She picks up her phone and dials the local luxe hotel, as he has suggested.

"I'd like to book a massage."

"Sure, have you been here before?" asks the receptionist.

"No, but my husband comes often," said Cass. "The last name is Connor."

A pause. "Yes, I see him right here. He was here last Tuesday."

"Oh," says Cass. "Right. He said it was wonderful."

"Fabulous," says the receptionist. "I'm glad the two of you enjoyed it."

"What?" says Cass. Something fills her throat.

"I'm glad you two enjoyed it."

"Oh, we did. We did," she says. The substance that clogs her throat has now spread across the surface. "Just confirming for my records. The two massages on Tuesday, and . . ."

"Tuesday, the third, Tuesday, the seventeenth. And the couples massage last week."

"Two massages or the couples massage?" asks Cass.

"The couples massage last Tuesday."

"Right. Of course," she says.

"People really seem to love the 'his and hers' package."

Cass manages a few more words before hanging up. The thing that fills her throat—rage, shock, terror—is now making it hard for air to enter. The call ends, and she buckles, reaching the ground in stages until her head is resting between her knees, palms against the floor, trying to figure out whether it has fallen away or remains directly beneath her.

She takes a long breath, straightens, and dials the same number.

"Reservations, please. Hi, this is the assistant for Ryan Connor. I'm calling to confirm the bill for a recent hotel stay. Great. Could you read those dates back to me? The third and the seventeenth. Thank you."

She hangs up the phone. Paralyzed with repulsion. She touches her wedding band in disgust. Bile rises from her stomach.

Ryan is set to land at eight o'clock this evening. At 8:16, as promised, he texts Cass to let her know he's landed. But Cass, now fortified by hours of futile searching, days during which to digest her shock and formulate its byproducts, rage and understanding, knows enough to second-guess Ryan's every assertion.

"Just landed," he writes.

After receiving the text, she picks up the phone and dials the airline. She is not surprised to find a discrepancy between her facts and his fiction.

"Just calling to check on the status of Flight 342. Jamaica to Portland."

A pause. An endless pause during which Cass tries and convicts her husband.

"Still in flight," says the voice. "Scheduled to land in forty minutes. Rerouted due to storms in the Caribbean."

"But my husband just texted to say he'd landed."

"You sure you have the right flight?" says the voice.

"Flight 342," says Cass. "Jamaica to Portland."

"Scheduled to land in forty minutes."

"Thank you," says Cass. She hangs up the phone. She scrolls to Nora's number, but something stops her. Pride. Shame. Humiliation. Staving off panic, she gets very still and quiet. Another hour passes without a word from her husband. Finally, just after ten, the sound of the doorknob turning, the rustle of his jacket as it is hung on the hook, and the clumsy, irregular footsteps of an intoxicated person.

She is sitting on the living room sofa as Ryan stumbles toward her. He kisses her in a way designed to stop further conversation.

"Shitty flight," he declares.

"Yeah," she says. "You look it."

He collapses onto the sofa.

"Took you a while to get back," she says. "From the airport."

"I texted you as soon as I landed."

"You meant to," she says. "But you didn't."

"Oh, Cass. You're so pretty. Why do you frown so much? It makes you look so much older." He furrows his brow, turning himself into a cartoon of consternation.

"Couple more drinks than usual," says Cass. "For a short flight from Jamaica."

"I told you it was a bad flight," he says. "Turbulence. You wouldn't have liked it." He is referring to Cass's flight phobia, for which she is mocked in the Connor household. She is constantly told it ages her, makes her stodgy, boring, the antithesis to his fun-loving companion who, she imagines, loves nothing more than to climb into a ramshackle puddle jumper, scarf tied over her head, peering out into the great unknown a mile above the horizon.

"You texted to say you'd landed, but the flight on your itinerary was still in the air. I'm trying to figure out how that happened."

Ryan is lying down now, sprawled across the sofa. He looks up slowly, first curious, then grinning. "Oh, you're good, Sherlock. Now you're really getting going."

"Go fuck yourself," Cass says. It feels as good as she hopes.

Ryan remains lying down in a calm show of defiance, a body-sized middle finger stretched out across the sofa.

"Remember the turbulence I told you about? There were storms all over the Caribbean. Some sort of hurricane brewing. I knew you would freak if my flight was delayed, so I found one that went through Orlando. It only cost a few hundred bucks. Some thanks I get. You're welcome."

"Did Stephanie like Jamaica?" Cass says. She regrets it as soon as she says it, but something happens to her restraint when her husband lies. Anger and speech are intimately connected.

"Oh," he says. He sits up now. "You're going for the win tonight." There is a new look on his face, something lighting the stupor. He still wears the stupid grin of a drunk, but now his eyes are shiny, like a hungry animal.

"Stephanie says she likes to fly," she says. "On her Facebook page, she says she loves adventure. She went to Negril three years ago. For spring break. Her senior year of college."

Ryan stands up now. He falters as he does this. "You know what's really pathetic? A grown woman stalking a twenty-four-year-old girl who could be your little sister."

Cass straightens her back. "You're the one who's fucking her."

Ryan's face changes forever in this moment. The goodwill that remains might as well be heated water. It leaves his body and is replaced by something different altogether. His face is transformed, contorted with the bile of hatred.

"You like to look at pictures of her? You like to watch her?"

"I may be gullible, Ryan, but I'm not stupid. This is the last time you'll make me doubt myself. This is the last time you'll blame your victim."

"Oh yeah? What makes you so sure?" Now he is walking toward her. "If you ever say that name in this house again, this will be the last night we spend in this house together."

"You can threaten me all you want," says Cass. "But I won't be censored. Maybe I should ask your boss. With all the recent news in the press on sexual harassment, I don't think they will take too well to the threat of litigation."

Of course, she doesn't mean this. Not with any true intention. It is more of an accident than a bluff, but it forces him to admit the scope of his deception. She realizes, after saying it, that it has been too effective, achieving two things quickly: inciting a volcanic amount of rage and the fear behind it, the fear of a guilty person—and incensing Ryan such as to send him off the reservation. Before she has time to react, Ryan is upon her, his hands clenched around her neck, his cheek against her cheek. His spit is flying into her mouth. His face is touching her face, not an inch between them, and he's whispering into her eyes, as though her eyes can hear him.

"Life as you know it is over." His fingers compress around her neck.

And then, by way of punctuation, he shoves her against the wall. And stays there, slowly pressing.

"I'm having terrible thoughts," he whispers.

"Thoughts about what?"

"Thoughts about killing you and chopping you up. Hiding your body in the backyard. You've driven me to this, Cass. Can't you see what you're doing?"

The fight spans several hours. She remembers it in fragments. She remembers a scuffle over his phone. She remembers him pinning her against the wall. She remembers promising to tell his boss, and then, his hands on her shoulders, bashing her head against the wall. She remembers, with the shock of this blow, a simple revelation, that her husband has an unknown skill, that he knows how to turn their own wall into a deadly weapon. He knows how to turn her haven into a homicidal weapon.

A temporary détente is called by way of cell phone. Cass tries to call the cops, but he pries the phone from her. Ryan, always tactical, uses his phone to dial them. Both regret the call equally when the cops arrive ten minutes later. Remembering a cautionary tale about a wife who called the cops on her husband only for both to land in adjoining cells for the evening, they minimize the fight to the officers at their doorstep and agree to sleep in separate rooms and talk it out in the morning. Ryan sleeps in their bedroom, and Cass curls up next to Alice. The kids have miraculously slept through the evening's bout of violence.

It is very late now, well past three in the morning. Cass sits on the bathroom floor, dazed but determined. She is in her private torture chamber, studying images on her phone and computer. She is focused on Stephanie's Facebook page, scouring for clues, logistics. Her face changes as she is confronted by a new photo: Stephanie surrounded by seven girls, huddled together in front of Big Ben. "Greetings from London!" This deflates Cass completely, calling everything she believes into question.

It is dawn in Cass and Ryan's bedroom. The house is still and quiet. The only noise is the sound of breath. In. Out. In. Out. Air invades and escapes with more freedom than any of the residents. Ryan lies in bed, awake, watching zombies. Cass silently gets into bed, turns away from her husband, and lies like this, listening. Moaning. Eating. Dying. Her right temple is throbbing. Her ribs are tender.

"I love you," she says. Why does she say this? She does not feel it at this moment. She says it for one reason: because she needs to hear it.

Ryan says nothing.

"I love you," she says again. It is a question, not a statement. She knows, even as she says it, that she has lost some part of herself, some essential facet of being human and replaced it with something that seeks her own destruction.

More silence. She pulls the sheets from her waist to her shoulders.

"Why won't you say it?"

"Why do you need me to?"

"When you're married, it's common parlance."

"It's not common to make someone say it," he says.

"I'm not making you," says Cass. "I just wish you would say it of your own volition." She hates herself for saying these things, for caving so quickly. But she has lost her discipline—along with other qualities that seem to be depleting: her self-respect, her common sense, her peace of mind, her leverage. She has come to fear her husband's hand less than she fears his rejection.

Ryan says nothing. His knees are up, feet flat on the bed. His legs are so beautifully muscular, so perfectly proportioned.

"When did you start to hate me?" she says.

"Why would you say that?" says Ryan. He does not say that he doesn't.

"Your whole way of being has changed. The way you talk to me. The way you look at me. Your body language."

"Body language?" Ryan says. "Now you sound like Alice."

"Ryan, please."

"I don't like to be pushed, Cass. You know this about me. And yet you still do it."

Cass turns toward him, a plea made by her body. He flinches ever so slightly.

"Love is like this." He holds up a stuffed animal that belongs to the baby, a droopy matted elephant—long ears, shaggy. "Made up."

"We make it up together."

"Why would you want to hear something made up?"

"We decide what it means. We define it together."

"It's still made up," Ryan says. He holds the animal above her.

"The kids need to pretend, Ryan. It's how they figure out what they believe."

"Who decides what it means," he says.

"Most people agree on this one."

"What does it mean to you?"

"Warmth, admiration, commitment. A promise for protection."

Ryan turns away again, goes back to his movie. Zombie sounds continue in contrast to the quiet house. Moaning. Gnawing. Begging.

"We might as well start praying to this." He waves the elephant over her head. "An imaginary fuzzy being."

"That serves a purpose too."

"Such as?"

"Hope, morality, peace of mind."

"Now you're making this about God. Come on, Cass. That's offensive."

"God and love are the same," she says. "Concepts that are defined by us and how we treat them."

A pause, a pause that is long enough for Cass to wonder if she has finally gotten through to him.

"Why do you always have to be so heavy? Can't you just relax and enjoy a movie?"

"Yes, of course." No such luck. Not even when he seems to have heard, when she can feel him in the act of empathy, compassion.

"Thanks," he says.

More zombie sounds. Cass rolls over, turns her back to him.

"I love you," says Ryan. It's the standard bedtime version.

She turns to him quickly. "Then why wouldn't you just say it?"

"Because I object to you trying to make me."

Cass nods and turns back to the wall. "I love you too, Ryan."

NINE

The sound of clanging pots wakes Cass in the morning. The Connor family is back at the family project. She walks downstairs to find the house in a state of busy planning. Ryan and the kids have just returned with a massive load of groceries. The counter is piled high with overstuffed bags, and spirits are even higher. Ryan has commandeered the kitchen with his typical ardor, enlisting the kids to prepare an elaborate breakfast. Alice has been tasked with whisking eggs. Pete rinses berries in a strainer. Sam sits on the counter, banging two wooden spoons and repeating his father's orders like a tyrannical parrot. Better still, they have treated Cass to a rare luxury, sleeping late on a Saturday morning.

Ryan is like a man who has undergone a religious conversion. It is as though he is trying to set the record for world's most devoted stepdad. His energy is palpable, almost manic. He's got big plans for brunch—and, if everyone behaves, a crowd-pleasing dessert later. Today is the beginning of better times for the Connors. They are going to start cooking again—grilling, juicing, smiling. They are going to make up for lost time, make good on all their promises. They are going to do everything on their list—finish the house, hike more, bike more, cook more, read more, laugh more. They are going to attain the quality of life they came for. It is hard to resist the message, the hypnotic force of the rhetoric. And like all great missionaries, he's converting while he's talking. Like all great chefs, he's talking while he's cooking.

Cass sits down at the dining room table.

Ryan places a glass in front of her, a frothy pink mixture. "I made you a smoothie."

"Thanks," she says.

"Almond milk," he says. "Supposed to be healthier than dairy."

An apple is chopped with a large knife. Bacon crackles in a pan. Scalding water is poured over ground coffee. Ryan walks to the table, setting a plate in front of Cass—eggs, bacon, golden toast, and a fresh cup of coffee.

"Fresh start," he says. "Deal?"

Cass smiles. They are back here now.

"I love you, babe," he says.

"I love you too, Ryan."

"You need to take better care of yourself. I need to take better care of you also."

She palms the cup on the table, surveys the milky liquid. The heat of the mug burns her hand but she smiles anyway, eager to affirm Ryan's kind gesture. She takes a hearty sip and makes a show of how much she loves it. In fact, she doesn't like it at all. Cass drinks her coffee black, if she drinks it. She prefers tea any day—Ryan knows this. But perhaps it is a failing of hers that she can't appreciate the gesture. Or some sort of test designed to see if she is grateful.

"That's how they drink it in Jamaica," he says. "With lots of cream and sugar."

She smiles and takes another sip while Ryan is watching. It is sweet and warm from all the cream, lacking the potent kick of heat she looks for in her first sip of the morning. This time, the sweetness is too much and she spits it out on the table.

"What's wrong?" he says.

"So sweet," she says, wiping the spill with her sweater. "You know I don't take sugar."

"So pour it out. Geez," he says. "No good deed goes unpunished."

The kids have moved to the living room to begin their own project. Pete is building a replica of the White House with LEGOs. Alice is making sure the portico has the right number of pillars. Sam is toppling pillars as soon as Alice plants them. Cass balances three distinct tasks, none of which complement the other: ensuring each child has eaten breakfast, quashing bickering before it erupts into sibling warfare, and furthering the investigation that has become her compulsion.

But before she can devote further thought to this subject, the baby is grabbing her phone, and there is a new, more pressing demand on her attention.

"Tef," he says.

Cass snatches the phone out of his hands.

"Tef," says Sam.

He is pointing at the image from Stephanie's Instagram feed: bikini training shots of her ass from the side and behind, splayed out like a dead bug on a windshield. And a flurry of inspirational quotes—today's pain is tomorrow's power—and, even better, her handy food blog—did you know that chicken and oatmeal make a power-packed pre-workout breakfast?!!

In her rush to reclaim the phone, Cass loses hold of her cup of coffee, spilling the contents onto Pete's structure. Brown liquid pools on the unfinished White House to form a chocolate river. Like climate change, fifty years in the future after all the rivers have flooded over.

"Tef," the baby says again.

Cass has reclaimed the phone and shoves it into her pocket. She rushes back to the counter, grabs a wad of paper towels, and struggles to sop up the mess before Ryan and the kids notice the chaos.

"Tef," the baby says again.

Cass looks to Ryan. "What did he just say?"

"Hell if I know."

"Yes, you do," she says. "The baby just ID'd your girlfriend."

Ryan shakes his head now very slowly, as though normal bodily movements have been slowed by his revulsion. "I thought we were done with this," he says. "You're not going to ruin another morning." He turns to Alice and Pete, transforming his face. And then, like a camp counselor, rousing the troops, "Okay," he says. "Who's hungry?"

"I am!" says Pete.

"I am!" says the baby.

"Who wants to get some real breakfast?"

"I call pancakes!" Pete says.

"Pancakes," says the baby. Sam has no trouble saying this word, no issue with concept or enunciation.

"Go get your shoes and jackets."

The kids evacuate the room. Ryan lingers. Cass can see herself as he sees her, from his perspective, still in pajamas, sitting on the floor, undignified, like a beggar. Why would anyone want to be with her? When did she become this person?

"First one dressed gets to pick the place," Ryan calls out. He is really hamming it up now, playing the fearless leader, as though he knows every unit of joy enacts another unit of pain in Cass's psyche. He gives her one last withering look before following the ruckus.

"You coming or what?" he says as he leaves.

Cass is nodding. Right now, she will follow, but there is no more room for denial.

They set off as a family with Ryan leading the group. Alice and Pete duke it out over the destination, debating the merits of doughnuts versus pancakes. Pete is an able negotiator and Alice is very persuasive, instinctively offering or withholding the few possessions he controls that his sister covets—an invitation to his birthday party in seven months, a month of riding shotgun. By the time they have reached consensus, Ryan has chosen the destination, stopping at a hardware store on the way to buy supplies for his latest renovation. Today, the contents of his bags include the usual sundry items: paint thinner, joint compound, chalk paint, and a box cutter. This weekend, he proudly tells the clerk, he has grand ambitions: to paint a chalk wall for the kids so that they can draw on the wall and Cass can keep a master family schedule. He needs joint compound to fix the wall before painting. The box cutter is anyone's guess. She marvels at how easy it is to procure such a sharp weapon.

The next stop is Tucker's, a small but well-stocked market at the town landing with table and counter seating. It is renowned for its quarter-pound lobster roll, and its generous size-to-cost ratio, as well as its friendly staff and assortment of necessities from ice to aspirin. The lobster roll, that pinnacle of Maine delicacies, can here be enjoyed in a quintessential seaside setting with views of the glittering bay and the craggy islands. There is no pretense at variety: the rolls are served cold in cardboard boats, on buttered buns, lightly tossed with mayo. The only garnish is a wisp of wax paper and the occasional stray chop of tarragon. For the kids, there are apple-cider donuts and Coca-Cola in glass bottles. A lobster roll at Tucker's, and its frugal ten-dollar price, is a fail-proof family pleaser, all the more enjoyable when eaten on the dock—buoys and napkins included. From September to May, after the busy tourist season, the clientele at Tucker's is all locals, and it is once again the ideal spot to enjoy the particular palette of Maine: blue water, green trees, gray cloud cover.

Cass sits with the kids, placing their orders. Ryan excuses himself to go to the bathroom—and stays there for several minutes. She could have sworn he just went at home. He must be texting Stephanie, planning their next meeting.

But when he returns, he's sweet again, and he's got a present. He slides a lobster roll across the table. "Your mother loves these," he tells the kids.

"Yuck," says Pete.

"I know," says Ryan. "It's the old salty dog in her."

"Mom, you're an old salty dog," says Pete.

"Don't be mean to Mom," says Alice.

Cass looks from Pete to Ryan. Does this call for a reprimand? Is she supposed to laugh now? She has lost her social compass. She is drifting, floating, drowning, watching from a distant planet. Why is he being playful again? Is this a sincere gesture? Did she imagine the morning's affront? And the lingering question: Is *she, not he*, the problem? Smiling, she accepts the gift and asks the waiter for a to-go container.

An hour later, the Connor household has regained equilibrium—Ryan is on a ladder, pounding the wall with a hammer, and the kids are taking turns rolling across the living room on a skateboard. Childhood is a chilling oxymoron. The threat of danger lurks behind every corner. Joy sometimes seems a clever cover for the constant threat of violence.

Cass wanders into the kitchen to make the baby a snack. She opens the fridge and takes out the lobster roll. She takes a bite to acknowledge his thoughtful gesture, as though the first step in her rehabilitation is learning how to accept what he says at face value. Reflexively, she spits it out. The taste is sharp and shocking. The outside of her mouth goes numb, and her tongue is burning. It is a wholly unfamiliar feeling, as shocking as touching a hot stove or being drenched in ice water, an assault on the senses.

"Mom, what's wrong?" Alice says.

"Must have gone bad," she mutters.

Alice, still sitting on the skateboard, watches her mother.

"Alice, does this smell weird to you?"

Alice walks over and sniffs the lobster, wrinkles her nose in revulsion. "Yeah," she says. "But that stuff always smells disgusting."

Cass confronts a new but unmistakable feeling. The effort it takes to thrust doubt from her mind is met with a doubly powerful force, the buzz of intuition.

"What's up with the food you bought me?" she calls out. Ryan is upstairs now. She can hear his footsteps in the hallway above her.

The footsteps stop. "What did you say?"

"What's wrong with this food?" Cass says.

"Beats me," says Ryan. The acoustics of the house are such that sound carries up and down the stairs with only the slightest muffle. "Must've gone bad. Throw it away."

Cass reseals the plastic container. She walks to the trash to dispose— obeying on automatic—but she is stopped by her gut again. She turns and walks back to the fridge and places it on the top shelf, where none of the kids can reach it.

TEN

Cass stands in her bedroom, staring into her closet. She steadies herself on the door, trying to piece together a costume. Strife has made her weak. Discord has made her nauseous. Jean has corralled the kids upstairs in their queue for the bath, and pajamas are laid out for bedtime. Ryan and Cass are going to the party for Nora's fortieth birthday. "Grown-ups in costume," the invitation said. "Abstainers are not welcome." Everyone is supposed to dress up as an "eighties icon." No sexy witches or naughty nurses. Extra points for rock stars and political figures. Lots of self-congratulation. Ryan is not amused by the theme or the prospect. He's been grumbling about it since Cass mentioned the commitment.

"We should leave in half an hour," says Cass. She hears herself talking, but she does not recognize herself anymore, this timid, scared person.

"Playing dress-up with a bunch of aging yuppies?" he says. "Thanks, but I think I'd rather stay home and play dress-up with the children."

His mood does not shift as they drive. The city is gray always. The party is raging when they arrive. Drunk yuppies in full regalia. Waiters carry trays that contain an assortment of ghoulish pleasures: plastic flutes dripping with orange champagne, tarts with wriggling mushrooms, pigs in blankets tinted black, stabbed by toothpicks with black fringe like witches on broom-back.

For Cass, the effect is hallucinogenic—smiles stretch a little too far, volume pitches and recedes. The costumes and chaos add to the feeling that now follows her, that she and her husband are in the special purgatory for spouses on the verge of breakup, and that this isolation will follow her wherever she goes until she fixes her perception or elicits a confession.

Ryan returns from the bar with champagne tinted orange. He hands a glass to Cass and takes up residence in a corner, a perfect position for watching the guests and mocking the whole idea of public recreation. A guest walks by dressed as Kurt Cobain. Shaggy hair, plaid flannel, tweaked disorientation.

"Wrong decade," says Ryan.

"Technically, the band formed in the eighties," says Cass.

"Poor guy," says Ryan. "You know what happened to him."

"What?" says Cass.

"Wife drove him to it."

"I wish you would socialize," she says, "instead of glaring in the corner."

"I wish you would leave me alone," he says, "instead of trying to control me."

"Did you take your meds this morning?" she says. She already knows the answer.

"That's none of your business," Ryan says.

"It is when you behave like this."

"Get out of my head, Cass." He says this at a whisper, but it has the intensity of a scream. And then, at a regular volume, he adds, "I don't see any reason for us to stay together."

Cass pauses when he says this, but not because of the content. There's something theatrical about the statement, something distinctly scripted, outside of the realm of normal speech and human behavior. It is as though he is a director on a set and Cass is his actor; he is giving her motivation, trying to influence her next move, to spur her to report this comment to a friend, to run to the bathroom in tears, to escalate the fight from a couple's quarrel into a public spectacle or otherwise react in a way that will be witnessed and recorded.

But Cass is determined to make the most of this occasion. She leaves Ryan on his own, scowling at the table, and makes her way through the crowd to locate Nora. She finds her standing in the center of several icons: two Madonnas, a Mr. T, and Ronald and Nancy. Nora wears a white lace bow tied around her head, looped large like the ears of a bunny.

"Virgin Tour?" Cass asks.

"Radio City Music Hall, 1984."

"Nice," says Cass. "I was there too. Black lace, black midriff tee, black rubber bangles."

"What's your costume?" Nora asks.

"Battered housewife," says Cass.

"Nicole Simpson is so nineties." Nora leans in close now, eyes widened for emphasis. "Did you call him?"

"Yes," Cass whispers. "I felt like I was in a spy caper."

"I know!" says Nora. "Isn't he amazing? When will you have it?"

"Shh," says Cass. She checks her back, ensures their conversation is private. "Soon," she says. "He said he would be in touch. It was all very cloak and dagger."

"He's incredible. Every woman should have him on speed dial."

Suddenly, Cass's smile flattens.

"What's wrong?" says Nora.

"I just got this wave of . . ." Cass trails off. A swirling sensation snakes from her throat to her stomach, followed by the tingly feeling she gets in her legs when an elevator is descending very slowly.

"You're drunk already?" Nora says.

"No," says Cass. "I only had one drink. Just feeling kind of queasy."

"Then you need another!" says Ryan. He has emerged from hiding. He holds two more glasses of champagne, lifted from a nearby tray.

Cass accepts the glass. Perhaps they can start the night anew and enjoy the party together.

"To playing dress-up!" Ryan says.

"To acting like our children!" says Nora. "When we're not with them!"

"To pretending," says Cass. She takes a hearty gulp of champagne and smiles, carried by the moment.

The party is over, and Cass and Ryan are walking, heading to their parked car through the streets of downtown Portland. The city is in a perennial state of rainfall. It is always either about to rain or about to stop raining.

The cobblestones in the old part of town are slick, and the brick on the buildings looks mossy. Ryan walks with the halting steps of a broken robot. The car is several blocks farther, on a small side street called Cherry. The walk is challenging for Ryan given the number of drinks he has had, the wet cobblestones, and the manic energy of oncoming trick-or-treaters.

They reach the curb as the light turns red, and just as cars rush toward them, Ryan touches Cass's back, pushing her ever so slightly into the path of oncoming traffic.

"I'm gonna have to do it this way," he says, "because you clued into the lobster so fast."

"Hey! What are you doing?" Cass regains balance and stumbles back to the curb. She is more shocked than scared, more confused than outraged. The push was a gentle shove, as opposed to a forceful thrust, but it was a surprise nonetheless—as was the rush of headlights speeding toward her. "What the fuck, Ryan. Are you trying to kill me?"

"Oh, Cass, you've always got a theory." He says this in the usual way, his demeaning demeanor, with all the usual implication. He says this as though there are two distinct ways to push someone into traffic—one humorous and one homicidal—and that she has jumped to the wrong conclusion, disappointing him once again with her shitty sense of humor.

"Are you trying to kill me?" she says. "You're trying to kill me."

"Yup," he says. "And I know exactly how I'm going to do it. I'm gonna make it look like a suicide, and everyone's gonna believe it." He is smiling like a mischievous child who has successfully stolen a cookie.

"Fuck you, Ryan," Cass says. "Fuck you. That's not funny." Cars are rushing past them now, making the threat of the act all the more potent. Cass hurries to the car, opens the door, starts the engine. She is pulling out of their parking spot as Ryan gallops toward her, fumbles to open the passenger door, and collapses into his seat in a fit of laughter.

The car is silent as they drive home, away from the city of Portland, over Back Cove and Tukey's Bridge, into the dewy suburbs. The only sound is Ryan's breath. In. Out. In. Out. A request and a rejection. A threat and a promise. A death threat or a diabolical joke. A mind game or a confession? Cass watches the light recede as they approach Cumberland, holding the light in her gaze as though the city is safety and every mile she drives away, she is farther from it.

Cass knows about liars. She has read up on the subject. She grew up in a home where lies were just as likely as truthful statements. Liars like to brag. Liars love attention. Liars have a love-hate relationship with the people who catch their falsehoods. Liars rely on their listeners, both to suspend their belief and to validate their triumphs. Cass is a veritable expert on the subject because she has spent her life calling out her father's.

Cass understands liars' inherent paradox. As much as they want to obscure their lies, liars want to broadcast. It is for this reason that so many lies end up with a confession—because, as much as they love to succeed, they hate just as much to get away with their lies in private, without the thrill of an audience. Cass has read all the research, presented by the experts. Liars give themselves away with their satisfaction, a smile at the corner of their lips, the unmistakable flash of pleasure. Storytelling is no fun without someone to listen. Knowing this, the deceived are armed with one surefire mode of detection: liars eventually betray themselves. To a liar, deception without exhibition didn't really happen. It, just like a lie, could be a feat of the imagination.

Liars are storytellers first and foremost, and a story without an audience is a tree falling in a forest. Liars, like the rest of us, answer to compulsion. All human beings narrate life and share their tales with others. And so liars can be waited out. Liars can be baited. A liar will eventually hang himself on his own need for confession.

The feelings begin later that night with maddening vagueness. It is like the beginning of being high but without the euphoria component. Her hands twitch ever so slightly, but her hands sometimes do this when she is nervous. And she can't tell if they are twitching now—these electroform movements that make her fingers look like jellyfish in a tank—because her brain is making them twitch, because the nerves that control them are dying, or because she is freaking herself the fuck out about something that is not happening, and her body is short-circuiting from the anxiety.

It must be around midnight now. It may be six in the morning. Time feels subjective, tangential, like the ever-changing color of the sky in Sam's drawings.

"I have to go to the ER," she tells Ryan.

"Don't be dramatic," he tells her.

"That's what you say to your wife after you try to kill her."

He snorts in the way he did before when he was laughing, then rolls over and falls asleep so fast that Cass can no longer tell if he was laughing or snoring.

"I need to go to an ER," she says, now louder.

"You're freaking yourself out," he says. "Stop with the drama. Why would I tell you I wanted to kill you if I was actually going to do it?"

"You were wasted at the time."

"Go," he says. "By all means. I'm not trying to stop you. I'm just trying to save us money. They'll keep you there all night, tell you it's nothing, then charge you a thousand bucks for the trouble." He closes his eyes, then opens them again. "Besides, if I were going to kill you, I wouldn't use poison," he says. "Too easy to find in an autopsy."

Cass is perturbed, not comforted by this statement. He has given this too much thought—both the method and the alibi. And the more he tries to quell her fears, the more he sounds guilty.

Now, the physical sensations are growing more certain. The brown medallions on her sheets—sheets she usually finds soothing—are making her dizzy. The dim light coming from the hall is harsh to the point of blinding. Nausea has taken up residence in her throat and stomach. She crosses the room and walks down the stairs, clutching the railing. She opens her bag and rummages through. Her keys and her wallet are missing.

"Where is my wallet?" she calls out.

But all she hears now is the sound of his breathing. How can she hear it downstairs? Is this a hallucination?

By morning—it must be five by now—Cass is throwing up in the toilet. The feelings are more specific: overwhelming nausea, nausea that drags her to the ground as though a magnet at the center of the earth is drawing the iron in her blood to be its companion. Vomit that starts as chunks of food, recognizable items. The leafy green remnants of lettuce. A pasty white mass of chicken. Followed by a pinkish-brownish substance that looks like an internal organ. She is hunched now on the floor, throwing up on the cold tiles. She tries to rise from the ground and throws up into the bathtub. The vomit is followed by a pain that emanates from her center. Burning in the throat. Dizziness that won't be quelled by stillness. Nausea that does not lessen after she vomits. Pain that has no onset and no end. Pain that has no locus. Pain that is not something she feels but rather something that controls her. She is the pain's puppet. Pain is her God, her master, and her organs are its disciples.

"I need help," she tells Ryan. The irony of this statement is not lost on her, its inconvenient object. But there is no one else to tell. She doesn't want to call Nora with this crisis. Her family is over three hundred miles away. Her friends are scattered across the country.

The rest of the day proceeds in flashes, moments out of order—or at least, that is how she remembers it, or remembers remembering it, or reminds herself to remember it later. Time is moving up and down, backward and forward, around and behind her. Time is marked, not by moments but by sounds and sensations, not like beads on a necklace after the clasp has broken but like beads in a tower, piling up, then scattering. It is unlike anything she has known. It defies description, like the time she smoked pot in college with the girl who used a briefcase as a backpack who told her she had "the good shit" from "the gold coast" and promised "it will just relax you" and the two of them ended up seven hours later, in adjacent beds in University Health Services, trying to get the nurse to understand that the athletes in the next room, icing their swollen ankles were, in fact, the four horsemen of the apocalypse. Needless to say, after this, she swore off marijuana forever.

Now they are riding bicycles together as a family on the path that hugs the bay with all the happy people. The trees move past them in a haze of green and golden flickers. The wind sifts through their hair like a thousand tiny fingers. The sunshine is warm on their shoulders. Every shoulder feels this sunshine. The raindrops that fell on the roof last night. Everyone in this family heard these raindrops. Everyone in this family is connected by these memories and the feelings that follow. Cass cannot tell if she is happy or high or dizzy. Everything is blurry. Everyone is dizzy. Everything is dizzy and everyone is blurry.

Now she feels clear and light again as they round the bend of the bay, as they slow down and park their bikes in a clump of spokes and metal. They are dashing through the woods like a litter of puppies, a group linked by one soul, bound by a psychic connection, in other words, a family. As they frolic in the park, Cass stomachs a new conviction. Ryan has staged this winning performance for public consumption, as an alibi, a witnessed family portrait, with scads of people to view his upstanding citizen act, the doting husband and father. And still, even as she clocks this version of the day's events, she is equally unsure if they have left the house yet, if any of this has occurred on Casco Bay or in a hallucination.

It is nearing noon, and Cass needs a second opinion. The kids are watching a movie in her bedroom. The sounds of canned joy from a cartoon punctuate the silence. The kids are safe and settled for now, and she needs another person, both to provide a reality check, to dispel or validate her symptoms, and, if the latter, to help her get out of the house intact with all the children.

She fumbles for her phone and calls the most recent number.

"Even if it were a joke," says Nora, "nothing about this is normal. And given the way you sound right now, I think you should call the cops, and an ambulance."

"Nora, I need your help," she says. Her voice is distant, foreign. "I need you to come and watch the kids while I go to the hospital."

It's later again. Minutes have passed or hours. Cass is standing on the stairs, confronting her husband. But she's not just accusing him of fucking someone. She's accusing him of attempted murder.

"You're not just a cheater. You're a killer," she says.

Does she say this or imagine it?

"I'm done living with you," he says. "Done living with your sickness."

He pauses, unsure where to go, walks into their bedroom, then turns and sprints upstairs. Heavy objects fall to the ground as he rummages through a closet—a basketball, a suitcase, golf clubs. He hurries back, carrying a large gray box, and pauses in the bedroom, as though weighing his options; then he seems to make a decision and marches down the stairs and out the front door with the kids trailing behind him. Shoes are shoved on. Jacket grabbed. The coat hook nearly dislodges. He bursts out the front door and heads to the car, scored by the children's crying.

"I'm sorry," he says as he starts the car. "Your mother is not well." He has the panicked look of a man jumping off a capsized boat, pity for those he leaves behind and terror for himself. Cass is struck by the most incongruous memory at this moment. Ryan is underwater, hair floating above him like a halo. He is deep-sea diving with sharks, weaving between pink and orange fish, mermaids in the shadows.

Time accelerates again as Ryan turns the ignition. He yanks his wedding ring off his hand and throws it across the driveway. The spectacle is incongruous in the quiet town of Cumberland. The car lurches forward across the driveway, and the kids follow it up the hill until it turns the corner. Cass crouches to the ground and weeds Ryan's wedding band out of the grass. It is one task she can complete in a world that defies comprehension.

She unclasps the necklace on her neck, takes the wedding band that she is still clutching, and laces it onto the chain next to her heart-shaped locket. The ring lands just outside the heart, like a ring around a planet, just like any other fool, both trapped and protected.

She sits and tries to soothe the kids and regain composure.

"You are safe," she tells the kids. "It's going to be all right now." She wants them to believe this. Would that she could also.

Part II

ELEVEN

The hospital is blue, blue in every direction. The color is adding to Cass's sense that she is swimming against a current. The night has not brought clarity to the prior day's confusion. The uncertain feelings in her head have grown more certain. She is wholly overcome by a feeling that defies description. Colors in the waiting room have the deepest saturation. The blue is the blue of nightmares, a photograph submitted to the strongest filter. The beige of the walls is the brown of mud. The sickly green stripe on the walls is the uniform color painted in hospitals around the world, as though to immortalize the color of bile in the patients. Sounds are loud and then very soft, muffled and then echoic.

Time has totally changed its ways. It no longer moves in predictable chunks, marked by seconds and minutes, but unpredictably, like a child who is walking a long distance, sometimes exhausted, sometimes energetic. People's faces morph without rhyme or reason, their smiles curling up in the corners, their eyes bulging as they move from the periphery into sharp focus. All these things amount to a vaguely surreal world, as though its contents—human beings, nature, and inanimate objects—have changed their genetic makeup like a frog with a mutation, too subtle to notice at first until the webbing reveals a fifth finger. At the moment, the metal handrails of the stretcher parked in the corner appear to be respiring while the man asleep on top seems to have lost the same power.

Adding to these bizarre qualities is the way they defy description. When the things of the world change the way they impact the senses, and the senses themselves seem to be broken or altered in their essence, perception changes meaning, not only the things that Cass sees but the notion that *she* is perceiving. It feels more like she is the witness of someone else's perceptions, a fiber in the optic nerve of a much larger being. It is as though a circuit has shorted in the brain's translation system, connecting nerves in the eyes and hands, and the nerves in the brain to which they report their observations. The glitch reveals her tininess, her relative insignificance, and also a glimpse at her role in a much larger system. It all amounts to the sense that Cass is not Cass anymore, that her senses are not her senses, that her soul has vacated her body as though evacuating a smoking building.

"State your name and date of birth."

Cass Phillips Connor.

"Your address, please?"

This is harder. She states it in reverse or hears it backward while stating it correctly. Hard to tell the difference.

"Do you know what year it is?"

She does, and she declares it. "Can we move past the small talk?" she says. "My husband tried to poison me. I need you to test my blood before it leaves my system."

The nurse who is asking the questions turns and looks to a different nurse who is sitting at a computer. They exchange a loaded look, a look that means something specific. Cass assumes it is disdain for her tone, or the clothes she is wearing—leggings, and the fraying oxford shirt that she wears on the weekends, a shirt that once belonged to her husband. It occurs to her that her style of dress, typical of the busy working mothers in Cumberland, may not extend past county lines and that she looks, to these nurses, decidedly disheveled.

"How do you know he tried to poison you?" asks the nurse. This is the one sitting at the computer.

"He told me," Cass says. She nods and raises her eyebrows, as though to say *gotcha*.

"Why would he tell you what he was going to do, if he was trying to kill ya?"

"Apparently, homicidal people all have a moment where they state their intention. It's called having a plan. That's why ERs and shrinks are required to ask a patient if they intend to hurt themselves or another person. Turns out it's a pretty good indication. So part of it was probably that he wanted to brag. Liars love to broadcast. Or he thought I'd soon be dead and wouldn't live to tell it. Like he said, he already had an alibi: to make it look like a suicide and convince people that I was crazy. Also, he was drunk at the time. And, as the saying goes, there are three things that never lie: drunk people, children, and leggings." She laughs at her joke, waits for the nurses to share their appreciation.

"Why would he think you're crazy?" asks the nurse sitting at the computer.

"Oh, he doesn't really. He just says that to kick up dust when I accuse him of some fucked-up thing he's done in order to throw me off the scent and win an argument. His first defense is turning the tables. He always says that. You know that saying: deny, deny, deny. He takes it a step further: deny, deny, deny, then shift the blame to the accuser."

"Gotcha," says the nurse sitting at the computer.

"How would he convince people?" says the one asking questions.

"Excuse me?" says Cass.

"You said he was going to convince people you were crazy. How would he do that?" she says.

"Oh, easily," says Cass.

"Easily?" says the nurse.

"By acting like I'm paranoid every time I clue into some new lie, every time I discover some new underlying connection."

"I see," says the other nurse. They exchange another look. The look is no longer suggestive. It has become more certain. But Cass just thinks they are a little thick and confused by the situation. She does not see this connection until they have asked her to stand and follow them out of triage, to walk down a long blank hall to a room that is near the waiting area, but not in it, until she hears the door of this room close and lock behind her, until she is seated in a chair in a row of seats in pinkish-brown pleather. A receptionist sits behind a glass window, her long gray hair in a ponytail that falls on either side of her neck. The sound of ranting pierces the quiet, occasionally growing so loud as to vibrate the glass partition.

"Where are we?" Cass asks.

"You're in Mercy Hospital in Portland, Maine."

"Yes, I know that," Cass says. "But where are we inside it?"

"You're in the psych ward of Mercy Hospital. You called 9-1-1, and an ambulance brought you here. We're just going to do a quick evaluation."

"But I just went through triage," she says. "I came here voluntarily. I need you to test my blood for poison," she continues. "I need to get proof of my husband's crime, and, depending on the amount, I probably need to get it out of my system."

"Right," says the nurse. "We will do that if we feel it is merited, but first you're going to go through a psychiatric evaluation."

There is a new nurse now, a man wearing a white jacket. "Don't worry, we're going to draw your blood, but first we're going to ask you a few questions. Please give us your belongings and cell phone, and we'll return these to you when we determine it's safe to do so."

Cass looks down at her bag, the cell phone she is clutching. This is not good. Not good what is happening. She leans down and releases her bag. She does this slowly. This is an important maneuver, she knows, in which there is the possibility for terrible misunderstanding. Now she must release her phone, her access to the world she knows, to someone who can vouch for her, to state the facts of a sensible world, access to her children. Before she must release her phone, she sends an SOS to Nora.

"Need help ASAP. They have me in the psych ward."

A man arrives to take her phone. Just before, a text arrives. "Stay calm and speak slowly," says Nora. "Scared people are scary."

Cass forces a polite smile as the man confiscates her belongings.

Understanding dawns now with a physical sensation. People describe a heaviness with shock, a weight, something sinking from the head to the stomach. For Cass, it feels more like heat, the way it slowly emanates from the top of her head to her shoulders, from her shoulders to her fingers, from her fingers to her organs, except here the sensation is not warm and sweet. It is the opposite of pleasure. She is in the mental ward of Mercy Hospital in Portland. She is locked inside against her will, and this detainment is legal. Her children are likely getting tired, waiting for their mother and their nightly bedtime ritual. Her children are likely getting scared, wondering what has happened to her, what has happened to their parents, why their world has shattered in an instant. She is trapped in a cage of Ryan's design that extends far beyond anything he or she could have imagined.

With this understanding come other revelations. It is essential to remain calm. She must act and appear normal. Any appearance of losing composure, any resisting or protest, will only play into their concerns, the suspicions of these people, and increase the likelihood of the diagnosis that is already their thesis. The irony of this situation is wholly apparent. It is *their* paranoia, their suspicion, the visceral fear caused by her allegations that has made these witnesses paranoid, crazy with suspicion, while they try to assess the same thing in Cass. It is this very process, the violence incited by fear in another person and the need to predict future violence, that turns friends into enemies, police officers into murderers, peaceful into warring countries, human nature against human nature, human beings into barbarians. This is why a person must move slowly when a cop tells her to put her hands up, Cass realizes, because minor misunderstandings are made in the nanoseconds of confrontations, and those misunderstandings can have the gravest of consequences. Because nine times out of ten, the misunderstanding is the expectation of evil.

"You can't give me meds against my will," she says. She knows this from her basic knowledge of ER dramas, from her time as a journalist covering the space between lunacy and the legal system, the overlap between medicine and the law, the people trapped in this ghetto.

"Not unless you get out of control," says the nurse with the gray ponytail.

Cass takes a deep breath and tries to slow her breathing. In. Out. In. Out. Historically, this has offered solace, some measure of meditation. No such luck at the moment. Instead, she must perform, give an Oscar-worthy performance. At the moment in her life when her body most wants, needs to panic, she must achieve total calmness.

Ryan has set the course, and there is no getting off it. She is on a plane locked on autopilot, careening into the mountains. Her panic and tone did not help her, nor did her gender. Cass has found herself in a new world that does not presume innocence—but rather presumes madness. She has landed in enemy territory, on the border between two distinct communities—victims of attempted murder and people with paranoid delusions.

Two hours have passed, and Cass still sits in the waiting room of the locked psych ward, listening to the sound of her own breathing and crazy people ranting. Is it rude to think of them this way, she wonders, the most absurd of snobbery? Is it foolish to think she is somehow exempt, that she has been falsely imprisoned, that everyone around her is nuts when *she* is currently detained for a psych evaluation? Is this her delusion? In. Out. In. Out. The distinct sound of these two acts—one higher and one lower—and the fact that they can be predicted, allows Cass to focus on the only thing that makes infinitely more sense than the place in which she is sitting. Finally a young doctor emerges. He seems to be a doctor—white coat, stethoscope, patronizing smile—but given the current state of things, she must test all assumptions. In. Out. In. Out. He just has a few questions.

As she begins to speak, she gives herself a few instructions. Speak slowly. Be precise. Say what happened word for word—but not too many words because that can sound like ranting. Begin with Ryan's threat to her life, the alibi he shared with her—suicide, madness—and the defense that he promised and predicted—that people will believe she is crazy—would enable him to get away with murder (had the attempt succeeded) and (despite its failure) is miraculously foiling her attempt to report it since she has lived to tell it.

Simply saying the word *poison* seems to incite suspicion, seems to cast doubt on Cass faster than a criminal record. Ryan has, in a sense, poisoned her mind, her body, and her surroundings, not only with the slow insidious steep of his cruel words and deceitful behavior, with the toxic effect of his lies and carnal betrayals, the contamination of the trust that is the center of a marriage, but with the subsequent crime and its narcotic effect on her audience, the first line of responders, tinting their objectivity like food coloring in water, until their bias all but precludes an objective reception.

Murderers have a host of alibis available to them. Victims do not have these. Victims have two options: to be believed or dismissed. Deemed credible or crazy. And if dismissed, to be eligible for a new crime, something with its own hefty sentence. An unreliable witness. Credibility, like sanity, has no alibi, no objective criteria, other than projection. One need not look at the history of gender, race, or sexuality for proof that projection often results in false and dangerous assumptions.

Ryan has chosen the perfect crime and the perfect weapon—although he was not wholly successful—not only because this weapon avoids messy fingerprints altogether, but because it has the ability to transmute suspicion from the hand of the attacker into the face of the victim, turning people against Cass, or at least unleashing skepticism in a way that even Ryan could not have predicted.

Attempted murder with poison is unlike a crime with a gun or knife. Poison is more like rape in that it penetrates the system, leaving behind a malignant scar with little trace to prove it. In a legal realm, poison, like rape, tends to impugn both the perpetrator *and* the victim. It has the power to turn supporters into critics, doctors into skeptics, shattering the credulity of those one needs so sorely for protection. Poison has turned her first line of support into a front line of opposition, all but ensuring those she needs for help become unwitting accomplices to Ryan's mission. Unfortunately, were she to state this theory right now, it might seem like paranoia. She tries to think of the movie in which the falsely accused seems guiltier with every assertion of innocence. "Don't protest too much" is all she can remember. And a lyric from a well-known song: *Talk less. Smile more.*

Cass smiles at the doctor and tries to find composure. She thinks of a prisoner cuffed to a chair. Resisting will only tighten her binds. The best— the only—thing she can do is relax into the chair and hope the ropes loosen. She crosses and uncrosses her legs, tries to make herself smaller. The leather, if it is leather on the chair, squeaks as she does this. Searching her brain for the perfect lede, she calls on her reporter's instinct. She clasps her hands on her lap to hide a splat of paint on her shirt. Would that she had changed into nicer clothes before leaving the house this morning.

"My husband made a death threat," Cass begins slowly. "He told me he would get away with it because—" She stops herself quickly. She should not volunteer Ryan's alibi—so far, this has not worked for her. It sounds like an admission. It seems only to bolster Ryan's version.

"It's okay," says the doctor. He seems to sense Cass's discomfort. "I've heard a bit about your situation, and I've spoken to your friend." He gestures out the glass window in the door to the larger waiting room. Cass follows his gaze to find a familiar face. Nora sits on a chair, eyes long and exhausted, head bowed in sleep or prayer. "Your husband sounds like a bit of a scoundrel," says the doctor.

Cass nods emphatically. Does this doctor have a sense of humor? She opens her mouth to say more but decides against it. She knows this from her days as a reporter: less is always more when trying to elicit a response from a subject. Never cut a person off before he has finished his comment. And, most important rule: a source has never finished his comment.

"Either he's trying to kill you or scare you," says the doctor. "Neither one's very nice."

"No." She shakes her head and tries to minimize the scope of her movement. She shifts her weight from one leg to the other, hears the sticky release of the leather.

"We can run some tests here," says the doctor. "Blood work and urine."

"What will you test for?" Cass asks.

"We'll run for household chemicals, narcotics, heavy metals."

Cass's brow furrows.

"Not like the music," he says, smiling. "Lead, mercury, arsenic. The stuff they used in the olden days to kill Victorian woman. And the things that lurked in every household until the EPA wised up and cleaned our pipes and attics."

Cass nods and smiles. She is grateful for the doctor's kindness, grateful to be getting closer to facts, to data, to trade all this hazy speculation for the scientific method.

"Bleach, ammonia, the oxides. Those are the worst things you tend to find in the house. Especially when they're combined. The seven-screen is a panel for basic narcotics—pot, coke, booze, hallucinogens. The only one that's not on it is LSD. Not sure why. PCP's the one that lands people here. Talk about poison." He shudders. "That seems like the right place to start given your symptoms. You'll just have to wait here a couple more hours. We can't release you until the lab sends back your blood work and urine."

"In here?" she asks.

"Nah," he says. Another merciful smile. "We'll get you out of here in a minute. You can sit out there in the big waiting room with all the really crazy people."

"How many hours?" Cass asks.

"Five or six."

She shudders.

"I suppose you could leave now and get these tests run by a private doctor."

"I'll do that," Cass says quickly. She fields and decides to ignore a message from her better judgment. Intuition tells her to stay, to get these tests done immediately, that she will come to regret any delays to this decision. But she is suddenly overcome with a rush of emotion, the feeling that is the strict and universal domain of all mothers, a feeling too intense to be called *sadness* and too specific to be called *heartbreak*, the feeling that comes from time spent away from one's children—whether a matter of days or hours. And the memory of the locking door, the nonconsensual sleepover she has narrowly averted.

"One last thing," he says.

She looks up, dread rising from her stomach.

"Urine is better than blood for the heavy metals panel. It only stays in the blood for a few days. It shows up in the urine when the body is trying to excrete it. They take about a week to come back. Sometimes longer."

Cass nods and tries for a polite smile on this foul subject.

"Good luck." The doctor smiles. His smile is no longer patronizing. It seems to be heartfelt.

"Thank you," says Cass. The door opens, and Cass walks quickly through toward Nora. She has never in her life been so happy to see another person.

Cass sits in the passenger seat of Nora's family schooner, watching the silver bay speed by like a syringe delivering salvation. As she rides back to Nora's, she takes comfort in familiar sensations, the seep of wind through a slit in the window, the whirl of the massive engine, the purr of the tires as they race from the road onto the bridge's smoother surface. Something about a brush with death and the relief of her friend's embrace alights an overwhelming impulse to call home and talk to her father. She regrets it as soon as she hears him.

"So," he begins their conversation, this time with a devilish sparkle. "To what do I owe the pleasure of a call? Let me guess. You're worried your husband is cheating again."

Cass digests the tone, the battle she is facing. Calling him was a bad idea. Now it will take time to extricate herself from this situation.

"Yes, he is cheating again," Cass says. "But that's not why I called you."

"Did you find something? A matchbook? Suspicious receipt from a hotel bar?"

"As a matter of fact, yes, Dad."

"You always have a theory, Cass. I always thought you'd make a great detective."

"I have proof of a couples massage that did not involve me, hair in my shower. It's not a suspicion, Dad. It's physical evidence. There's nothing subjective about it." And then, because she can't resist, "And I am a good detective. I won the Columbia Award for Excellence in Investigative Journalism." At forty she can still be reduced by her father to an adolescent.

"So what if he's cheating?" her father barks. "Every man is entitled to a couple of girlfriends."

Cass struggles not to respond. It takes physical force to do this.

"Everybody cheats," he says. "It's not a reason to end your marriage."

Cass waits in silence for outrage to pass through her. It takes all her strength to resist telling him off in the most florid language. Luckily, she is too nauseated to find the words as quickly as usual.

"You want some advice?"

"No," she says.

"Stop being so nosy. If you weren't such a snoop, you'd be happily married."

Again, Cass struggles to squelch the bile rising from her stomach. *Do not engage*, she tells herself. *Ignore his provocation. Don't instigate. Don't take the bait*—as she tells her children. There is no sense debating a man who is immune to reason, a man with no respect for monogamy, and less for women. It is like trying to explain the concept of language to a table. Luckily, she is too distracted by his comment, and the logic issues within it, to begin her rebuttal. She cannot decide which is worse: that he blames her for uncovering Ryan's infidelity, or the fact that he thinks her best bet is to turn a blind eye to betrayal.

Revelation travels the same path as nausea in reverse, warmth descending from her throat to her stomach. "Oh, I get it," she says. "This is about money. You're worried that if I end up alone, I might become a burden."

"Worried?" he says. "That's a simple fact. Let's face it. You're not a college girl anymore. You don't make a lot of money. You're forty years old and you have three children. You do not have options."

Cass has always known her father to be a misogynist. He believes women have utilities, as opposed to merit. "We disagree on this subject," she says. This is the best she can manage. "I think we can agree on the simple fact that we have different values."

"Has that worked out so well for you?" His rage is palpable, a vibration.

She faces and foils a strong impulse, the urge to be loved, to be believed, to be cared for and nurtured. To be harbored by her father, to be told everything will be all right, that he will stop at nothing to bring justice to her attacker, that he will stand watch at her door with a rifle. A daughter's impulse for a father's love is a hard habit to break, like curing a dog of the urge to bark, or a bird to migrate in the winter. But she will not find this from Marty Rosen. She should know by now: he is not that kind of father. He is not that kind of person. He is not that human.

"You still haven't told me why you called," he says.

Cass musters the strength to speak, the most credible explanation. As a journalist, she knows the most direct approach is usually the best one. State the facts. Plain and simple. Who, what, when, where, how, why. Then, the counterargument.

"I just got back from the ER, Dad."

"Why is that, Cass?"

"Because Ryan tried to kill me."

"Don't be ridiculous," he says.

"I wish I were kidding."

Marty says nothing for a long time. When he does, the sound of his voice has changed from disbelief to derision. "Oh yeah? How did he try to kill you?"

Cass struggles to find words that will not estrange her father. She has lived through this presentation enough now to know that simply stating the facts does not yield the support of her audience, but rather makes her vulnerable to a different kind of suspicion. She thinks of something her father once said when describing his success in business. Deals are closed with facts, he said. At least until the signature. "He tried to poison me," she says.

"He tried to or he did it?"

"He did it," she says. "But I survived. He used enough to make me sick but not enough to kill me."

"How?" Marty says. He is listening now. "How did he do it?"

"He put it in my food and coffee. And possibly in the house. I'm not sure what it is yet and where he put it."

"What?" Marty scoffs. "Don't be absurd."

She can hear the cogs of his brain grinding through the analysis, working out the likelihood on a statistical basis of Cass's statement, other possible explanations. For a moment, the warmth of hope begins to creep into her body. She imagines a flicker in her father of something like empathy, horror. But she is wrong. She has mistaken outrage at Ryan for outrage at his daughter.

"That's preposterous," he says. "You sound like a crazy person."

"I'm sorry you feel that way, Dad."

"Don't ever say that again," he says. "Or they'll cart you off to a mental institution."

"It's true," she says, "that people could easily mistake this statement for a delusion. I learned that all too quickly. But in this case, they would be making a grave error, dismissing the pleas of a person who is in clear and present danger. Dismissing the eyewitness testimony of a victim of an attempted murder."

Marty listens now with a new sentiment altogether. Skepticism has turned to something else, confusion laced with anger. He has undergone the switch, the same conversion she witnessed in triage, in which a victim's cries for help alienate the listener, turning a source of help into a source of derision, converting a needed ally into a new source of opposition. "I've told you this before," he says. "And you never listen. You've always had an active imagination, Cass, but this time you've gone too far. Your husband is fed up with you. Your family is fed up. And if you don't stop this nonsense, you will have no one."

"He tried to kill me, Dad. You are having the wrong reaction. Your anger should be directed at him, not your own daughter. This is when the father says he's gonna guard our door with a shotgun."

"Don't be ridiculous," Marty says. "This man saved you from a miserable life. Without him, you would be a lonely, aging widow."

"I think you mean financially independent single mother."

"You know what I mean," he scoffs.

Cass shakes her head, crushed by her father's reaction. "My husband tried to kill me." Repetition is her only source of power, defiance.

"Well, I do not believe you."

"That's very disappointing," says Cass. She trails off. "It's shocking."

And then, a final insult. "I don't care if he tried to kill you," says her father. "Just don't say it."

That people are abandoned at the moment they most need protection is unfortunately all too common. As improbable as it seems, it appears to be the default setting of human nature. Still, when it happens, it is baffling to the person seeking assistance. Cass struggles now to understand her father's reaction. It is the opposite of her most basic instinct as a parent—to love, protect, and nurture. But now, as she listens to her father—her own father—and digests his reaction, she considers a possible explanation for his callous treatment, for what can only be described as his own delusion. Perhaps it is so painful for him to imagine the harm of his own daughter that he simply refuses. Instead, he prefers to think—can only think—she did something to cause this, which in turn allows him to blame her "active imagination," spare him the pain of imagining harm—and worse, his role in allowing such a thing to happen. She hangs up, gutted, convinced of one thing only: that she understands human nature less than she did an hour prior.

Cass is lying in the guest room of Nora's Cumberland mansion. Everything in this house is beige. It is like a giant hotel room. Three other people share this bed. Daughter. Son. Baby. In. Out. In. Out. Alice, Pete, and Sam look like a trio of kittens, their limbs and hands entwined in one spectacular knitted being. Cass draws her children close and pulls up the blankets. She feels hollowed, halved, carved out like a cantaloupe before chopping. She has lost her love and faith in love. She has lost her home and her faith in home. She has narrowly escaped death and detainment. That her three children lie in her grasp is why faith remains at all.

She tries now to steel herself, to draw on previous means of meditation, to make a list in her head of consolations and desolations. She listens to the sound of her breath, tries to find the virtues in her situation. It is not easy, but here goes nothing. One: she has survived an attempt on her life, brought her children to safety. Two: she has lost—and left—a man who subjected her to intolerable cruelty. That she misses him is only proof of the depth of his degradation. Three: she has averted a misunderstanding that nearly resulted in forced incarceration. Four: her children are in her arms, and they are breathing.

Surrounded by all that matters in the world and somewhat sedated, she pulls out her phone, that trusty lifeline—and goes back to work, continuing an investigation that has risen from petty and prurient affairs to attempted murder. She begins where every detective starts, amateur or licensed: that infinite source of information, clues, facts, and misunderstandings, the World Wide Web, specifically, Google, Mayo Clinic, WebMD, Poison Control, and the website for the Centers for Disease Control and Prevention. She types the only thing she knows: *poisons, undetectable,* and *heavy metal* for good measure.

A knock on the door. She looks up to find Nora standing in the doorway, holding a cup of tea and a stack of white towels. Dear God. Thank you for small mercies.

She rises to sit without stirring the kids. "What would I do without you?"

"Please don't thank me," Nora says. "I'm just glad I got your text in time. That could have been hairy."

"I got yours just in time. I was starting to lose it."

"Anyone would in that situation."

Cass adds a new item to her list of consolations. Five: she has dear friends, and they are dear to her. It is true, she is finding, that hard times reveal who your friends are. It is not true, she has learned, that blood is thicker than water. If the last twenty-four hours are any indication, family has nothing on the kindness of strangers.

"What happened in there?" Nora places the tea on a table and sits on the edge of the bed.

"It was scary," says Cass. "I was locked in that room. I didn't know if they were going to let me out of there."

"But you passed the test." Nora smiles.

"Apparently," Cass says.

"That's my girl," Nora says. "Making friends and taking names in psych wards across the country."

"I should have seen it coming," Cass says.

"How could you?" says Nora.

"He's been teeing this up."

"How could you know?"

"How could I not?" says Cass. "He did exactly what he said. The threat was a statement of his plan. He just kept his promise."

"Look, honey, Cass." Nora takes the particular tone women take when they're about to get angry, the sudden increase in volume, the rising pulse, the tenderness that precedes indignation. "It's natural now to doubt everything. Everything around you. But you've just been through hell, my dear. Nothing feels safe to you right now, but that doesn't mean you should heed all your instincts."

Cass straightens. "It doesn't mean I should dismiss them either."

A moment passes between the friends as they digest a difference of opinion. "It was a mistake to go," says Nora. "I had a feeling this might happen."

"You had a feeling *this* could happen?" says Cass.

"Not when I told you to go," she says. "But now, after spending time in that place. I learned a lot from the nurses and doctors in that waiting room."

"What did you learn?" Cass says.

"Just about trends of presentation."

"What do you mean?" Cass asks.

"Turns out there are two kinds of people who show up in emergency rooms with fears of being poisoned. Victims of domestic violence and paranoid schizophrenics."

Cass leans forward on the bed, to prevent a rise in volume. "What are you saying, Nora?"

"Just that you need to be careful now. You need to watch what you say and to whom. There's a world outside this room ready to judge this, ready to judge you. An avalanche that will smother you if you don't get out ahead of it. You saw that tonight."

"Yes, I did."

"Who knows what would have happened if you hadn't reached me, if I hadn't been able to come."

"This sounds like more like a reprimand than a warning."

"I'm just making sure you know what this is, Cass. This isn't like reporting a pickpocket or a burglary. You know what happens to girls who report assaults, even when they do have bruises. These women get taken down," she says. "They get victimized by the press, by the cops, by the lawyers, the courtrooms. It doesn't matter if it's a rape, abuse, assault, or drugging. 'She's crazy,' they say. 'She made it up.' 'She wants attention, money.' 'She's a slut who wore too short a skirt.' 'Why was she there so late at night?' 'She drank too much.' 'She asked for it.' 'She wanted it.' 'She deserved it.' I'm surprised they don't say more often that she did it herself, shoved a wine bottle up her crotch and injected the semen. Women get brutalized, Cass. For reporting brutal crimes against them. They're DOA before they can even make their statements. And that's not even thinking about what happens to their children."

"And what do you suggest I do to avoid this brutalization?"

"Hell if I know," Nora says. "It just seems to me that reporting a crime can make things worse, that the systems there to protect us actually fail us more often. Only you can decide what to do. I guess you just have to ask yourself what you gain by speaking out. Ask yourself if it's worth it."

"I am trying to protect myself, find safety for me and my children. I am not 'speaking out.' This is not a political statement."

"You know that's not what I mean," says Nora. "I'm just telling you the box is open now. You have to be very careful."

Cass begins to feel it again, the heavy sensation of dread descending over her being, followed by a new weight, an array of questions, possible outcomes, catastrophes, permutations. And she asks herself: This feeling that has taken up residence in her heart—is it paranoia or intuition?

"Right, of course," Cass says. In. She takes air into her lungs. She needs to dull her emotions. She needs her friends and their belief in her. She needs their love like she needs water. It is going to be a cold winter, and she needs to preserve her resources. "Thanks again for everything."

"Anytime," says Nora. "Anything." And then, just before closing the door, "Clean clothes are in the drawers if you need them."

But the light tone they try for now underscores a bleak reality. Cass turns off the lamp, but she is already submerged in darkness.

———

The symptoms begin later that night with a new vengeance. She immediately wishes she had stayed in the hospital, not only because they would believe her now—now there would be no confusion—not only because she needs proof and proof is now abundant but because the symptoms are so extreme as to bring her to her knees and render her helpless, to cause her to beg for mercy, to beg God to make himself known and forgive her for calling on him only when she needs protection. The nausea has its own unnerving cycle—first, an overwhelming urge to gag, a gag that is both a source of pain and a harbinger of vomit, followed by a violent eruption of the esophagus. *Peristalsis* is a fitting word, conjuring the halting, wormlike contractions of this serpentine organ. The only respite from the experience is to make yourself tiny, to face the coldness of the floor and try to remember a different sensation.

But the most disturbing symptom of all is not a physical ailment. It is an affliction of the head, a feeling in the brain that can only be described as a swelling. A mental illness of sorts. But unlike mental illness, it is caused by something outside the mind, as though by an infection, an intrusion from the outside that causes an internal inflammation, a burning up of the cerebellum. Imagine the most you've ever had to drink, the feeling where the room begins to spin, that awkward parting with the knowable world when the walls and the floors lose the distinction between their two separate axes. Now double the greatest dosage of alcohol you have ever ingested, and try to complete executive functions. Smile, speak, open your mouth. Find your keys, bag, wallet. These are the simple instructions Cass gives herself when she is awakened later by pain that spreads from her throat to her gut, from her gut to her brain to her toenails.

It must be three or four o'clock when she wakes with a shudder. Her chest feels cold, as though her lungs were dampened and then frozen. The muscles in her face are stiff, encrusted. She is unsure if this sensation is the result of fear and sadness, the poison coursing through her blood—or some indistinguishable mixture, like sugar and water, that has blended together into a new substance. She reaches over her sleeping children to collect her phone. The baby and Alice are to her right, still tangled like a skein of yarn—arms, feet, round tummies—and Pete is cuddled up on her left, clutching her forearm. A new surprise greets her on her phone, an email in the unmistakably officious tone of a lawyer. Ryan has retained a divorce lawyer and petitioned for custody of Sam. Before this information has traveled from her eyes to brain cells—the malice, the betrayal, the mental leap required to fathom nights without her baby, a baby who still fed from her breast not two months prior, the cost, the calls, the meetings, the heartache, the decisions required—Alice and Pete begin to stir, and Cass must rise to action and switch into a functional state and her morning version.

She must move this new reality from one part of her brain to another, and so she begins the tasks required to get her children dressed and brushed and ready before eight fifteen this morning. She scans the room for clothes that will support this transformation—pants, sweater, clean socks—and removes them from the drawers, grateful for Nora's suggestion. She moves on to the bathroom to begin the bathing process. She turns the faucet and submerges her face, hands, and fingers. The water starts the day again, resetting her senses. Would that it were so easy to turn time on and off like this, to start yesterday again such that it would not end in this bizarre new reality.

So little time has passed, and yet so much is different. What could she have done differently, she allows herself to wonder, to prevent them from ending up here, in this house, in this world that is almost familiar and yet strange and inhospitable? Right now, it takes all her energy to remain standing at the sink, hands submerged under the faucet, so powerful is the force of nausea swirling from her gut to her throat, so hazy are the thoughts in her head as to feel that they—the thoughts themselves—have been drenched and blurred like newsprint by water.

It will be a triumph if she can dress all three kids and get them out the door for school without forgetting the name of that school, and the directions to it, without crumpling to the floor and landing in a pool of her own vomit. Luckily, thanks to the grace of God and her children's resilience in a crisis, all four of them stand in Nora's front hall, looking vaguely presentable twenty minutes later.

An hour later, the kids are dropped off, safely delivered, content for the next six hours. Cass is in the car, headed home. Sam is beginning to doze in his car seat. With the baby sated and the big kids safely at school, Cass calls the only doctor she knows and asks for a morning appointment. She is beginning to feel a measure of hope as she pulls out of the school driveway. Her children are safe. The baby is calm. It is not raining. The dark green firs that line the road will survive this winter as they have every other before it. Flowers will bloom in the spring no matter how harsh the winter—tulips, magnolias, cherry blossoms. The bay is still on her right, absorbing the winter sunshine, and the ocean is just farther east beyond it. She has survived an attack on her life. She is strong and resilient. What she needs more than anything now is proof. Blood work, urine tests, numbers on a page. She needs unassailable evidence, objective fact, empirical data. Surely, this doctor will provide this.

At the Connor home, a young woman sits on the front step, hair brushed, eyes shiny. She looks neat and prim. She wears leggings and a checked oxford shirt, a gray cardigan sweater rolled up at the sleeves, lace-up Victorian-era boots that tie above the ankles. A tattoo peeks out from her sleeve, a subtle incongruous question: Nice or naughty?

But today, she is almost exclusively nice, even dowdy, hair pulled back into a bun like a surgeon prepped for focus. It is twenty minutes past eight right now, and she is patiently waiting. Marley has reported to work. She is here to watch the baby. She has brought a canvas bag filled with crayons and colored pencils, books with cheerful bindings. She is ready to put the last nanny to shame. She is a veritable Mary Poppins, if Mary Poppins were a mint julep.

Cass fights the gnawing sense that something has been forgotten. It will be hours before she remembers the girl sitting on her front step, a small mercy, like dollars found in a coat pocket, that will get her through the next few weeks, these endless hours. Help has arrived in the form of Marley Lyons, an ally committed to Cass alone, every day, rain or shine, for ten to twelve hours.

TWELVE

Cass is sitting in her gynecologist's office. This doctor's office is pink, not blue. Pink as a baby's bottom, pink as a bouquet of spring flowers. This is the only doctor Cass knows in the city of Portland. Were she still in Brooklyn, she would have had a list of options, a second and third alternate on speed dial, specialists for ears, noses, and throats at all the various hospitals. But she is still a virtual newcomer to this city and has not yet amassed the go-to Rolodex collected over years as a grown-up, and the confidence that comes with having such a list, however false, that you are safe from injury or accident. Conversely, Cass feels right now particularly prone to disaster, balancing the baby on her lap while talking to the doctor and trying to prevent Sam from grabbing the prescription pad off the doctor's desk or using the doctor's jar of pens as the foundation of a tower.

"Well, that's creepy," the doctor says. This is her response to Cass's now-familiar synopsis, what she has begun to think of as the short version.

This doctor has a bedside manner that is decidedly not treacly. She speaks with the businesslike tone of a lawyer, and Cass likes her for this.

"It was," says Cass. "It is." She lets out an unexpected burp and, with it, embarrassed laughter. Is it possible her body is expelling the toxic substance, that she is now the lucky beneficiary of the body's miraculous self-correction, that her body has begun the inelegant but efficient purge of its gastrointestinal system?

"The miraculous human body," says the doctor.

Cass looks up quickly. Did she say that out loud? Did the doctor hear what she was thinking? She pushes the thought from her head and continues through her list of questions. "They told me I should get these tests with a private doctor, so I'm wondering if you can run them. He said to start with household chemicals, heavy metals, and basic narcotics. He said to do blood work and urine."

The doctor nods and sits in silence for several seconds. Cass begins to wonder if she has not heard her. She wonders if she has said something wrong, something inadvertently offensive.

"Oh, hon, I don't have the tubes," says the doctor. "I wouldn't even know where to send them."

"Oh," says Cass. This is unexpected. "Can't you just draw my blood and send the tubes to the lab and ask them what tests to run then?"

"Unfortunately, I cannot." She smiles at Cass and looks at her oddly. It is the look of a person who knows she is doing something sketchy, if not something wrong per se, then certainly something high on the unethical spectrum.

Cass nods slowly. She is getting the same feeling she gets at the airport when they weigh her luggage, as she realizes she is the butt of a joke, that the weight of her bag will no doubt correlate to the amount she has to pay to keep her clothing. "Why not?" she says finally. She is starting to favor directness.

"It's a liability thing," says the doctor.

"I see," says Cass.

"I'm responsible for the follow-up care of any test I order for my patients. I don't know anything about this. And I can't say I want to. It's not every day that people come in here suspecting they've been poisoned by their husbands. Which is good, of course, for most people. That it's not an everyday occurrence. But bad for you because there are not many experts on this subject. At least not in the city of Portland."

"Got it," says Cass. Did you not take the Hippocratic oath, she wants to say, which compels you to help any patient in need, regardless of creed, class, or complaint, regardless of whether her affliction is in your field of expertise or a rarer version? Does that oath not compel you to pick up the phone to investigate the question or, God forbid, try Google, WebMD, or Wikipedia before giving up altogether?

"You need a specialist," says the doctor.

Again, Cass fights the feeling that the doctor has heard her thinking. "What kind of specialist?" she says.

"Someone who knows about poison."

"Right."

"A toxicologist."

"Got it."

"But this will not be easy to find. They tend to work in emergency rooms, not in private practice."

Cass sighs. It is a deep exhale that expels both her hope and worry.

"I'm sorry I can't be of more help."

"Thanks anyway," says Cass. She gathers her jacket and rises.

The doctor watches her leave with an exaggerated look of compassion. Then, as though offering a consolation prize, she adds, "Go ahead and leave a sample on your way out. I'll see if the lab can run the test you want."

Cass gratefully accepts. She stops in the bathroom, empties her bladder into a cup, and writes her name and the date in thick black letters.

"Cass Connor. 11/5."

She leaves it on the metal shelf with the other waiting samples. Like an uninvited guest, hoping to crash a party.

She stops at the reception desk on her way out of the office. A vase of lilies competes with a bulletin board papered with photos of recently delivered babies.

A nurse greets Cass with a saccharine smile. "No charge for today's visit."

Cass smiles, endeared and surprised by the doctor's compassion. She is halfway down the elevator before she understands it. The doctor did not charge today for "liability reasons." It was not an act of kindness, but rather an "act of insurance," so as to ensure there is no record of the visit.

Cass pulls into her driveway and opens the car door slowly. Sam has fallen asleep again, lulled by the cold wind in the trees, the ceaseless glitter of the bay just outside the window. She begins to lift him from the car, focused on the delicate removal of a sleeping child from a car seat, but her concentration is interrupted. A woman is sitting on her front step, a woman she cannot place or name after the recent chaos. Marley stands and smiles, smooths her shirt. She is prim and put-together. Her ponytail has loosened slightly, and her eyes have dulled—she has been sitting here for over an hour. Her face comes back to Cass before her name does, and Cass begins the awkward apology for forgetting her entirely.

"Oh, God," says Cass. "I'm so sorry. It's been a long weekend."

Marley shakes her head and nods. It is an oddly confusing gesture but somehow makes sense to Cass. She looks at Marley now and remembers why she chose her. There is something about this girl, a decisive presence. She begins to feel the cautious relief of a reunion with an old friend or younger sister, that what she could not face alone will now be possible to accomplish. Just when life seems untenable, she is sent a tool, a talisman.

"I'm really sorry," Cass says.

"Oh, goodness. No worries."

"How long have you been waiting here?"

"Not long. Couple of hours."

"I'm so sorry. I'm going through a bit of a crisis."

"No need to apologize to me. I'm here to help."

At first glance, Marley has the basic features of prettiness—big eyes, high cheekbones, nice proportions. But on closer inspection, there's a manliness, a rugged quality, like a person who was raised on a farm who has had to contend with intense weather, or a child who knew a rougher world, in which she'd had to fend for herself—and fight—if the occasion required. Her jawline is more angular than most women's, her arms more muscular. Her hair is thin but styled to look girlish with a curl of bangs and a barrette pinning them off her forehead. And the accent, Cass now remembers, the Southern drawl, though charming at first, has a slightly cloying quality, like a performance of a Southern belle. Cass can't help but wonder if it will wear on her, if all the "yes, ma'ams" and "oh, my goodnesses" will start to sound a bit precious.

Cass struggles with the lock, still carrying the sleeping baby. Marley opens her arms to help, but Cass pauses on reflex, reluctant to hand over her baby. An ongoing struggle with the key makes the decision for her. With an awkward laugh, she drops her bag and hands her sleeping child to Marley so as to better face this newest obstacle.

Cass's frustration and embarrassment grow in tandem. The first key jams, fails to work. Same with the second. She rummages through her bag, growing more frantic.

"I think my husband took my keys."

"That wasn't very nice of him."

"No," says Cass, "it wasn't."

"Did he forget his?" she asks.

"No," says Cass. "He didn't." She tries another key and jams her finger in the process.

Foiled, she looks to Marley, who still holds the sleeping baby. But unlike her, Marley is calm and composed, drawing on the endless reserves of the millennial generation, saving the day with her cell phone.

"Here we go," she says, flashing her phone like a badge. "Local locksmith. Speedy and professional."

Cass exhales and smiles. "Great," she says. "I needed to change the locks anyway."

Cass takes the baby back into her arms and sits down on the floor on her porch. Marley sits beside her. The perch is oddly grounding. A call is made to the locksmith of choice, and they begin that special female gift of making conversation.

"Rough day?" Marley asks.

"You have no idea," says Cass.

"Sorry to hear that."

"Thanks."

"Tomorrow can only be better."

Cass turns to look at the stranger sitting beside her, amazed by how quickly strangers can turn into friends in extreme situations. And amazed, in these same situations, by how friends can turn to strangers. "You have a great attitude," says Cass. "I should be more like you."

"Don't say that," Marley says. "You're an incredible woman."

"The kids are gonna love you."

"Someone's always got it worse," says Marley. "And someone's got it better."

"How'd you get so wise?" says Cass. "You're barely . . . what . . . twenty-five?" She recalls, of course, that Marley has a terminal illness.

"When you watch kids die, it's hard to feel self-pity," she says.

Cass turns to her quickly, taken aback by the morbidity of her statement. But surprise also makes her smile. This girl talks like a Hallmark card, albeit a blunt version, but she is nonetheless a font of inspiration.

Time passes slowly as they wait for the locksmith. This slowness, this new pace of time, more like its normal regulation, is a relief to Cass after its recent acceleration. She watches in a passive daze as the locksmith arrives. He turns from one woman to the other.

"Which of you lives here?"

"I do," says Cass. "With my three children. And my husband."

"May I have some proof that this is your house?"

Cass takes a sharp breath, unnerved by this reminder of the tenuousness of her presence. But again, she must prove her right to her belongings, her claim on things she previously took for granted. She riffles through her bag and produces her driver's license.

He still seems uncertain.

"That cat meowing right now," says Cass. "Her name is Ginger. She belongs to me also."

The locksmith smiles, chided. He commences jabbing, breaking the lock and installing a new one. The baby also sleeps through this. Only Marley seems alert as the locksmith produces two new sets. "Now, you have an extra set for the next emergency situation." He hands one set to Cass and one set to Marley.

Cass opens the door and walks upstairs with the sleeping baby. The house, in its raw unfinished state, now seems shocking, barren, ravaged. She suddenly cannot believe that he—and she—have been raising a family in this inhospitable environment. The facets of the house she days ago saw as potential, she now sees as hazards, terrifying possibilities waiting, sure to happen.

Wires dangle from the walls, inviting electrocution. Walls exposed with torn Sheetrock blow dust into the halls with no concern for the demands of respiration. The stairs removed so hastily and walls torn down with rapture—it all just seems a sanctioned exercise in self-destruction. How far gone was she that she failed to see this? What incentive did she have to buy into his vision? She sees this now with clarity, how deeply immersed she was in the Ryan delusion.

Walking through her empty house, she thinks of other instances of denial. The carrots and the sticks that cause people to uphold fictions. In matters of addiction, there are clear rewards and punishments—stop the drug and lose the fix, deny the problem and keep it. But what about those instances of collective denial, when one group puts up with another group's torture? What happens when this occurs across an entire culture, when a people look away while another is exiled, killed, exterminated? Is it any different in the privacy of a man and woman's bedroom?

What punishment do people face for voicing wrongdoing? Conversely, what incentive do they gain for its toleration? She thinks now of a story she read as a young journalist about a man who posed as a Rockefeller. For years, he maintained his fraud, collecting friends, disciples, and believers. They followed him around the world as he squatted in strangers' homes, displayed his "original" Rembrandts, actually framed posters, and fooled most everyone he met that he was someone special. What struck Cass most about those people who had followed, the ones who felt the most disgrace for buying his whole falsehood, was not that they were gullible, not that they were foolish, not that the fraud was so clever, not that they were threatened or feared their own self-preservation, but something more insidious, something more disturbing. These people had incentive.

Why maintain a friendship with this clearly made-up person, a person they later came to see as nothing more than a con man? What did they have to gain by claiming a friendship with this person? Joining him at his stolen homes, commenting with authority on his art collection. *What did you have to gain?* Cass asks herself as she wanders through the empty halls of her disemboweled home. *What did you trade for your peace of mind, in exchange for your safety? What was your kickback?*

Marley is tidying up when Cass returns to the kitchen. She has already figured out what is where, toured the upper and lower cabinets. She has cleaned the sink and begun the dishwasher's cycle. She has wiped down the counter. She is boiling water in the kettle. She has found and removed a glass from the pantry and filled it with water. Cass walks in just as she raises the glass and lunges to thrust the glass from her hands, nearly knocking her over.

"Don't drink from that."

"Oh. Okay." The poor girl looks startled.

"You can't use the glasses or dishes," Cass says. She tries to say this in a soft tone, but it sounds more like admonishment.

"I won't," says Marley. She slowly puts the glass back on the counter and begins to clean a puddle of spilled water. The task complete, she puts her hands down at her sides, then clasps them.

"Everything needs to be cleaned," Cass says. She is at a loss now. She does not want to scare the girl but needs to convey the severity of the situation, and meanwhile preserve her fragile credibility.

Marley stands politely like a soldier at attention, waiting for Cass to share more information.

"I don't want to freak you out," she begins, "but something bad went down here."

"Oh no," she says. "I'm sorry."

"Yeah, me too," says Cass. She pauses, unsure how to proceed.

"Try me," says Marley. "I don't shock easily."

"I'm going through a divorce. My ex became violent. He made some threats. He acted on some. And it seems he had access to poison." Cass watches Marley's eyes, as she does when her children open presents, more interested in their reaction than the contents.

Marley is strangely unfazed. Either she is unflappable, as she claims, or she has not understood Cass's statement. She looks from Cass to the glass, the water spilled on the counter. "Note to self," she says wryly. "Do the dishes."

Cass smiles. She has understood. She just isn't frightened.

"I may just buy new ones."

"Paper plates?" says Marley.

"Exactly," says Cass.

"Wow," says Marley. "That's scary."

"I told you it was creepy." A new series of thoughts floods Cass's head.

She must give this girl an out. She cannot get other people mixed up in Ryan's intentions. "I completely understand if you no longer want the position."

"No," she says. "It's not that. I'm just amazed at how many of us have been through this."

"Been through what?" says Cass.

"Women," she says vaguely. "Violence."

Understanding comes now with its usual sensation. Concern turns to compassion, alienation to affection. "You too?"

"Here's where I flash my badge."

Cass smiles. She thinks Marley is speaking figuratively, but as she smiles, Marley opens her mouth. She nods to Cass to come toward her, like an alligator inviting a frog, and reveals a tooth near the back of her mouth that is fully shattered.

"Oh, my God," says Cass. "When did that happen?"

"He clocked me in the jaw," she says. "Uppercut and under." She points at the faint bluish bruise on her collarbone. "And the worst part is he stayed in our house while his friends took me to the hospital."

"I'm so sorry, Marley."

"Abusive relationships follow a standard pattern. First, it's all the charm. You're the prettiest girl in the world and he's the perfect romantic. Then the degradation starts. You didn't make the house look right. He doesn't like your clothes. He's jealous of your friends, your job. Then the isolation. It's routine and systematic. Friends, family, lifeline gone in a matter of minutes. And then the escalation—minor quarrels are now rages. Did you know that 90 percent of verbal abuse eventually turns violent? Most women are attacked at the end, after they leave the relationship."

"You seem to be an expert," says Cass.

"I learned the fun way," says Marley. "Experience is the mother of education. Unfortunately, in this case, expertise does not breed better judgment. It took me a while to get out, as it tends to in these situations."

Cass nods. No disagreement. It is as though this girl has torn a page from her own handbook.

"I've thought about getting it fixed," she says. She slips her tongue to the back of her mouth, points at the tooth again. "But I decided against it."

"I know why," Cass says. She clutches her chest on instinct. "I understand completely." She lifts her necklace from her chest to flash her own talisman, her own prized symbol. A ring around a heart. Is it trapped or protected?

The two women stand in silence, united by their secret.

"It's two fifteen. We'd better go. I'll show you the route to school. I don't teach on Mondays. Tuesday and Thursday, I teach in the evenings. Wednesdays and Fridays are mornings. On days when I teach late, you'll do the school pickup." She turns and heads back up the stairs to collect the sleeping baby. She clocks a note of gratitude for the timely arrival of Marley.

Cass, Marley, and Sam walk through River Park in comfortable silence. The sky is bright and atypically blue. The air is cold and caustic. Cass feels more functional than she did in the morning, enough to notice details she didn't notice earlier, enough to focus on something other than the nausea.

"I like your tattoo," she tells Marley. Sam is dancing in the trees, chasing his shadow. He pulls the shadow off the ground and traps it in his pocket. It is the most uplifting thing Cass has seen in ages. It is almost worth the last few weeks just to see him do this, to see her child find this proof of his place, to see her child discover the elusive nature of freedom.

"Thanks. I love to draw," she says.

"Wow. You designed that?"

"This was one of my first drawings. I made it for a girl who passed away. And now she's always with me."

"When did you get leukemia? If you don't mind my asking." She feels clumsy asking like this, but she prizes directness. Whether it's the reporter in her, or the amateur detective, she is unfailingly direct, no artifice or manipulation. Better to tackle things as they are than patronize her subject. That would be dishonest.

"I was twelve. My sister was nine. She got skin cancer. I got blood cancer."

"Dear God. I didn't realize."

"It was 2004 in rural West Virginia. Cancer wasn't understood then the way it is now. Wasn't yet treated with these complicated cocktails. My parents ended up with two kids with cancer and only one income between them."

"So what did they do?"

"They couldn't do much. They certainly couldn't pay for our treatment. So they applied for a grant and made noise until the NIH noticed."

"What do they think caused it?" Cass says. "For both of you to get it?"

"Something in the water."

"Really?" She can't tell if Marley is being facetious.

"We grew up poor. Where poor people live, the EPA doesn't notice until you make it their problem."

Cass stares at Marley, moved by her story. "But how? Did they ever figure it out? It couldn't just be coincidence."

"Mining was the main economy where I grew up. When the earth is assaulted like that, metals in the earth's crust seep into the water. It's even worse with fracking. It was everywhere. In the wood. In the food. In the water. Nobody knew the extent."

"My God. That's horrifying," says Cass. The coincidence is noted. And perhaps because of it, she has more interest, more compassion. "How could a whole generation miss this?"

"The seventies were the Dark Ages for environmental policy. And, as it turns out, a renaissance for the manufacture of toxic building materials. Think of all the ranch houses that cropped up for the boomers, all of them made of compressed wood, eat-in kitchens with particleboard cabinets, decks for outside-inside living treated with toxic chemicals. All the crappy wood they used. Decks, cabinets, floorboards. When your house is built with it, it's in the air you're breathing. It seeps into the ground. If you use a well, then it's in the water you're drinking."

"The ultimate irony," Cass says. "Your home is actually your hell. Your haven is your coffin."

"So my parents made it their problem. Got us into a trial program for new medications. And two kids whose parents made about forty grand between them suddenly had the best medical care in the country. Paid for by good taxpaying citizens, people like you and your husband. Excuse me. Ex-husband."

Cass startles at Marley's words, the sudden aggression, but she quickly forgives the slight. She is entitled to her indignation. She shakes her head, moved by the tale, shamed by the implication. "It's an amazing story," she says.

"Just the life I'm living."

"And you and your sister recovered?"

"As far as I can tell, we're still standing."

"What's the cure?"

"There is no cure. You live with it forever. It's always in your body, but you can slowly tamp it back. With drugs that kill everything in sight—the good cells and the bad cells. Taking them is living hell—nausea, hair loss, brain fog, vomit. It's a full-frontal assault. But if they work, they work real good. There's a reason the best-selling cancer drug is called Cytoxan."

"Chemo sounds just awful."

"It was worse when I was a kid. Now I barely notice. And the drugs have gotten better. But we made do in the hospital. You make friends. You draw. Learn to play the guitar. Get interested in medicine. You learn that some-one's always got it worse. And someone's always got it better."

"God. You are incredible."

"I try not to say that."

"I don't mean to be patronizing."

"No. G-O-D. You say it a lot."

"Oh," says Cass. "I'm sorry."

"I try not to say the Lord's name in vain."

"Oh, shit. I mean—I'll try not to."

"No problem, ma'am."

"Oh, don't call me *ma'am*."

"Sorry, I can't help that one. Remember, I grew up in the South. Good manners are just habit. Especially when speaking to an older woman."

Cass stares at Marley now, at once offended and apologetic. Something odd has happened here, an unspoken reversal. But before she can give it further thought, she faces a new obligation. Sam barrels into her arms, wav-ing his latest capture. His shadow is trapped in his pocket, fluttering like a wounded bird, and he wants his mother to see him grasp something so rare and elusive. Moved, she hoists her son to her arms and smothers him with kisses. She feels pride and pity both, pride in the victory he claims and pity for his inevitable disappointment.

THIRTEEN

A day and night have passed, and Cass is still standing. She has survived an attack on her life and the death of her marriage. She is now in a world without the man she'd planned would be her friend for life, her love, her partner. It is as though she has taken a flight and landed in the wrong country. But the rules of travel have changed. She has been banished from her home, condemned to indefinite exile, with no means of return, no money, no ticket, no passport. She has one cause for gratitude, and it is the thing for which she is most grateful. The only familiar facet of life is the most important. Her three children are in her grasp. They are shaken, confused from the weekend's upheaval, but they are sturdy and resilient. And thankfully, Cass has Marley now, the mercy of her arrival. She will be held up by a circle of women, women who have also suffered. They will get through this together.

Cass and Marley meet Alice and Pete at the school doors. The children greet Marley cautiously but only for a moment. Within minutes, they are deep in conversation, quizzing her about her tattoos, demanding that she teach them guitar, mimicking her accent. They race her back to the car, all of them yelling, "Shotgun!" Cass stops at the store on the way home, claiming she needs to restock milk. But the milk is just a prop. Instead, she buys supplies: vinegar, bleach, dish detergent, a stack of paper plates, and plastic utensils. And rubber gloves. Knowing little about what and where the toxin is, she cannot be too careful. She notes the bizarreness of this new world she has been thrust into, her crash course in household remediation: how to keep the family safe in a house that may be doused with unknown toxins.

Marley helps them get back home, tending to the children while Cass makes dinner. She prepares a simple supper: mac 'n' cheese from a box, broccoli, chicken nuggets. Today, this is the best that she can manage. The afternoon reveals a new flower in the bouquet of her symptoms. She sits on the toilet in her bathroom, huddled over her knees, waiting for the nausea to begin its cyclical recession. She reaches down and wipes to find the toilet paper is dyed a bright shade of red, the color of spring tulips—or blood from internal organs. Concern turns to panic when a wipe of her ass produces the same color. Bright red blood pools from her ass and vagina. Unnerved, she walks back downstairs to ask Marley if she can stay later. She needs to see a doctor.

"Is there any way you can stay late?" says Cass. "I left something important at work and need to run back and get it." No need to involve her in any more of the gory details.

"Shoot," says Marley. "I'm so sorry. Any other night, I would, but I promised my friend I'd walk her dog, and she'll kill me if the dog has an accident."

"Oh, of course. No worries," says Cass. It is too late now to say her real reason. Bracing herself, she signals the kids to head upstairs for bath time. She will have to go in the morning.

Marley laces up her boots and gathers her belongings. Cass thanks her once again and closes the door behind her.

In the bathroom, Cass fashions a homemade diaper using toilet paper, maxi pads, and several pair of underwear. She steadies herself as she runs the bath, shepherding the kids through their nighttime ritual. She observes them closely as they bathe, checks for any anomaly. They seem okay, if slightly riled by the sudden disappearance of their stepdad. Pete masks any concern with a convincing performance of indifference.

Cass ushers the kids into her bed, piling everyone in for a story and snuggle. She will stand on ceremony tonight, rest on the power of ritual. She opens the book and begins to read in the lightest tone she can manage, "Miss Puddleduck considered her nest to be the tidiest of her neighbors." She barely finishes the sentence before Alice interrupts her.

"Mom, is everything okay?" says Alice.

"All is well," says Cass. She nods in a definitive way, designed to feel conclusive.

"What about the trip?" says Pete. "You promised, Mom. You said we were going."

"Pete, it's been a challenging week. I promise to do my best. I'll do some more research this weekend." She turns back to the book, continues with the first paragraph. "Miss Puddleduck often said—"

A door swings open downstairs. The rush of night and drizzle.

"Daddy!" says Sam.

They all turn toward the door.

But it is only the cat downstairs, moving from the stairs to the kitchen.

By half past eight, the house is quiet. Again, the sound of life on hold. In. Out. In. Out. The children are safe and sleeping. Cass collapses on the bed, curling herself into a fist, hopeful that stillness of the body will result in the stillness of her thoughts. Where is her husband right now? Is he nearby, in a friend's guest room, watching her downstairs lights go off? Or is he somewhere distant now? A new head resting on his chest? Or his, in a tangle of blackish hair, splitting open another woman?

There is one thing Cass needs right now, in addition to clarity about the crime, evidence, and medical attention: a new pair of jeans. Hell if she knows where and what is the toxin, but she'll be damned before she becomes the next on the list to innocently don a dress only to croak from cardiac arrest minutes later, dying of "unknown causes." Would that simple

tasks like this were as easy as they had been a week prior. Driving to a bou-
tique near school feels nearly insurmountable. Parking alone mystifies her.
Her right and left sides seem to have reversed, or the impulse that connects
her brain to physical actions.

"Can I help you?" a graying lady asks as a jingling bell signals Cass's
entry. "All the jeans are half price today."

"Thanks," says Cass. She walks to a neatly organized rack with an array
of hanging apparel. As she palms through the various shades, she notes
one of her hands is shaking. The jeans look intensely blue to her, and yet
she cannot seem to distinguish the numbers for any of the sizes. She senses
the stare of the saleslady, and realizes she is wondering if she can afford to
shop here. Finally she locates a pair that resemble the approximate size of
an old pair. She removes several hangers at once and walks directly to the
desk to pay for them.

Over the course of the week, Cass's symptoms worsen: nausea, twitching in the hands, bleeding from the ass and vagina, a rash that spreads
from her neck down her back, burning in her throat when she drinks, and
most bizarre of all, sporadic inelegant belching. At night, in the bath, hair
falls out in clumps. But worse than the physical manifestations, worse than
these creepy and painful symptoms, she feels as though she has been
drugged by a powerful substance that alternates between the effects of a
black-market amphetamine and a hospital-grade sedative. The dizziness is
pervasive. Simple movements make her seasick. The nausea is a constant.
She is increasingly baffled by basic executive functions. A Google search
of her symptoms alone reaps several accounts of cancer patients describing
a round of chemo.

It's Wednesday, and Cass sits in the passenger seat of Nora's family
wagon. The Portland sky is a wall of gray, threatening rain or sunshine like
a parent promising reward or punishment depending on the child's behavior at the dinner table. Nora, helpful as ever, has convinced her doctor to
see her friend despite his reluctance. She has spent the last few days doing
her own research, scouring the internet, calling doctors. She dials a number
on speaker with Cass in the car. Yet another doctor joins the chorus.

"The Clearview emergency room has the best toxicology department in
the state."

Cass shakes her head. No way. Not going.

"Do you know any private doctors?" says Nora. "She says she's not going back to an ER."

"Why not?" says the doctor.

"Bad experience," says Nora.

"I see," says the doctor. And in these words, Cass feels a shift in his perspective. "Your friend just walked into a minefield," he says. He doesn't know he is on speaker.

"Why?" says Nora.

"Two types of people show up in emergency rooms complaining of being poisoned."

"Who?"

"Very unlucky people and paranoid schizophrenics."

Cass shrinks into the seat, deflated by his comment, and the now-familiar dismissal that is sure to follow. Nora senses all these things and prepares a succinct rebuttal. "Right, but what's that phrase?" she says. "Just because you're paranoid doesn't mean you're not being followed."

"Those with paranoid thought disorders usually have other coinciding beliefs."

"Like what?" asks Nora.

"Grandiosity. Ongoing suspicions of pursuit. Auditory hallucinations."

"Well, that's good news," Nora says. "She doesn't think she's the pope. Do you, Cass?"

Cass musters a smile. "Nope. Not the pope," she says. "Beleaguered saint, maybe. I've known Joan of Arc? St. Catherine?"

"I've known this girl awhile," Nora adds. "She can be a raving bitch, but she's not a raving lunatic."

Cass turns to her friend, her eyes wet, grateful. In the span of three days, Nora has become an expert on the subject.

"I'm sure that's true," the doctor says. The phone scratches through a hazy part of reception. "I'm just telling you what you're up against. And what she may encounter."

A pause.

"Let me put it this way," he adds. "The first question on the psych eval is 'Who are the enemies against you?' Followed by 'Are you being poisoned?'"

Cass makes a mental note: look out for leading questions.

Nora thanks the doctor for his time, and the call is ended. A moment passes in silence, bay passing, sun shining. When Nora turns to Cass, her tone is different.

"I think we should go to Clearview," she says. "He says they have the best toxicology department in the state of Maine."

"I need to find a toxicologist with a private practice." Cass looks at her friend with sincere adoration. Hardship amplifies emotion. Sadness deepens one's reserves, the depths of compassion. Nora has a friendly profile, snug features, and businesslike freckles. She drives as she does most things, with an air of authority that is soothing to all around her.

"No," says Nora. She takes a sharp breath, the breath of someone who expects a reaction. "I spent all morning looking. They only work in emergency rooms. Turns out there is no such thing as a toxicologist with a private practice."

"Sorry. No. I can't," says Cass. This is her new reflex. Trauma turns even lesser scares into full-blown emergencies.

"Then you won't find an expert," Nora says.

"I'm sorry. I can't risk it. Not after Sunday."

"Suit yourself, Cass, but I've put a lot of time into this, and I can tell you now, you're not going to find a better option."

Cass considers Nora's advice, the shrill of rising tension. As much as she hates to let down her friend, she simply cannot risk another accidental incarceration. The terror was too great. The dangers too uncertain. The possibility for some impermeable shift, being driven to the actual brink by the supposition that she might already be there. The sound of the locking door too fresh, metal turning on metal. The narcotic seep of terror, like water freezing in a damp root. Her panic driving her to yell or scratch in defiance, only to confirm their diagnosis, invite their binds, their own narcotics. No, this was not a risk she could take; neither she nor her children could afford the worst-case scenario. Better to stanch the flow of blood with homemade diapers and count on her body's inherent strength, its innate impulse for cleansing, excretion.

Cass is sitting with yet another doctor. Nora has outdone herself and found a new expert. This is not a toxicologist per se but an oncologist; her family friend told her he is likely to know about toxic substances due to his work with chemo and radiation. His office is decorated with inscrutable abstract art, an explosion of jewel tones. A prim Filipino nurse leads them through the office warren. An older male doctor sits at a desk, waiting for Cass to be seated.

"I have good news for you," he says. "Your blood work is basically normal."

Cass's face falls. She tries to smile but knows her feigned relief only betrays her disappointment. "What do you mean by basically?" Cass says.

"Well." He shrugs. "Your CBC is essentially the CBC of a healthy person. A CBC is a complete blood count."

"I know what it is," says Cass.

Nora, sensing her friend's anger, puts her hand on Cass's shoulder. "She's very well-informed."

"Right, good. Your CBC is normal but for a few minor irregularities that could be nothing at all, and basically fall into the standard deviation."

"What irregularities?" says Cass.

"Your monocytes are a little off."

"What are monocytes?" she asks. "And how off are they?"

"Just a bit," he said. "Your potassium is below the norm. And there's a slight abnormality in the hemoglobin, but it's likely nothing. Nothing more than standard deviation."

"Oh," says Cass.

"You sound disappointed."

"No," says Cass. She is becoming incensed, but she tempers her reaction for the sake of Nora. Her friend has devoted the last week to her care. "It's not that. It's just that I was looking for some sort of . . ."

"Evidence?"

"No," says Cass. "A path forward. Some sort of clear direction. What are monocytes?" she asks again.

He exhales. "Monocytes are a type, or rather a part of the white blood cell."

"What could cause them to be low?" Cass presses this point despite his clear annoyance. She is regaining her inner strength, her reporter's instinct.

"Any number of things," he says. "A compromise to one's immune system, leukemia, virus, toxins. But to be honest, even I barely understand them."

"So it can be associated with toxins," she says, "the ingestion of a toxic substance. Possibly a substance that is hard to detect, otherwise impossible to trace in the system."

The doctor pauses for a moment, looks directly at Cass, as though he is considering her statement, but it quickly becomes clear he has arrived at another thesis. "You realize that most of the symptoms you report can be caused by stress and anxiety."

Cass draws a sharp breath. "I'm not hysterical, Doctor," she says. "Frankly, I find the reflex to ascribe a woman's symptoms to stress—to psychosomatic symptoms or the imagination—to be, at best, a medical error and, at worst, a sexist compulsion. Only a woman could state her account of a crime and have it called a delusion."

"Then it seems you have a good understanding of the overlap of the mind and body."

"I get that you think I'm imagining it." She shakes her head and sighs, but it is not despair she feels. It is terror. It's the panic of being in a small room and watching the walls close in around her.

"I don't think you're imagining it," says the doctor. "I just don't know what caused it."

Cass opens her mouth to speak but something wisely stops her. She has realized one facet of her situation is its tragic irony—the more she insists what she knows to be true, the more she is discounted. Given that the credulity of others now stands between her and her safety, it is necessary to censor herself, to silence both her facts and her indignation. Both have the power to foil the very thing she so desperately needs: assistance.

"I'm sorry I can't be more helpful," he says.

"No worries. Hopefully, I'll stop bleeding out of my asshole."

The doctor gasps in quiet indignation. "If it persists, please make an appointment, and we will assess the merits of doing a colonoscopy." He hands her a copy of her labs, a small pamphlet of papers. Cass leafs through her CBC, a seven-screen, the test for the top seven drugs and narcotics, and her heavy metals panel. Her eyes stop on two rows with the letter *H*. "The arsenic is high," she says.

"Not really," says the doctor.

"It says the normal range is zero to fifteen. Mine is nineteen."

"Hmm," he says. "Do you eat a lot of fish? Such excellent seafood in this region."

Cass ignores the question. "You don't find that odd?"

He shrugs. "It's a naturally occurring element in the dirt and on the seafloor. There are trace amounts in lots of things. Fish. Rice. Vegetables. Apples. Almonds. Red wine."

Cass nods, unconvinced. In the last week, she has barely consumed more than tea and toast.

"Your mercury is on the high side too. That would indicate something in your diet."

"But I don't eat any of those things in excess," she says.

"Good," he says. He forms a patronizing smile. "Then you should be all set."

Cass gathers her belongings as Nora thanks the doctor.

But the doctor has one more pearl of wisdom. "If we spend our lives avoiding every possible hazard, we might all die of starvation."

Cass idly considers which would be worse: starving to death or being poisoned. She leaves the doctor's office in a state of agitation. She and Nora sit in silence all the way home from the doctor, and Cass wishes she could return to lighter concerns, like what to make for dinner. Nora focuses on the powder blue sky that has graced Portland. Cass tries to still her nausea by focusing on the air rushing through the window.

Nora pulls over in Cass's driveway. Cass turns to her friend.

"Where would I be without you?" she says.

"Locked up in a padded room somewhere?"

Cass smiles, rolls her eyes. Thank God for Nora and gallows humor.

As the car pulls out, she looks down to find a missed call on her phone from a blocked number. No number, no message other than a short text.

"The item you ordered is ready."

They say it takes weeks for a habit to form. Six weeks to kick a drug. Half the length of a relationship to forget a lover. That grief follows phases like the moon, from denial, to anger, to sadness, to acceptance. Whether anyone ever accepts a loss—that is a different question. All these clocks and calendars are set by culture, consensus, comparison. No such luck for Cass. She is deeply confused by the basics right now, by the geography of her home, by the route from her home to the children's school, by right and left, by facts and falsehood, by schedules and logistics. The darkness brings all these questions to the surface.

The car arrives, and Cass moves from her perch at the window. She leaves the room with purpose, descending the stairs without a sound, putting on an old sweater of Ryan's, slipping on the large black boots that sit underneath the red coat hook. In this odd outfit—pajamas, boots, and a man's sweater—she looks something like a hunter on an expedition. She pauses in the hall before she leaves to double-check the children, and then she crosses the path from the house to the curb and joins the man in the running car, slipping noiselessly into the passenger seat beside him.

He hands her a shiny new phone.

"This should work."

"Thanks," she says.

"Right now, just texts and emails."

"No way to see calls?"

"Not right now. I would need some more time with it. Do you have his iTunes password?"

"No, but my daughter might. She's always buying movies."

"Can you get it now?"

"She's asleep right now."

"Oh, I see. I'm sorry." He seems embarrassed by the query. "Maybe ask her in the morning."

She thanks him and opens the car door, hurries back inside with the new phone in her possession.

Once inside, she places the phone on the empty space on her bed. She watches it as she falls asleep, waiting for the first text. It is almost like being with Ryan—and therefore, equally comforting and sad.

The first text rolls across the screen. It is shocking—magical, even—like watching a butterfly burst from a cocoon. But the content brings her down. Quotidian life, once again.

"Mr. Connor, your dry cleaning will be ready for pickup at 4:00 P.M. at the Cherry Street location."

She scans the room for a spot that will escape the curiosity of her children. Then she slides the phone underneath the bed, in between the mattress and the box spring. As she falls asleep, she thinks about the perks and price of prophecy. And for the first time in days, she sleeps through the night soundly.

FOURTEEN

Cass types two words: *family* and *law*. She assembles a list quickly, using the simplest criteria: the one with the most pleasant-sounding name (Matthews and Jeffreys are good), the one with the highest number of stars, and the ones who look the most affordable. By ten in the morning, she has contacted four adequate options, two of them named Becker. By eleven, she has spoken to two of these people. By noon, she sits in the modest office of a young man who graduated from law school after Sam was born. His office is a space he shares with an immigration agency. As a result, it is sometimes hard to hear him above sporadic shouts in Cantonese and Mandarin. She focuses on the name on his degree. Seems convincing enough: Matthew Becker.

Marley busies the baby in the waiting room while Cass and Matthew speak in private.

"How can I help you?" Matthew asks. His skin reminds her of the kids' Play-Doh. He wears winter snow boots with gray pinstriped pants. His accent is thick and hard to place—Massachusetts? Jersey? His office is unadorned—no photos of loved ones or children. Stacked with messy piles of paper and a large antiquated computer. He is not the lawyer she would have imagined arguing her case in a courtroom. But until today, she did not expect to be standing in a courtroom with an adversary who was, a week ago, her husband. He is not the lawyer she would have chosen for herself under normal circumstances, but nothing is normal now.

Cass summons the energy to begin, tries for the short, sweet version. Matthew puts his pen to his notepad.

"My husband is trying to get custody of our child."

"Are you amenable to this?" he asks.

"No."

"Why not?"

"Because he has lost his way, and he's prone to violence."

"Why do you feel this way?" asks the lawyer.

"Because he tried to kill me."

The statement stops the lawyer, but to Cass's surprise, he does not give her the now familiar look. "I'm sorry to ask you to do this, but I need you to start from the beginning."

Cass summons the strength to talk. It is like scraping a bloody wound with a pick, but somehow, every time she digs, the skin underneath grows more numb. When she has finished, they sit through a long pause. The lawyer looks unnerved.

"You need to file an order of protection. And petition for sole custody."

"I'm not sure I'm ready for that," she says. "He needs a shrink most of all. Psychiatric intervention."

"With all due respect, you have to do what's best for you and your children. Not what's best for him."

Cass nods, then shakes her head.

"It's going to be painful and confusing. There's nothing I can do about that, but I can help you through the legal system. That is something I can do. We need to move quickly. We need to file a petition for custody. We need an order of protection. And we need to get the food tested."

Cass nods. It is a relief to be with someone who recognizes the severity of the crime and wants to see it proven. Her self-led investigation, while compelled, at first, by emotional reasons—confirmation, vindication, jealousy, even—has become necessary for practical reasons—for safety and survival. Proof precedes charges; charges yield protection. But she cannot do this on her own. She needs corroborating witnesses, data, photographic evidence. Proof of method, motive, weapon. Proof of the source, proof of purchase. In other words, the resources and manpower of a criminal investigation.

"I agree. That's why I saved it."

"Where is it now?"

"It's still in the fridge."

"We have to be very careful with it. There's a whole process. And they'll try to get it thrown out regardless."

"Sorry. I don't follow."

"Chain of custody," he says. "The rules of evidence in the courtroom. How evidence is deemed untainted and admissible in a trial."

Cass nods. "I thought I understood these things, but I'm learning how much I didn't."

"Is there anything else you need to tell me?" he says.

Cass pauses, weighing the wisdom of this disclosure.

"You understand that you have privilege," he says. "Anything you tell me in this room is strictly confidential."

"In my efforts to prove his crime," she says, "I may have done something illegal."

He nods. "Go ahead. Tell me."

"My friend knew this guy."

"A guy," he says.

"He's something of a computer specialist."

The lawyer understands right away. "Hacking is a felony."

"Does it matter if I didn't know that?"

"No," he says. "Knowledge of the law has little bearing on charges against those who break it."

"Got it," says Cass. She looks at her wrists, imagines them in handcuffs.

"Did you learn anything from the specialist?" He allows this one question.

"I'll let you know next week."

This does not elicit the smile Cass hoped it might garner.

"Tell no one else about this man, what he is doing."

"Should I get rid of it?" Cass says.

The lawyer pauses. "My legal advice is yes. Dispose of it. Immediately." Another pause. "Off the record . . . depends on what we can learn from it."

The baby's voice precedes a knock on the door from Marley. They have run out of paper or energy or both. Matthew's attention veers toward her, his eyes traveling from her face to her hips, from her hips back up her torso. He needs a few more minutes with Cass, so he excuses himself for a moment, leads Marley to the stash of office supplies, and sets them up in an empty conference room with paper, pens, and some cardboard boxes of copy paper, which Sam gleefully topples.

"I'm glad you have support right now," he says as he returns to Cass in his office.

"That girl is superhuman," she says. "She looks very young, but would you believe she's actually a licensed nurse practitioner?"

"A nurse practitioner? Really?"

"That's what she told me."

"She's licensed to practice?"

"I believe so."

"How old is she?"

"Twenty-four, twenty-five?"

"That's fast for medical training."

"Must have started her first year in college."

"They can write prescriptions also."

Cass nods. "That could come in handy."

Matthew stares at Cass, fixated on something. "Why is she working in child care?" he asks.

"She's been through some hard times," Cass whispers. "She's been told she can't have children."

"I see," he says. "Sorry to hear that." But he is stuck on something. "How much do you pay her?"

"About $500 a week."

"Not bad, but there are better ways for a licensed nurse to make money."

Cass looks directly at Matthew, tiring of the questions. "I'd be happy to introduce you," she says.

"Oh no, it's not that," he says. "Just sort of an odd career path."

Cass drives quickly from downtown to school pickup. Winter has settled on Portland. The light has bleached the red hues of fall. The clouds are low and chiseled. Silver tinsel and twinkle lights have begun their three-month occupation of storefronts and streetlights. Sam is fast asleep by the time they cross Tukey's Bridge and enter leafy Cumberland. Cass parks at home and carries the baby in to his crib, successfully depositing him without a flinch. She whispers a quick goodbye to Marley along with a handful of instructions and then hurries to school to pick up the older children.

A man stands on the sidewalk outside her house, directly in her path. She struggles to connect a name to the face, either because her brain is a blur or because he has not made enough of an impression to form a memory. Suddenly, memory and meaning intersect. It is her neighbor, Aaron, the self-proclaimed insomniac, the little boy's father, the weird dad at the playground. He always seems to be coming when she's going—or going when she's coming. This would bother or alarm her were she not in such a rush at the moment.

His house is the tall, graying Victorian with the peeling white shutters. Until moving to Cumberland, she thought of shrubbery and potted plants as arcane suburban status symbols. But now, as she thinks of this man's house, she wishes he would tend to it as a courtesy to the neighborhood.

"Hey, how are you doing?" he says.

She has come to hate the word *hey* when used in this context. "I'm good," she lies. "How've you been?"

"Great." He seems to have missed her deception. "We should get that playdate on the books."

His thick black eyebrows and big dark eyes exaggerate his expressions.

"Definitely," Cass says. "I'm just in a bit of a rush now." She fishes her car keys out of her bag, signaling her hurry.

"No worries. I'll come and get you," he says.

She looks up quickly, startled by his word choice.

"I'm more interesting than I look," says Aaron.

"I'm sure you are," says Cass.

"I did some cool shit in my misguided youth."

Cass nods. All she wants right now is for this man to keep walking.

"I heard about you and your husband," he says. He seems to say this as a last resort, as though he knows this will force her to pause. "I just wanted to say I'm sorry."

"Thanks. I really have to go."

"Just let me know how I can help," he says. "Anything at all. I could mow your lawn, cook the kids' dinner. Just know that your neighbors are here for you." His eyes are full of emotion.

Cass sees this, and it affects her. And perhaps because she wants to believe, needs to believe that neighbors can be counted as friends right now, she chides herself for dismissing him and promises to schedule the playdate sooner rather than later.

She is only five minutes late to school pickup. The sight of her children restores her, erasing all other thoughts from her head—their enormous eyes, their clean, healthy skin, their earnest demands. As usual, they both want to go in different directions.

"Can we go to the park?" asks Pete.

"Can we please get ice cream?" says Alice. "I have a massive quiz tomorrow. I need energy to study."

And despite the chaos, the impossibility of fulfilling everyone's immediate desire, Cass is comforted. Her love and attention is all they need; their health and happiness is all she needs for survival. They are her air and water.

Cass pulls up the sheets, their softness stiffened by the cold. She removes the cloned phone from her pocket, scrolls through Ryan's correspondence. She feels no guilt for this act, only relief. This will have to suffice as a trade for their old ritual, in which they exchanged accounts of the day's events, hand grazing arms, or toes touching toes, before falling asleep side by side in the same bed together.

The afternoon has brought a haul of new information: an email to Ryan from his lawyer, discussing strategy, an email between Ryan and Cass. A slew of useless finds: another notice from the dry cleaner that his shirts are ready for pickup. The sludge of work emails. An ad, it seems from a pharma co, Rx.com, with an obtuse message. And then the relevant emails and these, of course, are painful.

"Re: Custody"

"Re: House"

She cringes as she reads his words, marvels at his cruelty. When did he change? What changed him? What happened to the man who loved her and her children? Was he still intact, his mind mis-wired, his soul eclipsed, riled by traumas decades old, unhinged by skipping his dosage? Drugs and rage and memories that overtook him? And if that man is still intact, can he be rescued? Despite all he has done, all the pain and the destruction, she loved Ryan recently, loved Ryan deeply. And it is only habit to wonder what his state is right now. Is he taking his medication? Has he found some solace?

Now Cass reads her own email to Ryan on the cloned phone. It is the closest she will come to understanding his perspective. It is as though she has become someone else, a different person, her own audience. A wife is making a plea to her husband that they meet and talk about the end of their marriage. She is begging him to take any means to avoid a legal battle, asking that they make a compassionate plan among themselves. In the email, she accedes to his suggestion for how they will share the baby until they reach a formal settlement. He will pick up the baby every third night until they work out a permanent schedule. It is excruciating to be apart from Sam at all, but some part of her—either the diseased or the still healthy part—believes Sam needs and deserves to see his father.

By force of habit, she walks up the stairs and stands at the door of her children's rooms. Sam is sleeping in his crib. Alice is snoring loudly. Pete is sleeping in the same position he favored as a baby, bottom up, head under the pillows. Reassured, she turns to go, but something grabs her attention. A color in the periphery. A bag she has not seen before. She walks to it, examines it, unzips and drops its contents: women's panties, lacy ones, a pair in black and purple. A handful of women's T-shirts, one bearing the name of a local gym, and a bathing suit one would wear to swim laps, as opposed to one for sunbathing. And strands of hair that are dark and brown, not unlike the hair she found at the beach house. It is a bag that contains the gym clothes and several changes of clothing of a young and medium-sized woman. She racks her brain to think of a possible reason for the presence of such an item in her house, but no such reason surfaces.

She texts Marley to see if she has any information.

"Gosh, no," she writes. "I don't know anything about that."

Cass puts the phone down now, unsure how to respond. "What an asshole," she writes. This suffices at least to expel some of her humiliation.

"I'm so sorry," Marley writes back. "No one deserves to be cheated on. Men are such bastards."

Cass puts down the phone. There is solace in knowing heartbreak does not discriminate, and that others have survived this.

It is evening now and getting cold as Cass rushes from class, dodging students as she leaves and driving over the speed limit. The bay is a silver arrow, drawing a path for her. She opens the front door at home with the usual reflexive bracing, expecting the chaos of the dinner hour, squabbles over proprietary rights—food, toys, and attention. But the house is in an unexpected state when she arrives. Pete and Alice sit at the table, making an elaborate art project with all the colored markers. Alice draws the heads of animals while Pete draws the legs and bodies. Elmer's glue in hand, they adorn the creatures with glitter and feathers. The kitchen gleams from a recent scrub. A thick red sauce simmers on the stove. Laundry circles upstairs. The dishwasher murmurs. Marley has the house under control, exactly as promised. If Cass were not so relieved, she might feel a pang of jealousy. The only glaring problem in this house is the absence of two of its main residents.

"How did the hand-off go?" Cass asks.

"No issues," says Marley, smiling.

"Did Ryan ask you anything?"

"Nope." Another cheery smile. She places a feather on the body of something between a bird and a tiger. "Oh, he did ask for my number so he could make arrangements without having to bother you."

"And what did you say?" says Cass.

"I gave it to him," said Marley. "Was I not supposed to?"

"You shouldn't have done that," says Cass.

"Oh, goodness. I'm sorry."

"He and I will coordinate the schedule. Or the lawyers."

"Got it," says Marley. She looks down, an expression of contrition.

Cass softens and checks herself. She must not lash out at her allies. "I can't tell you what a relief it is to have someone I trust here. With things as they are." She stops, unable to finish the thought, relieved that Marley understands.

"Anything you need," she says. "Please let me know how else I can help. If you ever need me to stay overnight, just let me know."

Cass drops her bag by the door, takes a seat at the table with her children. In their company, she feels something like hope. She is fed by the sight of them, their joy, their health, the smiles on their faces. Their contentment will get her through this night, her first away from Sam. She will hold them close tonight, and this closeness will ward off their little brother's distance.

Marley stands and watches as Cass and the kids begin to eat their supper.

"Feel free to head home," Cass says. She yearns for privacy with her kids in a way that feels primal.

Marley walks toward the door and then stops and turns back to the table. "Oh. I almost forgot. I was wondering if it would be okay if I come in a little late tomorrow morning. I have a doctor's appointment."

"Sure. Everything all right?"

"Should be fine. My meds haven't been working quite right. Probably just need to up the dosage. If it's okay with you, I'll go see my doctor when his office opens first thing in the morning. Should be quick. I'll pick up Sam right after and be here by ten o'clock."

"Sure," says Cass. "I don't teach till noon tomorrow."

"Thanks," says Marley. "Thanks so much."

Marley smiles and walks to the door, laces up her ankle boots, pulls on her jacket. She turns back just before she leaves, her hand already on the doorknob. "Ryan texted, by the way, and asked if I could bring the baby to him a little bit early on Friday."

Cass looks up at Marley. She's on the floor, steadying a bridge in Sam's tower. "No," says Cass. "No, it's not okay."

"I told him it wasn't my place to decide," said Marley. "That I had to check with you first."

"Thanks," says Cass. "That was the right response." Cass watches Marley now, studying her gestures. "Get home safe."

"Thanks," she says. "It shouldn't take long at this hour."

"How are you going?"

"Probably take the bus."

"I thought you said you drove here."

"Oh," she says. "I usually do. But today, I parked at the bus stop because of the weather."

Cass is accosted by a familiar sensation. Instinct and intuition converge in what amounts to a loud buzzer. Something here does not compute. Something is not like the other. But before she can delve further into the sensation, the conversation is diverted. The children are anxious to have their mom to themselves and recount the day's adventures.

"I got ten out of ten on my quiz," says Pete.

"Way to go, Pete," says Cass.

"Miss Reyes liked the model," says Alice.

"Atta girl," says Cass.

Alice smiles, then looks down. "Mom, I miss Sam."

"I know, sweetheart," says Cass. "I do too. He'll be back tomorrow."

FIFTEEN

A night away from a two-year-old is a special kind of torture. In her heart, she knows Ryan would never harm their baby—on the contrary, his love for Sam has found its mirror in his hatred for Cass. He has told himself, she can only assume, that he is fighting for his child. That he would kill for this baby. That this is a virtue. But he has never been alone with Sam before, not for more than a few hours. He has never been pressed to feed, bathe, or snuggle him in the absence of his mother. And so she lies awake this night in a state of focused worry. She is comforted by a strange paradox: knowing her husband is capable of murder and yet still, despite this—because of this—a loving father.

Cass palms the phone and scrolls to the text between Marley and Ryan. On first read, it is benign, but a second look reveals a discrepancy, and perhaps something more malignant.

"Marley?" he writes.

"Yes. It's me."

"Can you bring Sam to the office early?"

"Sure!" she writes. That's all she writes. No mention of "checking with Cass first." None of the conversation she reported.

"Great!" he writes. The exclamation point doubles the insult.

Cass stares at the exchange, trying to understand the scope of the betrayal. Her mind is a scribble of theories now. She begins to unravel. At the very least, Marley has lied to cover a minor transgression: she made a plan with Ryan without checking with Cass. This would be a telling but forgivable sin, an attempt to ingratiate herself to both parents. Also possible: Ryan has gotten to Marley, begun to "flip" her, launched his charm offensive, the process by which he curries favor and allegiance with most people. But there is yet a third alternative, a far more sinister thesis: that this is not Ryan and Marley's first correspondence. That they have known each other a while, much longer than either one has acknowledged. With this in mind, two possibilities are equally likely. Did he already sleep with her, in the four days since she began her employment? Or—and this occurs to Cass now—did they know each other long before she sent her winning and, come to think of it, tailor-made application? Did they hatch this plan in bed, already lovers, while musing about their star-crossed love, and joking about how to stay together, how to off his pesky wife without a messy breakup?

Unnerved, Cass dials Matthew. She is speaking before he greets her.

"Can you run a background check on my nanny?"

"I'm not really supposed to—"

"Marley Lyons. West Virginia. There should be a license."

Matthew says nothing. Cass waits during an interminable silence.

"That name doesn't come up anywhere," he says finally.

"It doesn't come up anywhere?"

"Did you check her references?"

"The site I used does background checks. It said she was pre-vetted. She had some sort of badge."

"I think you can pay for that. Did you speak to any of her references?"

"I was in such a hurry to hire someone. Ryan threw a fit about the previous person. He insisted I hire . . ." She trails off. "He insisted I hire someone quickly."

"No medical license comes up either. And no evidence of marriage, which would explain a name change."

"This is not good," says Cass.

"Look, it could be nothing. These data searches are imperfect."

"No medical license? She said she was a licensed nurse practitioner."

Another pause. "Nope. No proof that this person exists at all. At least not the name we're searching."

"Dear God," says Cass. Her body feels weightless.

"Like I said, this could be nothing. The worst thing you could do is to jump to conclusions. She seems like a nice girl and a huge help. And right now you need all the help you can get."

Alarmed, Cass hangs up the phone, thoughts racing. She takes to her computer now, launching, from her rumpled bed, an alarmed mother's, abandoned wife's, and a seasoned journalist's equivalent of a criminal investigation. She begins with a routine search of email, text, and social media. Facebook, Twitter, photo sites, readily accessible data. She begins with the facts she knows—or thinks she knows—like a child assembling like colors, all the blues, all the whites when beginning a jigsaw puzzle. These are the first few pieces: tattoos, guitars, rescue dogs, leukemia, illustration. Ryan was right. It's amazing what you can find on Google. Within minutes, Cass sees a persona rife with contradictions. Within hours, it is clear that little Marley has said is true, from her name to her medical license. By morning, Cass has come to the chilling realization that the woman who has been caring for her kids is not only a stranger but a trailer park con. A match made in heaven, she now believes, with her scheming husband.

Marley's Facebook page presents a schoolmarmish persona, a smiling sweetheart photographed with her dog, baby pictures of girls in bows and smocked dresses, snaps with grandparents on exuberant family vacations—bungee jumping, skydiving, a cruise through the Caribbean islands! A girl who has recently graduated from college and moved to the big city. A second, more candid Twitter feed reveals a contrasting body of information, the band in which she plays the guitar, an obsessive interest in acid, and a motorcycle she proudly rides on which she suffered a recent wreck. A selfie from the hospital, eyes glassy and gown falling below a bruised collar bone. "Eat me, Accident!" she boasts. "At least the bike's not broken." Cass is not amused by her cavalier presentation. This is the girl who spent the afternoon with her baby? This is the dutiful nurse? This is the bruise she claimed as proof that she, too, emerged from the depths of domestic violence? Cass quickly assembles the portraits of two disparate persons, or rather, one young woman who enjoys constant reinvention.

Now she delves into the archives of Marley's Pinterest apothecary, a page devoted to her hobby, homemade herbal remedies. She sings the praises of ginger, its use in Chinese medicine, the virtues of milk thistle and dandelion root as natural blood cleansers. Parsley, cilantro, and watercress are the most potent leafy greens for heavy metal detox, possessing the power to clean the blood of impurities as disparate as dirt and lead and mercury. Even good old orange juice cannot be underestimated, as calcium contains, Marley extols, the ability to strengthen the bones and aid in the blood's oxidation. And then, an entry on the list that catches her attention: arsenic, killer or cure? Invigorating health tonic or old-fashioned murder weapon? A couple of keyboard searches later, Cass is an expert.

Arsenic is unique in its dualistic nature, its capacity both to heal and to harm, to act as a cure or a killer. In small doses, it has a medicinal effect. At higher levels, it transforms from helpful to fatal. It is an example, perhaps more than any other substance, of the inextricable relationship between medicine and poison, endowed with the power both to revive and to destroy, to giveth and to taketh. Like two sides of the same coin, or the cruelest lover.

In ancient Chinese medicine, it was thought to be a cure-all, treating conditions from colds to rashes, even prescribed as an aphrodisiac. In ancient Rome, it is credited with ending the syphilis epidemic. In the Victorian era, it gained fashion as a health tonic and, later, as an ingredient in cosmetics—until lovely ladies, seeking to beautify, began to drop like butterflies. Then came its ubiquitous use as a dye and color enhancer, appearing in the lustrous Paris green paint and the brilliant pigments in wallpapers that turned a generation of women into shrinking violets.

But over time, it gained notoriety for a more sinister purpose, earning the auspicious title "the King of Poisons." By the Renaissance, many embraced its two-sided nature, deploying it as a murder weapon in royal feuds or to expedite an inheritance. In the late 1800s, it was used with alarming frequency as a weapon for suicides and murders. Its claim to fame was twofold, its potency as a killer and its difficulty of detection. On the periodic table, arsenic is one of the heavy metals, which means the electrons in the atom outweigh the protons and neutrons. Its molecular structure causes it to bond quickly and with abandon. It is a literally a malleable metal. But its greatest attribute as a weapon is its speed of delivery. It is rapidly circulated by the blood and absorbed by the vital organs—the lungs, the heart, the brain. It stays in the blood for mere minutes before being absorbed—causing death by heart attack or stroke—never to be detected.

In World War I, it made its way from boudoir to battlefield, when arsenic compounds were developed as agents of chemical warfare, lewisite and adamsite. Much later, it would find a surprising home as a household preservative, preventing the atrophy of wooden floors, cabinets, decks, even playgrounds, and in construction materials from paint to plaster. It ultimately found its most common use as a pesticide, killing insects on crops and pesky mice and rodents. But the strangest thing about arsenic is the way it flips from medicinal to toxic. It is Dr. Jekyll, then Mr. Hyde. A personality split between the capacity to do good and evil. Of course, it is true that any substance consumed in large amounts can wreak havoc—all good things in moderation—but arsenic turns from angel of life to angel of death in a hot minute. It is tasteless as a powder, colorless as a liquid, and scentless as a gas. Readily absorbed by skin, ingested by mouth, or inhaled through the nose. It saturates every surface it touches—whether a poison cloak, in the case of Jason by Medea, or old lace, as with Agatha Christie. The victim dies of seemingly natural causes within minutes of pulling up her britches.

These same attributes led to its use in the most unlikely of places. Arsenic has come to be widely used in modern cancer treatment. Chemo drugs and corticosteroids are the chocolate and peanut butter, the wine and cheese of the modern cancer cocktail. One is used to kill the cancer and everything in its midst, while the other is used to revitalize the red blood cells and other agents of the body's own self-healing mechanism, to give the body a round of revitalization after the attrition. Corticosteroids, Cass discovers just before sunrise, are a blanket name for a variety of drugs, which include among them many hallucinogens and psychotics, such as regular steroids, anti-inflammatory drugs, and more typically used recreational drugs like LSD and its newest designer versions. Their chief purpose is to help the body rebuild after the devastation of chemotherapy with the added benefit of curbing nausea, reducing discomfort, and preventing the patient from puking up her medicine.

It is six now, and sleep will soon relieve the pain of these frenzied hours, but before Cass closes her eyes, she makes one last curious connection. Arsenic trioxide is the favored treatment for one cancer in particular: acute myeloid leukemia. Like so many substances used in the treatment of cancer, arsenic is both a killer and a cure. It has the power not only to end the division of the cancer cells but to kill off most everything in the surrounding area. It is like a nuclear weapon in this way, leveling the enemy at the cost of civilization.

By dawn, Cass has sketched a vague outline of a person, composed of facts she has gleaned, learned, and dismissed in the last eight hours. She still believes that this woman is, in fact, afflicted with leukemia. This seems to be one of the only true things she has told her. The details have the ring of truth, more consistency than the others. But her name, last known address, date of birth, names of parents, relatives and friends, even the references she provided on the sitter application—all of these things are false. And so by seven o'clock, Cass feels afflicted, not only with the mania of sleep loss but with the growing sense that she is closer to and further from the facts than when she first started.

She entertains two possibilities now, both equally compelling: one, this woman is an abject liar with the most insidious of intentions; two, she is a typical twentysomething, testing boundaries, acting out, and otherwise behaving within the realm of acceptable social convention. Cass thinks back now to their first meeting in the coffee shop. She remembers saying to Ryan that night, "She's either a real-life Mary Poppins or a professional con."

"You and your theories," he'd said. "Time to call the doctor." Followed by: "Promise me you'll hire her."

The memory is quickly shunted by a pressing obligation: the patter of padded feet on the stairs—these sounds are morning vespers. Time, she begins to understand, heals all wounds, not only on its own merit or with its glacial accrual—with its derivative proof that all things do eventually pass, that birds sing, suns set, and moons rise every night just as people heal from heartbreak and grief and losses. Climbing to the top of the stairs, she greets Pete and Alice.

"How'd you sleep?" she asks them.

Wordless grunts convey indecision.

"Ginger was up all night," says Alice. "She misses Sam also."

"He'll be back today," says Cass.

Alice and Pete smile. And that is all Cass wanted.

She embraces them as though it has been weeks, not hours, since she last saw them. Satisfied that all is intact, she heads downstairs to assemble breakfast. They need to eat their scrambled eggs, ask for more OJ, pull on socks and shoes and jackets. She must guide them through their morning needs, watch them walk through the school door, and then, once she sees the school door close, she must reclaim her youngest.

And so she attempts a performance as she sits at the table with Pete and Alice. She performs peace of mind when she feels none, calmness when she feels only terror. She stills her trembling hands as they sit at the breakfast table, the kids eating eggs while she drinks her tea, no milk, no sugar. She runs through Pete's new vocab list. She helps Alice gather her books for her backpack. She tries to shore up the foundation of their shattering world with the simple act of being together.

"Loquacious?"

"Wait, I know this one."

"Endeavor."

"Try hard."

"Copse."

"Dead body?"

"No! A group of trees."

"Gosh, Mom. Why so jumpy?"

She forces a smile, moves on quickly.

Cass is waiting for Marley's text, consumed with worry. The plan was for Marley to go to her "doctor's appointment" and then pick up the baby at Ryan's office, to text Cass the moment she meets Ryan and has the baby back in her possession. It is ten past ten when the text arrives and with it, the awful buzz of reinforcement.

"We have him," Marley writes.

Cass stares at her phone. She focuses on the pronoun.

"Who is we?" Cass writes.

A minute passes before the next one. "I meant I just got him from Ryan's office. Where would you like me to bring him?"

"Bring him home right now." This does not satisfy Cass's concern—it only raises questions. Pronouns do not lie. They are the brain's first and most accurate mode of self-presentation.

An awful moment passes during which Cass imagines her husband fucking this young girl, sitting underneath her, tongue in her lips as she stands above him; this young girl sitting in their car, in the seat that is usually hers, silver bay on her side, enjoying the gaze of her two-year-old, playing the role of Cass in the life she has stolen.

By the time Marley and Sam arrive, Cass is consumed with panic. She takes the baby into her arms as though she is rescuing him from a fire.

Sam clings to his mother, legs sprawled around her hip, one arm laced around her neck. The strength of his grasp is forceful.

"How was your doctor's appointment?" Cass asks. She is not asking in earnest. She is collecting information—lies, gestures, reactions.

"It was good. Thanks for letting me go. I was waiting for him when he got there."

"That was smart," Cass says.

Marley smiles and busies herself, prepping for a day of child care. She sits down on the rug where Sam plays, dumps a basket of blocks, and begins to lay the foundation for a new tower.

"Everything all right?" Cass asks. For a moment, she feels something like concern, and then she remembers the doctor is likely a fiction.

"Yup. Basically a routine visit."

"You said you might need to change your prescription."

"Oh yeah," Marley says. "He just decided to double my dosage."

Sam, tempted by the sight of his blocks, motions to be put down now. Cass does so reluctantly. He walks to the rug and places a block on Marley's structure.

Another minute passes before Cass begins her interrogation. "I called two of your references," she says, "from your application. None of the names or addresses you gave seem to be valid."

"That's strange," says Marley, without looking up. "Did you call the Blakes or the Barbers? They're probably just really busy. I'm sure they'll get back to you later." She remains sitting on the floor, focused on the tower. Cass stands above her.

"Probably," says Cass. "In the meantime, would you mind providing some basic information? A home address? A recent phone number? Your mother's name? Your father's? You said you had a brother."

"Sure," she says. "Don't you trust me?" She rises slowly from the floor and meets Cass's gaze with a mixture of apology and anger. "My mother's name is Mary Lyons."

Cass walks to her laptop, places it on the kitchen counter, and logs in to her standard directory, types the name Marley has supplied. The baby sits on the rug, trying to build a bridge on his tower. "There's a Mary Lyons in San Diego, California. I thought you said she lived in West Virginia."

"You must have the wrong one," says Marley. "It's a pretty common name."

Cass looks at Marley now with rising aggression. Marley meets her gaze and stares back. Her gaze is not as strong as Cass's, but hers is reinforced by apparent indignation. And then, a masterful performance. With tears welling up, she stares back and says, "I lost my mother six months ago. This is really offensive."

"Want juice," says Sam. He topples the tower and cries when it tumbles. Cass, on high alert, walks to the rug, picks up her child, and walks back to the counter.

"I'm sorry that you're offended," says Cass. "I can see why you would be if you have been honest. But I hired you to take care of my kids, and therefore I have the right to demand basic verification. If you've lied, what you've done is not a minor offense. Fraud is a misdemeanor. Breaking and entering is a felony. God knows what other crimes you've committed. Hopefully, we can clear this up and everything you've told me can be easily corroborated."

Marley looks back without flinching. It is a contest between two forces, two alpha females, one younger and one older, one aided by the power of intuition, a career spent honing the art of questions, the subtleties of information and its misrepresentation; the other bolstered by youth, the arrogance that comes with it, the indignation of the falsely accused, or the strident sneer of a sociopath with no morals and a good motive.

"Perhaps you can find someone to call and verify the facts you've presented. You mentioned a brother, a friend in Portland. You can call one of them and put them on the phone. Or you could just give me an ID. You must have something in your bag with your name on it."

Marley shakes her head as though renewed in her disdain for human nature. She fishes theatrically through her bag in search of the proof Cass has requested. "Looks like I forgot to bring one today."

"You don't have any ID? A bank card? Driver's license?"

"I left the house in a hurry."

"Then you need to call a friend or family member. I need some proof of who you are. Nothing you're saying is checking out. It's very concerning."

Marley looks at Cass now with utter revulsion, as though Cass, not she, has paid an unforgivable insult. "Everyone I know is at work."

"That's fine," says Cass. "But I'm going to have to call the police if you don't clear this up. It's fraud to fake your identity. It is a felony to fake a medical license. Neither of these things is acceptable for someone working with children."

Marley shifts gears suddenly from her previous tactic. She abandons the act of fishing through her bag, looking for ID, and begins theatrically scrolling through her phone. "I'm trying to find someone who can get my ID from my apartment." She dispenses with an injured look, designed to convey the greatest injustice. Sniffling, she crosses the room. "Excuse me. I need to go to the bathroom."

Cass moves quickly now, fueled by adrenaline and outrage. Still holding Sam, she walks to the front door, locates Marley's jacket on the coat hook, and removes a stash of crumpled papers from her coat pocket. She rifles through the papers, searching for relevant information—a receipt, a bank card, so many cards for Starbucks, a receipt from the morning's doctor's visit, replete with a different name from the one she has given. Mary-Lynn Logan. This appears to be the real name of this young woman, different from the one she used on Facebook. Now Cass has a new last name, theoretically a correct one, to check against the false one.

She leaves the jacket on the coat hook and palms the phone in her pocket. She walks back into the kitchen now. The first call she makes is to her lawyer. However young and inexperienced he may be, he is the only one who can help her at this moment.

"There's something wrong with the nanny," she says. "She's a fraud. Completely bogus."

"Head downtown right now," he says. "Meet me at the District Court. The family division."

"Why family court?" says Cass.

"I want to get you an order of protection. Short of an arrest, it's the fastest way to move this forward."

"I'll have to bring the baby."

"No," he says. "You can't do that. Can you ask a friend to watch him?"

"I'll try," she says and hangs up the phone.

She stands for a moment, baby on hip, waiting for Marley to emerge from the bathroom. But before a plan forms in her mind, the rush of winter air enters the house, and the sound of the front door closing.

Ten minutes later, Cass pulls into Nora's driveway and hurries to her doorstep. She stands outside with a bundled Sam, her face twisted in desperation.

"Nora," she says, "I'm sorry to ask. Can you watch Sam for a few hours? I have to go to the courthouse. Something was wrong with the nanny."

The request is met with silence. Cass cringes, fearing that Nora is nearing her limit. But without a word, her friend takes the child in her arms. "Hi, cutie! Who wants to watch a movie with Aunt Nora?"

Cass drives at top speed from Cumberland to downtown Portland, propelled by a new determination. Fear and vindication numb her to the nausea that has become a constant companion. Downtown Portland has an odd quality at this hour. It is a city in the midst of a transformation. It has the vestigial remnants of an old port town—the narrow streets, the crumbling brick, and wet cobblestones—and the shiny taller structures of a city that has sprouted up in the last decade.

The court buildings sit at the top of a hill on Newbury Street, surrounded by a few grand old hotels and an assortment of places to buy bail bonds and wire money, dirty magazine stores, and unsavory storefronts. At the highest point in the city, the Superior Court boasts a view of Casco Bay and the surrounding lakes and forests, juxtaposing the courts of law with these massive growths of nature. Every other building has signage written in an Asian language, usually paired with misspelled English words. *Passport Picks, Soovenirs, Cendy.*

Cass finds a parking spot in front of a building that can only be a brothel or a crack house and makes her way up a very steep hill until she is standing on the wide white steps of the courthouse. The rolling topography of downtown, always an adventure in incline, particularly after rainfall, is even more challenging today as Cass struggles to take in the necessary oxygen. Her chest feels tight and her breathing is labored. She is out of breath by the time she reaches the top and stands, facing the court in all its marble and bronze glory.

Matthew is sitting on the steps when she reaches the building. His brow is furrowed into a zigzag. His knees are bobbing up and down the same way Ryan's would do when he was up late, working on a deadline.

"Thank you for rushing here," she says.

"This is important," Matthew says, standing.

"I couldn't do this alone," she says.

"No. Not at the rate things are going."

She smiles, grateful for the levity.

"We need to get the food tested. Any food or drink he gave you. Find the source. Establish a link. Proof of purchase."

"I agree," says Cass.

"Where is the food you told me about?" he asks.

"I put it in the freezer."

"Make sure no one touches it."

"Obviously."

"I mean for purposes of chain of custody. For the integrity of the evidence. Was there any other item," he says, "that you think he may have contaminated?"

Cass considers. "He made me coffee the other day. Was acting very suspicious. A couple of drinks at the party. God knows where else. From what I've read, some of these toxins can also be transmitted through dermal absorption."

"What does that mean?"

"Through the skin. In bedding, clothing, and fabric."

"You've done your research."

"Ever heard of Agatha Christie?"

He shudders. "You need to find any item that may have come into contact with the toxin. Cups, plates, silverware, water. Clothes. Bedding. We need to get it tested by a reputable lab. With witnesses present to testify to the integrity of the evidence. Either way, they'll try to destroy it."

"What about me?" Cass says.

"What about you?"

"The evidence in my body."

"You should get tested again," he says. He pauses. "But there's a problem with that evidence. It's not like a bullet or bruise. That evidence has no fingerprints. There's no way to prove who put it there. They'll say it could be anyone. They could even say it was you."

Cass shakes her head. "He looked me in the eyes and told me what he was going to do."

"That's testimony, not proof."

Cass takes a sharp breath.

"We're going to try to get you protection now. He'll be out of your life soon."

Together they walk up the steps of the courthouse. It is impossible not to feel self-conscious in such a formal setting. The grand monolithic pediment, supported by Doric columns, causes her to feel they have walked onto the set of an epic political drama. She has fashioned a makeshift suit out of a blazer she often wears to class—and the jeans she has been wearing since Monday. Her hair is pulled back in a tight ponytail, a proxy for composure. It is a noble if not entirely successful effort. She focuses on the simple need to put one foot in front of the other. She follows Matthew into the lobby, through a security system, emptying bags and electronics, then into an elevator, crowded with anxious people. Even after emptying her pockets, removing her rings and jewelry, Cass sets off the metal detector. This happens several times before she is patted down with the wand, before the guard finally lets her pass, assuming it is the machine's malfunction.

"You have fillings?" the guard asks.

"What?" she says.

"Dental fillings," he says. "Metal."

"Not that I know of," she says.

"Lots of people have them and don't even know it."

Cass nods and considers as the detector buzzes. Something in her body has set off a metal detector? She runs her tongue over her teeth. She has no cavities and one root canal, but it was done recently enough to assume they must have used a more sensible substance than iron, lead, or some other heavy metal—plaster, silicone? But new demands promptly usurp the scientific method. Meanwhile, the alarm continues to sound. The metal detector at the court seems to know better.

Cass and Matthew emerge on a floor that looks like any other municipal waiting area—a passport office or the DMV, filled with women of all ages, a handful of restless children. These women mill about or wait in chairs affixed to the ground while others approach a glass window when their name is called. An hour later, Cass and Matthew are called to this window. An hour after that, they sit in a small windowless courtroom, facing a prim female judge with coiffed brown hair and pearls, a whispering lawyer, and a clump of uniformed court officers.

"Stay calm," says Matthew. "Tell the truth. And speak slowly."

This is the only thing he says before the court is called to order. Cass is instructed to swear in to the courtroom. The judge asks Cass to state her goal and the reason for her appearance. It is hard not to be humbled by the judge's robes and the formality conferred by the setting. She takes a deep breath.

"Judge, I am asking for custody of my child, and an order of protection from my husband. On November 1, he made a death threat, and then he acted on this threat. He pushed me into traffic. He informed me he had been poisoning me and that he intended to make it look like a suicide. Since that time, I have experienced severe and painful symptoms, including nausea, vomiting, mental confusion, vaginal and rectal bleeding. I don't feel safe in my home. I fear for the safety of my children. I am asking for a protective order for the safety of myself and my children."

It takes several minutes to recover from the rush of speaking in the courtroom. Her heart speeds. Her hands are numb. Nausea is momentarily eclipsed by adrenaline. The rest of her time in the room is a blur except for the memory of Matthew saying, "Good job," the knowledge that she needs to stand and exit, and the relief that comes from learning she has finally been believed, that she has broken through the recent days' dismissal, and that she has succeeded in her goal, gaining a measure of protection for her and her children.

They stand outside the courtroom now in a room that resembles a marble mausoleum.

"Most people freeze up," Matthew says. "You ever done this before?"

"I've had to pitch before," she says, exhaling.

Matthew explains the outcome in more detail now. The judge has granted, ex parte, a temporary order of protection. *Ex parte* means in the absence of the defendant. This order must now be served to Ryan. Then he, with his lawyer, will have the chance to defend himself against the allegation. The judge has not ruled on custody. This will happen with both parties present. They will all return to the court in a week. Ryan, Cass, and their lawyers. Until then, things will proceed as they were with Ryan getting Sam the following night, as scheduled.

"It's a start," says Matthew. "The restraining order will deter him."

"Let's hope," says Cass. "But we need to wait to serve it. I want Sam back with me first."

"That makes sense," says Matthew. "Call me as soon as you have him."

Cass walks to the car, grateful for the silence. Everything feels different. Everything is altered. It is mid-November, and the sun is out in Portland.

Back at home, Matthew arrives with three people—two witnesses and a notary. One is a short, overweight man with a balding head and greasy scalp. From his prominent brow and thick lower lip, he could easily be Matthew's brother. The other appears to be the receptionist from the immigration agency that shares his office. But Cass is too grateful for help to quibble with the details. She is grateful for someone to steady her hand while she removes the lobster roll from the freezer, to witness this bizarre procedure as she places the food in the special tube designated for "animal tissue," for someone to sign his name on the line that says "witness," for the notary to make this event official, to prove that it happened as it did without any evidence corruption, by putting his rubber stamp on this document. It is a far cry from the cheerful family meals assembled on this counter, and she shudders as she considers her husband's latest ingredient.

She is grateful that someone is here to use phrases like *chain of custody* and *contamination*, to explain the technicalities involved in this process when she is too sick and sad and confused to remember much more than the names of her three children. Matthew intends to "establish a link" with Ryan's fingerprints on the container. To obtain proof of purchase of the lobster roll and the toxins he placed in it. To prove the delivery of the weapon with medical labs taken from Cass's system. To prove a crime not unlike rape, a crime with no witnesses, the only proof that it did occur, the victim's bruises, trauma, terror, and, if she's lucky, her attacker's semen. A rapist warps an act of love into an act of violence. Except here the semen is poison. No DNA to speak of. Ten minutes later, the food has been safely transferred to the appropriate container, the container placed in a sealed envelope, the envelope ferried to overnight mail for delivery first thing in the morning, and these three strangers have left her alone in a house that was once her haven and is now her very own crime scene.

SIXTEEN

It is morning, and Cass works to restore a sense of normal. Because of the issues with child care, she calls in sick and cancels her afternoon class with a perfunctory dashed-off email. She shudders to think of the complaints of her students, who treat the last-minute absence of a teacher as a cause both for celebration and a passive-aggressive note to the dean of students. "We didn't pay this tuition to have our teacher cancel at the last minute." Alice and Pete are safe at school. Sam is fed and contented. Now Cass stands underneath a wooden plank bridge while Sam roars with laughter, running back and forth, shrieking with delight as he instructs his mother to "be the monster." Several trips later, another little boy about the same age climbs up the ladder and asks for an encore. She recognizes him vaguely from his mop of curls and unusually wide-set eyes but does not remember who he is until she turns to see his father.

"Be the monster!" Sam says.

Cass obliges.

"Be the monster, Mommy!"

Cass performs another growl, to the delight of both children.

"Impressive," says Aaron.

"Thanks," she says. "I've spent years honing my monster impression."

"You've got three, right?"

"Yes," she says.

"Don't know how you do it."

Cass smiles. "I'm very lucky."

"You smoke?" he says.

"What?" she says. Does he mean what she thinks? "Oh, no. Not since college."

"You and Ryan never lit up a joint? Bottle of wine on a Friday night. After the kids finally conk out?"

"Nah," she says. "That stuff never agreed with me. I don't need any more reasons to be suspicious."

He waits for her to elaborate. She immediately regrets making this joke with this near stranger.

"If you ever change your mind," he says, "I could hook you up."

"Thanks," she says. "I'll do that." Her eyes are on Sam as he gains momentum on the plank bridge.

"Don't go thinking I'm some drug dealer. I just know people who can facilitate should you ever need it."

She pauses. *Facilitate*. Why is it that druggies always use such overwrought vocabularies? "Not for me. Besides, I'm thinking of doing a cleanse. Got enough junk in my system."

"What kind of junk?" he says.

"Oh, you know." She regrets the disclosure. But everything is so dark right now, there is something reflexive and cathartic about gallows humor. "You know how it is with an old house," she says, retreating. "There's always something in the paint or the pipes or the water."

"Fuck, we can't do anything anymore. Can't breathe in the house because of the lead paint. Can't eat seafood because of the mercury. Forget about the great king crab. Filled with arsenic . . . sick bastard."

"I didn't know that," she says. She is eager to end this conversation, but something holds her in her place. Loneliness or morbid curiosity.

"I'm something of an expert," he says, "in the science of foreign substances."

"Oh yeah?" she says. "Why's that?"

"Wow, that sounded macabre."

"It did," she says, "but now I'm curious. What kind of expert?"

"I was that kid, experimenting with baking soda to make explosions in the kitchen. Then I was the science geek in high school, working the Bunsen burner. Majored in chem in college. After that, I spent my twenties finding myself in the American Southwest, where I learned about the science of the drug trade—meth, ecstasy, acid—and I gained the dubious distinction of being one of five people present at Timothy Leary's deathbed."

"Leary as in LSD, the professor?"

"The one and only. Turn on. Tune in. Drop out. Think for yourself and question authority. Father of the movement."

"How did you have occasion to meet?" Cass says. She feels her journalist's instinct kicking in.

"Truth be told, I used to sell a bit. Paid my way through college. You know. My wayward twenties. The search for purpose. I read his books, wrote him a letter, went to visit him in the desert, ended up sticking around a few weeks. That turned into a few years. I think of that time as my master's in chemistry. You can learn a lot about science—chemistry and the brain— from real-life experiments." He smiles. "I mean from the manufacture and combination of various substances."

"Wow," she says. It is all she can say. She is repelled and intrigued in equal part. But something keeps her standing there—loneliness, voyeurism, perverse interest.

"They're using it now for everything. Alcoholism, trauma, depression. Terminally ill patients. Did you know recovering addicts on acid trials have a lower rate of relapse than the ones who go through rehab? You should hear what it does for trauma patients. Thirty years of therapy in six to eight hours."

Cass nods. No other response comes to mind.

"But of course, you know what they say . . ."

"What do they say?"

"*Sola dosis facit venenum.* It's the dose that makes the poison."

"Right," says Cass. "I thought it was 'everything in moderation.'"

"Santos is the laboratory where it all started. Two self-taught druggies-turned-chemists making LSD in a New Mexico basement. Now Monsanto is the largest pharmaceutical company in the free world. Chemo drugs and pesticides. Both made from the same darn stuff. Pretty awesome when you think about it. The same thing that saves the lives of the terminally ill kills every little fucker that lands on our precious agriculture. And then we use those crops to feed our children. Ironic, huh? Nuclear warfare on a micro-scopic level. And to think this little underground lab became the biggest of Big Pharma."

"Fascinating," says Cass. "I had no idea you were so knowledgeable."

"I'm just the weird dad at the playground."

"Just the weird dad." She smiles. "Weird but interesting."

A burst of laughter from the bridge where the kids are playing. Cass beams at her son, arrested by his elation.

"They play well together," says Aaron.

"Yes, let's do this again," she says. She is not sure about this, but she wants to go now. And the truth is this is the first time in weeks she has spent ten minutes in sunshine, distracted from abject darkness.

"If you ever change your mind, you know where to find me." He nods at his house across the street. "You seem so stressed. Everyone feels better after a little vacation."

Cass collects Sam from the plank bridge, re-zips his puffy blue parka, hoists him to her arms, and quickly leaves the playground. Given the strange nature of life of late, this conversation seems relatively less bizarre than it might have weeks prior. Stranger still: as she walks home, she is actually considering Aaron's offer.

It is afternoon, and Cass tries to uphold a semblance of normal. At the Macon Dance Center school, she and the kids pass the time in a state of diversion, Pete calmly reading a book while Sam locates a similarly athletic toddler and enlists him to climb onto various chairs and tables. Every several minutes, the flailing and adorable legs of tweens fly across the class-room window in flashes of black and pink spandex as Alice and her classmates perfect the routine for their upcoming winter recital.

As Cass sits in the crowded lobby, Ryan's phone lights up, revealing a bizarre text exchange between Ryan and Marley.

"I am very sorry to say I had to resign from my position," writes Marley.

"That's unfortunate," Ryan writes. "Are you available to discuss this?"

And then, a few minutes later, from Marley: "I'm at a doctor's appointment now. I'll call you when it's over."

"Please do," he writes. "Please call at your earliest convenience."

Cass stares at the phone with budding awareness. There is something off to the exchange, something rehearsed, scripted. Too wordy, grammatically proper. A pretense of formal. Texts tend to be more cursory, shortened by urgent, clumsy fingers.

Cass considers again the various theories of their involvement: either Ryan is pursuing Marley now or a greater intimacy and longer history exists between them. If the latter, this message is nothing less than a criminal's alibi, a rig designed to obscure a more complicated structure. Still, Cass checks the impulse to draw too many connections. But she cannot discount the possibility that Ryan and Marley were lovers, that he placed her in their home as a plant, a marriage of motive and accomplice, a chilling hybrid of Dr. Jekyll and Mrs. Doubtfire. This would be truly sinister, a whole other level of deranged and psychopathic.

The night still holds a series of decisions for Cass. She has not yet authorized Matthew to serve the restraining order, and so as far as Ryan knows, he will receive the baby later tonight at their scheduled transfer. She faces a throng of opposing emotions on this subject: rage compels her to hurt him back, to deprive him of the thing he wants most, their most precious shared possession, and common sense tells her he is not in his right mind, that he is not competent now to be around children. And yet her pure and weakened heart wants no revenge, no malice, and, like some old broken toy, yearns to make him happy.

Now Cass scripts her own message, one designed not to convey but elicit information.

"Some bizarre behavior from Marley yesterday. Turns out she was a total fraud. Fake name, fake references, fake everything. It was pretty scary."

Several minutes pass, minutes during which he is either distracted or deciding on the most appropriate reaction.

"You ran off another nanny," he writes. No mention of Marley's message to him, no mention of any prior knowledge.

"The girl was a psycho," she writes. "We're lucky nothing happened."

"The nose always knows," he writes back. "Lucky you're such a good detective."

Cass fights a new impulse to double over in anguish, but finds a new diversion; anguish activates anger.

"Don't come to the house tonight," she writes. "I'm not willing to give you the baby. Our lawyers can talk on Monday and figure out a long-term solution." Her fingers hover over the phone, about to press Send on this nuclear message. But something stops her—fear, self-doubt, compassion. She erases the message to start from scratch.

Ryan writes before she revises. "Meet me at home," he writes. "I'll come to the house to get him."

Cass is ready now to tell him not to bother, to greet him instead with a note on the door: your new restraining order. But the cycle of their relationship is a wave with a fearsome undertow. She is a swimmer, wading back to shore, and he is the wave that carries her under.

By the time they reach the house, the kids are agitated and grumpy. Hunger and day's-end fatigue converge to make them edgy and prone to sudden movement. They have reached the crucial zone before dinnertime during which a parent has mere minutes to nourish her children or else witness a rapid decrease of blood sugar, spirits, and inhibition. The urgency of the endeavor is heightened by the kids' divergent goals. Pete wants to play LEGOs and eat at home. Alice wants to go out to dinner. Cass wants to get the big kids inside before Ryan's arrival and delay the transfer of the baby as long as possible. Conflicting goals converge as they emerge from the car into the driveway.

Ryan arrives in the midst of all this chaos. The car rolls to a stop, and the door opens. He gets out quickly. She watches his face for signs of which Ryan he will be. Loving stepdad? Company man? Estranged husband?

Seeing him produces a swell of emotions, so conflicting as to be combustive, soothing her just as it causes a surge that feels like a geological explosion.

"Can we talk for a minute?" Cass says. She cringes as she says this, words uttered by women for thousands of years, words that have caused generations of men to go spontaneously deaf to reason.

The kids freeze near the door. Ryan waves an awkward greeting. Pete waves back. Alice doesn't.

"Put the kids inside," he says. "We can talk for a minute."

He grabs the baby from Cass before she can stop him. Sam reaches out for his mother on reflex, but Ryan is quick to respond, distracting him with a steady stream of babble and promises. Startled, she turns and opens the door, eager to shield the older kids from the tension. Pete pauses for a moment, his chubby hand on the doorknob. He turns back to look at his mother and Ryan, confused by his feelings; one impulse tells him he hates this man, that he mistreated his mother. The other misses him terribly. Not two weeks ago, this man was a fact of his life, a playmate, a friend, and, for all intents and purposes, a father. The contradiction of these emotions— hatred and love, fear and desire, loathing and yearning—is too much for a seven-year-old, and, reasonably enough, it makes Pete angry at his mother.

He stares at Cass and Ryan for another moment and then slams the door and runs inside to pick a fight with his sister.

Cass looks at Ryan, as though waiting for an answer to a question, as though she can tell from his eyes whether he is still susceptible to reason. But reason is quickly leveled by the weight of emotion. "Do you realize how sick I've been?" she says.

"I know you're sick," says Ryan.

"No, not sick in the head. Puking my guts out. Bleeding out of my asshole. What did you do to me, Ryan?"

"Stress is a powerful force," he says. "It can cause serious symptoms."

"Spare me," she says. "I've heard it before. Do you have any idea what this has been like for the children?"

"You could have avoided this," he says. "But you wouldn't listen."

"You ended our family," says Cass. "Now we need a peaceful resolution."

"I'm open to peace," Ryan says. "I sent you a fair proposal. We have a child together. We both want to be with him. Neither one of us can get everything we want. This will be a negotiation."

"He's two years old, Ryan. He was still breastfeeding two months ago—"

"You know what?" he says, cutting her off. "I don't want to talk anymore." Without another word, he is walking away, toward his car with Sam. He has snapped from susceptible to impenetrable, again immune to reason.

Sam is crying now, unsettled by the tension.

"But you said . . ." It is too late now. Ryan is moving too quickly, fastening the car seat belt, settling into the driver's seat, as though trying to find cover before a storm. "Can I please say goodbye?" Cass says. This is more a wail than a whisper.

"I'd like to spend some time with my son. We can try to talk again in the morning."

Cass begins to crumble before the car leaves the driveway. The sight of her child being driven away is pain that defies description, watching his face recede, his eyes following her until they are obstructed by trees and distance.

Cass thinks back to their fight on North Haven—the brutality of the words, the volume, the threat she felt in her body. The strike of the words themselves, which echoed for days. The terror of being the object of her husband's hatred.

And then it was over, gone, a moment in time that passed with no proof. A crime with no evidence other than hearsay, a memory, the sounds in her head, and the scar of knowing, wondering if there is truth in what he said, if she caused it, deserved it, enjoyed it. Just as quickly as the world transformed, the world was replaced. His rage is a summer storm. All the evidence evaporates. No way to know if it even happened.

Now Cass turns and walks back to the house. She must find composure for the sake of the kids. "Alice, Pete, come on," she calls. "We're going out for dinner."

They are several minutes into the meal when things begin to fracture. Cass is standing over the bathroom faucet, washing Pete's hands with soap when she realizes she has been washing his hands for several minutes.

"Mom, the water's too hot," he says. "Mom, the water."

It reveals itself first in colors, the way they saturate and ripen. Then something happens to sound—it echoes in a way that only machines can mimic. Then it is something that happens to time, its shape—elastic and round—and its behavior—uniform and then erratic. Every moment has a duplicate, a twin moment, so that a person sitting across the room seems to exist in two disparate planets. Something peculiar happens to the faces of other diners, curling the corners of their mouths so that they look as though they all have the same genetic mutation. It is a full-scale assault on the senses, giving each a new purpose, as though sight has been tasked with smelling and taste with seeing images. It is a jarring shift to everything she knows, believes, and senses.

All red things are red as raspberries. All blue things are bluer than oceans. Clouds pulsate at the edges. Glowing circular orbs emanate from every light source. It is a new world that might be interesting had she had time to pre-pare for it, had it not been done to her. Instead she sits in the restaurant with her children, trying to act as though all is normal, trying to shield her kids from the fact that their mother is coming unglued at the center, she strug-gles to utter basic words as their waiter stops at the table.

"Can I get you guys anything else?" he asks. His collegial tone is now abrasive.

"No," she says. It is all she can muster. "Wait. Yes. Water."

He looks at her with furrowed brow. He knows her, and she knows him. These are not the manners to which he is accustomed.

"Now," she says. And while she wishes for better manners, it is this or else devolve into incomprehensible babble.

Their food arrives, and the children begin to devour it. Scrambled eggs for Alice. Pancakes for Pete. Did she tell them to order breakfast for din-ner? Have twelve hours passed in the last ten minutes? Is the food on the table real, or is every object in the room, table and children included, a fig-ment of her imagination? Terrified, she grabs her phone and thinks of an unlikely person. Conveniently, just down the street is a self-proclaimed ex-pert on hallucinogens.

"Aaron," she says. "It's Cass. Your neighbor. From the playground."

"I know who you are," he says.

"Something bad is happening. Something I think you would understand. I need help. Can you come meet us?"

Aaron, much to his credit, arrives in less than ten minutes. He exudes the calm and soothing command of an emergency medical worker and a bossy older brother. He distracts the kids with a story about his own toddler. He scores a box of crayons from the waiter, tells them to draw on the paper on the table. He tells Cass to drink her water, orders her another. It is im-mediately calming to be in his presence, a man acting as a man should, as a caretaker, a protector. His expertise on the subject at hand makes him uniquely helpful. He immediately identifies the most likely culprit—LSD or liquid acid—and fields Cass's questions with calm and comforting answers.

"Why does it look like everyone's smile is turning up at the corners?"

"Don't let it freak you out," he says. "It does something weird to faces."

"Time is all messed up," she says. "Everything is happening in two places."

"That's your cerebral cortex," he says. "Controls your sense of time. It's on fire at the moment."

"Why do I feel like I'm trapped in a hell and I might never come out of this?"

"That nightmare quality won't last long. That's the bad part of the trip. It gets worse if you stress out. The calmer you are the better."

"My throat is dry," she says.

"Common effect. It will pass. Drink water."

"Why do I feel like I'm connected to every person in this restaurant, all the raindrops on the window?"

"That sensation of universality," he says. "That's Be Here Now. Turn on. Tune in. That's why people do this shit, to experience the connectedness of all people, things, and nature. For that exact revelation."

The kids have regained a measure of calm, transforming the paper table-cloth into a colorful mural. The waiter has abandoned niceties and seems to be avoiding the table. Aaron sits in the spot that would usually be occupied by Ryan. He has assumed the role of babysitter, only he is looking after the adult as opposed to the children.

Either because he is kind or because he is an expert in this particular substance, Aaron provides the soothing assurance that this will soon pass, that all is not lost, that Cass and her faculties will return in six to twelve hours. She trusts him as a child trusts a parent. She willingly submits to his help, leans on him to shepherd her and the children out of the restaurant, follows him back to his home, docile and grateful, while the world continues to look like the cover of a Grateful Dead album.

The children fall asleep in Aaron's guest room despite the night's upheaval. They are young enough to enjoy the unexpected and thankfully not yet wise to a world in which evil can be imagined—at least not in any more concrete terms than games about monsters and dragons. Aaron's wife and son are asleep nearby in their bedrooms. The house is unapologetically cluttered with yellow walls and features from the seventies—dark cabinets, Formica counters, and vinyl flooring. The effect is heightened both by a vaguely sour smell and Cass's current state of intoxication. It is familiar but indistinct— pot? Baby's diapers? She spends the next several hours pacing Aaron's living room with Aaron offering guidance and consolation. By dawn, she has re- gained the coherence to return to the guest room and fall into the bed that contains her children.

Alone again, surrounded by two of her three children, she chides herself for misjudging this man, for the danger of condescension, the errors of her judgment. Running through the events of the week, Cass struggles through her stupor, to piece together a narrative, to make sense of all the nonsense. She comes to the bizarre but compelling conclusion that Ryan placed the substance on the doorknob, inducing her to touch it and dosing her with a hallucinogenic substance. But why would he do this? Just as a means of ha- rassment? What would he gain by causing her to behave like a tweaked-out teenager at a summer music concert?

The answer comes to her as suddenly as the question. If Cass were to behave in a bizarre and unhinged manner in public, it would corroborate Ryan's chorus, his claims of mental illness. A silver bullet for his defense. It would discredit her as a witness. It would effectively neutralize any claims she makes against him and, if deployed correctly, help him to gain custody of the child they have in common.

"Put the kids inside," he'd said. "We can talk for a minute."

She struggles to recall the moments of the previous evening, summons her memory as though ordering items on a menu. She remembers opening the door, watching Pete and Alice set down their backpacks, then closing the door and walking back outside to Sam and Ryan. She remembers seeing Pete in the window, staring at her and Ryan, his eyes large and somber. She remembers a story Ryan told her once about his girlfriend in college. She grew up on a hippie commune. One night she and the other kids got into the grown-ups' stash of punch spiked with acid.

"Did they take you to the ER?" Ryan had asked.

"No," she said. "Of course not."

"What did they do?"

"They gave us crayons."

Is Ryan capable of such a prank, such a crime against her? She pictures him now as he was in their home, the man she loved. She pictures him standing over the stove, laboring over the latest concoction—the best batch of almond milk, the perfect scrambled eggs, the fail-proof roast chicken, the magic, pot-infused cookies he made, a "little Jamaican magic." Yes, he is capable, she decides. She knows it in an instant. Not only is he capable of it, he would enjoy it. An act like this would delight every facet of Ryan—builder, tinkerer, chef, chemist, architect, rebel. An act like this would thrill him.

Before she falls asleep, she summons the energy to write one last email.

"To Whom It May Concern," she writes. "It has come to my attention that a sitter I hired from your agency supplied a false name and false references. She claimed to have a medical license that is nonexistent. Everything she told me was a lie. Obviously, I'm quite alarmed that the agency failed to catch this and, most of all, that this woman was in the presence of my children. Please respond at your earliest convenience."

SEVENTEEN

It is Thursday, and Cass has a busy day before her. She must change the locks and pitch the food, clean the clothes, and empty the closets. She must purge her house of everything that could be toxic: food, sheets, clothes, all the floors and every surface. Forks, spoons, knives. Dishwasher. Washing machine. Oven. She must scrub and scour every inch with the most stringent solution. She must call the lawyer and call the cops. She must prep for court again. She is like a soldier on a raid, except stronger. She is a mother.

Before she drives the kids to school, she writes a text to Ryan that is devoid of emotion. It is almost suspicious, she notes, how literal and unadorned her wording. If he were half the sleuth she is, he would immediately know that something was different.

"See you at Tucker's at 4:00 P.M."

He does not respond for several minutes.

Panic rises in her throat. It matches the burning sensation that has taken up residence in her intestines, the swirl of nausea that rises from her gut to her mouth and the burning that stings her esophagus every time she takes a sip of water.

"4:00 P.M." This is all he writes. But it's enough to quell her nerves and to cause her to drive faster.

She checks his phone for something new, some morsel of evidence. Nothing since the last exchange, the painfully scripted dialogue between Ryan and Marley. She'd seen better writing on daytime television. She scrolls more frantically through the phone, texts from friends and colleagues.

"Meet up for a drink this week?" says the guy who works in the next office.

"Reminder to pay your cell phone bill before it is disconnected."

"Mr. Connor, your dry cleaning will be ready for pickup at 4:00 P.M. at the Cherry Street location."

Nothing new, nothing fruitful. But one text draws her attention now, from Ryan to an unknown number. It is dated late September. It is neither a love note nor a sext, but a more plaintive missive. A selfie of Ryan in repose, pouting in a way he seems to find terribly alluring. But more incriminating still than this exchange is the picture below his own photograph: a photo of a guitar. A gift, it seems, for a woman with a penchant for "all things strings." The muse and the "lyre."

A quick draw on her database reveals an unsettling detail. The unknown number belongs to an Ohio address with a name that lists only a first initial. *C. Alloy.* Cass racks her brain for some possible association. C. Claire, Christina, Catherine, Charles. Then it strikes her: Wikipedia.

C-Alloy: a synthetic man-made compound comprising more than one metal. Alloys are used in commercial production due to their excellent corrosion resistance and prove to be useful in a number of applications such as flue-gas desulfurization, chemical processing, and food processing and storage as well as pharmaceutical applications.

Ryan is standing outside when they reach the restaurant. Sam looks unsettled as well. His clothes are the same as he wore the day before, and his hair looks unwashed.

"Want milk," he says and reaches for her. He whimpers as he does when he's tired.

Cass can see it in his eyes—the redness at the edges, the jerky quality to his movements. This is not the fluid, playful Sam who leaps into his brother's and sister's arms, the child whose joy is contagious. Cass fights the urge to ask, to play the detective. Where did he sleep? How many hours? Who else was in the bed last night? Nothing she says will yield the truth or useful information. Right now she has a more important objective. She must act entirely nonchalant. She must stay calm until she has her child, and then she can run, then she can scream, then she can call for help. Hopefully, this time, someone will listen.

"You guys have a nice night?" she asks.

"Yes," he says. He is being curt. This is the brevity of anger.

"Thanks for taking good care of him," she says.

"Don't thank me," he says. "He's my son. It's not something I do for you."

"Of course," says Cass. "Just a figure of speech. Hi, sweetheart. I'm so happy to see you." Without another word, she reaches for her child, hoists him under his armpits, turns, and walks back to her car. She opens the door to the back seats, where Alice and Pete are sitting, and begins the process of getting Sam buckled into his car seat, which, even on a normal day, requires some strength and maneuvering. She can feel Ryan watching her move, feel his eyes on her. The buckle snaps into a lock as he calls her name. She has given herself away. Both of them know now.

"Cass," he says.

She does not turn around. She closes the back seat door. She keeps moving. She opens the driver's seat door.

"Cass," he says.

"Yes, Ryan," she says. She drops into the driver's seat. She closes the door. She turns the ignition.

"I get him tomorrow at five," says Ryan. "As per the agreement."

"Yes, Ryan," she says. "That's the agreement." She turns and glances at the back seat, registers the alarm on the faces of her children.

"Cass," he says. His volume has changed. This is anger. This is suspicion. "Cass!" he shouts.

She closes the window. It rises slowly.

"Cass!" He knows that something is wrong. Something is different. He senses she has turned on him, that he may never again see these children. "I would kill for that child," he says. "If you take him from me, I will kill you."

But her foot is on the gas. Now the car is moving. She is pulling out of the parking lot, peering in the rearview. Ryan is running behind, eyes wild and arms churning. But she doesn't really see him. All she sees are her children's faces. Alice's eyes, solid and blue, open in terror. Pete, covering his eyes as though hiding from a monster. Sam, gazing out the window, watching his father with a curious look as Ryan chases after the car long after they turn the corner. Three reasons to fight, to be strong; three reasons to be believed. Three things to believe in. Three faces in the rearview. Their faces are tight with fear, their eyes blank, their mouths flattened. But they are together, and they are safe. She drives with new purpose. She has Matthew on the phone before she reaches the next stoplight.

"Serve it," she says. "I have him."

"Glad to hear it," Matthew says. "I'll call his lawyer."

"I need to go to the cops," she says. "We need real protection."

"You sure you want to do that?" he says.

"Why wouldn't I?" says Cass.

"For many reasons."

"Like what?"

"First of all, they're the cops. They can do whatever they want. They could take you into custody. They could take your kids. You could be questioned. This man is the father of your child. Are you sure you want him locked up? I know this may be crass to say, but if your husband loses his job, he can't pay alimony and child support."

Cass scoffs, too repulsed to dignify the notion.

Cass and Matthew sit in Portland's third precinct. Pete and Alice are in school. Sam is with his new best friend, Aunt Nora.

"You're sure you want to do this?" Matthew asks. "Attempted homicide is a serious allegation."

"Please stop asking me that," says Cass.

"It's my legal obligation to remind you that the cops can do whatever they want. They can take you in for questioning, take your kids into custody. Both of these things are possible."

"Why would they take my kids?" she asks.

"Because this is a confusing mess," he says, "and he will make counter-allegations. The state can do whatever it wants when it comes to the interest of children."

"Why would it be in the interest of children to take them from their mother?" Her volume is rising now.

"I'm just telling you they can make any interpretation. They will also question you if they start an investigation."

Cass turns to look at Matthew with barely suppressed revulsion. "I have nothing to hide."

"I know that," he says. "But he will try to destroy you regardless."

"We live in a world that hates women so much that they would sooner blame a woman for reporting a crime than punish a man for committing it."

"They always start with the person reporting the crime. In matters of rape and assault, that person is usually the victim. You know how that can go. In crimes without physical evidence, it's a matter of hearsay. His word against yours. What he and you can do to support—or destroy—the credibility of the witness."

"They'll have to take my word for it."

"You're accusing a man of attempted homicide, Cass. This will not be proven with one statement. Even for them to charge him, this will have to meet a high burden of proof. You'd better believe they'll question everyone in the town of Cumberland."

Cass stares at Matthew now, considering his statements. "He is guilty," she says.

"I know that," he says, "but they don't yet."

She looks at him another moment, then shakes her head.

"Besides, given the man you describe, how do you know he didn't plant something in your house? Or get some bogus witness to testify that you did it? You ever heard of false alibi corroboration?"

Cass shudders as she makes new considerations. She is not a stranger to the basics of criminal justice. She knows that the systems in place to protect innocent people from false charges can also protect the guilty. She knows the burden of proof is on her, that meeting the standards of probable cause will take more than testimony and circumstantial evidence. But before she can give any further thought to the obstacles before her, she is following a burly female cop up a small stairwell with peeling blue paint and prepping herself for yet another rendition of her story.

"We don't get involved in cases like this," says the cop before she has finished.

"This kind of case?" says Cass.

"Domestic dispute. Assaults without physical proof. Battery with a chemical weapon? I don't even think we have a code for this one."

"There's a sample," Cass says. "We sent a portion to a lab. The rest is still in my freezer. Can't you do something with it?"

The policewoman gives her a new look. "Oh, honey, we don't send samples to the lab unless the victim comes in on a stretcher."

"Got it," says Cass.

Matthew nods. "I guess you should consider yourself lucky."

The officer issues a look designed to signal the end of the meeting. Matthew and Cass stand to leave, gather their belongings.

"Besides," says the officer. Her tone has changed to something less collegial. "You have a chain-of-custody problem."

"Excuse me?" says Cass.

"If you were poisoned," the officer says, "the evidence would be destroyed when it was ingested. That means no fingerprints. No wound or bruises. No smoking gun."

"But if medical labs show it is in my system . . ."

"Then you're the smoking gun," says the officer. "Still no links between the weapon and the perpetrator. If it even is a weapon. Lord knows what's lurking in the environment these days. You've heard of Flint, Michigan."

"Yes, of course," says Cass. "And there well may be criminal wrongdoing there as well. But in this case, the poison was not an accident of the environment. Someone put it there."

"Maybe," says the officer. "But who? There is no way to attribute it to anyone—him, you, or a third party—without an eyewitness. Why should I believe you any more than him? He could say you put it there. That you did it to yourself, or worse, that you put it there to frame him."

"But I am the victim," Cass says. "Why would I make this up when it costs me so much to say this?"

"You say that, but I don't know it."

"I experienced this, the violence that led up to it, the violence that he threatened, the violence that he carried out. The pattern of abuse, the threat, and the crime. I am the eyewitness."

"I thought you said you were the victim."

"I am."

"You can't be both. There's a very big difference between a victim and an eyewitness."

When she finishes, Cass is depleted. She regrets going to the cops, her naive expectations. Luckily, neither she nor Matthew considered the reception they do receive from the PPD: utter disinterest.

They thank the officer for her time and quickly leave the station with Matthew visibly unnerved and Cass renewed in the knowledge that she is essentially on her own, left to her own devices. The protections she assumed to be in place, the unflappable institutions—precincts, hospitals, courtrooms—are, in fact, vulnerable to the same things as anything else—corruption, bias, incompetence. Same story. New uniform. She is very much alone in this new reality. Her only hope of protecting her kids is proving Ryan's crime to meet probable cause for arrest with her own investigation. Motive, method, weapon. Blood, urine, vomit.

EIGHTEEN

Cass is back in the part of the city that looks like a foreign country. The silver bay and the glass of the new skyscrapers are indistinguishable. It is raining, raining always. The strangeness of this part of town is amplified by the fact that the familiar world now feels dangerous and foreign things are, at least, untainted by known dangers. The air is cold and assaults her face with every step toward the courthouse. She thinks of something her father told her as a child, how foolish his words sounded at the time, how maudlin: "You can't trust anyone." But this has come to make good sense. No one—not the cops, doctors, not even her husband or father—none of these people make sense anymore. Perhaps he was simply pointing out the fact that no one is immune to brutal and corruptible human nature. Anyone can be trusted to turn under the right circumstances.

"Wear something nice but not flashy. Blue, not black. Pretty, not sexy." Cass has heeded Matthew's instructions.

She wears a knee-length gray tweed dress with a square neckline. She looks appropriately demure, more formal than she does in real life. But she cannot hide the fear she feels, the hunted look in her eyes. It makes her look—and feel—likely to pounce, a threat in her own right. And so she tries to soothe herself, to funnel her fear into focus.

She arrives at the Portland family court and walks down a maze of hallways. The hallway ends at a wood-paneled room that looks more like a coffin than a courtroom. The judge appears in his robes. The lawyers riffle through their papers. The court is a theater, and everyone in it betrays the anxiety of performers. The feeling is contagious. Ryan and Cass are sworn in. They are two opposing sides. This is Cass versus Ryan. Connor versus Connor.

Her lawyer is asking that the court continue her order of protection.

"Your Honor, this woman is afraid for her life," says Matthew.

"This woman is delusional," says the lawyer for Ryan.

"This woman implores the court for protection."

"This woman is certifiable. This woman should be committed."

Ryan wears his favorite suit, a perfectly tailored gray flannel. He is clean shaven with a new haircut. He avoids her gaze—either to deter the flow of emotions or because he no longer feels them.

Cass struggles to stay clear, to stave off the flood of sorrow that threatens to buckle her knees beneath her. She does her best not to look at him, rather than give him the satisfaction, but she is not trained for such pretense. She speaks and listens carefully. She tries to make a mental record of the allegations, the rebuttals, the judge's comments. And then, just as suddenly as it began, it is over. The judge rules down the middle, discontinuing the order of protection, and delaying the issue of custody until a trial. For now, things will continue as they are, with Sam splitting time between his mother and his father.

Ryan storms out of the courtroom in a state of fury. Cass breaks down in tears due to sheer exhaustion. She has taught a class on this, studied this very phenomenon. She has written pieces on this: "Season of the Witch: The Rise of Institutional Misogyny from Politics to Precinct." She has fought to understand, to educate others about this perverse affliction, but she never imagined she would live it, would find herself and her children trapped and threatened by the overwhelming compulsion to believe a man's testimony over a woman's. The court has effectively dismissed her concerns, placing her son in the hands of a man who tried to murder the child's mother.

———

At home, Cass tries to funnel heartbreak into action. She settles the kids upstairs in front of time-tested entertainment. Satisfied with their distraction, she leaves the room and storms the house like a looting soldier, pulling clothes out of closets, bedding off beds—sheets, pillows, blankets. One item at a time, she disassembles the underpinnings of their home, removing every piece of fabric not nailed to the furniture. She assembles a massive pile on the floor of the laundry room, like a prodigious beaver, a monument to her determination and a totem to his evil.

A Google search guides the next course of action. "Cleaning, Poisons, Toxins," she types. She is relieved to find a cleaning method that is shockingly simple, and more surprised to learn that she has all the materials she needs in her kitchen cabinet.

"Vinegar, dish soap, and water. These three substances, when combined, will remediate most toxins. Vinegar is an acid and dissolves metals. Dish soap provides the grit along with physical action. Water removes the substances, once they've been dissolved and broken down."

God love the internet for its store of DIY instructions.

Cass leaves her laundry room and hurries to the kitchen. She takes a bucket from the pantry, gathers the listed ingredients, and produces the simple solution—one part vinegar, two parts water. Then she gets down on hands and knees and scrubs the house from top to bottom. Satisfied that the floor is clean, she moves on to the tables and counters. Then she collects the kids' blocks and LEGOs in the cleaning bucket. Doused with the solution, and bleach for good measure, they look strangely like a cache of Halloween candy. She works quickly, with only the duration of the movie until the kids surface. The cheerful sounds of the children's movie float downstairs in contrast to her maudlin mission. Just like this, she conducts a one-woman purge, cleansing toxins from her home, knowing neither where nor what is the substance or source of the contamination.

The task complete, she walks upstairs to check on the children. She piles them into her bed, assembling their sleeping bags on the mattress.

"It'll be like camping," she says.

Thankfully, they are too delighted by the concept to demand further explanation.

Once they all are asleep, Cass returns to the laundry room, stuffs it with all the bedding and clothes she can fit within it. She knows she will be up all night, doing loads and folding. Exhausted, she sits on the floor and tries to sort her thoughts. Would that she could organize them as easily as laundry folded on the table. Now she takes out her two phones—hers and his—and considers her leverage. As much as she hates to admit her reliance on technology, the phone is the horse to her cowboy, not only her means of communication, the lifeline to those who can help her—friends, family, cops, doctors—but her magnifying glass, her Ziploc bag, the vault for her evidence. It is also her camera, her video recorder, and her security system. The phone is her shield and her weapon.

Wielding her phone, she leaves the laundry room, pads noiselessly down the stairs to the kitchen. She stands in the green glare of the fridge and surveys every item of food recently purchased by Ryan. Every word she types now leads to the same destination.

High in arsenic, high heavy metal content, potentially toxic. These are the results she gets now. Rice milk, almond milk, apple juice, kale, root vegetables, and shellfish, particularly crabs and lobsters, are among the most concentrated sources of naturally occurring arsenic. Either by chance or by design, Ryan has purchased a fridge full of foods all high in the same substance. And then, just for kicks, a search inspired by his other recent purchase: "chalk paint, joint compound, arsenic." Followed by the string of entries: "Various heavy metals can be found in common household products." "Arsenic is used in paints, paint thinners, and several construction compounds." Followed by the comforting addendum: trivalent arsenic is readily absorbed through the skin and sixty times more toxic than the pentavalent form of the element.

Unsettled, she deploys her phone for its other greatest power, not only to identify evidence but to document it for cops, lawyers, and judges. One by one, she photographs every item in the fridge: cardboard boxes of almond and rice milk, drawers of dewy green vegetables, the remainder of the sickly greenish lobster roll, hidden on the top shelf. Her mind spins with a revelation. Ryan has created the ultimate Trojan horse. He has transformed a seemingly generous grocery list into the vessel for poison, doubling the noble act of a doting dad with a knowing act of murder. His dutiful list of provisions is the perfect alibi for an "accidental" environmental toxin.

Now, as she stands in the dark kitchen, Cass faces the starkest of questions, not only scrutiny of her own judgment but crucial strategic decisions. She must meet and surpass the burden of proof. She must provide not only photos, receipts, and proof of purchase—she must prove method (poison), motive (the baby and the house), and prove how he got the weapon. She must establish a link to the source, prove the connection to the weapon and its purchase, and, failing an eyewitness or video recording, elicit a confession from either the source or accomplice.

Click by click, she photographs the seemingly innocuous items. Each one is a shiny exhibit. On first glance, it is a normal grocery haul, proof of Ryan's paternal duty, his role as a provider. On second, it is an alibi, the source of what he could later claim was an accidental toxin, a hidden danger in the home environment. And yet, she is conscious, even as her suspicion grows into conviction, that he has again wrought, in his weapon of choice, yet another avenue for her dismissal. Who but the most ungrateful of wives, the most twisted and paranoid person, could see, in this bountiful grocery haul, such a sinister mission? She knows that these photos are not enough, that they, too, will be discounted. And so she must continue apace; the only way out is in deeper.

It's late now, and the strain of the day has dulled her nerves and spirit. Tomorrow she must change the locks and batten down the hatches. The locks, of course, were only just changed, but ever the trusting fool, she'd given a spare set to Marley. Cass will not sleep tonight. There is too much to consider. Did Ryan intend to kill her and fall short of the necessary dosage? With failure, he was condemned to discredit or dispose of a living witness. And so he dosed her again, this time to create a public spectacle, to drive her stark raving mad, or at least appear so long enough to discredit her as a witness. Or did Ryan remain unflinching in this goal, simply trading one toxin for another, expanding from one drug to a cocktail, all of which require time and repetition to build up in her system?

What was Ryan's alibi, what had he planned as his defense had he succeeded? The lobster roll, she assumes, was chosen because it could be ruled "accidental," the result of a freak accident, an environmental poison. Everyone knows that seafood contains all sorts of unwanted substances. But where else did he place it? In the food, on the floors, on the sheets, in the water filter standing in their kitchen? Is the substance potent enough that it need only be sprinkled on the floor, like powder used to kill a rat? Did it infiltrate the air so that no amount of cleaning would actually make a difference? Did he intend to affect everyone in the household so that when Cass died and the survivors were tested afterward, he could claim in solemn tones that the whole family was exposed to some ubiquitous environmental hazard, that the dust, the water, the air, the very fabric of their home was the culprit? What a shame, he would say. How tragic.

Now she looks more carefully into poisons and radiation, moving from general summaries on Wikipedia, forging on to medical websites like WebMD and the Mayo Clinic's, and then to more specific research from afflicted regions: Flint, Michigan, where residents reported problems with drinking water, where their faucets leaked metallic sludge for months before the government took notice, where city officials denied these reports while a community was poisoned. She looks at accounts from mining communities with compromised drinking water, fracking sites whose dirt and air was steeped in poison. Farming towns in Asia whose rice was foul, tainted, populations with skin and lung cancer on an epidemic basis. Adding to her horror is the most unsettling feeling, something like a déjà vu but without the inherent pleasure. The random searches lead Cass back to the most unlikely of places—the American Cancer Society website where she'd started her research on Marley.

Arsenic trioxide, declares an article, "Approved by the FDA for Trials in Acute Myeloid Leukemia." Was this Marley's salvation? Was the treatment of her own disease the inspiration for the murder method? Arsenic was hardly a modern invention. The eighteenth-century scientist Thomas Fowler ran with his eureka moment, creating a paste used topically in skin and breast cancer patients, and naming his ingenious salve Fowler's Solution. Not one to stop at invention, he contributed both product and philosophy to science, making the intriguing statement, "Sola docit venenum." It's the dose, not the poison. In other words, poisons in small doses are the best medicines, and the best medicines in too large doses are poisonous. Cass lies in bed, considering this chilling statement.

"Topical applications of arsenic," she types. "On skin." A flurry of entries arises.

> Ancient Chinese remedies often used arsenic compounds in ointments. However, traditional Chinese medicines must be administered with care due to the frequent incidence of death in those receiving arsenic compounds in their treatments. Many substances thought to have a curative effect have steep curves of diminishing returns, reversing from a tonic to a toxin above a certain level.

"Arsenic absorption through skin," she types, looking for greater detail.

Though often used as a cure-all in ancient Chinese medicine and recently approved for use in chemotherapy for specific cancer treatments, arsenic must be used with care as a therapeutic agent. The pentavalent form of the arsenic compound is absorbed through the intestine. The more toxic trivalent form is best absorbed through the skin.

She thinks back to high school chem. Trivalent. Three electrons available for bonding. Pentavalent. Five electrons.

"Best test for arsenic," she types.

"Heavy metals panel. Urine, blood, or hair sample," says one website.

Cass ponders for a moment. Inspired, she bolts out of bed, hurries to the bathroom, and removes a pair of scissors from the cabinet. Standing at the mirror, she appraises her appearance. Her heart-shaped locket still grazes her collarbone. She has left it on as a reminder. The heart is still surrounded by his ring, caged, like her own vital organ. Her face is still a dissonant mix of delicate and determined. Slowly, she pulls her hair back, finds an inconspicuous spot near the nape of her neck, and cuts a half-inch swatch of hair. She walks downstairs to the kitchen and places the lock of hair in a small Ziploc.

She writes her name on the bag, walks upstairs, and places it under her mattress.

"Cass Connor. 12/5."

Another day. Another sickening sample. She will stockpile her own hair, another stack of proof with its own empirical data.

Hours later, Cass lies in bed, soothed by the whir of the dryer. She clutches Ryan's phone, braced for any communication, but she knows its contents by heart now: emails to and from work, texts to a confidante, dry cleaning notifications. Except for one exchange she has missed, a message to C. Alloy, written at 4:41 P.M. as he left the courtroom.

"Split," he writes. "I should have killed myself."

She reads it as both a cry for help and a confession. Indeed, they may be one and the same. A cry for help, like a threat, however feigned or performed, is always, in some way, a statement of intention. Knowing Ryan as she does, Cass hears his statement's implied referent. As though the word *instead* belongs at the end of the sentence.

She winces at the response. From C. Alloy: "Keep the faith. Stay focused. This is only the beginning."

NINETEEN

When Cass wakes up in the morning, which is to say two hours later, her phone contains an arresting message.

"Cass, I know I have not been good. I have been bad, Cass. But not in the way you think. Not in the way you're afraid of. I am guilty of not making you feel as loved as I do love you. I am guilty of failing to provide the comfort I wanted to provide you. I am guilty of making you feel alone in the home we built for our children. I am guilty of failing to give the only thing I wanted for you.

"We have built a home together. This is simple for many people. But you and I, we come from homes built on shoddy foundations. I didn't know how to make a home. I knew how to demolish and destroy, to pound a wall with a hammer. I knew how to hide in the shadows, how to withdraw in plain sight, behind work, my phone, the children. I knew how to make a good meal, but I didn't know how to feed a family. I myself did not feel safe—and so I could not make you feel safe—in the home we built together.

"It is not too late to save our home. To fortify the life we want for our family. Everything is still possible, Cass. A good life. More beautiful children. All we have to do is love. Just love. Just love each other. You were right, and I was wrong. Love is the only true thing. All we have to do is love. It's that simple. Please forgive me, Cass. Please give me a chance to be better. A chance to finish the home we built together."

Cass is close to tears by the time she finishes the letter. She cannot help but be moved. It preys on her deepest doubts and needs. This is the man she remembers. She misses that man and wants so badly to believe him. *She wants so badly to believe him.* But there is no time for fantasy now. No time for wish fulfillment. Will and belief are a powerful pair, enacting faith in the most unlikely places. She thinks of the famous experiment, the theory proposed by Melvin J. Lerner. The "Just World" Delusion. It explains why people celebrate others' good fortune—and justify their torture. A lottery winner "deserved" his good luck. A girl who got raped "had it coming." We cling so desperately to the idea that good prevails over evil, so desperately as to deny the facts, to explain away atrocities in backbends of denial.

Cass runs through a set of possibilities and permutations. On one hand, she knows she is being snowed, lulled into a story. This is Ryan doing what Ryan does best, selling a plan, telling a story. She is a sucker in a seat, watching a sappy romantic movie. She suspends her disbelief. It is reflexive and instinctual, like blinking and breathing. She fills in the gaps of Ryan's tale. She empathizes with the characters he describes. Her heart breaks for them. She yearns for a happy ending.

It is human to trust, to expect the best, to grant forgiveness, especially when so much is at stake: a man you love, a home you've built, three beautiful children. "Keep working on it," women are taught. "Stand by your man." "Don't give up on your marriage." But sometimes the soothing mantras create their own madness. Sometimes standing by your man is an act of self-destruction. And through it all, one glaring question remains: Is it possible that she is wrong, that all this is imagined?

Now Cass finds herself caught in a state of sickening confusion. If her mind were a map, there would be routes in every opposing direction. A scribble of goals and circuitous needs, inferences and deductions. She wants—my God, how she wants—to believe that she has been wrong about Ryan. The question is whether this will amounts to belief, her wish to a delusion. Whether she wants so badly to believe that she will defy her best judgment. But another want and another route is equally compelling: she wants, just as much, to prove her memory and perceptions, and to see her husband locked up as a result of his actions. She wants both things equally: to be right and to be wrong, to be rid of him and to be near him.

And so she allows competing truths to echo in her mind now. Competing truths that disorient her, like a child playing hide-and-seek, spun in circles. Love spiked by hatred. Fear mixed with desire. Emotion tempered by reason. All the while, the voices of doubt, however off-key, begin to sound like a chorus. The wisdom of crowds. The opinion of experts. She must silence them also. None of them feels what she feels in her gut. None of them saw what she saw in her bedroom, the hatred in his voice, the intention. None can measure or bottle the bile, the blood coming out of her organs. They can only assume. They can guess and condemn, tsk and tut, disapprove with knowing glances. They can sway her with something more potent than truth, consensus.

They can help her deny what she knows to be true. Lay the cement of denial. They can help her forget the strange surreal truth that took place in her bedroom. His cheek on her cheek. His voice in her ear. The gleam of his saliva. They can help her deceive herself just one more night while she secretly wonders. When she knows Ryan's crime better than her multiplication tables. Just like this, those who know and love her best can induce her to take back a killer. They can sanction and justify just one more night, one more chance to die for her husband.

The truth is there is no one truth right now. No single motive for Cass at this moment. It is true that she needs him to prove she is right. She needs incontrovertible evidence. An eyewitness. A nosy neighbor. A perfectly placed camera. In the bedroom. The hutch across from the fridge. On the kitchen counter. Or perhaps she can collect samples fast enough, her own bodily fluids—hair, blood, and urine—and bring them directly to the cops to prove there could be no other source than Ryan. She can follow him. Take photos. Find receipts. Bank statements. Cash withdrawals. She can wait until sleep, for the heaviest breath, take his phone from the bedside table. Read and forward every text and email. She needs this kind of evidence to advance the case, for him to be charged and convicted. Only proof will achieve this. Of course, she is conflicted. She is too self-aware to deny this. Of course, she yearns to be kissed and caressed, to be comforted and crushed by her husband. But, just as much as she wants to be wrong, she needs him to prove her correctness.

And so, the confusion of crisscrossing routes brings Cass to an unexpected destination. All routes lead back to the same place. In all cases, Cass needs to take Ryan back: to prove she is right or to prove she is wrong, to prove he is good or evil, to answer the questions in her head or to advance the case against him. The chorus of skeptics has not weakened her will, nor lessened her conviction. They have given her license to doubt and deny, to test her beliefs just long enough to make a bargain. She must take him back in either case. It is a win-win situation. If she takes him back and learns that she was wrong, then she saves her family and gets back her husband. If she takes him back and proves his crime, then she saves her family and gets him arrested. And if he has been bad and she takes him back, she believes this too—like so many women before her—there is a small chance she can fix him. The finest of lines between love and hate finds its highest tightrope in this marriage. In exchange for the chance to destroy him, she gets one small perk, that most lethal of trades, the most dangerous of addictions. One more night to fill her fix, the company of her husband.

But here, here she catches herself. No more. No more magical thinking. This man is not the man she knows, the man she fell in love with. This man is not Ryan. This is a sick, warped version. This man deliberately caused her harm. This man has built up a toxic level of poison in her system. This man is the reason she puked her guts out, hemorrhaged out of her asshole. This man is the reason her hair falls out in clumps when she gets out of the shower. And this man will continue unless she can prove it. She must meet the so-called burden of proof, shine light on the shadows of doubt, disarm the front line of skeptics. She must find the proof to see him charged and convicted. She must pull off a seamless bait and switch, snow him and seduce him. This man does not deserve her love. Not another moment of equivocation. He requires her most strategic attention. This man is not her friend or her love. This man is a killer. And she is going to catch him.

Now she makes a resolution. She will do whatever it takes to achieve this. She will take this killer into her home. She will neutralize him like Delilah.

Why? To obtain evidence of his crime, and to use this evidence to protect herself and her children. Why go to all this trouble? Why risk continued danger? Because she knows that if she does not, he will fuck with her for the rest of her life, and this is the only way to stop him. What better reason could there be? For love. Just love. Unjust love. Love for her children.

An hour later, at school drop-off, the children safely delivered, she walks with her friend toward their cars and shows Ryan's email to Nora.

"What do you think?" Cass asks.

"Utter bullshit," says Nora.

"He's full of it, right?" says Cass. "This is Ryan's favorite move. The Charm Offensive."

"He's after something," Nora agrees. "He's rolling the dice with custody. And he wants you off the scent of the crime." She assumes a melodramatic tone. "'I would never do it. And here are the three reasons.' That denial reads like something out of a law school textbook. When people are falsely accused, they're much less coherent."

"Good," says Cass. "Then we agree. I wanted your perspective."

"So what are you going to do?" Nora asks.

"Take him back," says Cass.

Nora stares at her friend.

"Get proof," she says. "Send the bastard to prison."

"No," she says. "You can't do that."

"I have spent the last three weeks reporting this crime to cops, lawyers, and doctors. None of them have helped me. None of them have stopped him. I need irrefutable proof. An eyewitness, a video recording, proof of purchase, or a confession."

"So what? You're going to take him in and hope that you can catch him?"

"I don't see any other option."

"You're playing with fire," Nora says.

"You would do the same," Cass says, "for the safety of your children."

"He's making the same bet," says Nora. "Winner takes all."

"He won't win," says Cass.

"But you could lose everything."

"We're in danger regardless."

Nora is shaking her head. "I don't know if you're being honest with your-self. It seems like you still love him. I know, if it were me, all I would want to do right now is collapse into the arms of my husband. As normal as that impulse may be, nothing about this is normal."

Cass pauses. She values Nora's candor, and she can't deny there may be some truth to her statement. "Of course, I love the man he was. Or the con that he presented. And yes, it takes time to trade that fiction for this person. But *this* man? No. No love anymore. Just a practical problem. It's not safe for Sam to be with him. I'll do whatever it takes to protect my son. No one else believes me, Nora. I have no choice but prove it."

Several hours later, Ryan and Cass have made progress. They begin to com-municate, she with caution, tentative power, he with passion, desperation, feigned or actual, and that ineffable gift for words, the tongue she fell in love with.

He asks to meet in person. He can't bear to be away from the children. He wants to rebuild the family, to sleep next to her in their bed, to finish the home they started together. She agrees to meet at a restaurant, buoyed by the safety of public witness. They will meet again tomorrow, on Friday. She cannot deny the excitement she feels, the wild exhilaration. She cannot deny the thrill she feels at the thought of catching her husband. But the predatory nature of her goals—and their attraction, the undeniable comfort of "collapsing into his arms"—pales in comparison to the prospect of some-thing more essential, something far more urgent: waiting him out and se-curing the proof she needs to send him to prison.

TWENTY

They decide on a restaurant in Back Cove, an old shipping neighborhood on the northern side of Portland. Back Cove is bordered by the dockyards, an abandoned bridge, and its replacement. The area has enjoyed the mixed blessing of hipster gentrification. Empty warehouses share sidewalks with treacly coffee bars and restaurants with names that sound like obscure rock bands. For a while, the area was populated by shipmen and junkies in harmonious coexistence. Now it is mostly home to hipsters seeking Saturday brunch or young families seeking condos. Even still, the big sky and abandoned bridge give it a desolate quality.

Ryan arrives first. Cass sees his car when she is locking her own. She pauses outside, checks her reflection in the car window. She wears a gray shirt dress, buttoned from the collar to the bottom. She looks the way she did on her first day of college, but her eyes show the wear and worry of the recent horrors.

Cass is arrested by the sight of Ryan, his striking face and features. He has always had this power over her, the power to freeze her in her place, to weaken her defenses. She feels the power of desire, the power of attraction. He is her poison. The only question is the dose at which he is fatal. But now, as she takes in the sight of this man, her lover, her tormentor, she must overcome conflicted goals: the desire to run from him, to collapse into his arms, and the need to destroy him.

"Cass," he says.

It is warm inside, but he still wears his jacket. His hands are deep in his pockets as though he is holding something—a gun, a recording device, more of the toxin? Cass places her jacket on her chair. Ryan doesn't falter.

Before a word is uttered, they have exchanged a thousand accusations, have alleged all manner of betrayal. And yet, they must pretend to speak in a common parlance. They must speak in terms others understand. Perform for the public record. They must act as though their connection is pure, not tainted and brutal. They must play familiar roles, archetypes: he is the contrite lover, the strayed lamb, the remorseful husband. She is the aggrieved wife, the long-suffering widow.

"Take me back," he tells her. "Give me a chance to be better." He grabs her hand and she lets him. And then, as though jolted by the circuit they have created, he unclasps her hand, spins her to him, and grabs her by the shoulders. He moves his hands from her shoulders to her face, as he did in their early courtship. They stare at each other for several moments, searching for trust, answers, predictions. They are like two injured cats, both conditioned by torment, braced for pain at every moment.

Does he love her? Does she love him? Is either one honest in his intentions? As Heisenberg famously asked: Does the act of measuring change the value of the thing being measured? Does the act of pursuing the truth change that which is being detected? Could Cass's efforts to prove his guilt compel Ryan to be *guilty*? Could she force a sincerely repentant man to resume his violence until he has no choice but silence her before she can prove his attempted murder?

As Cass looks into his eyes, she questions whether Ryan is more guileless than she is. That he is here to make things right, that, however horrid he has been, he now has good intentions. The only thing that can trip them up is whether or not she believes him, whether or not she trusts him to stop, and drops her investigation. If she persists in proving her claim, he will have no choice but harm her. And so the act of detection here finds its most bizarre challenge, because the act of measuring intent can greatly impact the outcome. Trust could compel Ryan to be a better man, whereas doubt could force him to give in to his worst nature. A trusting marriage finds new stakes on the age-old issue: happiness or homicide, confidante or killer.

"Let's go away together," he says. "Just us. Just the family. Like we were planning. To heal. To be together."

Cass neither declines nor accepts. She says she will consider. And they part with plans to speak in the coming days in a more private setting.

Cass watches Ryan leave through the restaurant window. He resumes a quicker pace as soon as he is out of earshot, as though he is rushing to make a pressing commitment. As he descends into his car and peels out into the drizzle, Cass cannot shake the feeling that she has just witnessed a brilliant performance, that she, not he, has been taken in, has suspended disbelief for faith in a falsehood, that she has been outsmarted.

The day ends as it often does with Cass alone in her bedroom, the endless chill of the bay beyond seeping in through her window. But tonight, a text arrives that opens like a colorful parachute in the surrounding darkness.

"Cass, I love you. Please give me another chance. Just love. Just love. That's all we have to do. I promise you won't regret it."

Cass cannot help but smile as she reads his message, but there is no room for pleasure now. Smiling, laughter, sweetness. These are frivolities of the past. Luxuries she cannot afford. These are lies, performances. Now she must be impervious, unmoved by emotion. She must maintain her resolve. She must put pleasure and sweetness behind. That life is over. This is her life now. A war in which losing is death and winning is safety for her children.

They meet again the following day. This time in the hotel room where Ryan has been staying, a hotel he seems to frequent. Cass takes some pleasure in the week's reversals, not only her transformation from mouse to cat but from the realm of wife to mistress. The door is ajar when she arrives. Inside, the sound of running water.

"Be right out," he calls out.

She pauses for a moment, sets her bag down, surveys the lush setting. Plump pillows. Cream-colored bedding. Then she lifts her dress over her head, slips her underwear to the floor, unclasps her bra, and walks into the bathroom. She steps into the steaming shower, faces her husband, and guides him toward her. Slowly first, then with increasing force, he thrusts himself inside her, holding on to her ass for balance, leverage, power. Both Ryan and Cass forget themselves for the moment, forget who is predator and who is prey, who is victim and who is aggressor, and instead they are merged in the abject pleasure of bodies that fit together. The pleasure is blinding, as intense as the poison is toxic, and she wonders for a moment if all drugs dance so dangerously between ecstasy and torture, or only just before the dose reaches a fatal level.

Just as quickly as she stepped in, she exits the shower, leaving him breathless and covered with her, slumped against the wall like some sort of dying Greek hero, post-arrow. Satisfied with her decision and its side benefits, she returns to the bedroom and sits down at the edge of the bed in the most proper posture.

"There's a Christmas shindig at work," he says, returning in his towel. "Hors d'oeuvres and ice sculptures."

Cass smiles in spite of herself. "Sounds fun," she says. "I'd love to."

"Good," he says. He lies down next to her. "I'd like you to be there."

She considers now a reason for Ryan's invitation: he wants to be seen with her at this party, wants to be seen in public. He wants a public record of him playing the good husband.

"I apologize in advance," he says. "I gotta put my time in." He puts his arm around her waist, pulls her toward him. "You make me look good," he says. "Looking so sexy in your dress, chatting up those boneheads about their vacations."

"Happy to be of service," she says.

He pulls her down to the bed and wraps his arms around her. She can't deny how good this feels, the perverse pleasure of being captive to her husband.

"Are you going to get your hair done?" he says. His hands are on her tits now.

"Wasn't planning on it," says Cass.

He pins her by the shoulders. "You've been through a lot lately. You deserve to treat yourself, babe. Do you want me to make an appointment?"

Cass pauses now before responding. Suspicion is alight again. Ryan is planning something. "Yeah, you know, maybe I will. I could use a little touch-up."

But whatever she plans to say next, whatever theory, resentment, or intention, is quickly eclipsed by the force of his weight as he pushes himself inside her. And she knows that she knows nothing in the face of this pleasure.

He holds her neck while he fucks her, his fingers curled around the back, his thumbs touching.

"Don't do that," she says.

He does not stop.

"Stop. That hurts. Don't do that."

He moves his hands to the back of her head and massages her temples, making tight circles.

"Ryan, what are you doing?" she says.

"It turns me on while I'm fucking you," he whispers.

"Why are you rubbing my head like that?"

"Cass, please shut up. You're so fucking sexy right now. Be quiet and try to enjoy this."

For the party, she buys a festive silver cocktail dress with a clean neckline. A haircut and highlights work their simple magic on her mood, reminding her of her beauty, and the power that comes with it. With her hair freshly cut and newly golden, her lithe figure displayed by the tailored silver, she looks something like a metallic Christmas ornament. By the end of the morning, she feels a measure of refreshment. And so she is somewhat deflated when she arrives back at home after school pickup to find a small shopping bag on her doorstep—blue tissue paper, black ribbon—and, instead of the usual delight she might feel for an unexpected gift, she feels something altogether different.

She opens the bag to find a sexy silk thing, low back, high neckline.

She holds it up to her body.

"You're so beautiful," it says on the card. "I can't wait to take it off you."

And playing the part—it seems only fair with a gesture like this—she sets aside her own purchase and instead hurries into the shower to change into the dress Ryan envisions.

An hour later, she stands in this dress at Ryan's office party, a surprisingly lavish affair for Portland. She stands alone at the buffet table, the sweat of the meatball caddy blurring her vision. A colleague of Ryan's she has met before approaches. Allen is coming to say hello, or does he simply want his own meatball?

"Hi!" he says. His apparent rush decelerates sharply. "How have you been?" He tilts his head in a way designed to signal something she can't pinpoint.

"Great," she says. "Really well."

"Good," he says. "I'm so happy to hear that. Ryan mentioned you've been going through something."

Cass pauses. What has Ryan told him?

"Thanks." And then, to put him at ease, "It's been a rough patch, but we're muddling through it."

"Nothing to be ashamed of," he says.

"Of course not."

"So many suffer silently," he whispers.

"It's such a shame," she says, "that there has to be such a stigma." What diagnosis did Ryan give her? Mental illness? Cancer?

"Anything we can do to help." He spears a meatball with a toothpick.

"That means a lot," Cass says. *Who is "we"?* she wonders. It's only the two of them talking. Does he have a wife, a husband?

"We have it in our family too," he adds. "Nasty illness with no regard for age or gender."

She nods. "I appreciate your saying that," she said. "Hardship reveals friendship."

He smiles, apparently pleased with how he's handled the situation.

"Have a great time on your trip," she says. "Ryan tells me you're going back to the Amazon. It's so wonderful you spend your own holiday giving back to less fortunate people."

He shrugs, smiles, bashful.

"You guys are amazing." This is what he wants to hear. It's all anyone wants to hear, that he is heads above the average asshole.

"Least we can do," he says. He smiles, looks down, shrugs again, takes a step backward.

Cass is enjoying herself now. "There are two kinds of people in the world. People who run from others' pain and people who run to them. Something tells me you're one of the good ones."

"You would know," he says. He takes another step away, but she is happy to see him go. She wants to find her husband and figure out what lie he has told these people.

Allen smiles again and gives one last look of self-congratulation before he turns and makes a hasty, relieved exit.

Cass scans the room now for her husband. She locates him near the bar, cornered by another man in a suit, likely talking about a surfing trip to benefit the marine creatures. She flinches as the vapor of meatballs wafts upward even while she is chilled by a new realization. Her conversation suggests a wider scope to Ryan's campaign. For the first time since his return, she wonders if she has made a fatal error. They are in a game of cat and mouse. But who is the cat and who is the mouse? He, not she, may have the upper hand now. She considers now that Ryan, ever the planner, has planned for all of this—her missing him, her taking him back, even her plan to prove his crime—and that he has confined her in a straitjacket of her own purchase.

They part ways after the party on their own doorstep. Ryan kisses Cass good night like a high school suitor.

"Can I book the tickets?" he asks.

Cass inhales, demurring.

"It will be good for the kids," he says. "It's good for them to see us make up. To learn that everyone makes mistakes and has the capacity for forgiveness. Besides, I made them a promise. I'd really like to keep it."

Cass pauses. His words are so convincing, but she reminds herself there is no truth in his words, only two incentives. "Okay," she says. "I'll talk to the kids."

He kisses her again. "You won't regret it."

Cass heads back inside alone and relieves Jean, the sitter, then returns to her bedroom, her haven and headquarters. She pulls the sheets up to her neck and recounts the events of the evening. As she lies awake, she is roused by a new vibration, a message on her own phone, a text from her neighbor with an urgent request to do laundry.

"Mind if I come over now?"

She cannot help but feel he is trading on his recent kindness, milking Cass's goodwill, compelling her to return the favor even though the field of reciprocity has already been leveled. She picks up the phone to better understand the nature of his request.

"Rachel is going to kill me if I don't finish her jeans before tomorrow."

"Can you come in the morning?"

"I would," he says. "But that might end my marriage. Unfortunately, she's telling me she needs them for tomorrow."

Cass stares at her phone, considers his insistence. Then, softening, she says, "My husband is weird about laundry too."

"Wouldn't have pegged him for that."

"I thought you knew each other," she says.

"I barely know the guy. We've never even had a full conversation."

She rises reluctantly, leaving the comfort of her bedroom.

Aaron is waiting outside by the time she turns the doorknob. She can't help but feel a pang of concern as he makes himself comfortable inside, dropping two large bins of clothes on the floor and smelling like a plume of marijuana.

"Thanks," he says.

"No problem." She takes some pride in the fact that she has kept her promise, that she has made this a policy, made kindness her religion.

Aaron laughs, then closes his mouth, then laughs again as though responding to a prior statement.

"What?" she says.

"Nothing. It's just . . ." He trails off, reluctant to continue.

She smiles to offer encouragement.

"It's just that, to someone watching, say from a neighbor's window, it might look suspicious, you know. Like *we're* up to something."

Moments pass before Cass understands. She smiles, then frowns, eager to shut down the idea and its visualization.

"We're going away next week," she says. "You can use the washer while we're out of town. Maybe I'll just give you keys and you can watch the place while we're gone. Water the plants. Feed the cat." She pauses, feeling suddenly guilty that she has turned a selfless act into something with a kickback.

"Where are you going?" he says. He seems not to have registered this as an imposition.

"Same place we usually go. To the beach. Just the family."

"Sounds like a fun vacation." The sarcasm is blatant.

"I'm looking forward to it," she says.

"I wouldn't want to be in *your* bedroom."

Cass issues a look designed to convey several things to Aaron: the conversation has gone too far, well beyond her comfort level, and the relationship has gained a level of intimacy she no longer wants and never intended.

"Look, I just don't get it," he says. "Last week, you were telling me this man was trying to kill you. Now you're going away with him on some cozy beach vacation."

"With all due respect," Cass says, "it's really none of your business."

"Look, I get that," Aaron says. "Like I said, I'm just your weird neighbor. But neighbors aren't neighbors if they don't speak up. When I see something that's not right, I can't sit by in silence."

Cass looks at Aaron with new awareness. She knows it is her fault he feels entitled to an opinion. She ostensibly consented to this when she went to him for help and shared so many details of a private situation. This knowledge—and frustration—compels her to share an even greater confidence.

"I'm faking him out, if you must know."

"Excuse me?"

"Collecting a war chest."

"What are you talking about?"

"Proof of the crime, witnesses, physical evidence."

"Oh, wow," he says, "I get it now. How Hitchcock of you. How incredibly romantic."

His sneer, Cass now realizes, is not the sneer of disapproval. It is the sneer of jealousy, a man who has developed feelings, the strength of which neither he nor she realized until this minute. But Cass understands the perils of desire better than anything, far better than the perils of friendship. Every woman knows what happens in the next instant: the moment when a man's desire turns to shame, how shame turns to rage, and how quickly rage, unexpressed, turns to violence. With this in mind, she changes her tone and redirects the conversation, trying to impart, in the same breath, both compassion and distance.

"Better get the laundry in," she says. She starts up the stairs, heading to the washer and dryer.

Aaron follows her up the stairs, subdued. The energy between them has changed from the easy rapport of two friends to something more like child and parent. They stand in silence in the laundry room while he empties the first bin of clothes into the washer and Cass, by default or instinct, helps him sort his whites and colors. Something about this simple act, sorting laundry with a man in a quiet house after midnight, instills trust again between them, dulling Cass's concerns with the sense that her mind has a broken circuit.

"I need you to do something for me," she says. It is a concession, a request for renewed confidence between them. She says this before she can weigh the costs and benefits of her question.

"Anything." He pours detergent into her machine, as though this is his home and she is the neighbor, or as though she is the wife and he is the husband.

"I need you to put cameras in my house," she says. "You know. Those cheap ones you can get now. So I can watch the house while we're away. I think you can buy them anywhere now. Tiny cameras to monitor your house. So I can watch what's going on from the privacy of my cell phone. I think this woman, the bogus nanny, is going to come into my house to do something for my husband, and I need to prove it. Is that possible?" she says.

"Anything's possible." He stares at her for a long moment. "Why would you take him back?" he says finally. "If you don't trust him." This is as much a plea as it is an assertion. "Why not spare the stress and expense and throw the bastard out of the house? There's no camera in the world that can protect you from this kind of trust issue."

"On the off chance that he's innocent," she says. "And the likelihood that he's guilty."

"Which is it?" says Aaron.

"I'm not entirely sure," she says. It may be the first honest thing Cass has said in weeks.

He stares at her intensely, then shakes his head in resignation.

Cass turns away and places his wife's jeans in the dryer. He puts his hand on her hand. She looks up, surprised, shaken.

"Delicate," he says.

"What?" A million possibilities occur to her in this moment.

"Delicate for denim."

Cass nods and exhales, understanding his cryptic assertion. Aaron seems to have made a choice, reconciled a trade-off. He will take Cass's credit card number, will do this favor for her, purchasing and installing cameras to monitor the movements in the house, any intruder or shadow, until the Connors are back home, safely returned from paradise.

TWENTY-ONE

School gets out on Thursday at noon for the holiday vacation. Cass meets the kids outside and greets them with a surprising announcement.

"Remember that trip we were talking about?"

"Yes," says Alice. "What about it?"

"I think we may go after all."

Pete bursts into spontaneous applause. Alice studies her mother.

"Are we going to the reef?" Pete asks. He is nearly shouting.

"I thought we'd go back to the Dunmore. We're due for a little sunshine. And some of those chocolate milk shakes."

"When would we leave?" Alice asks. She pauses, watching her mother.

"After Christmas," Cass says. "We'll go for a week and stay for New Year's Eve."

"Can I stay up till midnight?" Pete asks.

"I'll think about it," Cass says.

Alice continues to scrutinize her mother. She knows there's something more to this. Intuition, after all, is a trait shared by mother and daughter.

"Ryan would like to come," Cass says.

Alice's face wrinkles in confusion. The mixed relief and dread of confirmed expectations.

"Are you getting back together?" says Pete.

"No," says Cass. "No, we're not. But we'll always be tied to him because of Sam. And he says he wants to apologize, be a better man, and keep his promise."

Alice gives her mother a withering look. She is torn between misgiving and desire, torn between yearning for the past and her memory of Ryan's exit. Understandably, she is vexed by these conflicting feelings.

Cass meets her daughter's gaze. Her concerns are valid and Cass knows this. She understands the risks of what she is undertaking, but feels it is the only way to achieve long-term safety.

Pete bounds ahead to the car, determined to get home and start packing.

Soon enough, they are all consumed by the excitement of travel. On the car ride home, the kids devolve into talk of their beloved tropical haven, who will ride shotgun, which bathing suits and books to pack, whether this year they will surf or snorkel, and a heated debate over the merits of the vanilla versus the chocolate milk shake. They are the picture of a functioning family again—loving, fighting, reconciling, staying together. The picture, at least, on the surface.

At home, Cass makes a call. A precaution for the vacation.

"Hi, this is Cass Connor," she says. "We're so looking forward to our visit. Just wanted to confirm we have two separate rooms. In the main house." A pause. "Yes, five. Two twins will work well for the kids. And a queen and a crib in the other."

Once again, she questions the wisdom of agreeing to this trip with Ryan, but the risk of continued dismissal is too great, and the need for proof too crucial. They will be buttressed by the earshot of so many respectable vacationers. For now, she must rely on the safety of numbers.

It is late now, and Cass does her rounds as resident lamp-snuffer. She works silently in the children's rooms, choosing and setting their clothes in a pile, hauling shirts and shorts to the laundry room, locating swimming suits and sun hats, toothpaste and sunscreen, running the loads of laundry for a week's worth of clothing, placing her own and the kids' clothes in one large suitcase. The simplicity of the task calms her racing mind—grasping all they will need for the week, placing it in one container. Shorts, shirts, socks, shoes, bathing suits, sunscreen, diapers, books, crayons. This is her job, and completing it gives her purpose.

Cass walks into Alice's bedroom and sees that she is awake and restless. She sits down on her daughter's bed and runs her fingers through her hair, trying to restore her sense of comfort, but Alice is not consolable. She has a question for her mother.

"Mommy, what happened to Marley?" she says.

Cass pauses, unsure how to answer. She wants to reward her daughter for asking, commend her for knowing, but she doesn't want her to be scared, does not want to share things that a child should and could not fathom. "I just didn't think she was right," she says.

"I didn't like her, Mom. There was something weird about her."

"Yes," says Cass. She runs her hands through her daughter's hair, this time pausing with her palm on her forehead, as though she can take the worries from her mind simply by keeping her hand there. "What did she do that was weird?" She cannot resist the question.

"Just something about her," Alice says. "The way she kept bragging about her tattoos."

"That was a little annoying."

"And the way she kept trying to get me to do things I told her I wasn't allowed to. One day she tried to make me drink tea she said she got from her boyfriend."

"What do you mean?" Cass says. "Why didn't you tell me this sooner?"

"Because I told her we're not allowed to drink tea. And I kept telling *her* that, but she kept trying to get me to do it."

Cass takes a sharp breath. "You didn't drink it, did you?"

"No, of course not," Alice says. "I know we're not allowed to, so I got a little suspicious. And then, when she made us dinner, I didn't want to eat it, but Pete was really hungry."

"Alice." Cass takes another sharp breath. She does not want to appear frantic. "Did this really happen?"

"Yes," says Alice, "but don't worry. I made sure he didn't."

"How?"

Alice smiles, covers her mouth. "By putting hot sauce in it."

"You're kidding."

"Nope." She chuckles, unsure if she is due for praise or reprimand.

Cass exhales. "I'm proud of you, Alice."

"Why?"

"You did something awesome."

Alice is beaming now.

"Not only did you protect yourself, you also protected your brother."

"You said I should speak up if I ever think I'm in danger."

"That's right, sweetheart. You listened to your gut. You used your brain and your courage."

"Do *you* do that?"

Cass pauses. Her daughter is too smart for her. She hears this as it was intended, as a critique and a reminder. "My job is to protect you. That's my only purpose."

"And yourself," says Alice.

"Yes, and myself, but you don't have to worry about me. I'm strong and self-sufficient. It's the same thing your teachers tell you in school. If someone treats you badly on the playground, you tell them not to. And if they don't listen, then . . . ?"

"Then you tell the teacher."

A pause, as though all is solved, certain.

"But what if the teacher doesn't help?"

Cass takes her time now. This answer will be remembered. "When you can't count on the authority whose job it is to protect you, then you have a problem. At that point, you enlist your friends, your neighbors, strangers. You form a chorus. You lean on these people for the power of their eyes as witnesses and their hearts for support. And no matter what, you call for help—you yell the moment you feel you're in danger."

"*Was* I in danger?"

Cass pauses. This time, the pause is conspicuous. "You're safe now, sweetheart. That's all that matters." It is a clumsy dodge, but she feels it is the right one. She lowers her cheek to her daughter's cheek, attempts to impart all her love and strength through simple osmosis, and stops for one last kiss on her forehead. Then she stands. Alice needs to sleep. The day ahead will be exhausting. She kisses her plump little cheek once again and tiptoes across the bedroom.

"But what if you don't know?" Alice whispers. She has questions, and she wants answers. "What if you think you're in danger, but you're not? And you get someone in trouble. Or what if you are and you don't call out and the bad person gets away with something awful?"

Cass stands in the middle of the room, arrested by her daughter's fear, immobilized by her questions. She takes her time before she speaks. She knows she needs to give a very definitive answer.

"We all know about the boy who cried wolf. No one helped him when he needed it. And, as you say, waiting too long can be a recipe for disaster. So, if you're in doubt, the best thing to do is take ten deep breaths and get very quiet."

"Stay quiet?"

"Not *stay* quiet. *Get* quiet. Quiet for a moment. Quiet enough to listen to your gut, listen to your surroundings. Quiet so that when you speak, you say exactly what you mean and speak very clearly. I want to make myself clear: I am not advising silence. Never silence. You must speak up always. What I'm saying is take a deep breath first and then choose your moment. Time is information. The more information you have, the more likely you are to take the best action."

"But waiting can be dangerous."

Cass nods. The statement is chilling. "That's true, sweetheart."

"And how do you know which is which? Crying wolf or calling for help when you need it?"

"You don't, sweetheart. You don't always know."

"So how do you decide?" asks Alice.

"When your gut tells you," says Cass. "It will be clear. And when it is, you yell, 'Fire!'"

The sound of footsteps rustles in the darkness near the washer. A doe-eyed child, drunk with sleep, stumbles toward his mother. The commotion of his sister's fear, this late-night lesson, has stirred Pete from his dreams, sparing him from his own nightmares. He makes his way across the room and climbs into bed with his sister.

"Okay, you two."

"Where are you going?" says Pete.

Cass takes in the sight of her two strong, sizable children, nestled into a twin bed, enormous and yet still tiny. "I'm not going anywhere."

And before she has made a conscious choice, she joins them in their cramped twin bed and crumples herself in between her two oldest children, arms laced around each other, a mother and her kittens.

One last email demands her attention before sleep relieves her:

I've consulted a lawyer, and it's legal for you, as an owner of the building, to install cameras for your own safety. But I want something in exchange. A few hours of your time when you get back. Uninterrupted. Just you and me. To talk sense into you. Whether or not you stay with this guy, you've gotta admit he's messing with your head. As your friend, I want to spend some time talking with no distractions about the wisdom of staying in what I have come to believe is a very destructive and dangerous relationship.

Before she can go to sleep, one last act of preparation. Unpacking, more than packing. She cannot bring Ryan's phone. Too risky when he is so close to her and she is so close to knowing. No need for a crystal ball. Prophecy is both a curse and an asset. Cass takes the phone from its place under her mattress and walks upstairs to find a better place to stash it. She paces the hall for a moment before deciding on the best option and then places Ryan's phone in a dark, unreachable crevice behind the washer and dryer. It is a perfect hiding place, as one thing is for sure: Ryan has never done his own laundry.

TWENTY-TWO

Vacations are like medicine, working their magic even before the dose is ingested. The prospect of being secluded together for several days away from home, away from other families and distractions, cinches around the family like a belt, making them tighter and smaller. Brother and sister reinvent their notions of one another, reconsider the idea that they are stuck with an ally as opposed to the usual opponent. Husband and wife, too, are paired up, forced to reckon with the perks and price of their privacy and isolation. The Connors are headed to their favorite place, poised for sunshine, sand, and surf, and all the giddy promises that come with them: health, healing, and restoration.

In the airport, the kids huddle around their parents in a state of tweaked excitement. Cass does the mental math that parents do in a crowd, counting the children in her sight, calculating possible hazards, predicting suddenly closing doors, unexpected falling objects, and potential outside intruders. A last stockpile of candy, magazines, and sundry useless items, and then it is time to sprint down the terminal, cram into line to board the plane, and walk into the blinding maw of the jet bridge to begin their adventure.

Cass stares out the window and focuses on the sound of the engine. Pete and Alice sit on one side of the aisle, immersed in their snacks and headphones. Ryan and Cass are on the other side with Sam in Cass's lap. Ryan has borrowed a marker from the kids. He is also busily drawing.

Cass thinks back to the last time Ryan was in their home. It has been nearly one month since he slept in their bedroom, ate with the family at the dinner table, but he seems oblivious to the time that has passed since then.

"Please give me a chance to be better. A chance to finish the home we built together."

She nearly laughs out loud at the absurdity of his pretense. Then again, is she any better? They are both excellent actors.

"This is what we should do with the kitchen," he says.

He hands her a piece of paper. He is back in his obsession, demolishing and reconstructing, moving the stove, the toilet, the tub in infinite permutations. This is her husband, Ryan, the trained architect, the self-taught scientist, this grown-up dreamer, the builder and destroyer of the home they'd planned to share forever. He could teach himself anything: fix the tired plumbing, rewire all the fraying cables, cook a meal for twenty, lace it with poison. Could he teach himself to be happy again? Could he teach himself to love her?

As though in answer to this question, Cass feels a resurgence of symptoms. A powerful force splits her in half, sending an electrical current to her head from her fingers. Her hand convulses as though she has invited voltage into her mouth and her body has formed a closed circuit. She thrusts the paper from her hands before she understands the impulse. Her body has rejected it because it contains the substance. The paper is saturated with the poison. Or is it only her perception that is tainted? Seconds are long in this state. Seconds become minutes. Minutes blend into hours. But she has little sense anymore of the quantity of these units. Time is just another thing at the mercy of her beliefs, subject to her warped senses. The baby is crying now and needs her attention. He sits, facing her, on her lap, trying to get her attention. Ryan is standing above, asking her if she is all right. Her mouth is moving, but she cannot speak. He looks worried. It is entirely impossible to tell if he is sincere or if this is a performance.

"What happened to you, Cass?" he says.

She shakes her head and waits for words to join the lips that form them. "Not feeling well," she says. This is all she can manage.

"It's okay, babe," he says. "It's all okay. I'm here now." And then, as though in explanation, "We're all together." He extends his hand to her. She withholds hers on instinct. He smiles. The smile is loving, patient. Once again, she reminds herself why she has taken him back, embraced this violent person. This was her only option: to engage in this dangerous game, to collect the proof of his guilt and get this psycho locked away before he takes her life or her children's. Breathing deeply, she takes his hand. Or she thinks she does this. Reaching for his hand is the last thing she remembers.

When she regains composure, she is sitting at the gate in a different airport. She has lost time or lost her family or lost herself. One or all of the above is equally possible.

"You okay now, honey?" he says. Ryan is blurry. Ryan is getting closer. Ryan is circling. No, he is standing in the middle of the luggage carousel and, much thanks to Einstein, he appears to be revolving around her, as opposed to standing still in the middle of the luggage conveyor.

"Where are we?" she asks him now.

She hears Alice's worried voice. "Are you okay, Mom?"

"Everything is fine," he says. "You need rest, Cass. We're going to get you better." He says this in a loud, clear voice, as though for the public record. And then, in a lower voice, he adds, "Try not to look so upset. You look like you've been abducted. Someone might report me. And you're scaring the children."

She stares at him with knowledge now, knowledge and intention. Cass is done with doubt, doubt in herself and her perceptions. Cass is weakened, but she knows the truth of action and reaction, the truth of causal connections. She knows how she felt when she got in the car, how she felt when she entered the airport. She knows how it feels when the toxin enters through her skin and swirls through her bloodstream. She knows how she felt when she got on the plane, how she felt after he handed her the piece of paper. She knows how she felt when he held out his hand, that she hesitated to accept it. She knows what came before and what happened immediately after.

It may be true that she has ingested so much that she is compromised in her perception, so confused about right and wrong, action and reaction, that she has invited this threat, this malignant, evil person into the confines of her haven, but she has not lost the faculties of her senses, the ability to see, to taste, to touch, to feel, to know the difference between health and sickness, between calmness and convulsions, between her old self and the new creature she is becoming.

She looks at him with loathing now. The glare does not escape detection.

"Ouch," he says. "Some thanks for the guy who's taking you on vacation."

They wait for a second plane now, a puddle jumper from the mainland to the smaller island. Cass tries to still the feeling that the ground is shifting, as though she is on the plane already, not waiting for its departure. She tries again to focus on the faces of her children. They look contented in a way that soothes her slightly. Their gait already evidences the healing power of travel, a respite from the stresses of school and the hazards of the home environment. Alice and Pete are busy with a cutthroat game of spit. The baby is doing his best to join, sporadically removing and replacing cards much to the chagrin of his brother and sister.

The contrast between the jet and the commuter airline is immediately apparent as it rattles down the runway and launches into the sky as though it has been thrown there. Clouds rise like steam from a cup of coffee, clouds so welcoming as to invite passengers to reach their hands out the window as though they are sitting in a car, driving eighty on the highway, not cruising at an altitude of five thousand feet in a plane the size and make of an old jalopy. Now they are surrounded by blue, blue in every direction. Light blue, baby blue, powder blue, clear blue, cornflower blue, teal, turquoise, aquamarine, navy, and purple, blue so mesmerizing that they barely notice the sea and the dunes rising from underneath like naked drowned women.

Much to Cass's surprise, they land safely at the second airport. Now it is time for the journey's last leg, the challenges of which add to the travelers' sense of a well-deserved destination. The hotel is on a small exterior island, a spot of land just off the northeast coast, connected by a jetty at low tide, accessible by boat at high tide. The island is etched by a dirt road that runs the perimeter with a couple of cuts across it. Visitors welcome the fact that it can be traversed only on foot or in the occasional golf cart owned by the hotels and locals.

A boat must cross a busy bay that spills from the body of water they have just traveled. The boat is a small and sturdy thing that looks like a storybook tug, weighed down by the luggage of its travelers and manned by a captain who appears to be more interested in the waves than his passengers.

They arrive at the Dunmore at dinnertime, sedated and exhausted. The hotel has earned its role as cherished family destination, not only because of the chocolate milkshakes for which Alice would travel any distance but because of its understated elegance, because it is both beautiful and unadorned, and because it has earned the hallowed role of family tradition.

The hotel is owned and run by a stylish young couple—he cooks and she oversees the business. Every meal is served family-style on a chic bohemian terrace that overlooks a beach with rose-tinted sand, carved from the pink rubble of the coral reefs that surround them. The charming plantation-style house is a modest bric-a-brac mansion, filled with Moroccan tiles, fading Parisian sofas, and eclectic, colorful paintings that look like Gauguin could have painted them during his early training. The house is set in a band of beach with sand soft enough for building castles and long enough to run on, that casts an ever-changing kaleidoscope of rose and golden light depending on the sun's angle. It is, in turns, stirring and tranquil.

Cass stops to greet the hosts and exchange a cordial catch-up. She struggles to project her usual grace, but she has a more pressing problem.

"Great news!" says Claude. She smiles with delight. "You'll be happy to know that one of the cabanas opened up."

"No," Cass says too quickly. "I reserved two rooms in the main house."

"I know," says Claude. "But we had a cancellation this morning. And I remembered how much you loved the privacy of the cabanas."

"Claude, that's very kind of you," says Cass, "but we couldn't. Really."

"We insist." She smiles, enjoying her largesse, then adds, "Gratis. It's wonderful to have you back."

"Really, we prefer the main house." Cass is visibly unnerved by the change of venue. She had counted on the safeguard of public witness, the proximity of earshot.

But Ryan quickly intervenes, apologizes for Cass's brusqueness, explaining to their hosts in hushed tones that Cass has not been well of late and that the trip is designed to restore her nerves and temper. "The cabana will be perfect."

"You make me sound like some sort of convalescing Victorian lady," she says as they wander toward the cabana. "The ones they stashed in attics and found crawling around, sickened by the wallpaper."

"If the shoe fits," Ryan says.

"Ryan," says Cass.

But he darts ahead before she can protest, hoisting the baby to his hip, throwing his shoes off playfully, and disappearing down the sandy stairs that lead to the ocean. Alice and Pete peel off as well, scouring the resort for familiar faces. Cass exhales as they and Ryan peel off in opposite directions.

Cass finds their cabana and collapses into the new surroundings. It is a small two-room house on the beach with one room for the grown-ups and one for the children. It is close enough to the main hotel to facilitate every convenience, but far enough to afford the privacy for a couple to reconnect, for a family to fortify their bond, or, as the case may be, for a husband to murder his wife without an eyewitness. A wrought iron four-poster bed anchors the master bedroom. The walls are painted a bold shade of cobalt blue, and the sheets are a sumptuous combination of tufted white cotton and fruit-colored rattan linens. The second room has been set up as a children's nursery and playroom. Two twin beds draped with mosquito nets flank a crib in the middle. An extra cot stands at the ready for fort-building or last-minute sleepover guests. It is paradise for a family, except for the fact that all of them have vacated the premises.

A text arrives on Cass's phone. She knows the sender before she reads it. Subject heading is the usual fare, like a teenager playing the role of trusted confidante in a spy caper.

It begins, "Re: Surveillance."

"They're in," writes Aaron.

"Copy," writes Cass. Just to indulge him.

"I set your password for you," he writes. "Just type in your email. The password is: Santos."

"Thanks," she says.

"Password hint: lab where it all started."

"Cool," she writes. She does not mean it. She wants to end the conversation.

"Pretty soon you should be getting a live feed from your kitchen, bedroom, and basement whenever motion is detected. Let me know when it's working."

"Thanks," she says. She is relieved. She has been thorough, proactive. Perhaps she will catch something incriminating, a visit from a suspicious party—Marley rifling through her belongings, planting something in her bedroom.

A theory is starting to gel about Marley and Ryan's collaboration. Marley was a plant, her application scripted by Ryan, the details carefully crafted to match Cass and Ryan's child-care needs and parental aspirations. Hence, Ryan's vicious attack on the previous person, and his demand for her immediate replacement. Their goal in placing her in the house had two central intentions: one, to contaminate Cass's food, and two, to make false witness testimony about Cass's behavior had they succeeded in her murder. Marley would describe the fragile mental state of a "suicidal" woman, the mood swings, the tears, the deterioration. The dutiful nanny, questioned by the cops long before the autopsy. No need to question the husband when the death is deemed a suicide.

The hotel room has the particular echo of a room with only one person in it, but with the continued reverberation of people recently speaking. The children's shoes are peppered across the floor, along with their scattered plane clothes. Their bag has been hastily unzipped, stripped of its essentials— bathing suits, flip-flops, beach towels. Cass walks to the window, scans the beach in all directions. She can just make out a gangly leg, sprinting into her periphery, a shock of orange (Pete) and red (Alice) swimsuits moving toward the water en masse with a gaggle of other independent-minded children. But no sign of Ryan or the baby. They are out of view and earshot. Cass leaves the room and sets out for the beach, barefoot. The heat of clay tiles on the patio—and then the hot sand in her toes—helps to ground her to the earth, but instead of the usual relief, she feels increasingly alien.

Moving quickly toward the water, she surveys her environs. She scans the pink sand and the blue surf, her eyes a roving searchlight. As her eyes adjust to the sun, she can just make out patches of color in a pixelated daydream. Pink sand, white noise, shocks of red on the bathing suits of women and children, and the hypnotic blue of the vast Atlantic Ocean. Families, people in repose, commune with nature. This is what sunshine does to the brain. This is why people need water. Now she locates Alice and Pete, skittering up to the edge of the surf, stopping before the white part. These are her beloved children. They observe her rules even at a distance. But still no sign of Sam or Ryan. She calls their names without luck. He said he was going down to the beach. Where could he have disappeared to so quickly?

With new alarm, she leaves the beach and heads back to the main house. She traverses the grounds, the wind-worn stairs that rise from the sand, the freshly mowed grass that surrounds the main house, the dusty road that approaches. Her husband and her baby are in none of these places. Not in the lobby of the main house. Not on the green lawn that surrounds the hotel. Not on the hazy dirt road on which they arrived less than an hour ago. Cass grows increasingly perturbed as she scours the hotel grounds. After one more lap, she is frantic. She hurries back toward the beach to collect Pete and Alice, but as her feet meet the sand and she trudges toward her children, she faces, to her great surprise, the objects of her search, her baby and her husband. They sit on the beach in the very place she just recently circled, a bird's hop from their cabana, not thirty feet from their window. Ryan and Sam are so busy that they barely notice her arrival. They are hard at work on a sand castle, pouring, molding, constructing. The castle, however, is decidedly rough, more of a favela than a fort, as though it was constructed hastily with one or two dumps of a bucket to stand in for evidence, albeit shoddy, of the time they have been working.

"Where were you?" she says. Her tone is tight with worry and accusation.

"What do you mean?" Ryan smiles. His smile is bright and oblivious with a hint of outrage—indignation at her indignation.

"I've been looking for you two," Cass says. "Where were you?"

"We were right here."

"No, you weren't. I just walked by here."

"Look." He points to the sand castle, as though it ends all further debate, as though the crumbling tower is irrefutable evidence of the time they have accrued there. "We've been sitting here, playing this whole time." And then, the masterful shifting of blame. "We were waiting for you. You must have just missed us."

"No," she says. "I walked by here at least three times in the last twenty minutes."

Ryan exhales slowly, a struggle to expel frustration. "Did you expect us to sit in the hotel room? Would you like us *all* to go crazy? Try to unwind, Cass. That brain of yours needs to think less."

Cass does not respond. She is beset by confusion—and the certainty that her husband is lying, actively trying to debunk valid observations, working to cause her to distrust her own senses. Is it possible she was so engrossed in her search that she walked right past him? No, it is not. He is simply continuing his campaign to cause her to disavow her trust in herself, to doubt her own perceptions. In a sense, this is a separate crime, the assault on her confidence, the batteries on her self-respect, the theft of her instincts. What is a person who has been robbed of the power of her own convictions? A fool, a freak, a madwoman? If she acts like a freak and sounds like a freak . . . is she any different from the thing he calls her? No, she needs to focus now, to double down on her convictions, to refine her blurry but emerging understanding of his method, weapon, and intention.

"I need to lie down," she says. "Can you watch Sam for an hour?"

"Yes," says Ryan. "That's a great idea. Take as long as you need, babe. We're here for you, Cass. For you to get your health back."

He is a Method actor now, continuing his performance even after the camera stops. This performance is not for their audience, but rather for Cass and himself.

"Thanks," she says. She kisses the baby on both cheeks, inhales the smell of sunscreen. He is busy with his castle and barely notices her departure.

Cass hurries back to the room, struggles to regain composure. On her way, she stops again at the gaggle of older kids, issues reminders for more sunscreen and distance from the surf, to please be back by five to change, and more kisses to Pete and Alice. The sand is hot in between her toes, and her shoulders already feel burned. She notes these two reminders of her corporal presence as she opens the door to their room. The last thing she remembers is grasping the doorknob. Moments or minutes or hours later, she wakes up, facedown on the bed, her children traipsing back into the room, waking her to join them for dinner. He has expanded his target from her food, to her body, to surfaces.

They are sitting on the patio of the main house, waiting for dinner. Cass looks at the triangular tiles she admired upon arrival, only the patterns within each tile seem to be pulsating at the same rate as her heart. She is focused on the strangest things, but what is strange seems normal. Normal things seem peculiar, tinged with the indescribable silver tint of nightmares, cuing the subconscious brain that something bad could happen at any minute. She is doing her best to appear unchanged so as not to worry the children, watching Ryan's hands for evidence of sudden movement, for interference with the waiter, for placement of his toxin. But just watching, knowing, is not enough. She must prove it beyond a shadow of doubt, must find another witness. It is testament to how weakened she is that all of this seems normal, that a mother could spend a meal in this way, surrounded by her children, guarding her plate from potential attack by a homicidal husband.

They have nearly finished eating, a festive meal of sole, string beans, and mashed potatoes, when Cass witnesses the method. His right hand rests on the table or gestures in conversation. His left hand leaves the table and descends, first onto his lap and then into his left pocket. His left hand returns to the table just as dessert is passed. Dessert is a rich chocolate cake in a decadent crème anglaise sauce. As the plates are placed by the waiter, the kids commence their commotion. And Ryan, in the midst of this chaos, lifts his left hand over one plate—sprinkles powder as fine as salt—then hands Cass her slice of cake, the powder mixing easily into the viscous liquid.

She has no choice, she decides, but accept the plate and test her theory. How else can she know for sure if what she has come to believe is a fact or fiction? Should she willingly ingest poison if only to corroborate her theory, to cloak herself in the shadow of doubt, to meet the burden of proof she will face when she brings charges to cops, to a court of law against her own husband? Moments later, she has her answer: doubled over in her seat, nausea rising from her gut, body crumpled over in pain, fingers twitching as though to the beat of some Satanic drummer.

"Mom, what's wrong?" says Alice.

Pete studies his mother.

"I'm fine," she says and smiles. "Just ate too much chocolate."

Suspicion crystallizes now into revelation. He has made himself a living weapon, a kamikaze soldier. He is knowingly exposing himself to the substance, personally delivering it like a snake delivering venom, but he will stop just before his own intoxication reaches dangerous levels. His goal is to transfer poison gram by gram, ounce by ounce, until she reaches fatal levels, delivering the weapon in food, in drinks, in clothes, on surfaces, and, when necessary, by hand, on his own person. She thinks back to her research on one particular substance. Arsenic heals before it harms. Was used for wellness before it was used as a weapon. Arsenic, she remembers, is especially adept at dermal absorption and functions on a bell curve, treating the body to a speedy hit before it reaches diminishing returns and becomes a deadly cocktail. But Ryan is not one to spare drama in his adventures. His plan is to hold Cass's hands and run with her to the edge of a cliff and then, just then, as balance fails, to shove her over the rocky crag and let gravity do the work for him.

Somehow, in her dawning vision, Cass feels something like admiration. Leave it to Ryan to invent a new recipe for murder. A poisoner's handbook for killing your wife. Leave no trace whatsoever. Destroy her credibility meanwhile, immunize the poisoner to the reports of his victim so that her cries for help fall on deaf ears and, better yet, compound to damn her further. The recipe calls for one woman and a long, slow preparation. Place her in a cooling relationship for at least three years. Marinate with sweetness that tenderizes—sugar and salt in equal parts, equal parts kisses and tears. Then add salt to the sting of your wounds. Soak your woman in promises, dangle these above her head and hold just out of reach. Spice with generous helpings of rage—extra spicy for those who can bear it. Season with splashes of terror. Et voilà. A masterful recipe with the simplest of ingredients.

It is dark now, and Cass is disoriented. She is amped by the impact of his latest attack, her latest ingestion, her "voluntary" consumption. She will not feel coherent again until she is lying in bed later that night with Ryan mounting her from behind, opening her for his pleasure. Cass tries to shove him off as he lifts her from her stomach to her knees and begins rubbing circles into the skin behind her ears and on her temples.

"Stop!" she says. She pushes him off, but he doubles down on her.

"Cass, please be quiet."

"Ryan, please. Stop doing that!"

"Oh, baby, you're so hot right now. Please don't ruin this also."

Every time is the same. Every time is different. She tries to focus on the facts so as to report the details. She must be a journalist now, accurate and objective. She imagines while he is fucking her how she will describe it. The feeling that something foreign has entered her body, that her body must reject it. The nausea curling up her throat. The body's reflexive effort to expel, the electric nature of the convulsion. The amped, jittery quality in her brain, the vaguely silver hue around her. Every time is the same. Every time is different. Every time it is worse. Is it because she is getting sicker, or because experience is worsened by anticipation? Or because the poison in her body is approaching fatal levels?

Cass wakes later that night, breathless and sweating. She stands from the bed and clutches her phone, fumbles for information.

She finds several unopened emails, each one demanding her attention:

"Movement has been detected in your bedroom," it announces. The alarming headline is followed by an equally unnerving display. The fuzzy black-and-white image thickens from pixels to a solid. And now, an image of her bedroom, exactly as she left it, but for one fluffy orange cat, striding across the bed with all the pride of a Bengal tiger.

Another text interrupts Cass's surveillance. A new message from Aaron, as though he has somehow rigged her phone to alert him whenever she is opening her email. Is he getting these alerts also? His typically annoying subject heading has advanced from "Hey" to "Hey, you" to "Hey, I'm worried about you." She wishes there were a special chute for friendships you no longer want, for relationships you have come to find more troublesome than rewarding.

"See anything yet?"

"Nope, just the cat. She seems to be enjoying the run of the place."

"Cool," he writes. "Glad it's working."

"Thanks again for setting it up."

He responds with a smiley face, cementing Cass's annoyance. Emoticons should be outlawed, she feels, particularly for men over forty.

In her groggy state, she tries to assemble a log of each attack she remembers.

1. coffee
2. lobster roll
3. champagne
4. neck
5. dress
6. paper
7. cake
8. neck

She rereads it and scoffs, imagining a cop's response. Is there a better word for this? Assaults? Batteries? Drugging? Dosing? Assault with a chemical weapon? She thinks back to what the cop said. "I don't even think we have a code for this one."

Another email from Aaron arrives. The subject heading pisses her off even before she reads the content. "Subject: Re: Confirmation bias."

The email includes a link to an article on the concept. She clicks it, as requested. "When you have a hammer, everything is a nail," begins the writer. The subtitle of the article is "You're Not as Smart as You Think You Are." It goes on to present various examples of bogus or circuitous logic, in which a person who is overly motivated by a theory, goal, or expectation arrives at false conclusions, finds problems that do not exist, or misdiagnoses benign concerns with false positives—or worse, malignant findings. To wit: people seeking advice from psychics, wives looking for proof of cheating husbands, or doctors running tests on an otherwise healthy patient.

She scans the article quickly with growing resentment. She replies in a text. "Why the sudden change of heart? Please stop trying to dissuade me."

He writes back quickly. "I'm just trying to point out alternative explanations."

"Please don't," she writes. "I know what's he's done. I just need to prove it."

"Then what?" he writes.

"Then I go back to the cops. And I stay there until they listen."

"I don't think you should do that."

"Why not?"

"The cops will do one of two things: laugh at you or arrest you."

A pause and then an email arrives with another inscrutable heading: "Re: Dr. Lugner." Followed by an impassioned plea to consider the referral for a shrink in downtown Portland who specializes in "negative fixations" and, Aaron says as a final plug, "at the very least, might be someone who can help you work out why you are entrenched in such an unhealthy relationship."

Enraged, Cass signs off without ending the conversation. The doctor's name is familiar, but she is too put off by his sudden flip-flop—and his insulting suggestion—for any further consideration.

One last Google search before she allows herself a reprieve from the night's investigation.

"Space behind the ears," she types. "Temples. Neck. Absorption through skin."

And after a flurry of photos of various Jewish, Buddhist, and Roman temples, she finds something more relevant. Confirmation bias is a bitch. So is poison.

"Jugular vein," she reads. Followed by the definition. "One of the largest blood vessels in the neck that transports blood from the head to the heart. This vein runs from behind the ears down the neck and up to the temples. It is often used for injection or topical application of medications because it drains directly into the heart, allowing for the most expedient delivery of medication to the major organs." And then, the chilling addendum: "External jugular cannulation is the injection or topical application of fluids, medications, nutrition, or chemotherapy into a patient. It is an integral part of modern medicine, practiced in every health-care setting for rapid dissemination."

She closes her computer, sufficiently riled by this information.

Desperate for respite from the day, the nausea, the confusion, Cass walks to the bathroom and turns on the shower. She stands under the faucet, grateful for a familiar sensation, grateful for the simple connection between action and reaction. Hot water runs down her back. She wraps herself in a towel, embracing the comfort of the soft cloth against her shoulders. She sits on the bed, then lies on her back at a right angle to her husband and falls asleep next to Ryan, still in her towel, clutching her pillow as though it is a life preserver.

Nausea wakes Cass in the morning, nausea so intense it propels her from bed with its own momentum. She stumbles to the bathroom, knocking over a stack of clothes, tripping over the suitcase, leaving a trail of neon shirts and bathing suits that look like spilled jelly beans. She collapses on the bathroom floor just in time to vomit bile into the toilet. After, she crouches on the tile floor, hands to the ground, struggling to still the moving plane of all that is horizontal. The tiles are cold and hurt her knees. The floor is damp in patches. The puddles lead to a trail of footprints that extend from the shower to the door.

"Why is the floor wet?" she calls out. Her thinking is as viscous now as her stomach. She is making simple assumptions. She assumes that Ryan still lies in the bed, and that he—or someone—will answer.

"I don't know." His voice is hoarse. "Probably from the shower."

"But you just woke up," she says.

"Yeah," he says. Then, for clarity, "I woke up when you woke me."

"Then how would it be wet?" she says. "Everything else in here is dry. It's been hours since I ran the shower." She touches the clothes hanging on the hook, her bathing suit—and the children's. "The clothes are dry. The footprints are wet." And then again, "Someone was in here. In the last few hours."

"Who do you think it was?" he says. "Who is the culprit, Miss Marple?"

"You tell me," Cass says. She is on her hands and knees, her face inches from the floor as she inspects the wet shapes tracking from the shower.

A long pause during which Ryan digests or feigns frustration. "What are you saying, Cass?"

"I'm not saying anything," she says. "I'm asking."

Another pause, this one the pause of a man struggling to still his anger. "Are you suggesting someone broke in? That someone broke into our cabana?"

"I'm not suggesting anything," she says. "I'm telling you there are footprints that go from the shower to the door and asking you how they got here." With effort, she rises from the ground and crawls out of the bathroom.

Ryan is standing in the doorway when she crosses the threshold. "Don't do this, Cass," he says. "Don't ruin this vacation. This is how you wake me up? With your paranoid delusions?"

But Cass will not be bullied. She is done with intimidation. She struggles to rise from the floor, hobbles out of the bathroom, then opens the front door of the cabana, takes several steps across the grass, then drops to her knees to feel the grass, as though the dew, the dampness can prove who was in her bathroom.

Ryan stands at the door as Cass crawls across the grass. He is shaking his head with revulsion.

"You're crawling," he says. "Like one of those women."

She does not look up. "Watch out what you wish for."

"Get off the ground."

She does not move.

"Cass, look at yourself right now. Get off the ground, Cass."

"Someone was in our room," she says. "Someone was in there recently. I'm calling the front desk, Ryan. We have to tell them."

"Cass, do not call them. What are you going to say? You found your own footsteps, Cass, after taking a shower!"

"Stop trying to make me doubt myself," she says. "And basic facts of nature. Water evaporates, Ryan, after several hours."

"Do not bother them, Cass. You're going to feel really stupid when you realize these are your footprints."

"You're telling me this water has been here for over eight hours?"

Furious, she walks back inside, marches to the bathroom. She grabs her bathing suit from the hook where hers and the kids' are hanging. She wants to leave quickly, and her bikini top is closer than the bra that is still in her luggage. She puts it on, clasping the back, and then finds a dry blue sarong, a simple patterned fabric, and ties it at her hip to look like any of the other presentable, elegant mothers. She stops at the door, mouth poised to speak but freezes at the sight of the waking children. She and Ryan will have to wait to continue this conversation.

Alice and Pete sit on the floor, a pile of white shells between them. They are sorting and trading yesterday's haul, as they do with Halloween candy. Shells clatter on the tiles like coins in a pocket. The children's cheeks are flushed from the sun, their eyes bright with anticipation. Cass surveys her kids, oblivious in their laughter. She looks at the man that was once her love, her partner, the man that has become her tormentor. She thinks of what she told her daughter when she asked for her guidance. When you don't know what to do, get very quiet. *Get* quiet, don't *stay* quiet. Then scream bloody murder. The time has come to call for help. The time has come to end this madness.

Moving faster now, she leaves the cabana and heads to the lobby, but before she has taken ten steps across the warm sand of early morning, the feeling is upon her. Light so bright and silvery it looks as though the sun has gotten closer. Nausea pulls her down again with the convulsive release of all that was inside her. The force of it brings her to her knees, so that she is kneeling in the sand like a shipwrecked sailor.

She racks her mind now for the cause, the latest ingestion, the action and reaction. Was it something she ate, something she touched, something she breathed, something that is on her? And then, recoiling in horror, she realizes she has once again turned his weapon on herself, a voluntary dagger pointed at her breastbone. She gestures clumsily at her chest and fumbles at her clothing. Something that is on her. She is in broad daylight now, amid the morning strollers. She cannot rip her clothes off in the middle of the beach or else appear—and confirm his claims that she is—completely demented.

Frantic, she stumbles to the surf, desperate for any cover. She crouches into an approaching wave, untying her bikini top and dragging off the bottom. She wears only a sarong now with nothing underneath it. She gathers water from the waves and tries to cleanse her chest of the remaining toxin—whatever has not already been absorbed into her system, and already circles her veins, speeding from the jugular vein to her prefrontal cortex.

Holding the bathing suit by a string, she waits for another wave and rinses it in the water, beating it against the sand in the chop in the hopes that this will purge it of the toxins it has been soaked in. But this, too, seems a futile act, a pointless protest in the face of something that has grown massive—a force that is everywhere at once, inside and surrounding her. She hurls her bathing suit into the ocean—first the top and then the bottom, as though in offering to the sea, in acceptance of its power, and an act of defiance. The orange shreds of her suit flow out on the next wave. She watches them rise and fall once more before they are enveloped.

When she turns around, Ryan is standing behind her. "Look at yourself, Cass. You're practically naked."

She clutches her sarong to her chest, tries to run now in the sand, but her steps are slow and labored.

"Cass, stop."

She doesn't. She keeps moving.

"Cass, stop!" Ryan is faster. He reaches her in four large strides and grabs her by the shoulders. He spins her toward him and stares at her as though he can still hypnotize her into submission.

"We're leaving," she says. "I'm ending the vacation early."

"By all means. Take Alice and Pete. Sam is staying."

She looks up now. They are eye to eye, and his gaze is relentless.

"Sam's coming with me," says Cass.

"Not unless you want me to report you."

"To whom?"

"It's illegal to take a child out of the country without the approval of both parents."

"We came here together," she says. "I am his mother."

"You're in no state to travel," he says. "I'll have to inform customs."

She matches his intensity without flinching. "You can't stop me."

"No, I can't," he says. "But you can't travel without a passport."

Cass turns and trudges across the beach, fighting the sand to reach the cabana. Inside, she empties the bags in a frenzy, first the one with wallets and passports, followed by the luggage with her own clothes and the children's. Clothes unfurl across the floor in a pile of socks, books, and swimsuits. She drops to the floor on her hands and knees, rummaging like a beggar. Ryan has bested her once again. Pete's and Alice's passports are still in her bag, secured, as before, with a rubber band. Sam's is conspicuously absent.

TWENTY-THREE

The Connors sit together at breakfast on the terrace, cheeks flushed and spirits soothed. Two days into their vacation, their faces already evidence the salve of changed perspective. The kids eat eggs and toast and fruit, the colors of which are vivid enough to name Crayola colors—yellow mango, pink grapefruit, green papaya, brown toast, and red berries. To anyone looking at this family, they appear picture-perfect, a far cry from the horror Cass is living, which is, of course, she realizes now, exactly what Ryan has intended.

Ryan hands Cass a drink, a frothy white thing in a curvy glass, garnished with a cherry. He stares at her in a goading way, daring her to defy him. If she refuses, she acknowledges she knows his method, and, therefore, poses a threat to his freedom. Should she call his bluff and sip it as a show of trust or a pretense of ignorance? Or meet him with the tacit acknowledgment and refuse it? Surviving a crime can be more dangerous than being its victim.

But now a new problem. Sam, too, is tempted by the milky drink and the shiny fruit adornment.

"Want drink," he says, reaching for the glass. He plucks the maraschino cherry.

Ryan and Cass react in the same instant, swatting Sam's hand away from the drink and snatching the garnish. Sam bursts into tears, surprised by the reaction and the denial.

Cass stares at Ryan. Ryan stares back, defiant. The inference is not lost on either one. The drink was meant for Cass.

"Too sweet for Sam," Ryan says and quickly changes the subject. "Who wants to build a sand castle?"

The kids raise their hands at once. Diversion is a fail-proof tool. Enthusiasm—and bribery—are equally contagious.

He leads the children from the terrace to the beach after breakfast, each one gleefully taking their place in the usual procession, except now they are carrying pails and shovels, ready to make good on the promise of their heated conversation. A flutter of fear occurs to Cass as she imagines some unconsidered hazard—an accident of nature, a tidal wave or strong current, but her heart is buoyed by pride and relief as Alice and Pete build and play with furious determination. For the rest of the day, the Connors prostrate themselves to the trifecta of sunshine, sand, and water. Cass is strengthened by her children's joy. Her heart begins to pump more fully as she watches them dance across the beach, chasing each other across the surf like a school of dolphins.

A short trip to the hotel room to restock towels and sunscreen affords the opportunity to send an email to her mother. She is reluctant to do so, but it seems imperative. She knows, of course, that her mother is a fragile alliance. And now she understands the risks of speaking too soon to anyone. Reporting this crime has well-known repercussions. But so does silence.

Subject heading: SOS.

"Mom," she writes, "I need your help. The kids and I are in danger. We're on vacation in Bermuda. I need you to fly here as soon as you can and take Pete and Alice back to New York. I need you to keep them safe with you until I can fix a very bad situation."

She puts down her phone and opens her computer. Now a different message draws her attention: a new email from an unknown address in

Arizona. It opens with a single click and an elaborate Excel spreadsheet. On the left column is a list of substances. On the right, a series of numbers. First, the trace amount in which these substances might be found naturally in the environment, followed by the amount in which they have been found in the sample substance. She understands the numbers before she remembers the referent. It is the lab report from the toxicology test ordered by her lawyer. The lobster roll has tested positive for seven heavy metals on the periodic table—arsenic, lithium, beryllium, magnesium, cadmium, nickel, and mercury—all of them in toxic levels. But none is higher than the first— they are listed in alphabetical order. Arsenic: 350 mcg/L. A bouquet of metals. A compound. An alloy. C. Alloy.

She types all seven metals into her search. It yields the following definition:

Group 12 Elements. Transitional metals in the D-block of the periodic table. Likely to form bonds with other metals and often used in alloys. Low boiling points make them favored in the formation of metal compounds. Transformation to gas at lower points than most metals.

She quickly switches off the phone and hurries to her children. She needs to find someone, anyone to help them.

Certainty can be more confusing than any amount of wondering. Wondering leaves you with options, alternate explanations, and room for the lies we tell ourselves in order to live without fear and trepidation. Cass no longer has the luxury of not knowing. Time is no longer on her side. Time has joined forces with her husband. She joins her family on the beach, where Ryan is reclining on a lounge chair. Sam sits building mounds of sand in the shade of an umbrella. The older kids are farther down the beach with a gaggle of other children, their red, orange, and yellow bathing suits scattered like a handful of jelly beans.

"I'm going in," Ryan says.

He rises from his chair and starts toward the ocean, picking up speed as he passes Alice and Pete and taunting them to join him. Cass watches Ryan walk, surveys his sunburned shoulders. She scans the beach like a hungry bird and prepares to gather her children. Pete and Alice have moved slightly. They are combing the beach for shells at low tide along with the seagulls. Without delay, she rises and hoists Sam to her hip, taking him from his castle.

"No!" he wails. He tries to squirm from her grasp.

Cass holds him tighter. She walks briskly across the beach, calling the names of the older children, conveying from her gait and tone that there will be no negotiation. Soon she is walking, baby on hip, flanked by Pete and Alice, marching swiftly across the beach from the surf to the rambling stairs, up to the hotel lobby.

"Mom, what's wrong?" says Alice. The sun has turned her cheeks red, and her eyes are as blue as the water. She hoists her towel around her shoulders. "Mom, I was having fun. I don't want to go now! Mom, what's wrong?"

Pete is far more stoic, trudging dutifully up the beach, accepting this impromptu exodus.

"Nothing," she says. "Keep walking."

Of course they know it is something. She will not share the reason for her alarm, but her urgency is apparent.

"Then why did you make us leave?" says Pete.

"Just do as I say. We need to move quickly."

In the lobby, she stations the kids at a table with a stack of jigsaw puzzles, instructs them to stay and play at this table, and to keep the baby distracted. With the kids in her sight, she walks to the front desk and sets her plan in motion.

She approaches the hotel concierge, a young blonde too pretty to be indoors in such a tight-fitting jacket.

"Good morning," says Cass.

"Morning," she says. "How can I help you, Mrs. Connor?"

"There's been a change of plans," says Cass. "Is there any way you can help me change my flights?"

"My pleasure, Mrs. Connor. Do you have your flight information?"

Cass locates her phone in her cluttered beach bag, sifting past sandy bottles and books to find the email with this information.

"Is there an ideal departure date?"

"Immediately," says Cass.

"Absolutely," says the woman. She hides her surprise with a smile and quickly makes a phone call.

"Thank you," she says. Cass lowers her voice to a whisper. "My husband is trying to harm me."

The concierge regards Cass strangely, not with the shock she expects to summon with this comment but rather an utter lack of surprise, as though she has been prepped in advance for this very declaration. "He mentioned you've not been feeling well," she says. "I'm really sorry to hear this. Would you like us to call a doctor? There's a small clinic on the island. A handful of medical doctors and some very experienced counselors."

The weight of dread drops from Cass's throat to her stomach. "No," she says. "No, thank you. That won't be necessary. Just your help with the flights. And a telephone I can borrow." She smiles now in a way designed to convey composure, regretting her choice to confide anything more personal than flight information.

Cass's first call is to the number on the email. A man answers from what sounds, from the substantial echo, to be a very small space like a suburban garage or a basement.

"This is Cass Connor. I just received your email."

"Oh, hello," he says. "I've been waiting for your call. That was quite an interesting sample."

"Right," says Cass. She tries, with her tone, to curtail small talk. She looks to her children, who are for now playing contentedly at the table. But this must be quick; she is racing the clock of their attention spans, and it is only a matter of minutes before Ryan comes to find them. "Is there any way those metals could exist in nature?" Every fiber of her being is now steeped in awareness. And yet she tries, once again, to play devil's advocate, to consider some alternate explanation. It is either a default journalist's instinct or an attempt to submit her own findings to the same skepticism with which they have been met by others.

"Not at these levels," he says. "And not this constellation."

"What do you mean by *constellation*?" she says.

"The number of metals in the sample. This indicates . . ." He trails off. "This indicates . . . deliberate contamination."

"But how would someone do this?" she says. "What is the likely source here?"

"Hard to say." He pauses. "Some sort of alloy. All of them seem to be metals. Metals that bond easily."

"Where would someone get such a thing?"

"Industrial-grade chemicals, expensive synthetic drugs, or a very expensive chemistry set."

"What industry would that be?" she asks.

"Metals are used in many. The pharmaceutical industry in chemo drugs and preservatives. Agricultural in pesticides. Wood preservative. Construction, renovation, building supplies. Pulp and paper. Greeting cards for preservation. Textiles with dyes and tinting. Tattoos."

"And what about the levels?" she says. "Could any of them be naturally present?"

He pauses to cough. Cass waits for something clearer.

"Those levels were off the freaking charts," he says. "The arsenic alone was one hundred thousand times the trace level."

Cass takes a moment to digest this statement. She does not have the time right now for leisure or discretion. "Can you suggest any hypothesis for how this could have happened?"

Another laugh or cough. "Whoever gave you this food is not someone you want to have over for dinner."

"Right," she says, and then again, "so you can't think of any other explanation?"

"Like I said, I can't speculate on any criminal matter. In fact, it's probably better for you that I speak directly to your lawyer. Only way to retain privilege."

"Oh," she says. "I see." She is back in foreign territory, a world with new rules and jargon, a world with words like *chain of custody, privilege,* and *matter.*

"Good luck," says the man.

Alice joins her mother now. She has tired of the puzzle.

"Mom, what's going on? Did you say we're leaving?"

"Our plans have changed a little, honey. Everything's going to be okay. I need you to try to stay very calm. Can you do that for me?"

She nods, studies her mother's eyes. She is too smart both to be deceived and to defy her mother.

Sam, too, has reached the limit of his distraction. He is wandering from the table, and Cass needs to corral him. Pete is close to tears because he wants to be back on the beach, jumping in the waves, finishing the castle. Cass has her eye on the door, watching for her husband.

She looks back at the front desk where the receptionist is pretending not to listen, then back to the table where her kids have abandoned the puzzle.

"Excuse me, Mrs. Connor?" says the woman at the desk.

"Yes?" says Cass.

"I'm afraid I've been unsuccessful. Flights are booked through the New Year—that is, if you want to travel on the same plane as your children. We may be able to charter a flight to one of the Florida airports, but if you want to travel together, your best bet is probably to go wait at the airport and try to fly standby."

"How much does a charter cost?" says Cass.

"I'd have to call to get a quote."

"May I have the phone? I can do it." She has already done the mental math, added up the maximums of all the cards in her wallet.

The lady provides a small pamphlet with pink-and-purple lettering, an absurd portrait of an extravagant jet-setting couple. Cass grabs the paper and dials.

"Hello," she says. "I need to charter a plane for this afternoon. From the Bermuda to Miami or Atlanta."

She tries not to flinch when they quote the price, $2,000. She gamely removes a card from her bag and recites the numbers. She waits for one awful minute before they inform her that her card has not been accepted.

"But that makes no sense," she insists. "I paid the bill in late November. The limit . . ." She trails off. It's not worth it. It's all too clear. Ryan has cut off her finances.

"Thank you," says Cass. "Thank you for trying." She returns the phone to the woman and gathers her belongings. "I'm actually feeling much better," she lies. "Perhaps we'll stay through Friday, as planned. Thanks for not mentioning this to my husband. I don't want to worry him unnecessarily."

"Of course," she says. She smiles in a way that conveys an absence of feeling. "Shall I put you all on the dinner list for tonight's New Year's Eve celebration?"

Cass studies her face, as though a thorough scan will reveal the extent of her knowledge. "Yes," she says. "Yes, please do. We wouldn't miss it."

"Wonderful," she says. "They're roasting a lamb. Potatoes, creamed spinach. And chocolate cake for dessert."

"Scrumptious," says Cass. She musters a smile. "The kids will be ecstatic."

With effort, she summons the strength to feign composure a little longer. Gaining speed, she gathers the kids at what remains of the puzzle, praising them for their patience and good behavior. They have completed the corner of a cloud that looks unmoored without its center.

Flanked by Pete and Alice, baby on her hip, Cass marches from the main house down the rambling stairs to the beach, back across the cooling sand. The chalky clouds of an afternoon storm cast a shadow over the beach that makes the entire island look as though it is underwater. It is as though Ryan is being fed information, as though he has a clone of *her* phone. He has beaten her at this game also. Ryan knows that she knows and what she knows. He has begun an acceleration, and if she waits any longer, she and the kids will face even greater danger. She must pack their belongings, gather her children, and leave the hotel before morning. They will wait in the airport for the first flight to the States. From there, she will take the kids to New York, install them safely with her mother, then walk to the closest precinct. She does not have the luxury of completing this investigation. Not without becoming its first fatality.

The afternoon passes without any unexpected drama, the kids exhausted by the sun and consumed by a hearty debate about the night's celebration. Every year, bets are placed on who will stay up the latest—and who will fall asleep before the awaited hour. But this year, they have a fail-proof plan, no less sly than the one to stake out Santa, armed with brownies and alarm clock, parsley for the reindeer. This year, they will not be foiled. Rumor has it that the chocolate cake has special properties, and this will afford the energy to stay up long past midnight. Heated debate and friendly hazing continues as they shower. Cass takes advantage of the kids' distraction to assemble a pile of clothes. Three days' worth for both children—six shorts, six shirts, two dresses, two pairs of pants, and two skirts, six pairs of underwear, socks, and sweaters—which she shoves under the mattress. Ryan has remained on the beach, reading, napping, or scheming, affording Cass the much-needed time to plan their escape in private.

At seven o'clock, the Connor kids are teeming with excitement. Alice's hair is combed and brushed. Pete proudly wears a jacket. Sam sports his very first sunburn. Ryan returns from the beach, sullen and silent. He ducks quickly into the shower, delaying their departure, testing the outside limits of the children's patience.

"Who's ready for dinner?" she says. She feels oddly like Ryan when she says it, the fearless camp counselor.

"I am!" everyone exclaims at once.

From the shower, Ryan calls out, "I'll meet you up there in ten minutes."

Cass opens the front door, and the kids bound out before her. They topple onto the beach like puppies from a crate, tumbling across the dunes into the lavender sunset. The kids are blissful, unaware, but Cass knows this will be their last night in Bermuda.

"Wait," she says. She is speaking to herself and the children. "Where are your shoes?" She addresses Pete, who is wearing a clean striped oxford shirt, khaki shorts, and no sign of footwear.

He stops short, falling to the ground in a theatrical show of contrition. "I left them in the room," he says.

"Run and get them, sweetheart. They won't let us sit down without them."

Still smiling, Pete sprints back across the sand. Cass holds Alice and Sam at bay as he backtracks. The door opens and closes as Pete hurries in. Cass stares at the little house and marvels at its storybook proportions, imagines if this were their home. What if they had lived in this little pink house, silhouetted by these charcoal clouds and this peaceful sunset? Would they have been happier? Would things have been different? Not more than thirty seconds pass before Pete emerges and begins retracing his steps toward the stairs and his mother and siblings.

"You can hold them in the sand," she calls out.

But he doesn't hear her. She looks away to track Alice and Sam, who have started up the stairs toward the main house. It is hard to spot them now as the sun has fully set and shadows and bodies blur like lovers. Her heart catches before she spots them again, farther up the stairs, nearly at the terrace. When she looks back, Pete is gone. And the beach is washed in shadows.

"Pete," she calls.

He does not respond.

"Pete!" she cries.

No response. Only the increasing volume of the breaking waves. The tide always seems to come faster as soon as the sun sets.

"Pete!" she yells. Her eyes scan the beach with no success. And then, in her periphery, a dancing reflection of a tiny light, as the buttons on Pete's shirt catch the last of sunlight. When she reaches him, Pete is doubled over, rocking like a blind man. She grabs his wrist and finds his pulse. His pulse is speeding.

"Pete, sweetheart, what's wrong?"

He writhes on the ground, moaning. "Mom," he says. "Can't breathe."

"Pete, sweetheart. Can you talk to me?"

He opens his mouth, but a moan comes out. He raises his head but cannot lift it to an upright position.

She searches the ground for a cause, for some explanation. Her eyes search from his head to his hands, his hands to his feet. His light-brown bucks untied and loose around his ankles.

"Oh, my God," she says.

She grabs his ankle and yanks the shoe from his foot. She pulls off the other and throws it across the sand, far from them. Pete lies on his stomach, his arm twitching in a slow-motion convulsion.

"Ryan!" Cass yells. "Alice, Sam. Come down here! Ryan." Her voice is shrill, her volume higher than the pitch. No effort is made to sound normal. Only the hollow roar of a mother who knows her child's life is in danger.

Instinct tells her what has occurred, plays it out as though on a stage, as though she were sitting on the bed in the hotel room. Ryan emerged from the shower and, standing in his towel, spotted Pete's forgotten shoes on the floor. Thinking fast, he seized this moment, the privacy it afforded and the certainty that Pete would be back in moments—when his mother dispatched him to return for the shoes he would need for dinner—to place the toxin in the shoes of a seven-year-old child with the intention that he step into the shoes, soak in that substance, and fight for dear life as the poison absorbs in the soles of his feet, through the layers of muscle and skin, winding into his blood, heart, and brain, and causing the cardiac arrest or stroke that could kill him.

She picks him up like a baby, fighting the sand to get to the main house.

Questions of motive are often misplaced in the interpretation of violence. There is not always a reason why. There is not always an answer to satisfy the craving for explanation. But in this case, Cass can supply several, not least the vendetta of a psychotic man against the child of another man, nor his vendetta against that child's mother, and her increasing threat—and his rising terror—due to her knowledge of those intentions. *I'm gonna make it look like a suicide, and everyone's gonna believe it.* Or better yet, make it look like an accident, an unknown fatality of the environment. Just like Marley.

But these plans are too arcane for Ryan, not sufficiently Byzantine in their mode of torture. Ryan would do something more elaborate, Cass now decides. Ryan would do bigger. He would raise the level of arsenic in Pete's system so that he tests positive for the poison when his mother dies suddenly and others are submitted to testing in some lackluster investigation. She imagines the chaos after her death, her children's fear and torpor, her family traipsing up the East Coast like a maudlin armada. She can see the whole thing playing out like a fifties melodrama. The muted suspicion after her death, the halfhearted investigation, Ryan's stoic performance of grief, the hushed tones of the heartbroken husband. And then, once too much time has passed, once it is too late to detect the poison, the autopsy, the ambiguous results, the feigned effort to test the children, followed by the inconclusive decision that it must have been in the environment, some horribly botched batch of food, some hideously tainted groundwater, that this poor, lovely family fell prey to the worst of all tragedies, a senseless accident.

Cass looks up from the ground to find Ryan above her. His hair is wet and neatly brushed. His eyes are as shiny as his hair, like the mercury in a thermometer.

"What's wrong with him?" she says. It is not a question. It is an accusation.

"What do you mean?"

"What's wrong with him, Ryan? His heart is racing."

"Get ahold of yourself. You're losing it, Cass."

"Get the fuck away from me. He needs to see a doctor." She rises from the ground, hoisting Pete into her arms, and begins to trudge across the beach, carrying her limp seven-year-old child as though he is a newborn. He is heavy, too heavy to move quickly, but she gains strength with every step forward. Ryan watches, and he follows.

"Help!" she yells. "We need help!"

Alice stands at the top of the stairs as Cass approaches. Mother and daughter make eye contact.

"Get Sam," she says. "Follow me."

Alice nods and follows instructions. She hoists Sam to her hip. "Mommy, I'm scared."

"Don't be scared," says Cass. Her voice is low now, deep and fierce. "Everything's going to be okay. Just do exactly what I say. And stay close to me."

"Mommy, I'm scared," she says again.

"We need to move quickly and stay calm now."

They move together up the stairs, Cass holding Pete and Alice holding the baby. They are two women, one tiny, one tall, united in fear, united in their capacity for ferocious love and protection.

But Ryan is upon them. "Cass, what are you doing?"

"I'm taking him to the hospital," she says.

"He doesn't need a hospital."

Cass keeps walking. "It's okay, sweetheart. It's okay. Everything's going to be okay. Do you hear me, sweetheart?"

Pete holds on to consciousness, his eyes fluttering as Cass carries him. He lets out a rhythmic, breathy moan, as though his lungs are trying to expel whatever is in his system. He heaves and begins to convulse. Cass stops and kneels to the sand as he vomits green and yellow. "There you go, baby. Get it out."

A couple strolling on the beach wanders closer in the shadows. They stare, alarmed by the spectacle.

"Do you need help?" says the woman.

"No, thank you," says Ryan. "Just a family issue."

They keep walking, chided by his tone, trying not to stare as they hurry toward the main house.

Ryan grabs Cass by the arm. Cass flinches at his touch and wriggles out of his grasp. She nearly misses the next step but catches herself in time and holds Pete tighter.

She is walking faster now, approaching the lobby.

"Alice, give me the baby." He is following her, one step behind.

"Help!" Cass yells. "Somebody help! My son is not well! We need a doctor!"

They are nearing the cheerful pink stucco of the main house, and the New Year's Eve excitement is a stark contrast to the horror the Connors are living. Guests float past in cheerful attire, cheeks singed and hair yellowed, women boasting their browned cleavage, men, relaxed and clean-shaven, everyone wearing shades of blue and salmon. Chefs and waiters rush about, preparing the holiday celebration, setting the table with silverware, spruce, and candles. The kitchen door swings open, and a waft of deep, meaty air and baking bread swarms the lobby.

Cass rushes to the front desk, approaches the female concierge. "Please call an ambulance now. My son needs to go to the hospital. It's very, very urgent."

The hotel owner overhears, approaches the desk, and takes over.

"There's a clinic," he says. "Come with me. We'll get there faster if I drive you."

He fumbles for his keys, locates them in his pocket, and nods at a squadron of golf carts parked outside the window. "I'm ready to leave when you are."

Cass hurries out the main door and takes a seat in the golf cart, sitting in the passenger seat with Pete clutching her, face-to-face, like a koala. Alice follows her mother into the back seat with the baby.

"Cass, don't do this," says Ryan. "You're not thinking clearly right now." He turns to the hotel owner. "This really isn't necessary. We don't want to waste your time with a false alarm. I'm afraid this kind of thing happens often."

"Please go," Cass says.

The motor is running, and Cass, Pete, Alice, and Sam begin down the dusty dirt road as though they are merely taking a joyride around the island.

"Stop!" Ryan yells.

The driver brakes on reflex, and Ryan, without missing a moment, grabs the baby from Alice.

Cass has no time to react. She must distinguish between an emergency and an urgent situation. And so she allows the driver to keep his pace and watches her baby recede as they speed into the darkness. Once she has gotten help for Pete, she will come back for Sam. Once Pete and Alice are safe, she will have a better chance of escaping with the baby. She rests on one simple but chilling assurance, that while Ryan is capable of harming her, in spite of this, because of this, he will not harm their child.

The cart pulls up to a modest house close to the main harbor. The driver stops the cart and darts to Cass's side to help her carry Pete. With one hand, he shepherds mother and child. With the other, he takes Alice's hand and guides her. The four walk into a clinic that looks like a small suburban home. They are greeted by a woman in nurse's white and ushered into a larger room filled with small white beds and bottles.

The nurse conducts a frenetic triage. "How long has he been like this?"

"He collapsed on the beach about an hour ago. I took his pulse and it was 160."

Alice grabs her mother's arm. "What's wrong with him, Mommy?"

"We're trying to find that out, sweetie. Just give me a—"

The nurse deftly unbuttons Pete's shirt and begins to stick electrode sensors to his chest. "What hurts, hon?" she asks Pete. "Can you tell me?"

"Head," Pete says. "Tummy."

"Did he lose consciousness?" asks the nurse.

"Almost, but not completely."

"Any recent injuries?"

"No."

"Was he in the water earlier?"

"Yes, but no issues."

"Any history of—"

"No," says Cass.

"He's very healthy," says Alice. It is an offering and a plea.

"He ingested something," says Cass.

"By mouth?"

Here, Cass pauses. The truth has backfired too many times. She cannot risk delay or dismissal. She looks directly at the nurse. "He needs to be checked for arsenic. That's the cause. What is the most effective antidote?"

The nurse looks at Cass, conducts an instantaneous study. Then, moving quickly, she calls for help from another nurse, places a mask on Pete's face, and prepares his arm for an IV. "We'll put him on oxygen and run fluids to flush his system. There's no antidote for arsenic, but this should help to stabilize him."

Pete is quickly strung up to a circuit of wires, his small chest dotted by stickers with metal nubs at the center. The wires stretch from his chest to a machine that translates the activity of his heart. Cass sits next to her child, holding his hand, stroking his head, each brush of her hand a prayer that she might take his pain as her own. His eyes are little moons with dark crescents underneath, and his pink flesh is translucent. Alice sits at her mother's side, and Cass grasps her hand now. As she squeezes the hands of her children, she tries to impart her strength to them.

The nurse finds a vein and injects the IV. The fluids begin their cycle.

Cass follows her gaze to the screen. Tiny spikes dart across the screen like confused lightning. She stares at the lightning on the screen and makes a solemn prayer, the kind that only sinners make, in the absence of prior devotion, with knowledge of her own failures, promising any trade in the world in exchange for her son's safekeeping.

The next ten hours pass in a state of alertness and terror, feelings that have become all too familiar, as Cass sits by her son's bed next to her sleeping daughter, who lies on a cot wheeled in by the nurses. The nurse is joined by another nurse and, soon after, a doctor. She is grateful for the kindness and competence of this modest clinic. The medical care is far purer, the method more instinctive, not filtered through the lens of potential liability and lawsuits. As a result, Pete receives better care here than Cass has in Portland. There is no doubt, no disbelief, just a concerned and competent doctor. Slowly, by the grace of God, the spikes on the screen—and Pete's breathing—grow more stable.

The nurse returns to take blood and sends him to the bathroom with a cup to collect urine. They will run a heavy metals panel. Unfortunately, it will take days to get the results. Even in an American hospital, this is a send-away test. Double that on a remote island.

A thought occurs to Cass.

"Can you test mine as well?" she asks the nurse.

The nurse looks at her for a long moment. Then she hands her a second plastic cup.

Cass walks into the bathroom to produce her new exhibit.

"Cass Connor. 12/31." Like a signature on a love note.

Cass thinks of her mother now. She needs her help to survive this.

She takes out her phone and steps into the hall. "Mom," she says.

Alice looks up. She has never heard her mother say this before.

"Mom," she says. "I need your help."

"Cass," says her mother. "Is that you?"

"Yes," says Cass. She leans her forehead against the wall, as though to test whether it will support her.

"It's New Year's Eve, Cass."

"Yes, I know."

"Where are you?"

"I need you to come pick up the kids. Can you do that for me, Mom?"

"You said that in your email," she says.

"You didn't respond. Mom, I need your help now."

"I couldn't tell if you were serious." A pause. "Or being dramatic."

"I'm serious, Mom," Cass says.

"Where are you?" her mother asks.

"We're in Bermuda."

A long pause, during which Cass regrets the decision. This was a mistake, she decides, or will be a mistake at some point in the future. But before she can change her mind, her mother has assented.

Cass sits awake through the night, running through her options. It seems her best choice is to divide and conquer. When it is safe for Pete to leave the clinic, she will take Alice and Pete to the airport. She will meet her mother with the kids and put all three on a flight back to New York. The kids are not safe around Ryan, and she cannot risk another minute. Once Alice and Pete are safe, she will go back for the baby. She will fly back to Portland with Ryan and Sam, return to their jurisdiction. And then, at the first opportunity, she will take Sam and their still-packed suitcase and show up at the precinct. She will stay until they listen. She will present every shred of evidence and beg them to arrest her husband. Then she will fly with Sam to New York to reunite her children. And, once they are together and safe, she will slowly begin again. Again, she will start over. It is nearing daylight when she settles on this course of action.

By six o'clock, she has formed a plan and set it in motion. She has found the flight for her mother from New York to Bermuda. She has booked three one-way tickets to New York, using her mother's card. She has contacted Nora and Matthew to keep them posted on her actions. She has sent them all the evidence in her possession so that there are several copies of this information. Her mother will fly from New York at seven and land at noon in Bermuda. Cass will bring Pete and Alice by ferry to the main island. They will meet at four o'clock at the airport. Her mother will greet her children, travel with them to her home in New York, and she will keep them safe until Cass comes to retrieve them.

Now Cass must begin her performance. She must contact Ryan and convince him of her compliance. She must bait *him* now to take *her* back, just as he baited her to forgive him. She must delay his attack long enough to get Sam out of his possession. She must dangle a reward for sparing her life, an incentive for détente, a pause in the negotiation, by arriving with a wound that immunizes him against charges. This time will require a trade of sorts, an offering at the door as collateral. It will require dropping her weapon and entrusting him with something he can use against her. She must hand him her own poison pill. His very own signed retraction. An admissible exoneration. Without doing this, she will not last a night. He will have no choice but complete the attack. Her knowledge makes her too dangerous. She is as dangerous to him as he is to her. Both could end the other's freedom.

By dawn, Pete's heart rate has returned to normal. The twitching in his arms and hands has abated. Cass kisses his forehead, inhales his sweet scent, and thanks good God above that her son has survived this. At nine o'clock, she leaves her sleeping children in the hospital room and walks into the hall to call Ryan.

"Ryan," she says, "I've lost myself. I don't know what's up and down anymore. I'm like a broken compass."

"How is Pete, Cass?" he says. His voice is cold and officious.

"Stable," Cass says.

"I told you he was fine," Ryan says.

"You were right," she says.

"Good," he says. That's all he says. Ryan uses silence the way most people use words. To communicate and disable.

"You were right," she says. "I must have had a breakdown."

"Yes," he says. "You have. Admitting this is the first step."

She pauses to sniffle. "I'm coming back so I can heal. Regain my health. My sanity. I've asked my mother to pick up Alice and Pete so they don't have to see me like this. I've lost my way, Ryan." A long pause. During this time he gauges her sincerity, her intentions.

"Fine," he says. His voice is cold. He is suspicious also, but either he buys her act or sees the opportunity, a chance to immunize himself by discrediting her for good—or better yet, silence her forever. Two for one: eliminate the victim and the witness.

"They'll discharge us around noon," she says, "then I'll take the kids to my mother. I'll see them off on their flight and be back at the hotel by dinner."

"Do you want me to pick you up from the clinic?"

For a moment, she forgets herself and considers his question. But she catches herself in time. He cannot be near her children again. God knows what he could do now.

"No," she says. "But thank you. Take care of Sam until I get back. Give him a big kiss from me. Tell him Mommy is going to get better."

She hangs up the phone and returns to the room where her children are just waking.

Slowly, as the children rise, she begins to prepare them. She presses her cheek to theirs, whispers kisses and comfort and, once they are fully alert, she looks into their eyes and tells them the plan she has made to protect them.

"Guys," she begins. "I have some news that will be upsetting. We're ending our vacation early. Your grandmother is coming to pick you up and take you back with her to New York. I will stay behind for a day and fly back to Portland with Sam and Ryan tomorrow. You will stay with Gram for a couple of days, resting and playing. And when I am done, I will come for you with Sam, and we will be back together."

"Why?" says Alice.

"Because I need to take care of something, and I want you two to be safe while I do it."

"No," says Pete. "I don't want to."

Cass takes their hands. "I know," she says. "I understand, but it's very important."

She squeezes their hands tighter. "It's okay to feel scared right now. We went through something terrible. We went through something awful. But now you are safe, and I will do a better job of protecting you from this moment forward. Ryan has been very bad, and he will never again be near us. But I have also made mistakes. I stayed with him. I let him be near you. I should have packed up a long time ago, loaded the car with our clothes and toys, and driven us across the country. I thought I could fix this myself, but I was wrong. I didn't understand, or I wanted to believe, and that was a mistake also. Belief is a very powerful thing. It gives people comfort. A sense of purpose. It also gives people excuses. But I don't need belief anymore. You are my only purpose."

Alice and Pete are crying now. Cass fights her own tears, but the sorrow is too massive. She squeezes her children's hands as though they are part of one electric circuit. She tries to impart her hope and strength. And the solace of survival.

At noon, Cass, Alice, and Pete leave the clinic for the harbor. Pete is weak. Alice is visibly shaken, but she channels her fear into her gaze, which is steady and determined. The hotel owner picks them up and drives them from the clinic to the harbor. The same small boat carries them across the bay. The same captain holds their hands as they step from the rickety dock onto the gangplank. The same water that dazzled before with its various shades of blue is now different shades of black, cover for sharks and shadows. Cass gazes at her children, their faces glowing in the sun reflected off the pink houses that fortify the harbor.

Dale Rosen is waiting in the airport when Cass arrives with the children. The terminal is a small, humid room with twenty wooden chairs affixed to the floor and a small window with a plastic partition and a sign for coffee. Dale sits in one of these wooden chairs, drinking one of these coffees. She sips as though she is trying not to touch her mouth to the Styrofoam cup. Dale is a compact sergeant, surrounded by a phalanx of scarves. She peers through thin glasses that rest on her nose to greet grandchildren she has not seen since they were toddlers.

Mother and daughter embrace, and then Dale's grandmother's instinct takes over as Dale moves past Cass to shower her grandchildren with affection. After hugs and the diversion of so many useful presents—colored markers for the flight, new books, and sundry trinkets—the four sit quietly in the airport, heartened by the simple safety of being with someone bound if not by unconditional love, then by genetics. At five, Dale nods at Cass, signaling the time and their imminent departure.

A sharp breath draws pain into her chest.

"When will you come?" Alice asks.

"As soon as I can," says Cass.

"When?" Her voice is high and scared.

Cass takes another breath. "To be honest, I don't know. I don't think it will be more than a week. I'll fly home tomorrow with Sam and Ryan. And when I get home, I'll go to the police. And they will protect us also. Then I will come for you."

"Will he be arrested?" Alice asks.

"I don't know, sweetheart. I hope so."

"Mommy," says Pete. This is all he says. His eyes are big and wet.

"Sweetheart," she says. "I love you. Everything's going to be okay. You'll spend the week playing with Gram, and by the time you remember to think about me, I will be there to get you."

"And then what?"

Another breath. "And then we'll figure out what's next. And we'll keep going together."

"I'm scared," said Alice.

"I know, my love. What we've been through is scary. Now the worst is behind us." She gathers her children onto her lap as though they are babies. "Guess what?" she says.

"You love us," they say.

"Yes," she says. "I love you."

They nod and smile, comforted by their favorite chorus.

Dale nods at Cass now, signaling the time has come for their departure. And several hugs later, Cass's children are walking away, rolling their little blue and pink backpacks toward the door of the muggy airport, stopping to look back once, twice, three more times before disappearing into the sunlight.

And then they are gone, and the relief of knowing they are now safe is met with the sickening premonition that it will be lifetimes before she next sees them.

TWENTY-FOUR

Time passes in fits and starts as they wait for takeoff. White light saturates the plane as it reaches cruising altitude. Sam sleeps in Cass's arms. She strokes his hair and clutches him, listens to his breathing. In. Out. In. Out. A risk. And a reward. Ryan reads a magazine tucked into the seat ahead, a compilation of advertisements disguised as reading material. The airplane smells faintly like lotion. The flight back to Portland is tense but uneventful. Cass is consumed by thoughts of Alice and Pete, Pete's health, Alice's spirits, her mother's energy level—it has been years since she cared for children—and the task before her. But there is no room for fear. Only a winning performance. She must play the contrite wife, the rebuked hysteric, the broken woman. And so she rests her head on her husband's shoulder and burrows into the crook of his arm as though she is the disease and he is the medicine.

They land in Portland in late afternoon. Sam has reached the limit of his patience. It is a relief to be back on the planet, welcomed by the gray clouds of Portland. They make their way toward their luggage, and Cass falls behind to call to her mother.

"How is he?" she asks.

"He's fine," says Dale. "A little tired. Slightly nauseous. I have to tell you, Cass. This seems like a whole lot of nothing."

"You'll just have to trust me," she says. "I'm glad he's feeling better." There is no time to engage in debate. She is relieved to hear that Pete is recovering and that he is no longer in an acute situation. She shares a few quick instructions on favorite meals and bedtime rituals, asks her mother to deliver hugs and kisses, and hurries to the baggage area to find her loving husband.

On her way, she texts her student, Jean, to make plans for the following day. "Back from vacation early," she writes. "Any chance you can watch Sam for a couple of hours in the morning?"

Because of their early return, Cass has one more week of vacation. Ryan leaves the house the following morning, dressed and preened, as though it's any other Monday, any other day in the life of the Connor family, except today his mossy eyes are offset by a sunburn. Cass stands, holding Sam, on the porch, in her same-old silk nightgown. She waves at Ryan as he pulls out of the driveway, raises Sam's hand in his own farewell. She is the picture of a loving wife, a doting mother. She watches as Ryan's car climbs up the hill until the car disappears over the horizon, and then she rushes inside to prepare for the day, rapidly dressing herself and Sam as though for an evacuation. She puts Sam in a clean white shirt, blue corduroy pants, and a warm green sweater. For her, jeans, a collared oxford, and a clean gray sweater will have to suffice for propriety. She greets Jean at the door with Sam, issues a flurry of instructions, whispers endearments and kisses to Sam, then all but runs out the door, slips into her car, and turns the ignition.

Once again, Cass sits with Matthew in the PPD detectives' office. At first it is a shock to find that they are attentive. The reception now is different from when she visited in November. The evidence is still scant and mostly circumstantial, but it has three things in its favor: Cass's knowledge of the weapon, her understanding of the method, and her clear and consistent testimony, also known as "prompt outcry." This should meet the criteria of probable cause for an arrest. But probable cause, Cass is learning, is a somewhat subjective concept, subject to interpretation by whichever cop happens to sit in the precinct when a crime is reported.

Another hour, then several pass in the police precinct. Cass gives her complete report to a new detective, an older man with rubbery skin and a carefully groomed moustache. Having met with dismissal for so long, she is utterly unprepared for his response: total credulity, except with a new object of suspicion.

"Did you say your husband was cheating?" the detective asks.

"Yes," says Cass.

"How do you know this?"

"The usual ways," says Cass. "Emails, hotel bills. Women's panties. Hair in the shower."

He nods in a knowing way, nursing a new notion. "Did that make you angry?"

"I'm sorry," Cass says. "I'm not sure what you're asking."

"What I'm asking is if you had motive yourself. Motive for revenge. Motive for lying. How do I know *you* weren't trying to *kill* him? How do I know you didn't put it in there? Maybe you were angry because you found him cheating and you put it there to frame him."

"I'm sorry," Cass says, shaking her head. "That is just . . . outrageous."

"Lucky for both of you," the detective says, "I have no more reason to believe him or you."

"But it's in *my* body." she says. She is seething, coursing with frustration.

"Yeah, and I'm sorry about that," he says. "But I still don't know how it got there—if you put it there to incriminate him, if you put it there to harm yourself, or if you put it there to harm him. If any of those things are true, you could be arrested."

Outrage pools in Cass's chest.

"Why do you want him arrested so badly?" the detective asks now.

"To protect myself and my children." And then, to prevent herself from screaming in rage, she repeats, "To protect myself and my children."

But these comments should not surprise her. Attacks on her motives, her morals, her credibility, and her common sense. They are merely pages in a playbook written by a culture that prefers to believe a man's testimony over a woman's. Incredibly, this was not part of the plan Ryan first envisioned—

just a happy accident that immunizes him from any future charges. Four ways to discredit a woman. Delusion. Fabrication. Inculpation. Criminalization. Four fail-proof ways to destroy the testimony of a victim—when the victim is a woman.

"Well," he says with a patronizing shrug. "We could keep you here for questioning and see where the questions lead us."

Cass opens her mouth to speak, to yell, but Matthew grabs her forearm.

"There's absolutely no basis," says Matthew. "Unless you want a wrongful arrest suit on your desk on Monday."

The meeting ends in the same place that it started, a standstill created by the face-off between the evidence and the Fourth Amendment. The detective promises he will speak to Legal and look further into "the precedent" for a crime of this nature. Defeated, Cass puts on her coat and gathers her belongings. She had expected action, finality. Instead, she was met with more of the same. Doubt, delay, dismissal.

But Cass has stopped listening even before the detective explains the details. What do you do when the institutions designed to protect you, when all of these let you down, when all of them fail you? You have only one option: to use your own devices to protect yourself and your children.

It's a cautious and curious calm tonight in the Connor household, two friends, turned foes, feigning love. A portrait of a marriage. They run through the bedtime ritual as though everything is normal. All is calm. All is quiet. Laundry circles in the wash. The dishwasher murmurs. Something delicious simmers on the stove. Until a circuit breaks and the machine ceases to function.

Cass lies in bed, trying to focus on a novel. Ryan scrolls through his phone, feeding his unrepentant addiction. The only sound in the house is Sam's breathing in the next room and the sporadic moans of Ryan's favorite zombies. It is routine and ritual both, so sweet as to be deceiving. Cass steels herself with a simple reminder: the damage of doubt is here eclipsed by the danger of denial.

It is late, and they are falling asleep. It will be their last night together. Cass knows this. It is vile to be so close to him, to share air with this sadist, this stranger. She stares at the objects in their room, the cat curled up on the edge of the bed, her gray cardigan sweater, the sheets with the brown medallions. The poison has labored her breathing, and she listens to this faint wheezing. In. Out. In. Out. An attempt. And a failure. An escape. And an obstruction. A trial. And an error. An attempt, and another. A completed act of murder. Can you be a little bit poisoned, or does it effectively taint your system like a drop of red dye in a glass of water? Is an act of homicide called homicide when it happens to a woman? Uxoricide? Matricide? A woman killed for the crime of witnessing her own failed murder? What is the word for the systematic attempt to erase a mother?

She is awakened by the pressure of his cock inside her. His hips grind against her hips. His hands clench around her head, for balance, for power. There is no gagging now, no choking. That would be too primitive, too banal a form of torture. Why leave scrapes and bruises? Why leave evidence of his touch when he can leave no trace whatsoever? Instead, he wraps his hands around her neck, thumbs touching at the center, fingers stretched behind her ears, making tight circles. Just like this, he works his way through her. Thrusting. Convulsing. As though it is a nightly act of conjugation. In. Out. In. Out. A demand. And a rejection. A snake delivering his venom. For a moment, she nearly forgets and her body almost feels pleasure until that pleasure is replaced by a surge of hatred so violent it threatens to erupt within her. The conversion of sex to violence. A haven into a hell. A vital life into silence. The daily rotations of domestic life deliver poison. Her vision starts to cloud with the slow fade of a dimmer. Just before she loses grasp, a burst of rage fuels her and she shoves him off her.

Ryan rolls back to his side as though she has rudely rebuked an act of passion, then closes his eyes and feigns sleep like a man roused by a nightmare.

Cass sits on the edge of the bed, sucking air, regaining focus. She stands and stumbles to the bathroom. She braces herself on the sink, stares at her face as though to affirm she is still the same person. One pupil is larger than the other, nearly obscuring the blue of her eye. The other changes in size when she leans backward and forward. She runs through her memory of ninth-grade bio for possible causes: aneurysm, blood clot, stroke. She leans in and studies her eyes again. One pupil expands and contracts. The other is unresponsive. It looks instead like a large black sun, setting behind her eyelid. Panic surges in her chest, but panic is a luxury now. Breathing deeply, she opens the bathroom door and runs to the closest refuge.

When she arrives, the door is open.

"How did you know I was coming?" She is breathless, frantic.

"I saw you running," says Aaron.

"You saw me coming?" Cass says.

"I heard your door slam. What happened to you? Here, have a Xanax."

"No," she says. "I've got enough shit in my system."

He looks at her, assesses her state, plants her on his sofa. He walks to the kitchen. She hears water running. She looks out his window at her own house. He said he heard her door slam, but her door is wide open.

He returns with a blanket and a glass of water.

"Drink this," he says. "Water will help."

"No," she says. "No, thank you."

He holds the cup in front of her mouth. "Drink it. Don't be stubborn."

Ten minutes later, she is falling asleep on the floor of Aaron's living room. She is overwhelmed by drowsiness, as though her eyes are weighted. The house has the same sour smell. A radiator clatters. The last thing she remembers is Aaron's hands on her back, rubbing gently, followed by pressure on her neck, just beneath her ears, in tight circular motions. It might seem innocuous were it not the first time he has touched her and the very same way Ryan delivered the toxin. The jugular vein travels directly from the head to the heart, the fastest way to deliver a medicine—or poison.

She wakes two hours later, groggy and incoherent with a distinct lag in perception. *Drink it. Don't be stubborn.* Did he put something in her water? Terrified, she scans the room for her belongings—her coat, her phone, and her shoes, but all of them are missing. Did she forget them at home, or did Aaron move them? Frantic, she tiptoes across the dark room, looking for the lost items. The house is quiet, another home with its own working system. A mother and child sleep upstairs. Books line the shelves. Pots and pans fill the cabinets. She lived in a home like this only a few months prior.

She finds her phone in an outlet in the downstairs bathroom. The bathroom is painted yellow and has the same rank smell as the living room. At the sink, she splashes her face with cold water, tries to regain composure. Now she opens the medicine cabinet and surveys the contents. The shelves hold a store of typical supplies, random creams and bottles, and behind them, an atypically large selection of amber vials. A veritable pharmacopeia in her neighbor's bathroom. Each label has a single letter and the name of a "prescribing doctor." She extracts one and reads the name—Dr. Lugner. It is the same doctor listed on Ryan's meds. The doctor suggested by Aaron. To cure her of "stress and other negative fixations." Violence disguised as kindness. Not a friend, but an accomplice.

Through her intoxicated haze, she comes to a harrowing realization. Understanding happens in a series of revisions. Aaron is not her friend. Aaron wants to harm her. Aaron is a dealer. Aaron sells to Ryan. Aaron is not her ally. Aaron is Ryan's accomplice. Aaron is the source of the toxin.

She reviews the events of the last few weeks with new and blinding insight. The more she communicated with Aaron, the worse things grew with her husband. Her reports of Ryan's acts to Aaron were directly followed by Ryan's acceleration. When she told Aaron her plans to go to the cops, Aaron and Ryan shared a problem. All these things were connected—her mounting investigation, her disclosures to Aaron, and Ryan's heightened efforts to deliver the poison. She even recalls an instance when Aaron tried to issue a "warning," encouraging her to leave her husband, to break off a "dangerous relationship." A final act of mercy in the hopes that she would leave him? Or the first of many attempts to divert her investigation? Instead, she burrowed deeper. And so her loving husband and trusted confidant redoubled their efforts. Her clone of Ryan's phone now seems a paltry diversion. No need for a cloned phone when victim, killer, and accomplice all have the same information.

She thinks back now with disgust at her blindness and his pretense: his sudden interest in friendship, his convenient appearance, his apparent knowledge of her whereabouts. His encouragement, followed by his dissuasion. First, he plumbed her for information to assess her knowledge. Then, as she gained clarity of the crime and shared her plans to report it, he tried to disavow her of her beliefs and expedited the plan to harm her. All the evidence she shared with him—every secret, every deduction—was promptly shared with Ryan. She may as well have told her husband herself while lying in bed, unwinding. She wonders now if Ryan would have acted differently had Aaron not been reporting her progress, but there is no time for such questions now. For any more denial. Necessity and her trusting nature elevated Aaron from eccentric neighbor to trusted friend. Bad luck caused her to run from a murderer into the arms of his accomplice.

"Then I go back to the cops," she had told him. "And I stay there until they listen."

"I don't think you should do that," he'd said.

She reviews the chronology once again as she gains her bearings. Aaron offered her help while engaged in a plan to harm her, like a wolf dressed up as a granny, licking his chops before dinner. He filled a prescription more potent than drugs and likely promised testimony to invalidate her forever. She checks the theory against the dates, reviews the timing of his appearance, the pace of his help and reversals. His own disclosures. Aaron is a dealer. He told her on the playground. He laid bread crumbs like all liars. He sells controlled substances. Apparently with access to a garden variety. Ryan asked Aaron to fill a special order, not pot, nor pills, not opiates, nor expensive designer synthetic—an old-school upper with a steep curve to toxic. The crime reaches further than even Cass considered, from a staid Portland neighborhood to a trailer park in rural West Virginia, to the biggest of Big Pharma.

"Santos," he'd told her, "is the laboratory where it all started."

Aaron was never sincere in his efforts to help her, but rather pressed to dissuade, to silence, to discredit, and eventually to destroy her.

It occurs to her now that Aaron has been involved from the onset, guaranteed a cut of the house had Ryan completed the murder. Foolishly, she entrusted him with her heart and her house keys, asking her own attacker to set up a security camera. No matter. He already had access. He had already been in her home, contaminating her clothes, her sheets, the washer and dryer. This is why he infiltrated Cass's life, pursued an intimate friendship, and then reversed so suddenly, not because he was rebuked, not because he feared for her safety, but because Cass's growing knowledge made her a threat to his freedom. She grew steadily closer to the truth, all the while confiding her conclusions, sending him her results, her findings until he had no choice but flip from encouraging friend to vehement denier. When that failed, he took action.

"Confirmation bias," he wrote. "You're not as smart as you think you are."

Except in this case, the opposite was true. She was smarter than she realized and far more foolish. The opposite of paranoid: dangerously trusting.

How could she have made this mistake, running from the arms of one psychopath into another, chiding herself for doubting too much, believing to the bitter end. She will not make this mistake again: talking herself out of what she knows, censoring her instincts, inviting the enemy into her home, as though he is an honored guest as opposed to an assassin.

In the darkness, Cass searches for her most crucial belongings. Her shoes are nowhere to be found. Her wallet is under the sofa. Now a rustle of blankets and footsteps emerge from an upstairs bedroom. Frantic, she abandons the search and races out the front door. Without a coat or shoes, she does not look like herself. She looks unhinged, unraveled. She has played into their prophecy, at least, in appearance: a woman running, barefoot, across an empty residential street, wind and rain swirling, every bit the madwoman Ryan has described to others.

She lands at Nora's doorstep several hours later.

"Holy shit," says Nora, opening the door.

"Need help," Cass says. "And a better lawyer."

TWENTY-FIVE

It is Thursday, and Cass stands in the marble courtroom. A day has passed since she went to the cops. Two days since they returned from Bermuda. They are no longer in the family court but rather the Maine Superior Court, a combined criminal and family courtroom. Their goal, according to Matthew, is to report Ryan's crime, present the existing evidence, and, once conveyed, to ensure that Cass has custody of Sam. Cass thinks back now to her first time in a courtroom. She is sobered by the setting, but bolstered by her survival. She has gotten her children to safety, endured incredible terror, and she has a small pile of incontrovertible evidence to show for her effort.

The judge is a small woman, under five feet, her robes so big that she has to hoist them up when she walks. The courtroom, walled in paneled wood, feels like a collapsible chamber. This officious pomp and circumstance is meant to confer power, reason, justice. Cass recounts the reasons she finds herself in this situation: she is here to secure safety, her own and her children's. Nora is standing at her side, supporting her with her friendship. Cass's hands and fingers pulse as though to a rhythm. She struggles to breathe, to think, to stand. Her body is coursing with poison.

"Please state your name for the court."

"Cassandra Connor," she says. She swears to tell the truth, unadorned with falsehoods, the truth and nothing but the truth in all its tainted glory. Ryan stands mere feet away. He states his name also. Three new people are filing in. A small battalion of lawyers. Two people follow them—her mother and her neighbor. She stares at them in disbelief. Is this a hallucination? Comprehension comes in chunks. They cross to stand at Ryan's side. None of them makes eye contact. This is an ambush.

Several minutes pass before Cass understands what is happening, before her auditory nerve connects with her frontal cortex, before images convert to words and words accrue to comprehension. But before this conversion is complete, before she is capable of logic, she is being ushered into another side room.

"I'm going to adjourn this court," says the judge, "for an emergency psychiatric evaluation."

Testimony will be given, not before a judge but before a court psychologist.

Cass is led into a small room with a door that locks behind her. The office of a bureaucrat. Desk piled with papers. Windows lathered with handprints and smudges.

She offers the man a pile of papers to add to his towers.

The man glances at the pages and then begins to ask her questions. "Who do you think are the enemies against you?"

Cass clears her throat, but her throat is closing. She tries to imagine Nora's advice. She must lay out her theory of the crime, not appear to espouse a conspiracy theory. She must draw on the lessons she has learned. Brevity, calmness.

"I don't believe I have enemies. Or that anyone is conspiring against me. Rather, I have reported a crime. Acts of violence committed by one person." She pauses. "And the two people who aided and abetted the crime, the source and an accomplice." She regrets it as soon as she says it.

"Accomplice?" says the doctor. His eyebrows are raised in a small mountain of confusion.

"One to provide false testimony. The other provided the substance. But technically both of them committed the crime also."

"The crime?"

"Delivering the poison." She regrets saying *delivering*. It sounds absurdly clinical like a child pretending to be a doctor, but it seemed a better choice than *putting poison in my food, spraying the toxin in my home, sprinkling it on the floor, spraying it on the sheets and on my clothes so that I would ingest it through dermal absorption. Using his own hand, his own body to deliver the toxin.* That would have been a mouthful.

The man nods and scribbles on a pad of paper. One eye focuses on the page while the other roves across her. "False testimony?" he asks.

"I believe their plan was for her to testify that I was suicidal. If they had succeeded."

"Succeeded," he says.

Cass pauses. She is reluctant to sound maudlin, so she makes the universal sign for death, pantomiming the slash of her neck, replete with sound effect, knife tearing muscle.

"*Were* you suicidal?"

"Of course not," Cass says. "I was fighting for survival."

"Then why would she have said this?"

"Because this crazy bitch was planted in my home expressly to give false testimony." Another pause. "And to deliver the poison."

"Planted in your home?" he says. His eyebrows look like little seagulls.

"Yes," says Cass, "he had his girlfriend apply as a nanny, pretending to be a stranger."

"This is the 'crazy bitch'?" he asks.

Cass inhales. "Yes, sir. The one and only."

The man looks in Cass's eyes for the first time since they began talking.

"You believe this or you know this?"

"I know this," says Cass.

"You know because you have proof?"

"Yes," she says. "There's lots of proof. And I have something better."

"What's that?"

"Women's intuition."

His lips purse into a smile that betrays an absence of pleasure. "I thought you said you hired her."

"Technically, yes," says Cass. "He insisted I fire the previous person and then demanded I hire a replacement. This girl's application appeared a day later."

The man nods in the way that Cass has come to identify as a nod of dismissal. It only spurs her forward.

"His plan was to poison me. In which case, the accomplice would have testified that I was suicidal." A pause. "False alibi corroboration."

The man inhales sharply and jots this down also. "Are you suicidal?"

"You asked me that already," Cass says. "I'm here because I am fighting for safety. Safety for me and my children. Why would you take my report of a crime and simply turn the tables?"

"You are accusing *him*," he says. "I'm just trying to understand why you would make this accusation."

"My husband made a death threat. Then he kept his promise. I suggested what he would have used as an alibi had his murder attempt been successful. It seems to me I'm being penalized for understanding his crime. I've provided you with a motive, method, weapon, alibi, source, and accomplice."

"And what was his motive?"

"Our son. Gaining sole custody of our son. The idea of losing or even sharing him was unbearable." A pause. "The trigger was much more mundane. He was having an affair. I figured it out and confronted him about his girlfriend." Another pause. "Oh, and this bitch wanted a baby. To start a family with my husband and move into my life. Ryan and I were joint tenants on the deed, which means that if I croaked, he automatically got the house."

Another nod, this one more certain.

"Then it became more complicated. When he failed and I figured it out, he needed to shut me up. That was his secondary motive. Because I posed a real threat, not only to custody of our son but to his own freedom. You know what they say."

"What do they say?"

"'It's the cover-up, not the crime.'"

The man nods in a way that almost looks like consideration. "You mention an affair," he says. "Were you jealous of this betrayal?"

"It bothered me," says Cass. "As it would any woman."

"Did it bother you enough," he asks, "for you to consider retaliation?"

"No," she says. "I am not a vindictive person." A pause. "Besides, I'm a journalist. You know what they say about the pen and the sword."

The man stares for several seconds, making a new assessment. "You've thought a lot about this," says the man.

Cass does not flinch. "When someone is trying to kill you, understanding is all-important."

"Your husband testifies that you have not been yourself lately. He says he has suggested numerous doctors, but you have refused his efforts. Why?"

Cass catches her breath, forces oxygen into her blood flow. "Because I do not need it, and, of course, he knows this. What I need is safety for me and my children." Cass continues, "I need medical attention for arsenic poisoning, not time in a shrink's office. I am sound and competent. I have no mental illness. My husband's description of me is false, a deliberate mischaracterization, a tactic designed to obscure his crime and destroy the credibility of his victim."

The man nods slowly and resumes scribbling. "Your neighbor testifies that you showed up at his house at three in the morning. That he offered you a glass of water. That you fell asleep on his living room floor, then left his house suddenly. That you appeared . . ." He flips through the papers. "Confused and disheveled."

Once again, Cass is seized by outrage. The bile of injustice rises from her gut. "I was heavily intoxicated against my will, drugged without my knowledge. When I realized this, I bolted. It is certainly possible that I looked 'confused and disheveled.' Forgive me if I did not have time for a manicure and a blowout."

The man looks up in the middle of his note-taking.

"You seem very upset. It's obvious you're frightened. I see that you are convinced that several people are trying to harm you."

The weight is back. The weight of dread, often described as a sinking sensation. But now it is not dread alone, no margin of unknowing. Now there is only certainty, the knowledge that she has been outplayed by more powerful forces. She must try again to state the facts, the facts, unadorned by emotion. She ignores the tightening in her chest, a straitjacket cinching around her lungs, her throat, stifling her breathing. Cass is in binds. Her only hope now is to relax into the situation.

"I know that my testimony is hard to believe and evidence is easy to misinterpret, but in this case, I am honestly reporting a crime as it was committed. Method, motive, and weapon. Alibi, source, and accomplice. Poison in my system. Poison in food prepared for me by my husband. Poison in the sheets, in my clothes, in the water. Poison designed for ingestion by mouth, absorption through the skin, and airborne inhalation. Poison used with intent to harm, deployed as a murder weapon. And the pattern of abuse that preceded homicidal ideation. I understand that poisoning is not an everyday occurrence, but this is not a conspiracy theory. This is an honest report of a crime of which I was both a victim and a witness. Legally speaking, the name for this is 'conspiracy to commit murder.'

"Please," she says. "All I ask is that you attenuate his claims with the same skepticism you have applied to mine. Just because a man wears a nice suit does not mean he is blameless. Trust me that behind closed doors, Ryan Connor is a different person."

Cass returns to the courtroom less than an hour later to find a small crowd of people, people she once considered her loved ones, her mother, and her once-trusted neighbor, Aaron, testifying in a court of law against her in support of her attacker.

"She has not been herself for a long time," Ryan says with feigned compassion. "Terribly concerned about what she might do to herself and the children."

"Rapid deterioration," says Aaron. "Obsessional fixation. Ongoing fears of pursuit. Claims of poison in the food. Drugs in the water."

"She called me from a tropical island, insisted I fly to meet them. Convinced her husband was poisoning her, that the children were in danger," says her mother.

"Paranoid delusions."

And then, the fatal blow: "Though it is painful to admit, my daughter is mentally ill. I do not believe Cass's claim that she has been poisoned. However, I fear she is capable of putting poison in her food to frame her husband. I believe she is so enraged by her husband's infidelities—or her imagined fears about them—that she could do something in retaliation. And so, while I give no credence to her claim that she has been poisoned, I fear that she may put poison in the food in order to frame her husband. Obviously, this reckless act would cause great harm to Cass and her children."

This statement is made not by Ryan's lawyer but by Cass's mother. Women, it seems, are among the worst misogynists.

The court devolves into mayhem.

"Danger to herself."

"Danger to others."

"Danger to her children."

"The court must take drastic measures."

One by one, they incant the legal criteria for forced incarceration.

The paneled walls are closing in. Her chest, her lungs are in a vise now.

"Your Honor," says Ryan's lawyer, "we have one last piece of information. The petitioner and the grandmother have obtained a Mental Hygiene Warrant. This compels the Portland Police Department to arrest the defendant and bring her to a mental hospital for immediate evaluation."

"Your Honor," says Matthew, "this is an outrage. A breach of due process. This warrant was obtained on false premises and is now being used as a coercive document. Not one of these claims has been supported. Not one of these witnesses has been cross-examined! You cannot make a decision based on hearsay without a hearing or trial."

Cass grasps Nora's arm as she digests this announcement. Ryan has deployed the ultimate legal weapon. A Mental Hygiene Warrant allows the cops to cart her to a mental hospital in a state of forced incarceration. The defendant can be locked away for up to seventy-two hours, held indefinitely at the doctors' discretion. Under Ryan's direction and with his careful guidance, they have subverted the constitutional rights to due process (the Fifth Amendment) and protection from forced detainment (Fourth Amendment), walking into the Maine Superior Court, applying for—and obtaining—an arrest warrant, punishing Cass for reporting Ryan's crime with her own sentence. In the absence of the defendant, the absence of a trial, the absence of a doctor, they filled out a page-long questionnaire and gained the right to lock her up by checking the boxes:

Delusions?

Yes.

Aggression?

Yes.

Danger to herself?

Yes.

Danger to others?

Yes.

Inappropriate clothing for the weather?

Yes.

Do you think this person should be committed?

Yes.

That's all it takes.

No trial. No jury. Just conviction.

Ryan has not said a word regarding the accusations against him, neither a claim nor denial. He has avoided the crime of perjury by placing all these false claims in the mouths of others.

Cass sits in static shock as this nightmare unfolds before her. She has honestly reported a crime only to be falsely accused of another. She summons the energy to speak. She is weak as she addresses the judge. Her voice and fingers tremble.

"Your Honor, there is clear evidence of a crime in the testimony and exhibits I have submitted. It is crucial that you take me at my word, that you trust the evidence, that you charge the perpetrator of the crime for the safety of me and my children.

"I know that poisoning is very rare, outside of spy capers and novels, but just because something is hard to believe does not mean it didn't happen. Just because a crime occurred in the dark does not mean it cannot be proven.

"Your Honor, I am a mother. You are being asked to separate children from a mother. This is taking place without a trial, without cross-examination, without charges other than hearsay from my attacker, hearsay from people with motive to lie. People who planned a bogus story together. Planned to confirm one another's story. False alibi corroboration. I came to the court today for one reason: to seek protection. Protection for me and my children. My ex was arrested for a crime and began a counteroffensive. His strategy is designed to do two things: one, to obscure his crime, and two, to discredit his witness. It is cruel and unusual that his false claims would allow him not only to evade charges, but compound to new horrors. I implore the court to see through this act for the sake of safety and justice. He is not the first man to obscure his crime by attacking his victim. And I am not the first victim who refuses to be silenced."

A moment passes in the court with lawyers yelling from every corner. Finally, the baffled judge raps her gavel and brings the court to order.

"Though this woman appears to be normal by all objective criteria, the testimony of those who know her best reveal a different person, a woman undergoing a rapid deterioration, a woman with a serious delusion. It is the opinion of these witnesses that this woman could be a danger to herself and her children. As a result, this court will err on the side of caution. I hereby order all three children to be removed from the mother. The older children will be placed in the custody of their grandmother. The youngest child will remain with his father."

Trauma supplies certain safeguards for a brutalized person. Shock delays comprehension, parses it out like a drug on a drip for gradual digestion. Had someone told Cass a year before that any of this was possible, she would not have believed it. Had she been assigned to write the piece, she would not have taken the assignment. She would not have believed it possible. She would not have believed that her own husband would try to harm her. She would not have believed her own family would turn against her, that a man who attempted murder would be supported, championed, that she would be impugned while he evaded charges, that he would be treated as an innocent and she would be charged with "mental illness." That she, not he, would be sentenced, and this sentence would be cruel and unusual torture.

She stumbles out of the courthouse, huddled over Nora's shoulder. An alarm sounds as she leaves.

"What is that?" says Nora.

"Keep walking," says Cass. She walks faster.

"What *is* that?"

Cass walks, straightens. "Metal detector."

The alarm blaring as they leave may as well be a call to arms, for it will take the force of a revolution to reverse the damage. But Cass will find this strength. Cass will wage this war. Killers forget that when they fail, they train their insurrection.

TWENTY-SIX

Cass opens her front door and stands outside in silence. She waits for a moment, surveying her lawn, marveling at the loss, the devastation. Pete's bike still rests on the porch. Alice's books are still scattered across the dining room table—*The Adventures of Huckleberry Finn, To Kill a Mockingbird,* a cookbook. The cat taps anxiously on the inside of the door. She's hungry and sick of waiting. Cass marvels at the simple fact: life can change in an instant. All the world she knows is gone. All that was hers has been taken. The mind cannot forget, once learned, the fragile nature of these things—a child on a swing, a family meal, the stupid sparkle of the bay, those most precious and perfect things gone to dread and anguish.

This is what injustice feels like. Living through days with no refuge, every refuge is a reminder, every memory a horror. Acknowledging the deception of every joy, every normal situation. A bed that promised restoration is now a torture chamber. A meal that offered sustenance became a vessel for poison. Waking up shuddering in the night, in the morning, waking up to daydreams more gruesome than the nightmares. Walking through the once-known world aware of one's exception, smiling when you mean to scream, laughing when you're weeping, complicit in the grand delusion that good prevails over evil. Upholding, with this falsehood and the comforts that come with it, those things that we rely upon, things we count on to protect us—family, friends, doctors, lawyers, churches, temples, sunshine. Knowing these things care nothing for us. They only make assessments. Can you afford to act? Will you condone the violence?

These things know no discernment. No compassion. No order, reason. Just random luck in a world that neither loves nor disdains you. You are but a passenger. *You* is but a concept. *They* are just the other *you*, making their own calculations. Can they abide the violence? Will it jeopardize their pleasant day, their wallet? Split-second choices that result in life or death, collusion or defiance, based on simple questions: What is the upside? What is the downside? What is the perk of silence? And then the dreaded inference. Good and evil. What are they? They, too, are false distinctions, made-up concepts. And finally the most sobering fact: *they* and *you* are no different. Good and evil spout from the same source, reside in every person. They and you are equally capable of benevolence and violence. Benevolence and violence—these, too, are bogus constructs. There is only how you act in that moment.

This is life at its limit, a sauce cooked down to reduction. How the number one behaves as it approaches zero. Nothing looks the same once you've witnessed this transformation. You can spend the rest of your life hell-bent on forgetting. You can push it from your mind, but this awareness pervades every minute. You try, and though you succeed for a time, you are forever different. This pain, the lessons that come with it, this is a new hell of its own, awareness coupled with the knowledge that someone has fought to erase you as a person.

Proving the crime and vindicating herself is no longer a matter of survival. It is the difference between this abject hell and reclaiming her children. She finds herself repeating the chronology like a mantra: her husband committed a crime but used his defense to destroy her. A wife reported her husband's crime, but the wife, not the husband, was punished. The process, the steps, the days ahead are difficult to fathom. All she can do is listen to Matthew's advice, find comfort in Nora's hope, strength in her outrage, and show up in court again in a month with more evidence, witnesses, and eventually, a trial. She must count on due process. For now, she must complete the excruciating task of living through these hours.

The bleeding has stopped, and the nausea has receded to a dull constant. Her hair no longer falls out in chunks in the bath and shower. Her hands no longer twitch like invertebrate creatures. Now she holds them, clenched, as though to defend against an intruder. The world is forever changed, not only in its nature. The world has been shattered at its foundation. Total demolition. Cass is a mother stripped of her children. Cass's children were taken from their mother. And this grief, this unceasing hideous grief is a pain that defies description. It is a constant state of horror. It feels like facing death, except there is no ever after. There is only the knowledge that her children are alive, the prayer that they will be safe until they are reunited, and the understanding that her belief in her beliefs, her choices, and her actions prevented something more dire. Her children are alive. And her quest to reclaim them will consume every moment, thought, hour.

Everything is different. Everything is altered. And yet, standing at her front door, things look very similar, so much like the life she used to inhabit. The house is still the same dusty blue. The clouds still loiter on the horizon. The grass is still the same dewy green as the eyes of her husband. The mail is piled up on the doormat, a stack of exhibits of time's unflinching accrual. She leans down and flips through the damp envelopes. Bills from doctors, notes from school, random solicitations. A life that used to belong to her. A world she used to belong to. She crouches to gather the envelopes. A series of return addresses draw her attention.

Maine Medical Labs. Sitters.com. The North Bermuda Clinic. She tears them open and scours the results. The heavy metals panels run over the last two months, by Nora's doctor and her own, as well as the North Bermuda Clinic. Urine and hair samples. They show a flux from low to high, from high to excessive levels. It's true that Ryan committed a crime with no fingerprints, a crime with no scrapes and bruises, but he did not plan for the evidence of his crime to be harbored by her body. Nor that Cass would live to tell it.

November 5: urine 19 mcg/L
November 15: urine 41 mcg/L
December 5: 144 mcg/L
December 31: 568 mcg/L

And one for Pete, December 31: 40 mcg/L

No need for a smoking gun. Cass swallowed the bullet.

Another goodie in the mail to add to Cass's exhibits. A letter from the babysitter agency with its own admission.

A sitter you have employed has failed the identity authentication. She has been removed from the website. Please discontinue contact with this person. A member is removed from the site for one of three reasons: she is underage, she has failed a background check, or she has provided a fraudulent name and biographical information.

And last, a letter with an official address. She scans it in disbelief.

Maine Department of Health is the return address at the left-hand corner. A rapid tear and the letter is out. She sits down on her front step to read its contents.

Dear Mrs. Connor,

Due to the mandated reporting of medical labs in the state of Maine, your labs have been reported to the Department of Health. You have been placed on the Heavy Metals Registry due to your elevated levels. Those on the registry have exceeded safe and normal levels, usually due to unknown environmental toxicity or occupational hazards. Please call the number on this letter for more information. You may be entitled to free medical care for the remediation of heavy metals. Please find the enclosed info sheet to better understand how your job may be affecting your health.

She sits and stares at the letter for several silent minutes. Time is callous, she decides. Finding this here days after the court hearing. No matter. It wouldn't have helped her. They would simply find a way to say the findings were inconclusive or, worse, claim she is responsible. Maybe it is a blessing she didn't find it sooner. She reads the handy fact sheet about heavy metal poisoning, educates herself about her options. The pros and cons of chelation. The irony is toxic.

Something in the letter jogs a part of her brain that has been blocked. Chelation: the cleaning of heavy metals from the blood. Detoxification. Using metal ions to bond with metal ions, like using dirt to clean dirt, like to clean like, poison to cure intoxication. Quickly now, she fumbles for her key, wrestles her front door open. She drops her bag and sprints up the stairs, past her room and the children's, until she is on the top floor of the house, the areas she likes the best, where she has spent countless hours, nursing the baby, folding laundry.

She stands in front of the washer and dryer, panting, breathless, and crouching, reaches behind the machine to remove the phone she hid behind it. Seventy-four messages since she last checked. Ryan's phone is still working. She pours detergent into the slot, starts up a load from the hamper, taking immense comfort in the sound of the washer. Something delicious simmers on the stove. The dishwasher murmurs. The laundry circles. A perfect machine until a circuit breaks and the machine ceases to function. She sits down on the floor, her back resting against the massive metal machine. She studies the messages on his phone, re-reads all the emails. But she only reads the first few before intuition starts buzzing.

"Mr. Connor, your dry cleaning will be ready for pickup at 4:00 P.M. at the Cherry Street location."

"Mr. Connor, your dry cleaning will be ready for pickup at 4:00 P.M. at the Cherry Street location."

"Mr. Connor, your dry cleaning will be ready for pickup at 4:00 P.M. at the Cherry Street location."

But she always dropped off his dry cleaning. And the sitter pitched in with the laundry.

She scrolls further back to the correspondence with C. Alloy.

"It's working," he writes.

"We did it," he says.

"She's over."

Followed by a stream of lewd love notes and hearty congratulations.

Now Cass thinks of two people, her second- and third-favorite liar.

"Delicate for denim."

God knows what they put in this washer. And what they exchanged at these drop-offs.

Cass scrolls to the contacts on the phone. Locates the number for C. Alloy.

A reverse search on the Ohio address lands at a 304 number. A quick search reveals that 304 is the area code for West Virginia. Another search confirms her suspicions. The number is registered to Mary-Lynn Logan.

Once again, Cass finds herself re-filling the gaps of recent history. Ryan and Marley were having affair long before Marley's application. When Ryan went missing during her class. The clumps of hair in the beach house. The panties in the laundry room. So many texts and emails. All of the texts to this number, their little joke: C Alloy, an amalgam of heavy metals.

Right here under her own roof, Ryan brought his inspiration and accomplice. Not a nanny. But a plant. A home into a crime scene. A haven into a coffin.

Liars tell parts of the truth. Liars leave breadcrumbs. Liars twist and flaunt the facts. Liars need to broadcast.

A girl, poisoned as a child by her own environment. The cancer treated with an even more powerful toxin. Arsenic trioxide. Spared from death but back with a grudge. For the stolen years. The lost childhood. She wanted damages, payback. In Marley, Ryan found a willing partner and a shared incentive. Not wanting to lose his child or his home but dogged by the need to split them in a divorce, Ryan asked his doting lover a simple question:

"How can I kill my wife?"

She knew just the thing. Guaranteed to kill without the risk of detection.

Ryan fell for her tale of woe, her desperate rebellion. She fell for Ryan. Right here under Cass's roof, a Trojan horse was delivered: a can-do nanny with a penchant for "all things strings," and a killer craving for Cass's husband.

With certainty comes the satisfaction of confirmed intuition, followed by the knowledge that it's time to avenge her children. And while some part of Cass feels sorry for this disturbed woman, her own life is too hard-earned to forfeit to a trailer-park grifter. She cannot help docking one last lesson as she puts on her shoes and jacket: Always trust your gut. Ignoring your instincts is the surest route to self-destruction. Doubt, not belief, Cass decides, is the most dangerous delusion.

It is morning when Cass arrives at the university. Only a week has passed since she returned to Portland. Four days since her world was destroyed. But here nothing has changed. Office hours start at ten, and her first class is at noon. The students are back from the winter break, and they move through the halls with extra volume. A knock on the door and a rustle of denim as her first student hurries in.

"Oh, good, you're here," says Anna. It is bittersweet to see her students now. So young and already invested in redressing injustice.

"There an issue with the assignment?" says Cass.

"I'm really struggling." Anna sits down on the chair next to the desk and extracts her laptop from her backpack.

"What's got you stuck?" Cass says.

"It's hard to be objective when you feel so strongly about a piece."

"Here, let's take a look at the lede. What is the subject of the article?"

"Lenient sentencing in rape cases based on a ruling that the rape was 'solicited.'"

Anna hands Cass her paper. She scans the first page and then looks back to Anna.

"This is strong," Cass says. "What can you do with the verbs to give it more rhetorical power? Journalists hate a gerund."

Anna takes the paper, begins to make revisions.

Cass glances at her student. Recognizes her strength. Her ambition. "I'm actually working on a project. I could use some help."

Anna straightens. "Can you tell me more?"

"It's an in-depth investigative piece. Requires some strenuous reporting."

"Investigative?" Anna whispers.

Cass looks back at Anna's paper. Considers the ethics of what she is asking.

"Is it a political piece?"

"It's somewhat political," Cass says.

"Sex crime?" Anna whispers.

"In a sense," says Cass. "And drugs. Sale of a controlled substance."

"Trafficking?" Anna gasps, mouth agape. "A sex-and-drug cartel?"

"Not exactly," says Cass. "More of a domestic situation. With a bit of over-lap in environmental science."

"You mean like Flint?" Anna's voice rises an octave.

"Some things in common with Flint. Stonewalling. Cover-up. Heavy metals. Think Flint but with criminal intent."

"Whoa," says Anna. "Sounds juicy."

And then, because Cass cannot resist a good pitch, "An outraged victim, wrongfully accused, dismissed, disgraced, ripped from her children. A woman, charged and criminalized, tried without due process. No suspension of judgment. No burden of proof. An innocent, a victim sentenced for reporting a crime. All of this filtered through a feminist lens. But most of all, it's the story of every woman's fight for survival, a mother on a quest for her children."

"I'm in," says Anna.

"Really?" says Cass. This was easier than she'd expected. Or she is better at this than she realized.

"Sounds like a huge story," says Anna.

"It is," says Cass.

"The victim, dismissed and decried. The broken legal system. The baked-in misogyny that make a community complicit. It's like a bad light bulb joke. How many victims do you need to accuse a man of rape before one is believed? Before one man is convicted?"

"You get it," says Cass.

"I'm quoting your article," says Anna.

"Oh," Cass says. "Right."

"So when can I start?"

Cass takes a sharp breath. "You free now?"

Anna shrugs. "Yes."

Cass studies the girl, assesses her capacity for trust. "I need to make sure that you can maintain confidentiality."

"Of course," Anna says. "Your lecture on reporter's privilege was one of my favorites."

"We're going to take some liberties with our source."

"Really?" says Anna. She leans toward the desk.

"Our source is also our subject."

Anna nods slowly.

"I want you to witness a transaction and make your own purchase."

"Okay," says Anna. "I can do that."

"If it goes well, you can write about it. The story is yours. Single byline."

Anna nods. Her eyes are wide.

"Are you sure you're up for this?" Cass says.

"Absolutely," says Anna.

Cass scrutinizes the young woman's face. Her earnest eyes, her childlike blond curls, the wisps of hair grazing her cheek. Her ambition, her intensity. "What are you wearing under that jacket?"

She unzips a jacket to reveal a tight-fitting T-shirt.

"That'll work," says Cass. She gathers the papers on her desk.

"Whoa," says Anna. "Girilla journalism. Every arrow in our quiver. All the tools in our arsenal to slay the dragon!" She is nearly punching the air.

"No," says Cass. "You'll need that pocket for the recorder."

"Oh!" says Anna. She straightens her face, nods somberly. She takes her paper from Cass and stuffs it into her bag.

"Any other suggestions for my attire?"

"Nope," says Cass.

"Glasses? No glasses?"

"You're perfect as you are."

It is ten o'clock, and four women sit in a borrowed car. Cass, Nora, Anna, and Jean are half a block from the address on Ryan's "dry cleaning pickup," the Cherry Street location. They are close to downtown Portland, where the coiffed lawns and crime intersect, where the trees meet the city. Nora has brought a thermos of coffee. They have been sitting for over an hour. The air is cold and damp outside, and the heat in the car is blasting.

A man in a hoodie strides up the block, wearing headphones that look like earmuffs. His gait is immediately recognizable, hunched shoulders and long rhythmic strides, like he's moving to a beat. Cass has to restrain herself not to shout curses across the street. Her "concerned neighbor" is a common criminal.

Now Ryan approaches from the opposite corner. He pauses at the light, as though he is performing what it is to be an upstanding citizen. He is wearing his weekend attire, jeans, a baseball cap, and an oversize parka. His face is obscured by a few days' growth. He looks overgrown, unmoored, not the familiar presentable Ryan. The light changes, and he crosses the street. He follows Aaron into an alley in between two battered houses. A dog barks sporadically.

Now Anna gets out of the car. She stands at the curb as though she's looking for an address and then hurries toward the alley. Lacking a more sophisticated recording device, they have used what they've got: Anna has

Cass's phone in her pocket. It's on speaker, calling Nora. Cass and Nora sit in the car, listening.

A loud indiscernible sound and then Anna is speaking.

"A classmate of mine recommended you."

"Oh yeah? Which classmate?"

"She said not to use her name. Said she's a very good customer and that I could trust you."

A pause. The dog barks. No words for a long moment. Cass is breathless, focused.

"Do you think you could help me out?" says Anna.

"What would be helpful?" Aaron says finally.

Now Ryan. "He likes to be helpful."

"I got a really important paper," says Anna. "Gotta pull a bunch of all-nighters." Her voice is high, flirtatious. Sounds like she's smiling.

"He likes all-nighters," Ryan says. "Right, Aaron?"

"Love all-nighters." Another short pause and the rustle of fabric. Is he reaching into his backpack, producing options? "Regular or extra-strength?" he says.

"Extra-strength, please," says Anna. She giggles.

Silence as the purchase is made, the transaction completed. Cass waits for Anna to emerge from the alley, but Anna wants another quote. "What's your poison?" she says.

Ryan responds. "Oh, nothing too potent for me. Just a little something to take the edge off. I prefer to support local business rather than Big Pharma."

"Got it." Another giggle. "Thanks for your help," says Anna.

"Glad to be of service," says Aaron.

More silence as Aaron hands Ryan his purchase.

How many women have to report a crime before the crime is believed?

One victim. Three witnesses. Twelve medical labs. A photograph. And a confession.

A minute later, Anna hurries out of the alley. She is out of breath but smiling. She walks quickly, checks behind her, then gets in the car. Still flushed, she empties her stash on her lap.

"Well done," says Cass.

Anna is beaming. "That's the real high," she says.

"You've got your story," says Cass. "And a friend for life. Thank you."

"Thank you for letting me be a part of this."

"Ready?" says Nora.

"Almost," says Cass. She is still staring at the alley. She opens her door slowly. "Just need to do one last thing."

She watches as Ryan walks down the street. He is moving slowly. He passes the house with the barking dog, the empty porches. He pauses at the light and crosses the street. Then, he stops at a green derelict house, finds a key, enters quickly.

It is late when Cass returns to this door. The time when there are no witnesses. She is not supposed to be here now. But she is consumed by the force of her rage. The force of vindication. She knocks on the door. A steel door on a wooden house. She waits. She will wait until sunrise if she has to.

Mary-Lynn Logan opens the door wearing a tight white tank and jean cut-offs, a patch of midriff proudly displayed above a swollen belly. Her rabid face looks bovine now. Due to her maternal condition. The face of a dog, chewing a bone, smug with the satisfaction of a plan nearly completed. Nearly, but not completely. A life, a home, and a man she was willing to kill for. And a baby of her own as a bonus. Ryan follows, in his briefs. His face contorts into a dopey grin. But he is not happy to see Cass. It is the grin of a busted liar.

"Did you follow me here?" He stares at her with loathing.

"Just came to pick up the dry cleaning," she says. "It's such a shame we'll never get to see your big performance. I was so looking forward to seeing you on the stand, testifying to my 'suicidal ideation.' Were you going to break down in tears or play it really stoic?"

"You're breaking the law." A smile curls at the corner of his lips. A snarl. An animal's first indication of attack. "You're done. You're fucked," he says. "Now you'll never get your kids back." He thinks he can rage with impunity, but he is shaking. "I'm calling the cops." He takes out his phone.

"No need," says Cass. "I called them already."

Ryan is breathless, panicked now. He blocks the door on instinct.

Cass takes in their vile vignette. Two sociopaths standing at their door. A modern *American Gothic*. Cass's stolen child inside. A baby in Marley's gnarly belly. How close they came to taking her life, taking everything that mattered.

"You never loved me," Cass says. "You loved my life. You wanted what I created."

"I gave you a choice," Ryan says. "We could have shared him."

"Thanks anyway," she says. "Now you won't be allowed in his presence."

"You can't prove anything," Ryan says. His voice is shrill and desperate.

"A day ago, I would have agreed," she says. "But now I've got something better than proof. I have my beliefs back."

Cass reaches to the back of her neck as the sound of sirens rises. The sirens sound like weeping, the loudest wailing in the world. A mother for her child. A child for his mother. The clasp releases. A squad car pulls up and parks at the curb. Two officers open their doors. Ryan is handcuffed first, and then his trailer-park princess. And Cass watches with bone-deep relief as these two toxic people are quarantined and Ryan's freedom is finally choked by his ambition.

Cass tosses his ring to the curb as the car door slams behind him.

She looks down the street, where her friends are waiting. Jean holds her phone high, like a lighter at a concert, recording it all. Anna's got her camera. Nora stands, arms crossed, smiling.

Cass hurries in the house now to collect her child. He is sleeping on a bare mattress, oblivious to the chaos around him. She lifts him to her chest and carries him out. It is heaven to hold him.

As she walks, she takes out her phone.

"Yes, I know it's late, Mom," she says. "I'm coming to pick up Alice and Pete. I'll tell you in person." A pause. "Your four favorite words."

I told you so.

Cass watches the cop car recede, surrounded by her friends, her sisters. The sky is churned by silver clouds that look like inverted mountains. Light bears down from above, determined to restore order. The bay and the sky are a mirror and reflection. She thinks of what she has survived and what she will overcome. She thinks of what she knows now, the ways that she is stronger. She thinks of every woman ravaged by violence while her attacker is rewarded. She will fight for these women also. Killers forget that when they fail they train their insurrection. *Sola docit venenum.* It's the dose that makes the poison. And poison that makes the best medicine.

ⓂMAINE MEDICAL

Heavy Metals Panel

Connor, Cassandra
12 Russell Road
Cumberland, Maine 04021

Acct# 31793690
Phone: (207) 563-4567   Rto:93

PATIENT DETAILS	SPECIMEN DETAILS	PHYSICIAN DETAILS
DOB: 10/22/1977	**Date collected:** 11/15/2016	**Ordering:** G. Stern
Age/ym/d): 1977/10/22	1153 Local	**Referring:**
Gender: F **SSN:**	**Date entered:** 11/17/2016	**ID:** 13839904
Patient ID:	**Date reported:** 11/21/2016	**NPI:**1528149507

General Comments & Additional Information
Clinical Info: Spot Urine Sample
Clinical Info: D AT 8 AM ON 11/21/2016.

Alternate Control Number: B0021155537
Total Urine Volume: 2100ml

Alternate Patient ID: Not Provided
Fasting: No

ORDERED ITEMS
Arsenic Exposure Profile, Ur

TESTS	RESULTS	FLAG	UNITS	REFERENCE INTERVAL	LAB
Lead	0	–	mcg/L	0	–
Mercury	0	–	mcg/L	0	–
Arsenic	0	–	mcg/L	0	–
Cadmium	0	–	mcg/L	0	–
Chromium	0	–	mcg/L	0	–
Arsenic Exposure Profile, Ur	40		mcg/L	0-50	
Arsenic (Total), U				Detection Limit = 10	01
Arsenic, Urine 24 Hr	**41**	**High**	mcg/24 hr	0-50	01

Comment:
Seafood consumption 2-3 days prior to specimen collection can markedly elevate levels of total arsenic in urine. This
dietary form of arsenic is non-toxic and is comprised primarily of arsenobetaine and arsenocholine. For monitoring
exposure to the ore toxic inorganic forms of arsenic, the test for inorganic arsenic is appropriate.

Creatinine (Crt), U	7.3		g/L	0.30 – 3.00	01
				Detection Limit = 0.10	

01	BN	Nexo Lab	John F Harrison, MD		

For inquiries, the physician may contact Branch: 999-999-9999

Date Issued: 11/21/16 1505 ET	**FINAL REPORT**	Page 1 of 1

This Document contains private and confidential health information
protected by state and federal law. If you have received this document in
error, please call 999-999-9999

© 1995-2015 Maine Diagnostics
All Rights Reserved – Enterprise Report
Version: 1.00

ⓂMAINE MEDICAL

Heavy Metals Panel

Connor, Cassandra
12 Russell Road
Cumberland, Maine 04021

Acct# 31793690
Phone: (207) 563-4567   Rto:93

PATIENT DETAILS	SPECIMEN DETAILS	PHYSICIAN DETAILS
DOB: 10/22/1977	**Date collected:** 11/5/2016	**Ordering:** R. Miller
Age/ym/d): 1977/10/22	1153 Local	**Referring:**
Gender: F **SSN:**	**Date entered:** 11/8/2016	**ID:** 13839904
Patient ID:	**Date reported:** 11/11/2016	**NPI:**1528149507

General Comments & Additional Information
Clinical Info: Spot Urine Sample
Clinical Info: D AT 8 AM ON 11/21/2016.

Alternate Control Number: B0021155537
Total Urine Volume: 2100ml

Alternate Patient ID: Not Provided
Fasting: No

ORDERED ITEMS
Arsenic Exposure Profile, Ur

TESTS	RESULTS	FLAG	UNITS	REFERENCE INTERVAL	LAB
Lead	0	–	mcg/L	0	–
Mercury	0	–	mcg/L	0	–
Arsenic	0	–	mcg/L	0	–
Cadmium	0	–	mcg/L	0	–
Chromium	0	–	mcg/L	0	–
Arsenic Exposure Profile, Ur	40		mcg/L	0-50	
Arsenic (Total), U				Detection Limit = 10	01
Arsenic, Urine 24 Hr	**19**	**High**	mcg/24 hr	0-50	01

Comment:
Seafood consumption 2-3 days prior to specimen collection can markedly elevate levels of total arsenic in urine. This
dietary form of arsenic is non-toxic and is comprised primarily of arsenobetaine and arsenocholine. For monitoring
exposure to the ore toxic inorganic forms of arsenic, the test for inorganic arsenic is appropriate.

Creatinine (Crt), U	0.57		g/L	0.30 – 3.00	01
				Detection Limit = 0.10	

01	BN	Nexo Lab	John F Harrison, MD		

For inquiries, the physician may contact Branch: 999-999-9999

Date Issued: 11/21/16 1505 ET	**FINAL REPORT**	Page 1 of 1

This Document contains private and confidential health information
protected by state and federal law. If you have received this document in
error, please call 999-999-9999

© 1995-2015 Maine Diagnostics
All Rights Reserved – Enterprise Report
Version: 1.00

Ⓜ MAINE MEDICAL

Heavy Metals Panel

Connor, Cassandra
12 Russell Road
Cumberland, Maine 04021

Acct# 31793690
Phone: (207) 563-4567 Rto:93

PATIENT DETAILS

DOB: 10/22/1977
Age(y/m/d): 1977/10/22
Gender: F   SSN:
Patient ID:

SPECIMEN DETAILS

Date collected: 12/5/2016
1153 Local
Date entered: 12/7/2016
Date reported: 12/11/2016

PHYSICIAN DETAILS

Ordering: M Lapinsky
Referring:
ID: 13839904
NPI:1528149507

General Comments & Additional Information
Clinical Info: Hair Sample
Clinical Info: D AT 8 AM ON 11/21/2016.

Alternate Control Number: B0021155537
Total Hair Volume: 2100ml

Alternate Patient ID: Not Provided
Fasting: No

ORDERED ITEMS
Arsenic Exposure Profile, Hair

TESTS	RESULTS	FLAG	UNITS	REFERENCE INTERVAL	LAB
Lead	0	-	mcg/L	0	-
Mercury	0	-	mcg/L	0	-
Arsenic	0	-	mcg/L	0	-
Cadmium	0	-	mcg/L	0	-
Chromium	0	-	mcg/L	0	-
Arsenic Exposure Profile, Hair	40		mcg/L	0-50	
Arsenic (Total), U				Detection Limit = 10	01
Arsenic, Urine 24 Hr	144	High	mcg/24 hr	0-50	01

Comment:
Seafood consumption 2-3 days prior to specimen collection can markedly elevate levels of total arsenic in hair. This dietary form of arsenic is non-toxic and is comprised primarily of arsenobetaine and arsenocholine. For monitoring exposure to the ore toxic inorganic forms of arsenic, the test for inorganic arsenic is appropriate.

Creatinine (Crt), U	8.1		g/L	0.30 – 3.00	01
				Detection Limit = 0.10	

01 BN	Nexo Lab		John F Harrison, MD	

For inquiries, the physician may contact Branch: 999-999-9999

Date Issued: 11/21/16 1505 ET	**FINAL REPORT**	Page 1 of 1

NORTH BERMUDA CLINIC

Connor, Cassandra
12 Russell Road
Cumberland, Maine 04021

Acct# 31793690
Phone: (441) 723-4537 Rto:93

PATIENT DETAILS	SPECIMEN DETAILS	PHYSICIAN DETAILS
DOB: 10/22/1977	Date collected: 12/31/2016 1153 Local	Ordering: K. Baker
Age(y/m/d): 1977/10/22	Date entered: 1/7/2017	Referring:
Gender: F SSN:	Date reported: 1/11/2017	ID: 13839904
Patient ID:		NPI:1528149507
General Comments & Additional Information	Alternate Control Number: B002155537	Alternate Patient ID: Not Provided
Clinical Info: STARTE	Total Urine Volume: 2100ml	Fasting: No
Clinical Info: D AT 8 AM ON 11/21/2016.		

ORDERED ITEMS Arsenic Exposure Profile, Ur

TESTS	RESULTS	FLAG	UNITS	REFERENCE INTERVAL	LAB
Lead	0	-	mcg/L	0	-
Mercury	0	-	mcg/L	0	-
Arsenic	0	-	mcg/L	0	-
Cadmium	0	-	mcg/L	0	-
Chromium	0	-	mcg/L	0	-
Arsenic Exposure Profile, Ur Arsenic (Total), U	40		mcg/L	0-50 Detection Limit = 10	01
Arsenic, Urine 24 Hr	568	High	mcg/24 hr	0-50	01

Comment: Seafood consumption 2-3 days prior to specimen collection can markedly elevate levels of total arsenic in urine. This dietary form of arsenic is non-toxic and is comprised primarily of arsenobetaine and arsenocholine. For monitoring exposure to the ore toxic inorganic forms of arsenic, the test for inorganic arsenic is appropriate.

| Creatinine (Crt), U | 0.57 | | g/L Detection Limit = 0.10 | 0.30 – 3.00 | 01 |

01 BN Nexo Lab John F Harrison, MD

| Date Issued: 11/21/16 1505 ET | FINAL REPORT | Page 1 of 1 |

For inquiries, the physician may contact Branch: 999-999-9999

NORTH BERMUDA CLINIC

Gerrety, Pete
Address here

Acct# 31793690
Phone: (441) 723-4537 Rto:93

PATIENT DETAILS	SPECIMEN DETAILS	PHYSICIAN DETAILS
DOB: 6/24/2009	Date collected: 12/31/2016 1153 Local	Ordering: K. Baker
Age(y/m/d): 1977/10/22	Date entered: 1/7/2017	Referring:
Gender: M SSN:	Date reported: 1/11/2017	ID: 13839904
Patient ID:		NPI:1528149507
General Comments & Additional Information	Alternate Control Number: B002155537	Alternate Patient ID: Not Provided
Clinical Info: STARTE	Total Urine Volume: 2100ml	Fasting: No
Clinical Info: D AT 8 AM ON 11/21/2016.		

ORDERED ITEMS Arsenic Exposure Profile, Ur

TESTS	RESULTS	FLAG	UNITS	REFERENCE INTERVAL	LAB
Lead	0	-	mcg/L	0	-
Mercury	0	-	mcg/L	0	-
Arsenic	0	-	mcg/L	0	-
Cadmium	0	-	mcg/L	0	-
Chromium	0	-	mcg/L	0	-
Arsenic Exposure Profile, Ur Arsenic (Total), U	40		mcg/L	0-50 Detection Limit = 10	01
Arsenic, Urine 24 Hr	144	High	mcg/24 hr	0-50	01

Comment: Seafood consumption 2-3 days prior to specimen collection can markedly elevate levels of total arsenic in urine. This dietary form of arsenic is non-toxic and is comprised primarily of arsenobetaine and arsenocholine. For monitoring exposure to the ore toxic inorganic forms of arsenic, the test for inorganic arsenic is appropriate.

| Creatinine (Crt), U | 0.57 | | g/L Detection Limit = 0.10 | 0.30 – 3.00 | 01 |

01 BN Nexo Lab John F Harrison, MD

| Date Issued: 11/21/16 1505 ET | FINAL REPORT | Page 1 of 1 |

For inquiries, the physician may contact Branch: 999-999-9999

December 26, 2017

A sitter you have employed has failed the identity authentication. She has been removed from the website. Please discontinue contact with this person. A member is removed from the site for one of three reasons: she is underage, she has failed a background check, or she has provided a fraudulent name and biographical information.

MAINE DEPARTMENT OF HEALTH

221 State Street
11 State House Station
Augusta, Maine 04333-0011
Phone: (207) 287-3707
FAX: (207)287-3005
TTY: Maine relay 711

December 29, 2017

Dear Mrs. Connor,

Due to the mandated reporting of medical labs in the state of Maine, your labs have been reported to the Department of Health. You have been placed on the Heavy Metals Registry due to your elevated levels. Those on the registry have exceeded safe and normal levels, usually due to unknown environmental toxicity or occupational hazards. Please call the number on this letter for more information. You may be entitled to free medical care for the remediation of heavy metals. Please find the enclosed info sheet to better understand how your job may be affecting your health.

Sincerely,

Jean E. Hoff